THE BEG

J.B. Drake

Editor: Tim Marquitz

Proofreading: Julie Hoyle/Jericho Writers

Cover: Michael Gauss "Helmutt"

ISBN-10: 1723163139
ISBN-13: 978-1723163135

CONTENTS

PROLOGUE

I t was killing him and she knew it. The entire side of her robe was slick with his
blood, and yet the bleeding continued. She had to stop, bind his wounds anew,
allow him rest. She had to stop.

"Almost there, my love," she said instead, her every word tearing at her soul. Their
only chance, his only chance, was for them to press on, get out of the marshland
they trundled through, get out of the nightmare they'd found themselves in.

Gritting her teeth, she looked down at him as he hung limply by her side. Her
arms were heavy, almost numb. And the blood, gods, the blood, it was all she could
do to keep a firm grip about him. But she couldn't let go, she daren't, and as he
stared resolutely on, his breath coming in shallow snatches as he willed his feet to
move slowly onwards, one before the other, her heart ached for him. He was trying,
dear gods, he was trying.

"Almost there," she repeated hoarsely. "Please, stay with me. We're almost there."
It was a lie, like so many others she'd told since their escape from the compound.
But what else could she say? She raised her gaze up to their path. Everything was
corrupted now, everything. From the trees to the buildings, even the birds of the air,
nothing was spared, the stench of death and decay clinging to the both of them like
a defiling miasma. The town didn't deserve this. Gritting her teeth, she fought to

ignore the waves of guilt that had been threatening to drown her since the incident. She'd wallow in self-pity later. First, she had to get him away.

"Stay with me," she said as she adjusted her grip on her beloved's arm about her neck, the sweat in her palm weakening her grasp. She chanced a glance behind them. The screams had long since stopped. Was it their turn to be hunted, or were they now truly alone? As she stared behind them, however, she was oblivious to the dead root jutting out before her, and as she caught her leg upon it, a startled yelp escaped her lips as they both fell to the ground.

Cursing feverishly, she hurried to her feet, turning to help her beloved onto his.

"No…" he whispered, shaking his head weakly as he rose to sitting. "I need to rest."

"No, we have to keep moving," she replied, shaking her head as she spoke. "He's still out there. We have to keep moving. Come, please."

As she reached for him, however, he looked up at her, his eyes pleading with hers. Shaking her head briefly, she looked behind them, staring intently into the fog as her heart beat loudly in her chest. They were not safe. He was still hunting them. They had to keep moving. Once more, she looked down at her beloved, but as her eyes fell upon him, she realized they had to stop. Relenting at last, she helped him to his feet and walked him over to the large fallen tree whose root had caused their fall. With a grateful sigh, he sat upon it. Once more, she scanned their surrounds. Nothing. But her fear remained. Sighing herself, she looked down at her beloved once more. His lips were purple, and he'd paled greatly. He looked up at her, smiling sadly once their eyes met.

"I'm sorry," he whispered.

She shook her head at him.

"We both made this choice," she said as she grasped the edge of her robe. Tearing free a generous strip from it, she sat beside her beloved and bound his wounds anew.

"But I talked you into it," her beloved replied. "You were right, we shouldn't have done it. We tried to steal the power of the gods. We had no right."

"Save your strength, we—" she began, only for a lone howl to echo out from the mist. Its sound froze her heart as it chilled her soul. She looked at her beloved. His eyes were wide with the same terror coursing through her veins. Wordlessly, he offered his arms up to her. Their rest was over. Nodding, she let go of the torn fabric as she rose to help him up, but at that moment, as she took a single steadying step towards him, a huge, terrifying beast leapt up out of the very mist itself, knocking her away from her beloved as it crashed into him. But as her lover fell to the earth, he did not scream, he did not make so much as a sound, though not from lack of want or need, for the beast had wrapped its huge maw about his throat, ripping it open even as its bulk frame forced him to the earth on the other side of the fallen tree.

Stunned, she stared at what little of the beast she could see, her fear stilling her tongue as the beast gorged on its unholy feast, and for a time, the only sounds to be heard were that of rending flesh and crunching bone.

"Hello, Mother."

Startled back to life, she looked behind her, and the sight that met her gaze brought a sharp cry from her lips. Scrambling to her feet, she backed away quickly from the little child walking towards her.

"Stay back!" she screamed. "You stay away from me!"

The little boy smiled at his mother as he neared her. "Were you looking to leave without me?"

She stared at his eyes, her fear shortening her breath as she buried her lips in her hands.

"Please, just stay back," she begged as she shuffled away from him.

"That was very naughty of you, Mother, leaving your son alone like that. What would Father think of you?"

"You are not my son!" she shrieked as tears streamed down her face.

The little boy grinned. It was a soulless grin, an evil grin, one only the darkest of hearts could call forth.

"You are not my son," she repeated. "Just stay back."

The little boy laughed. He turned to stare at the beast, a hound of sorts, its body more smoke than flesh. But as the little boy turned his gaze from her, she seized her chance and ran, pulling up her robe and racing forth with all she could muster. Though barely had she gone five paces when an unseen hand held her fast where she was.

"Going somewhere?" the little child asked.

Though she tried to speak, no words came, her tongue stilled as her heart threatened to explode in her chest. Slowly, the unseen hand lifted her off her feet, turning her about before bringing her back to her son. The hound was beside him now, its lips dripping with blood.

"Well?"

She stared at him. She couldn't speak, for her fear bound her as tightly as the spell within which the little boy held her.

"No answer? That's quite rude, is it not?"

Still, she couldn't answer. Then the hound began walking towards her. She stared first at the hound, then at her son, her breath coming in snatches once more, but still said nary a word. Slowly, the unseen hand tilted her to the side, lowering her towards the ground until her head was level with the hound's. Tears streamed down her face anew as she shook her head desperately at her son.

"Please! Gods, please!"

The little boy stared at her as he smiled the same soulless smile. The hound drew near, stopping just beside her. Licking its lips, it opened its huge maw and brought it about her head.

"Please!" she shrieked, all control, all self-control lost to her.

Her son giggled as a dripping sound echoed about them. The hound's jaw was now in line with her throat.

"Somebody help me!" she cried as her gaze darted about her. "Please! Somebody help me!"

The little boy laughed with glee. "Nobody's coming to save you, Mother dearest; there's nobody left! You didn't think I let you live this long because I couldn't find you, did you?"

She looked back at the little child, her breath in snatches once again.

"Starlight," she said. "My darling Starlight, please, stop him. Please!"

Slowly, the little boy's face fell as he shied away from her.

"Please, my darling," she continued. "We didn't mean it! As the gods bear me witness, we didn't mean it! Don't listen to what he's said, we didn't mean for this to happen to you. Please, stop him! Help Mummy, please. Starlight, please!"

The little child stared at her as tears brimmed his eyes. Pouting, the boy sniffled as he held his mother's gaze. Time stood still as mother and son stared at one another, one with a pleading stare, the other with a teary gaze full of pain and longing. Then, the little boy wiped the tears from his eyes as he sniffled once more. He looked from his mother to the hound, but as he looked back at her, his face was set once again.

"Bye-bye, Mummy," the little boy muttered sadly, and as his mother drew breath to speak, the hound bit down.

"Bye-bye."

Uneven Brilliance

Merethia, wondrous Merethia. Hers was a majesty unrivalled in all the elven cities. From Aderelas in the northern highlands to En'tirien in the woodlands to the west, none could boast of such beauty, such serene wonder. It was a majesty that was hers by right, for she was the jewel of the elven lands, the pride of all elves whether they wished to admit it or not. It was a splendor made possible by the favor she enjoyed from the high elves of the Shimmering Tower, the greatest school of arcane learning in all existence. The elves of the Tower were known as much for their arcane masteries as for their love of beauty.

But, for all its unrivalled majesty, fair Merethia was not immune to the one ill that has plagued every city of every race since the dawn of time. Uneven brilliance. Like all cities, there were parts of her that shone with her fabled wonder, and parts that sat in shadow and despair. It was indeed a most familiar tale, an imperfect magnificence felt most keenly by those denizens living in those shadows. And as the sun made its way up the morning sky, one such denizen was huddled within his meagre blanket, sleeping away the night's worries within the back doorway of a local seamstress shop, his light snores a clear sign of the peace he felt. That was, until the seamstress arrived.

Stopping, the seamstress stared up the deserted alleyway that led to her shop, a deep frown upon her lips as she glared at the blanket huddled in her doorway. Shaking her head, she made her way towards the bundle, her frown deepening with each step as she muttered to herself. At last, she stood before the blanket, a deep and angry scowl twisting her lips as she glared at it, and with a frustrated grunt, raised her foot and began stomping and kicking the blanket with all she could muster.

"Ow, ow!" came a cry from within the blanket, but his cries merely served to spur the seamstress on, her anger mounting with each blow. At last, a little boy appeared from within the bundle, his face twisted in agony as he rolled over into a ball, hugging himself tightly as the blows rained down upon him with increasing ferocity.

"I. Told. You. To. Clear out of here!" she bellowed as she kicked and stomped on the little bundle. "Clear out of here! Clear out!"

"Leave him alone!" came a cry from down the alley.

Stopping, the seamstress looked round to see a young elven girl racing up the alley towards her, her eyes ablaze.

"I told you to clear out of here!" she yelled in response, turning to direct her ire at the young beggar girl. "This is not a hospice, it's a respectable enterprise! Clear out of here, damn you! Clear out, and take your rags with you!"

Without waiting for a response, the seamstress gave the little boy one last vicious kick before opening the door to her shop and storming inside, slamming it hard behind her. A stunned silence fell upon the pair as they stared at the door.

"You okay, Tip?" the young beggar girl asked as she broke her gaze from the door to stare at her little friend, going down into a squat as she did so. Smiling bravely, Tip nodded at her.

"Was just pretending," he lied.

"Clever you," the young beggar girl replied, smiling.

Tip's smile widened in response.

"Well, come on then," she said as she began gathering up their blanket. "No telling what that old bitch is up to in there. Let's get out of here while we can."

"Okay," Tip replied as he too began gathering up their blanket.

"Marsha…" Tip said after a spell.

"Hmm?"

"Where'd you go?"

Before she could reply, however, something tumbled out of the blanket and fell, clattering to the floor. It was an ornate golden dagger. Stopping to stare at the dagger, Tip's young friend looked up at him, only for him to stare back at her, a guilty frown upon his lips.

"Well, least we know where tomorrow's supper coming from," she chirped as she swiped the dagger off the floor before shoving it into one of the myriad pockets in her trousers. She looked at Tip once more.

"Come on, then," she said. "Grab the bag."

"Okay," Tip replied as he did as he was bid, and once they both had shoved the blanket into their little bag of holding, both began making their way out of the alleyway to face whatever trials the day held for them.

The older of the two, young Marshalla, strode on in front, her fiery mane bundled into a messy ponytail as she led little Tip onwards, her left hand in his right and her emerald eyes scanning the crowds they weaved their way through. Though no more than fifteen years of age, to look at her would be to think she was a woman full grown. But while many a girl prayed for the gift of such full and luscious endowment at such a tender age, to a street child like Marshalla, it was more a curse. A curse made all the more biting by her striking beauty.

Occasionally, as they made their way through the crowd, she would throw a glance back at little Tip. And with each glance, her gaze was met by an innocent, almost incurable grin, a grin Marshalla couldn't help but return. It was infectious, Tip's innocence. Even though he'd been living their cruel and unforgiving life for little over a year, he still held on to the innocent wonder one would expect to find in a child who'd only just wandered into Merethia for the first time. It was this innocence that, were Marshalla to be honest with herself, bonded her so tightly with the little elven boy, for it was one of the very few things left in her life that still drove her on, that still gave her a pure purpose. That and the eternal shame she felt about how she had treated such an innocent little child when their paths first crossed.

They'd weaved their way through the city to one of the more affluent shopping districts, stopping across the street from one that, judging from the wares on display, was more appealing to the arcane-minded.

"We going to Mardaley's?" Tip exclaimed suddenly. Grinning, Marshalla turned to stare at her little friend.

"Now, don't you—" she began.

"But he hates me!" Tip whined.

"Only if you don't keep your hands in your pockets! That's the..." Marshalla's words faded as her gaze fell upon Tip's hands.

"Tip, your left hand."

"Hunh?" Tip stared at his hands. His left hand was clenched. Frowning, he brought his hand forward before unclenching it. Within it lay a gold ring, one with two emeralds embedded within. Guiltily, he looked up at Marshalla.

"Tip..." she sighed as she deftly swiped the ring from his hand. "Keep telling you, hands in pockets when going through crowds. Going to get us killed one day."

Tip's face fell as his frown grew.

"Sorry," he mumbled.

Sighing, Marshalla ruffled his hair before turning and proceeding to cross the street, a contrite Tip in tow.

"Now, remember," Marshalla said as they reached the front door of Mardaley's

Glorious Emporium, "hands in pockets, okay?"

"Okay," he mumbled.

She turned to stare at her friend once more. "Stop moping, okay? Not mad, just—"

Her words were cut short as the front door swung violently open, a tall and very irate high elf barging right out of it. It was all poor Marshalla could do to stop herself from bumping into him.

"And another thing!" he bellowed as he turned to glare back into the store. "I expect my items delivered by no later than this evening, or I guarantee, come tomorrow, the agreements and accords you have with the Shimmering Tower will all be reduced to dust! Good day!" As he finished, he turned on his heels, only to finally notice Marshalla and Tip. Almost at once, his face screwed up in disgust.

"Always suspected Mardaley chose to surround himself with vermin," he growled.

"Hey!" Marshalla exclaimed. The high elf glowered at her in response, as if daring her to protest. But Marshalla kept her peace, choosing instead to glare back at him. Finally, he smirked.

"Pathetic," he muttered as he barged past Marshalla and Tip, almost knocking the poor little boy to the ground.

"You alright, Tip?" Marshalla asked after a brief charged silence. Tip looked from the receding figure to his friend, before nodding.

"Good," Marshalla replied. "Come on, then." Turning, she made her way into the store, Tip close behind.

"There you are!" A voice rang out to them as they walked in. Staring at the utterer, Marshalla's face broke out into a wide grin as she waved at the store's proprietor. Though it was rare for a human to be the proprietor of a store in Merethia, it was rarer still for the store to be as widely regarded and frequented as Mardaley's Glorious Emporium. Except, Mardaley Templeton was no ordinary human. Walking towards them, he glowered at the two newcomers, though the smile upon his lips softened the glare greatly.

"And what time do you call this, young lady?" he demanded as he reached them. None in Merethia knew just how old Mardaley was, or even where he came from, but all knew he had means and ways of procuring items of and for arcane use that precious few could match.

"Sorry, Mardaley," Marshalla said. "Got held up on the way to Tip."

At her words, Mardaley peered behind her at the cowering little elf, his bony left hand slowly stroking his immaculately trimmed silvery-white beard while his right hand was buried deep in one of the pockets of his silk coat.

Tip stared sheepishly back at him.

"He'll behave this time, Mardaley. Swear."

"You gave me your word last time, Marsha, and it wasn't enough to stop him from taking the sealing pin to those hellbats' cages."

"But we cleaned up the mess they made though, didn't we?"

"Hrm… quite." Abruptly, he turned and headed deeper into his store. With a grateful sigh, Marshalla turned and grinned at Tip, only to realize his hands weren't in his pockets.

"Hands!" she mouthed at him.

"Sorry," Tip mouthed in response as he placed his hands in his pockets. Mardaley was talking to them.

"You know, you still haven't told me how you knew Toriel wouldn't be showing up for work today."

Marshalla grinned as she turned to face Mardaley. "Oh well, you know, one of those things, just—" A sharp gasp from Tip cut her short as both she and Mardaley turned to stare at him.

"What is it, boy?" Mardaley asked.

"Nothing!" he exclaimed as he stared wide-eyed at the old man.

Mardaley stared at him with suspicion before casting a careful eye across the trinkets and items about the little boy. Nothing seemed out of place.

"Hrm…" he muttered as he squinted at Tip. Tip merely stared back, a ridiculous grin on his face. At last, Mardaley turned back to the table he was standing beside. As he did so, Tip's gaze fell to Marshalla.

"What?" she mouthed at him.

Grimacing, he pulled out from his pocket a bulging money purse. Frowning, Marshalla stared at it before she too went wide-eyed.

"Are you two actually listening?"

"Uh…" Marshalla began, turning to stare at Mardaley, "yeah!"

"Mhm, and what did I just say?"

"You… asked if we were listening."

"Before that?"

"Uh…"

Mardaley sighed as he turned to stare at them square. "Look, Marsha, if you want his position, you need to be focused, alright? My clients demand the very best at all times, and you cannot get any of their orders wrong, ever. Do you understand?"

Marshalla nodded.

"We got a job?"

Mardaley frowned as he stared at Tip. "Marsha didn't tell you?"

Tip shook his head.

"No time," Marshalla replied in her defense. "Had to get back here quick."

"Right, well… you can fill him in on the details of the arrangement later. Right now, I need you to make some deliveries."

"Anything for that elf just now?"

"Who, Thuridan?"

Marshalla nodded in response even though she barely heard the name. As she nodded, however, Mardaley stared at them from the corners of his eyes.

"Why do you want to go to him?"

Marshalla shrugged as nonchalantly as she could. "He's going to hurt your business, so figured we make a delivery to smooth things over." It was weak, but it was all she had.

An uneasy silence fell upon them all as Mardaley weighed her words. At last, he nodded.

"Wouldn't hurt to send that little fool something to shut him up. Last thing I need is for him to be making a scene over in the Tower. Right, well you can do his deliveries last. Come over here, I need to show you how to work this delivery sack, and where you're going."

Nodding, Marshalla did as she was bid, leaving Tip to wander the front of the store admiring the many curiosities on sale, or at least pretending to. And with his hands firmly in his pockets, of course. But even so, even with fear and guilt coursing through him, Tip still eventually lost himself in wonder at the many items in jars, bottles and boxes arrayed upon shelf after shelf. There was just something about the arcane, the mystical, that tickled his imagination and drew him in, and it wasn't long before he began wondering how the elbst scales on the top shelf above him would feel to the touch, or how it was possible to convince the chimera that owned the tongue in the jar beside the scales to part with it. How did it speak now? And, for that matter, would the phoenix that owned the magnificent tailfeathers glistening just outside his reach not be missing them, or did it have lots to spare? And, how come the feathers weren't setting the shelf on fire? Did they only burn when they were attached to the phoenix?

"Tip, time to go," Marshalla called out to him suddenly, breaking him from his trance.

"Hunh…?" he asked as he turned to his friend. She had the delivery sack slung across her and was nearing the door.

"Deliveries, remember? Work now, dream later."

"Oh." Tip smiled sheepishly at her. "Coming," he added as he hurried over to join her at the door.

"If you get back before the noon-chime, you can have lunch with me," Mardaley said as Tip reached his friend. At this, both Tip and Marshalla's eyes lit up.

"Deal!" Marshalla exclaimed as Tip nodded excitedly, and with that they both hurried out of the store before tearing down the street. Luckily, their first stop wasn't all that far from Mardaley's, and as they rounded the corner leading to it, Marshalla came to a screeching halt. She stared at the house across from them, as if trying to be sure this was the right one.

"That... the first one?" Tip asked between breaths. Marshalla nodded in response. Abruptly, she turned to stare at Tip, her face all seriousness.

"Purse," she ordered as she took the delivery sack off her.

Frowning, Tip drew out the money purse. "What you doing?"

Frowning herself, Marshalla looked up from the delivery sack, but once she saw the worry in little Tip's eyes, she smiled.

"Giving it back!" she exclaimed before returning her attention to the sack. Tip stared at her for a moment before finally realizing her intent.

"That the Thuridan man's house?" he asked.

"Mhm." Marshalla nodded as she fished out Thuridan's delivery.

"But Mardaley said we do his last, though."

Marshalla looked up at him, her lips pursed. "Tip, we stole his coin. By now, he's noticed. By now, he's called the peacekeepers on us, and the first place they'll go is Mardaley's. You think he'll keep us when he knows we stole from a customer?"

Tip's face fell as tears stung his eyes.

"Sorry," he mumbled.

"Oh, Tip," Marshalla replied as she let go of the sack, throwing her arms around the little elf before giving him a heartfelt hug. "Don't hate you, honest. But peacekeepers won't care if you mean to or not, so we just have to fix this before they get to us." Then, she parted from him, dropping her gaze to his face as she did so. "Okay?"

Pouting, Tip nodded as he wiped the tears from his face.

"Good. Now, think this the right package. Purse?"

Tip handed over the purse.

"Good. Let me do the talking, okay?"

Tip nodded at her.

"Good."

Slinging the delivery sack across her once more, Marshalla tucked the package under her right arm, and with the purse in her left hand, she turned and began making her way towards the house, humming a tune to herself. Pouting still, Tip fell in behind her. Before long, they were standing at the front door. It was an imposing structure, the house, even for the area it was in, its designs and decorations bordering on the garish. Rapping on the front door, Marshalla stepped a couple of paces back and waited, humming still. Before long, the door swung open as a smartly dressed man stepped out, his nose wrinkled in disgust.

"What do you want?"

"Delivery for..." Marshalla replied, pausing to read the label on the package under her arm. "Thuridan Grovemender."

"And who is it from?"

"Mardaley's Glorious Emporium."

"Hrm... quite. Well, give it here, I'll make sure the master gets it."

Marshalla shook her head at him. "No, supposed to give it to him and him alone."

The doorman held Marshalla in a cold glare for a scant few moments, his frown deepening with each passing moment. "Young girl, I have been serving Master Grovemender since before your mother made the grievous mistake of spreading her legs to your father, and—"

"That supposed to—"

"And I don't need to stand here and listen to the likes of you insult my honor or my dedication to duty. When I say I shall make sure the master gets it, the master shall get it. Now, hand it over and stop polluting my air!"

Marshalla glared at him. "You Thuridan Grovemender? No. So, get out of the way."

The doorman laughed at her. "Oh, my dear girl, if you think I will let you carry yourself past this threshold, you are very much mistaken. Unlike Mardaley's, we are *quite* particular about who is allowed in here."

Marshalla smiled at him. "Well, then, tell your master you the reason his delivery late today, okay?"

"And where are you going?" the doorman demanded as Marshalla turned about. Marshalla looked over her shoulder at him.

"Got lots of deliveries to make, and if you going to act like a constipated old bastard, fine. Going to make my other deliveries. Will be back to drop this off after. Mister Thuridan's expecting this though, so when he starts asking where it is, you'll tell him it's late because you were particular about who you let into the house, yes?"

The doorman glared at Marshalla, looking fit to burst, but before he could reply, a voice rang out from behind Tip.

"What's going on here?"

Turning, Tip's face fell as he stared at the two peacekeepers behind him, but Marshalla simply stared at them, shrugging as she did so.

"Making a delivery, but this old goat won't let me."

"Mind your manners, child!" the doorman bellowed.

"So, give it to him and get lost," the older peacekeeper grumbled.

Once again, Marshalla shook her head. "Not happening. Mardaley said to give it to Thuridan Grovemender and Thuridan Grovemender only."

Snarling, the younger peacekeeper stormed right up to Marshalla, shoving his face to within a hair's breadth of hers.

"Are you deaf, rat? Did you not hear what he said?"

"Heard what he said, but unless you wanting to cross swords with Mardaley, you best not get in my way."

Sneering, the younger peacekeeper leant back slightly from Marshalla. "Are you threatening a peacekeeper?"

Before Marshalla could respond, the elder peacekeeper spoke up.

"What's so special about this package that you need to deliver it to Thuridan himself?"

Marshalla turned to the man. "He dropped something, something he'd want back quick."

"I knew it!" the doorman exclaimed. "You're the two pickpockets the master was talking about!" Without waiting for a response, he turned to the peacekeepers. "It's them he called you for! Arrest them! Arrest them this instant!"

Marshalla stared at the doorman as if he'd suddenly grown a second head. "You gone mad? If we stole it, why in the hells would we be standing here and not spending the lot?"

"I've heard enough," the younger peacekeeper growled before grabbing Marshalla by the arm.

"Careful! The parcel!" she exclaimed. Which was just as well, for in that instant, it slipped from under her arm, and she was only just able to catch it with her other hand.

"See what you almost did?" she bellowed.

"Shut up!" the peacekeeper snarled back as he yanked harder on her right arm before reaching to grab her left.

"What's going on here?" a voice rang out from behind the doorman. At those few words, all present froze where they stood.

"We caught those thieves for you, my lord!" the elder peacekeeper exclaimed, suddenly coming back to life.

Thuridan arched a regal eyebrow at the elf. "On my doorstep?"

"Er, yes, well—" he began, but Marshalla cut him short.

"Mardaley sent us. He said—"

"Did I say you could speak?" His voice was calm, his tone even, but the venom behind them biting, nonetheless. Glaring, Marshalla kept her peace. After a scant few moments, he turned to his doorman.

"Well?"

"They… those two came with a delivery for you, my lord, from Mardaley's."

"I see."

He looked back at Marshalla. "So, Mardaley stole my money purse."

"No," Marshalla replied sneering. "You dropped it when you tried to shove Tip and me into the gutter."

"Watch your tongue, girl!" the doorman exclaimed.

"That's alright, Albrecht. Vermin like her have no manners." Abruptly, he held out his hand. Glaring still, Marshalla shook the peacekeeper's hands off her, walked over and handed over the package and the money purse.

"And I suppose you'd be wanting some kind of reward?"

Marshalla shrugged. "Why not?"

"Typical," he replied, sighing. He looked up at the peacekeepers behind Marshalla before a slow cold smile parted his lips.

"How about, for a reward, I let you leave here with your little sewer mouse over there before the peacekeepers decide to interrogate you further?"

Frowning, Marshalla turned to the two men behind her. She liked their gazes not one bit.

"Well?"

Marshalla looked back at Thuridan.

"Come, Tip," she said at last, reaching out for her friend even as her gaze remained on the haughty elf before her. And as they left, the mocking laughter of the peacekeepers rang in her ears. After a few paces, they both stopped and stared behind them. Thuridan was talking to the peacekeepers.

"Going to have to run now, Tip. You ready?"

With a grateful sigh, Tip smiled and nodded.

"Yeah," he said. "And thanks, Marsha."

Grinning, Marshalla turned to stare at her friend, ruffling his hair as she did so.

"Race you!" she exclaimed as she broke into a dead run. Laughing, Tip raced after her. And thus did they race away, he to keep up with his friend, she to get as far away from the two peacekeepers as she could.

*****

"Thank you!" Marshalla exclaimed as she turned away from the smiling elderly lady, the silver coins that were her reward a welcome sight in her palm.

"Think nothing of it, my dear," the kindly elf replied, grinning as she looked from Marshalla to Tip. "And you tell that scoundrel, Mardaley, I'm still holding him to his promise. I don't expect that sausage to remain rigid forever."

With her gaze springing up from her palm, Marshalla stared wide-eyed at the kindly elder elf who stared back at her with a mischievous smile.

"What sausage?" Tip asked, prompting a warning glare from Marshalla, and a humorous stare from the elf.

"We best get going, Tip, we—"

"Mardaley's, my dear," the noble lady said, an impish glimmer in her eye. "We speak of Mardaley's sausage. You tell him from me, I grow tired waiting for a bite of it."

"Oh, okay," Tip said, confused.

"Come, Tip," Marshalla said as she ushered Tip away, "need to hurry."

"Okay," Tip replied, his face a mask of confusion still, until suddenly, his eyes lit up as he spun to stare at the noble elf.

"Can bring some of Mardaley's sausage over if you want?"

"What?" she asked, frowning at the little boy.

Tip nodded eagerly at her. "Marsha and me going to get stuffed at Mardaley's if we get back before the noon-chime. Can come and give you some after!"

"What?"

Marshalla stared at Tip, utterly mortified.

"We're going," Marshalla muttered at last as she pushed Tip on. "Now!"

Confused once more, Tip looked from Marshalla to the elderly elf before waving farewell to her. The noble lady merely stared back at the little boy with a look of bemusement till they disappeared from sight. Shaking her head once they were out of sight, Marshalla stared at Tip, sighing as she did so.

"What...?" he asked as his heckles rose.

"Know what she meant by sausage?"

"Yeah, it's human food. Seen Mardaley eat it before."

"Right..."

"Right!"

"Right," Marshalla repeated as she continued her pace.

"She the last one?" Tip asked as he fell in step beside her.

"Hm? Oh, yes."

"How much did we get, then?"

"With her coins...think we have enough for proper meals for the rest of the week,"

Tip's eyes grew wide. "From just one day?"

Smiling, Marshalla nodded at him. "Still got to go to Priory tonight though, and the street kitchen tomorrow night, but that's it. For this week anyway."

Tip's grin stretched from ear to ear. "So that's why you got the job!"

Marshalla's smile widened as she put the coins away. "You like?"

"Yeah! We'll be rich quick like this! Buy a proper bed and everything!"

Marshalla giggled. "Well... one day, yeah. We do this long enough, it's off the streets for us."

"Lucky for us Toriel didn't show up for work this morning!"

An impish grin replaced Marshalla's smile. "Yes, lucky us."

But as her grin widened, Tip's grin dimmed. "Marsha, what you do?"

"Hm?" she asked as she looked over at her friend. Tip was frowning at her.

"What you do, Marsha?"

Marshalla's grin dimmed greatly as she stared at Tip.

"What's it matter?" she asked as she shrugged. "You don't even like Toriel."

Tip shook his head at her, but before he could respond, she ruffled his hair. Scoffing, Tip pushed her hand away.

"Oh don't, Tip, don't. Toriel's been going on about how much better than all of us he is since he got off the streets. So, taught him a lesson, that's all."

Tip wasn't convinced, and it showed. Marshalla sighed as she stared at him.

"Come, let's get back. Noon-chime'll sound soon. Come."

"Not fair what you did to Toriel."

"Don't even know what happened."

"Doesn't matter, you stole his job."

"You lecturing me about thieving?"

A stunned silence fell on the pair as they stared at one another, the shock in one's gaze reflected perfectly in the other's.

"Look, Tip, didn't mean…"

As she spoke, Tip's gaze fell as his lower lip began to quiver. Without another word, Marshalla took him in her arms and hugged him close. An eerie silence befell the pair as a wordless apology floated from one to the other.

"Come," Marshalla said as they parted at last, "noon-chime'll sound soon, come." Tip obeyed without argument, and the pair hurried back, but the air between them was greatly subdued. They walked on in silence, Tip with his gaze resolutely before him, Marshalla throwing the odd glance at her companion, until at last, as the noon-chime struck its tenth chord, they finally walked into Mardaley's store.

"Ah, there you two are," Mardaley said as they walked in. "How did it go?"

"Flawless!" Marshalla exclaimed, but Tip merely stared at him, or rather through him. Frowning, Mardaley stared at Tip for a spell before looking at Marshalla.

"Stomach's rumbling," she replied.

"Ah," he said. "Well, this way, then." As he turned, both Tip and Marshalla saw what lay on the table behind him, and as their eyes took it all in, even Tip couldn't help but grin. In a flash, they were at the table, seated and ready to feast. Chuckling, Mardaley took his place, and all three began taking from the feast at the table, with Mardaley standing to carve the venison.

"Oh, you'll never guess who dropped by not too long after you left," Mardaley said as he sliced some venison for Tip.

"Oh?" Marshalla asked in response. "Who?"

"Two peacekeepers."

In an instant, Tip looked over at Marshalla, but the slight shake of her head seemed to calm his fears somewhat. Though, if Mardaley noticed, he did not show it.

"What they want?" Marshalla asked as calmly as she could.

"It was the strangest thing. They seemed to think Thuridan had his money purse stolen when he was over here earlier." Placing the slices onto Tip's plate, Mardaley began slicing off some more venison. "You two don't know anything about that, do you?"

"No," Marshalla shook her head. "Why would we?"

Mardaley stopped and turned to stare at her. "Because they said the two of you stopped over at Thuridan's to return it."

Marshalla shrugged as nonchalantly as she could, but it was Tip who spoke up.

"It was me," he mumbled, his gaze on his plate. "Took it when he pushed me."

Mardaley stared at the contrite little elf in silence for a spell before standing tall, sighing as he did so.

"Didn't mean to," Tip continued. "Just…can't…don't know how…"

"He really didn't mean to, Mardaley, and anyway, no——"

"You really need to stay quiet now, Marsha," Mardaley interjected, his gaze on Tip. Dropping her gaze to her plate, Marshalla did as she was bid.

"Tip, look at me."

Pouting, Tip obeyed.

"Thank you, for being honest with me."

Not knowing what to say, Tip nodded.

"I need to ask a favor of you, however."

Confused, Tip looked at Marshalla before looking back at Mardaley.

"What?" he asked as he cast a sideways glance at Mardaley.

"Can you keep Marsha honest? Few things I hate more than lies. So, can you keep her honest for me?"

Frowning, Tip nodded.

"Good. Oh, and another thing."

"What…?"

"Hands in your pockets, except when you really need to use them. Alright?"

Again, Tip nodded.

"Good. Oh, and one more thing."

Tip couldn't help but smile, albeit a slight one. "What?"

"Your venison's getting cold."

Chuckling, the little elf tucked into his meal, his fears forgotten. Smiling himself, Mardaley sat, his gaze upon Tip till the very last. Once seated, he looked over at Marshalla. There was a sad, guilty smile upon her lips.

"So long as you tell me the truth at all times, Marsha, you have nothing to fear."

"Sorry," she muttered, but Mardaley waved her words away.

"What's done is done. Just learn from this."

Marshalla nodded at him in response.

"Good! Now, tell me about your deliveries? Anything else happen?"

"Well!" Marshalla began, before regaling Mardaley with the tales of their deliveries, from the short race between Tip and her at the start, right to their brief encounter with the noble lady, an encounter that Tip was far more forthcoming about than Marshalla. However, just as Mardaley was finally about to acquiesce to the pleas from Tip to explain what the noble lady meant, pleas that Marshalla had tried to stop, the front door was flung open as a figure raced in, disheveled and out of breath. Startled, all three looked over at the figure, and what they saw elicited a gasp from Marshalla while Tip looked over at her in worry. Mardaley, on the other hand, simply rose, his features deceptively calm.

"Hello, Toriel," he said, his calm unnerving.

Panting, Toriel headed over to them. "Morning, Mardal—"

"Afternoon."

Toriel stopped as he stared at the others, his gaze pleading with both.

"Didn't meant to be late, swear. Overslept this morning. Don't know what happened."

"Nor do I care, Toriel," Mardaley replied in the same calm tone as before. "I warned you the last time you did this, I told you, if you ever showed up this late again, I'd find a replacement for you, did I not?"

"Yeah, but—"

"And now that you have done it again, I'm afraid I have found a replacement for you."

"No, but—"

"So, I need you to leave my store now, Toriel."

"Please, Mardaley, can't—"

"I said now, Toriel."

Wide-eyed, Toriel looked at Marshalla. "Marsha, tell him what happened! He always listens to you!"

Mardaley turned his gaze to her. Marshalla managed a weak shrugged.

"Don't know what he's talking about."

"Liar!" Toriel bellowed and charged towards them. In an instant, Mardaley turned his gaze back to Toriel, his eyes flaring as he did so, and as his gaze fell upon the charging elf, an unseen force grasped Toriel roughly, dragging him back to the door before holding him rigid before it. Toriel stared at Mardaley in clear terror. With the same unnerving calm, Mardaley looked back at Marshalla, saying nary a word.

"You've got to tell the truth, Marsha!" Tip exclaimed suddenly. "Mardaley said, you've got to tell the—"

"Okay!" Marshalla snapped, throwing an angry glare at Tip before turning her gaze back to Mardaley.

"Was at Brok's tavern last night. Got Toriel to buy a few drinks."

"Liar!" Toriel screamed. "Got me drunk!"

"Did she force the drink down your throat?" Mardaley asked, turning back to Toriel.

"She kept telling me buy, buy, buy. Just keep buying and drinking, like it was a game, and—"

"Did she force the drink down your throat?"

"But it's all her fault! She tricked me! She—"

Shaking his head, Mardaley sighed, and as he did so, Toriel fell silent even as his lips moved. Soon after, Toriel truly fell silent.

"Did she force the drink down your throat? Yes," Mardaley nodded at Toriel, "or no?" then shook his head at him.

Almost immediately, Toriel nodded.

"Truly? Even though she's half your size?"

Again, Toriel nodded.

Mardaley shook his head in response. "No, Toriel. You chose to drink, knowing full well you had to be here in the morning. If our arrangement wasn't important enough to you to have you say no, then I made the right decision in letting you go. Now, begone!"

And with that, Toriel was gone.

"Where he go?" asked a startled Tip.

Mardaley turned his gaze to Marshalla. "That was a supremely underhanded thing you did. I trust you will never stoop so low again under my employ."

His voice was calm, but his tone cold. Marshalla nodded guiltily at him.

"Good," Mardaley said before sitting once more.

"Where he go?" Tip asked.

"Sent him back to wherever he'd awoken. Now eat up, there are more deliveries to be made."

Both did as they were bid, but there was no longer any joy in their meal.

As the day began giving way to night, Marshalla and Tip finally bid Mardaley farewell, and for both, it was a time that could not have come soon enough. They were exhausted, truly and completely, for the deliveries covered the length and breadth of Merethia. But, more than that, they were both glad to be away from Mardaley and his darkened mood.

Yawning, Tip stretched his arms as wide as they would go before rubbing both eyelids.

"Sleepy?"

Smiling, Tip looked up at Marshalla. "No, just tired."

Marshalla grinned back at him.

"Long day," she said, nodding. Tip nodded back as they walked away from Mardaley's store. Then, as his eyes lit up, his lips were split by an enormous grin.

"But we got to ride a carriage! Four times as well!"

Marshalla chuckled at her dear friend. "Good as you thought?"

"Better!"

Marshalla chuckled once more.

"Want to know the best part?"

Shaking her head, Marshalla started grinning at the little bundle of energy beside her.

"What?"

"Guess."

"Oh, go on, tell me."

"The Gardens, Marsha. The Gardens! They let us in! Us!"

Marshalla laughed aloud at this, though in truth, Tip's joy was understandable, for the Gardens of Tait were the jewel of Merethia. They were the pinnacle of all that was Merethia's beauty, and a bold statement to the world of its status and stature. And though the Gardens were meant to be open to all of Merethia, in truth, vagrants and vagabonds had always found their way blocked by the peacekeepers that guarded them.

"Want to know my favorite part?" Marshalla asked as she adjusted the straps of the bag she carried.

"What?"

In response, Marshalla clasped one of her pockets and shook it, the sound of jingling coins ringing gloriously within.

"Woah!" Tip exclaimed, his eyes going wide. "How much in there?"

"Enough to keep us fed for this week and next, I think, if we're careful."

"Wow."

"That's just from the deliveries. There's still the coin Mardaley gave us," Marshalla said as her grin widened. At her words, Tip's eyes shone brighter as his mouth watered. But it was fleeting, the wonder in his gaze chased away by worry.

"You think Mardaley wants us back after what you did to Toriel?" he asked. Marshalla's own grin dimmed greatly at this.

"Think he'll forgive us," she replied, "but only if we don't do anything to make him mad."

Tip nodded at her.

"Hands in pockets, always," he promised.

Marshalla nodded at him. "Good. Come, our turn at the Priory tonight. Going to have to hurry though; should be supper soon."

"Oh, right!"

Quickening their steps, both hurried down the winding streets until they stood before the simple, but homely, entrance of the Priory of the Kind Goddess.

"Think we're too late?" Tip asked, frowning as Marshalla pushed open the door, but the delectable aroma that wafted out told a different tale. Grinning, both raced in, darting past the priests at the entrance as they hurried to the main hall.

Bursting through the double doors of the main hall, both elves stood panting slightly as they scanned the hall within. Stretched right through the center of the main hall stood a single mahogany table around which sat many of various races and ages, male and female, all of whom shared the misfortune of extreme penury. It was a simple arrangement, but an effective one, and judging from the ongoing commotion, those within were still taking their seats.

"Hey, look!" came a cry from within. "Marsha and Tip made it!"

Grinning, Marshalla's gaze went straight to the utterer before she and Tip made their way to her.

"Thought you already had your time here this week," Marshalla said as she sat beside the one who'd called out to them.

"Hi, Maline," Tip panted as he scrambled up on the other side of Marshalla.

"Hello, my darling," Maline replied. Smiling, she looked over at Marshalla. "You keeping well."

Marshalla smiled back. "You too. They change your day back to today, then?"

Smiling, Maline shook her head, but Marshalla could see the smile was forced.

"No, was just passing. Drumold said they had space at supper, so came in."

At her words, Marshalla's smile dimmed as her gaze hardened.

"He beat you again," she snarled.

"Gods, Marsha," one of the others across from them spoke up. "Don't have to say it like that."

"Still care for him, Marsha," Maline muttered as she dropped her gaze to her hands. "Not that easy to let go."

"Maline!" Marshalla exclaimed as she fought the urge to shake some sense into the older elf. "He's always drug-addled, or drunk, every single time! He spends every coin you both make!"

Frowning, Maline stared at her hands for a spell longer before raising her gaze to stare down the length of the table, her teeth clenched. Frowning herself as her gaze softened, Marshalla slipped a hand into Maline's, the elder elf's calloused hand rough to the touch.

"Maline and Fargus fight again?" Tip asked suddenly.

"Only a small one," Maline replied, looking past Marshalla as she spoke. But the worry in little Tip's eyes was hard for her to behold, and before long she shifted her gaze back to Marshalla.

"Where you sleeping tonight?" asked Tip.

"Here," Maline replied, turning her gaze to him once more. "Drumold said there's a spare bed."

Tip moved to speak, but a commotion at the far end of the table drew all eyes, and the sights that greeted them drew a smile on every lip.

"Really got here just in time, Tip!" Marshalla exclaimed as four priestesses walked towards the table, laden with servings of a most mouth-watering broth. However, as she stared, grinning, Marshalla felt a tug on her tunic.

"What?" she asked, turning to Tip.

In response, Tip merely beckoned her closer.

"What?" she whispered as she leant in.

"The dagger, from this morning," Tip whispered. "Let Maline have it."

Marshalla frowned deeply at her friend.

"We got a job now," he added. "She needs it more."

Marshalla stared hard at Tip, then glanced over her shoulder at Maline.

"Let her have the ring instead, eh?" she begged, turning to Tip once more.

Tip shook his head at her. "The dagger, Marsha. It's prettier. Will get her more."

Marshalla frowned at Tip as he stared pleading with her.

"Okay," Marshalla replied at last, before turning her gaze back on Maline, whose gaze was firmly on the priestesses. Reaching into one of her pockets, Marshalla pulled out the dagger before leaning into Maline. As the elder elf turned round to her, Marshalla pressed the dagger upon her thigh.

"From Tip," she whispered.

Confused, Maline looked down at her lap. The moment she laid eyes on the dagger, however, she looked over at Tip, stunned. But Tip merely grinned back. With no words to call forth, Maline smiled at him before returning her gaze to Marshalla.

"But you stay away from him," Marshalla demanded.

Nodding, Maline grasped the dagger.

"Promise," Maline said as she pocketed the gift.

"Good," Marshalla growled, and as the woman breathed deep, the pair turned to the priestesses approaching.

Soon, the priestesses reached them, laying before each their own delicious-smelling broth. It was a good few moments before any spoke.

"How'd Drumold know he'd have space anyway?" Marshalla asked after a spell, sucking on the succulent piece of chicken in her mouth. "They don't do the count till after supper."

Maline looked up at her, a stick of green bean sticking out of her own mouth. Shoving the whole stick into her mouth, she looked round at those about them.

The others around them were staring at her.

"What...?" Marshalla asked, her heckles rising.

In response, Maline looked over Marshalla's shoulder at Tip. He was clearly engrossed in his broth. Frowning, she leant closer to Marshalla.

"Tip's friend, Adalla," Maline whispered.

"What about her?"

"They found her this morning, in the Gardens."

The apprehension in Maline's voice called forth a ball of fear from within Marshalla.

"Found her how? And how in the hells did she get into the Gardens?" Marshalla found herself asking.

Hesitating, Maline looked over Marshalla's shoulder once more before continuing.

"Peacekeepers found her. Don't know for sure how she got in, but... Someone ravaged her bad, Marsha, real bad. She was bleeding and everything. Sometime last night. They beat her too, even took her bag and things."

With some effort, Marshalla kept her emotions from her face as she looked over her shoulder at Tip. She and Adalla never truly got along, but Tip adored her, and it was easy to see why, for she was a most pleasant creature, quick to smile and quicker still to laugh, one who seemed to have time for everyone.

"She okay?" Marshalla whispered, turning her gaze back at Maline.

"She dead, Marsha. Peacekeepers said she tried to crawl to the gate, but... the cold... and her wounds... She dead." Marshalla gazed deep into the ether, making nary a sound, until at last, she held Maline in a hardened glare.

"That why you came by?"

"Oh, don't you dare, Marsha," Maline snarled, her own gaze hardening as she spoke. "Don't you dare! Didn't know about her till Drumold said... would *never*... don't you dare!"

Marshalla's gaze softened. "They know who did it?"

Maline's gaze softened as well. "Peacekeepers think one of her patrons."

And that was the crux of Marshalla's dislike of Adalla, for though Adalla matched her in beauty and body, while she'd fought tooth and claw to keep her body her own, Adalla had chosen to sell hers to whoever would pay.

"They think he took her in there for a quick one, then called in some friends. But she never does groups, does she... *did* she? Must've said no too much and they... just..." Maline shook her head, a sad sigh escaping her lips as she did so.

"Nobody deserves to die like that," Maline continued after a brief spell. "Not her, not nobody."

"What you two gossiping about?" Tip asked suddenly, his giggles not far away. Marshalla and Maline both forced a smile as they looked at him.

"Lady stuff," Marshalla replied regally, to which Tip promptly pulled a face and went back to his broth. But as the women's gaze fell on one another once more, their smiles dissipated.

"Think they'll catch who did it?" Marshalla asked.

"Do you?"

Marshalla pursed her lips as her gaze darkened. Gritting her teeth, she turned her gaze to her broth, but her hunger was no more.

"Here, Tip," she said, pushing her bowl to the slurping youth beside her, "have mine."

"Not hungry?" Tip mumbled, lentils and quail crammed into his mouth as he spoke. Marshalla smiled before shaking her head. Shrugging, Tip pushed forward his now-empty bowl and pulled Marshalla's closer. Keeping her thoughts to herself,

Marshalla let Tip and the others dine in peace. The news imparted upon her had filled her heart and her head with hate. But she kept it all away from her face, keeping instead a serene smile as she watched Tip dine.

Before too long, Tip finished her bowl too, and, burping loudly, turned to Marshalla.

"Finished."

Marshalla chuckled at him. "Yeah, we guessed."

Tip grinned at her. "Sorry."

"Really?" Marshalla asked, smiling as she rose.

"No," Tip replied, grinning still as he too rose.

"Where you two off to, then?" Maline asked. In response, Tip looked at Marshalla.

"Off to find Drumold," Marshalla replied. "Tip's going to keel over soon, so best get him to bed quick."

"Hey!" Tip exclaimed as Maline chuckled. "Not sleepy, just tired!"

"Right," Marshalla replied, then, giving Maline's hand a quick squeeze, headed towards the kitchens, Tip in tow.

High Priest Drumold Etherspire was indeed in the kitchen, for it was well known that his love of food and its preparations was dwarfed only by his love for the goddess Diyanis.

"Ah, Marsha!" he exclaimed as Marshalla and Tip entered, his gaze lifting briefly from the chopping board. "Come to continue your tutelage?"

Marshalla smiled. "Not just now. Come to ask where we bed down tonight."

"Oh, right, of course. You weren't here during the allotments, were you?"

"No, sorry," Marshalla replied, grimacing.

"No matter, you're here now. Before you bed down though, how's the bag? Is the enchantment on it still functional?"

Marshalla nodded.

"And the blanket? The enchantment still keeping you warm?"

Again, Marshalla nodded.

"Good, should make it easier to clean, then. You're on the second floor tonight, third one on the left. Leave your bag in the usual place, would you? There's a fresh change of undergarments in the new bag in your room, for the both of you. We've run out of cleansing towels again I'm afraid, so you'll have to come back tomorrow. Don't worry, you and Tip are front of the queue."

Marshalla smiled at the portly priest.

"Thank you, Drumold," she said and spun round to leave.

"Before you go," the high priest replied, "can you and Tip take the waste out to the back? We're going to start washing soon; we'll need the space."

Marshalla grinned at Drumold. "Never get used to how much that lot waste."

Drumold grinned back at her. "Me neither."

Chuckling, she looked at Tip. "Come on, then."

"Oh, by the bye, Toriel was over earlier," Drumold continued, his words freezing the pair where they stood. "He said something rather disturbing."

Slowly, Marshalla turned to stare at the kindly elf.

"It's true, isn't it? You stole his place at Mardaley's."

"Didn't exactly *steal* it, just—"

"That post was his, Marsha. We've been through this."

"Yes, but—"

"No, Marsha, no buts. Mardaley's a dear friend. How do you think what you did reflects on me? If you were Mardaley, would you want to take on anyone else from here?"

"But Toriel was causing Mardaley grief, you said so yourself, many times. And Mardaley gets on better with us than Toriel. Saved you face if anything!"

Drumold pursed his lips at the rebelling elf. "You need to give Toriel what is rightfully his."

"But—"

"No buts. It's his role, not yours."

"But Mardaley was going to let him go anyway."

"And if Mardaley does do that, then yes, you can step in. But how you got this posting is wrong."

"But—"

Abruptly, Tip pulled on Marshalla's hand. Frustrated, she turned to stare at Tip, who simply stared back, nodding. A few moment's silence passed as an unspoken accord passed between the two. At last, she turned to Drumold with the look of one defeated.

"Go take out the waste. I'll summon Toriel tomorrow. All four of us will go see Mardaley. Alright?"

"Okay," Marshalla muttered.

"It's for the best, Marsha."

With a dejected nod, Marshalla headed over to the waste bucket while Tip opened the back door. Before long, both were standing behind the Priory, the waste bucket between them as they moved it towards the Priory's waste devourer.

"Step back," Marshalla muttered, pulling Tip gently away from the bucket. Tip did as he was bid just as Marshalla moved to stand behind the bucket.

"It's for the best, Marsha," Tip said just as Marshalla began tipping the bucket towards the devourer. "Was nice while it lasted."

Marshalla smiled before running her hand through Tip's hair. But, just as she was about to turn her attention back to the waste bucket, a figure stepped out from the shadows.

"Well, well, well, look who's here."

Startled, both Marshalla and Tip spun round to face the utterer.

"Toriel!" Marshalla exclaimed. And, indeed, it was Toriel, but this was a drunk Toriel, an angry Toriel. This was a dangerous Toriel. Stumbling forward, Toriel wiped the drool from his lips as he leered at Marshalla.

"Good thing you finally showed," he continued, "was getting bored waiting. You know, if you wanted that job so bad, could've just bought it."

Backing away from him, Marshalla kept Tip behind her as she made her way towards the door behind them, towards sanctuary.

"Look, Toriel," she replied with far more fire than she felt, "what's done is done. Okay, fine, it wasn't fair…"

Toriel scoffed at her at this, his slow advance unwavering.

"…but Drumold'll take us to Mardaley, get Mardaley to—"

"That fat old bastard? You think he can talk Mardaley into taking me back?"

The door was now within arm's reach, but so was Toriel.

"No, Marsha," Toriel continued, "no. No, you just have to pay up."

"Not got any coin."

Toriel smiled at her as his eyes dropped to her bosom.

"Not after coin," he replied, and without warning, lunged at Marshalla, grabbing her left bosom with his right hand before shoving his left hand between her legs while forcing a kiss upon her.

Gritting her teeth, Marshalla steadied herself before swinging her right knee in between Toriel's legs, the sudden pained gasp from the drunken elf bringing strange comfort. But she knew full well it was fleeting, and as Toriel staggered back, Marshalla spun round and shoved Tip at the door.

"Run!" she shrieked.

With his heart pounding in his ears, Tip dove for the door, but as he did so, a second shriek stopped him cold. As he turned, he stared in horror as Toriel pulled Marshalla towards him, her hair grasped firmly in his right hand. Then, he watched as Toriel spun his dear Marshalla round by her hair, only to crash a clenched left fist into her stomach.

"Leave her alone!" he bellowed, lunging at Toriel.

Snarling, Toriel turned to face Tip square, but in his drunken state, he was too slow to stop Tip from wrapping his arms around his leg, or stop Tip from digging his teeth deep into his flesh.

"Argh!" Toriel cried, before bringing his left fist down like a hammer onto Tips head, hard. The blow was enough to stun the little elf, and with an angry grunt, Toriel picked him up before swinging him at the waste bucket.

"Tip!" Marshalla cried as Tip crashed into the waste bucket, sending it careening towards the devourer, while Tip himself landed on the cold stone floor, head-first, then lay still where he fell.

Seeing her beloved Tip lying almost lifeless was too much for Marshalla to bear, and as the red mist descended, she threw herself at Toriel, clawing, biting and slapping for all she was worth. But, even in her rage, she was still no match for Toriel, and clenching his left fist once more, he smashed it into her stomach once, twice, thrice, before pulling her down onto her back.

Only, Marshalla was not one to admit defeat so easily, and even as he clambered upon her, she scratched him still, and it wasn't until he clasped her hands with his right and smashed his left fist into her temple with all his might that she finally did succumb, for it was at that point that darkness claimed her, too.

It was the throbbing in her left temple that finally brought her round, and with a groan, she slowly stirred back to life.

"She's coming to."

Groaning once more, she opened her eyes, and as she began to rise, a pair of gentle hands helped her up to sitting.

"Thank Diyanis!"

It was High Priest Etherspire.

"Where…?" Marshalla began as she searched about her, but as her eyes fell upon Tip sitting not far from her, she calmed a spell. He was staring at her with tears in his eyes, and by his side was a priest from the kitchens, comforting him.

"What happened here?" Drumold asked her. Groggily, she looked at him. It was then she realized they had draped a cloak about her. Irritated, she made to discard it, but the priestess beside her stopped her.

"What happened here, Marsha?" Drumold repeated, but Marshalla ignored him. The gaze from the priestess had carried with it a most unsettling meaning. Lowering her gaze, she stared beneath the cloak, and it was then she noticed that her blouse was torn so badly both her bosoms were freed. And not only that, her trousers were torn and pulled down almost to her knees, as was her undergarment. Toriel. As a sickening wave of shame washed over her, Marshalla pulled the cloak tighter as she hugged herself. At least she couldn't remember any of it.

"Marshalla," Drumold continued. Marshalla looked at him. "What happened here?"

"Toriel," she said softly. "He was waiting for us. He… did this to me."

At her words, High Priest Etherspire looked first at the priestess beside Marshalla, then at Tip.

"What?" Marshalla asked. It was the way they were staring at Tip. And as she stared at Tip herself, it was then she realized the priest with him wasn't so much comforting him as restraining him.

"What?" Marshalla glared at the priests in turn.

"We found him on top of you," the priest beside Tip replied. "He doesn't remember what happened."

Marshalla stared blankly at him for a spell, but as his words sunk in, Marshalla felt her anger rise. Toriel. She stared at Tip once again, but he couldn't look at her. Snarling, she looked at the others.

"What you say to him?" she demanded, but before they replied, she turned her attention to Tip once more.

"Tip, look at me."

Tip did not. Instead, he began softly weeping.

"Tip," Marshalla pleaded. This time, Tip obliged.

"Thank you."

"What?" Drumold asked. She glared at the high priest in defiance.

"Tip fought Toriel off. That's why he was on top of me. He was protecting me."

"Wait, Marsha—"

"No! Tip fought him off. He stopped Toriel from hurting me."

"But—"

"No! Tip stopped Toriel. Toriel didn't hurt me, Tip stopped him!" Abruptly, she looked over at Tip. He'd stopped crying.

"It's okay, Tip, it's okay. Don't feel bad. You stopped him. You stopped him!"

"But...don't remember."

Marshalla smiled at him. "Doesn't matter. Doesn't matter, hear? You stopped him."

Tip shook his head in response.

"But—" he began, his voice quivering as he spoke, but Marshalla shook her own head at him.

"Doesn't matter what they said, what any of them said. You stopped Toriel. Don't care if you don't remember, doesn't matter. You stopped him, thank you."

Tip stared at his friend as he whimpered still.

"You go in with Drumold, okay?" Marshalla continued. "Go with him. Be in soon. Okay?"

Mutely, Tip nodded.

"Come, Tip," Drumold said as he reached out his hand. Rising, Tip took his hand as he, Drumold and the other priest headed in. Stopping at the door, Tip turned to stare at Marshalla. Marshalla smiled at him.

"Go on, be in soon."

Tip stared for a spell before finally doing as she bid, but as the door closed, Marshalla's smile faded to nothing. Turning, she stared at the priestess beside her.

"Help me, please."

Nodding, the priestess obliged, a sad smile upon her lips. But, as the priestess began helping Marshalla with her clothing, neither noticed the figure in the shadows slip away into the night.

PUPPET AND MASTER

Yawning, Thuridan placed his tome upon the reading table beside him before draining his goblet.

"And this is why you never send a fool on an important errand, Thuridan," he muttered as he placed the goblet on the table. Sighing, he rose, shaking his head as he walked over to the door, but as he reached for it, he heard the main door open and a voice drift to him that instantly drew his ire. Gritting his teeth, he swung the door open, stepping out into the corridor just as his son was undoing his coat.

"What time do you call this?" Thuridan asked as he walked over to his son, his hands crossed behind him as he lifted his chin in cold anger.

"Hello, Father," Thalas replied, his calm gaze matching his father's freezing glare. A brief moment of suffocating silence fell on both as the few servants about disappeared from sight. They all knew what was to come, and knew better than to be around when it did.

"Where have you been?" Thuridan asked at last, standing only two paces from his son. His voice was calm, but his tone biting.

"Watching Mardaley's like you bid me to."

"Mardaley's store closed ages ago. And I do believe I smell drink on your breath."

Thalas smiled slightly. "Yes, well I ran into some friends and—"

Abruptly, Thuridan raised his hand.

"Am I to understand you decided to go off gallivanting about town while on an errand of mine?" he asked, before placing his hand back behind him.

Thalas shrugged. "I had nothing new to report. Mardaley's still falling over himself looking after those two gutter rats, and this Toriel, whoever he is, is still the object of Mardaley's ire. It's all as I told you yesterday, and the day before, and the day before that, so…I didn't see the harm in—"

Again, Thuridan raised his hand. Though his gesture was enough to silence his son, it wasn't enough to still the frustrated sigh that escaped Thalas' lips.

"Firstly, if I find out you and your friends have gone out and done something stupid with another street whore, I assure you, son of mine, you will be cleaning that mess up all by yourself."

"You're never going to stop making me—"

"And secondly—" he continued, bringing his hand back behind him once again.

"I told you, repeatedly, she refused to do what we paid her to do. It was not our intent—"

"And secondly! When I send you on an errand, I expect you to treat it as the important task it is. Is that clear?"

"She brought it on—"

Once again, Thuridan raised his hand. "Is. That. Clear?"

Gritting his teeth, Thalas nodded at his father.

"Good," Thuridan said, placing his hand behind him once more. "I already have low expectations of you, Thalas. Actions such as these merely serve to lower them further."

"Oh, woe is me," Thalas growled as he stared at his feet. Thuridan glowered at his son, but Thalas remained unrepentant. After what seemed like an eternity, Thuridan stretched out his hand to his son. Thalas stared at his father's hand for a spell before reaching into his pocket, pulling out a small, smooth stone.

"Is it still working?" Thuridan asked as Thalas placed the stone in his father's hand.

"Why don't you put it to your ear and find out?" Thalas snarled, raising his gaze to glare at his father, but the cold gaze that met him dissipated his glare before forcing him to stare at his feet once more. Staring at his son for a scant few more moments, Thuridan finally turned on his heels.

"What's so special about those gutter rats anyway?" Thalas asked. "Yes, the little one stole coin from you, but so what? The servants steal from us all the time."

Stopping, Thuridan turned to stare at his son in disbelief.

"Thalas, it's not the house help who steal from me, it's your friends."

"Now hold there, Father, they—"

"And besides," Thuridan continued, "the little one didn't steal coin from me; he stole my purse right out of my pocket without me feeling it, or him feeling any ill-effects."

Thalas frowned. "The whole purse? You never told me that."

Thuridan blinked at his son. "Why would I?"

"But… the enchantment," Thalas said, choosing to ignore his father's barb.

"Precisely," Thuridan replied. "They not only stole it without my noticing, but kept it on their persons for quite some time. Neither of them felt worse for wear."

"Was the enchantment still active?"

"Thalas…" Thuridan replied, sighing. "What did I just say about you lowering my expectations of you?"

Thalas glowered at his father in silence.

"Of course it was active, I checked it the moment the girl handed it over."

"But then, how could they have stolen it?"

A condescending smile parted Thuridan's lips. "If I knew that, I wouldn't be having you shadow them, would I?"

"How do you know Mardaley didn't teach them?"

Thuridan shook his head slowly at his son before sighing. "Teach them what, precisely? The enchantment was still active, Thalas, it was active. It was not tampered with or dampened, and not one of the wards woven into the enchantment was dispelled. You truly think that human is capable of such?"

Thalas held his peace.

"Besides," Thuridan continued, "I'd changed many of the wards since the last time I went to Mardaley's, so that would've been the first time he would've seen them. No, it's the boy. It must be."

"Hold, Father, you said the girl handed over the purse."

"Yes, she did. But it was the boy I bumped into."

"Perhaps the girl pushed him into you so it would appear—"

"Thalas, shut up."

Fuming, Thalas did as he was bid.

"I intend to learn how that boy got around my enchantment and my wards, Thalas," Thuridan said after a moment's silence. "I intend to learn how that little gutter rat got around them all without affecting them in any way. Can you imagine what such knowledge could do for us? Can you imagine the doors it could open? Literally." Thuridan could see from his son's gaze he did, but he could see another thought forming in his son's mind.

"Don't," Thuridan said simply.

Thalas stared, confused. "Don't… what?"

"You were thinking of learning the secret for yourself. Don't. I'd hate to hurt you for it, boy, but I am never gracious to those who cross me, no matter who they may be."

"I would never—"

"Shut up," Thuridan replied tiredly. Once again, he turned away from his son.

"Your brother returns in three days," he continued as he headed back towards the reading room. "Can I trust you to stay on this one simple errand till then?"

A silence fell on the pair once again, and as he reached the reading room door, he stopped, turning his head to stare over his shoulder at his son.

"Of course, Father."

"Good," Thuridan replied, then entered the reading room, unperturbed by the pure hate in his son's gaze.

*****

Leaning back against the wall, Mardaley watched as Marshalla sorted and wrapped the deliveries. He couldn't help but smile. It was only just seven days previous that he'd shown her how, and here she was flying through it all with the skill of one who'd been at it for months.

"Ow!" Marshalla exclaimed suddenly.

"What?" Mardaley asked as he hurried over to her side. She looked up at him as he reached her, her thumb in her mouth. But as he reached her, he realized at once what had happened. Kneeling beside where she sat, the elderly storekeeper pulled her thumb free.

"No, it's deep," she protested as she tried to pull her hand free of his grasp. "You'll get blood everywhere."

Mardaley paid her no heed. Instead, he leant forward gently as he brought her thumb towards his own lips, and breathing onto it, whispered words of arcane upon it. As the words left his lips, the deep cut on Marshalla's thumb slowly healed away, leaving behind not even a scar. At last, he let go of Marshalla's hand. It was then he realized she was glaring at him. Smiling, he rose.

"Oh, don't look at me like that, Marsha. This is Merethia after all. You cannot avoid magic forever."

"Could've managed without your magic," she growled.

"Oh, I believe you. Except, would you have been able to heal the cut so quickly?"

Marshalla chose not to answer. Instead, she glared at him some more as she wiped her blood off the blade she'd been using to cut the wrapping twine. Mardaley couldn't help but snicker at her.

"You okay, Marsha?" Tip asked, staring at them from the shelves near the door. His voice was soft, subdued, far more timid than usual.

Smiling, Marshalla nodded. "Yeah. Mardaley used his silly magic on me, that's all."

A slow smile parted Tip's lips before he turned and returned to watching the cleaning broom sweep the store unaided.

"He still hasn't gotten over it, has he?" Mardaley asked, his eyes still on Tip as a worried frown crept across his lips. Marshalla looked from him to Tip, then back at the wrapping, his sadness reflected in her eyes.

"No," she replied.

"But *you* have at least." It was more a question than a statement.

Marshalla shrugged in response. "Not the first time it's happened, won't be the last. Can't change that, so might as well get used to it."

Mardaley's frown deepened. It always troubled him when she spoke so callously. He looked over at Tip once more.

"He's not getting used to it though, is he?"

Marshalla looked up at Mardaley once more before looking back at Tip. A brief silence fell on the pair.

"First time he seen it happen."

Mardaley looked over at her, surprised. Marshalla returned his gaze briefly before shrugging and returning her gaze to Tip.

"The other times, some were before Tip and me met. Others, managed to get them far enough away for him not to see it. That or he was sleeping."

Mardaley stared at Marshalla in silence as she stared forlornly at the little elf.

"Didn't help that the priests thought he was the one who done it though," Marshalla said after a brief spell.

Mardaley shook his head at her. "Such a stupid thing to accuse Tip of. As if anyone would believe it."

"Tip would."

There was a sadness in her tone, one with a slight undercurrent of fear, not much, but enough to force the hairs on the back of Mardaley's neck to stand tall.

"Meaning?" he asked, turning to face her square.

Marshalla looked at him before looking back at Tip.

"Tip gets… blackouts… sometimes. Goes off wandering. Doesn't remember where he goes or what he does. Scares the very life out of me it does. Doesn't do it often, mind, just never remembers doing it. But Toriel knows. Helped me look for Tip one time, so had to tell him. He put Tip on me so Tip would think he hurt me in one of his blackouts."

Abruptly, Marshalla turned to stare at Mardaley. There was a fire in her gaze.

"What he did to me, fair enough. A treasure for a treasure. But what he did to Tip…" She looked back at the little elf. "No. He'll pay, he'll pay big."

At last, she rose, scooping up the wrapped deliveries on the table into the delivery sack beside her before lifting it and heading over to the little stairs leading to the front of the store.

"Come, Tip," she called out as she hurried down the stairs.

"Aww!" Tip replied in complaint.

"Tip, don't start. Watch when we get back. Come."

"But it'll be done by then," he whined as he rose to join Marshalla at the door.

"Well, then, be good for the rest of the day so Mardaley will bring it out again."

"Aww!" Tip repeated, pouting deeply as he did so.

"Buy you a tasty treat if we finish quick."

All at once, Tip's eyes lit up, and after throwing a single excited glance at Marshalla, he raced right out of the door, an act that elicited a knowing grin from Marshalla and a deep chuckle from Mardaley.

"Come on, then!" Tip exclaimed as he poked his head back into the store before disappearing once more. Sighing, Marshalla shook her head and hurried after the eager little elf, her delivery sack already slung over her shoulder.

Once they began however, the deliveries turned out be nothing less than whirlwind. It helped greatly that the total deliveries themselves were less than usual, but still, Tip's eagerness truly was infectious, and before long, it was Marshalla who was hurrying Tip along, racing ahead and calling out to him to keep up. And by the time the pair finally sat to rest, a sizeable serving of delicious savory treats between them, it was undoubtedly a well-deserved rest.

"Mmm," Tip sighed as he licked the sticky seasoning from his fingers, his mouth stuffed to overflowing with all manner of meat and vegetables.

"Good?" Marshalla mumbled, her own mouth in much the same shape. Looking up from the pack to his dear friend, a toothed grin upon his lips, Tip nodded, then reached into the serving bag.

"Hey!" Marshalla exclaimed. "Swallow first!"

"Look who's talking!" Tip shot back, gesturing to the fresh skewer of assorted savories in Marshalla's hand.

Grinning, Marshalla ruffled Tip's hair in response.

"No!" Tip exclaimed worriedly as he ran his free hand through his hair. "Don't want sticky stuff in my hair."

"Oh, shush you," Marshalla replied. "Used my clean hand."

In response, Tip pulled a face at Marshalla as he swallowed before immediately tearing off some more meat from the skewer in his hand with his teeth and working it into his mouth with his lips. Shaking her head, Marshalla shuffled deeper into the bench they sat on as she turned her gaze onto the river of people and carriages before them.

"Marsha…" Tip began after a brief moment of calming silence.

"Hmm?" Marshalla replied distractedly, her gaze still upon the throng.

"Think Toriel will ever come back?"

Stiffening slightly, Marshalla stifled a gasp. This was the first time Tip had spoken Toriel's name since that fateful night. With the greatest of care, she turned to him, staring hard at him as she tried to read the intent behind his words. But his gaze was on his hands.

"Don't think so," she replied at last.

Tip looked up at her. The relief in his eyes eased her fears greatly.

"Why not?"

"Because he knows Mardaley'll hurt him if he does."

Tip stared at her for a spell before nodding, dropping his gaze to his hands as he tore off another chunk from his skewer. Then he looked up at Marshalla once more, grinning widely this time.

"Mardaley can be really scary, can't he?"

Marshalla smiled. "Very."

Tip chuckled as he chewed. "Remember how he made Toriel stand by the door? Thought he was going to wet himself!"

Marshalla laughed. "Yeah, he looked very scared, didn't he?"

Eagerly, Tip nodded. "Yeah, very!"

Grinning, Marshalla turned her gaze back to the throng.

"Going to do that one day, Marsha. You'll see."

Confused, Marshalla turned to stare at Tip as he stuffed the meat in his hand into his mouth. He was still staring at her.

"Do what?"

"Be scary like Mardaley. Going to be strong and scary like Mardaley one day, then nobody will hurt us, not ever again."

As she stared at the little elf, the intensity of his gaze bore into her. Tip had always had a great fascination for all things arcane, part of the reason for his almost perpetual sense of wonder, but this was different. And unsettling.

"But you're already strong now, Tip," Marshalla replied, choosing her words with great care. "You chased him away, remember?"

Frowning, Tip dropped his gaze.

"Not strong enough…" he mumbled bitterly before looking up at Marshalla once more, the intensity of his gaze undimmed. "But will be!"

Marshalla smiled, unsure of what else to do. She'd never seen Tip like this before.

"That would be nice," she said at last. All at once, the fire in Tip's gaze dissipated, replaced by the innocent joy she knew him for. Nodding once again, he turned his gaze to the throng and tore off the last of the pieces on the skewer, pulling it all into his mouth as he reached into the bag for another. Marshalla stared at him for a spell longer, her mind awhirl as her heart slowly climbed up her throat. At last, she too turned to stare at the throng.

Not long after that, all the savories were devoured, and with a long collective sigh, both rose and, swiftly descending into the gossip and inane banter both enjoyed, began heading back to Mardaley's. So engrossed were they in each other's company that neither noticed the little boy standing in front of Mardaley's until they were almost at the store. It was Tip who first noticed him, slowing slightly as he stared with some curiosity at the boy.

Though clearly young in age, he was a boy immaculately dressed. From his perfectly trimmed hair to his impeccably well-polished shoes, this was a boy born into great wealth, a boy who would want for nothing. As Marshalla stared at him though, she soon realized it was not the boy himself that held Tip's attention.

As they neared him, both watched as he dispelled the fireball he'd summoned forth with but a flick of his wrist.

"Do that again," Tip gasped, his face alight and his eyes bright.

Frowning, the little boy turned to Tip.

"Go on," Tip urged, his lips split into a wide grin. "Do it again."

Frowning still, and tilting his head slightly to the side, the little boy obliged, raising his right hand as he whispered some words of arcane. As he spoke, a ball of pure flame burst to life just above his open palm, spinning almost of its own accord. Poor Tip was beside himself with wonder, chuckling and clapping all at once. Fighting to suppress a smile, the little boy stared hard at Tip. Abruptly, Tip looked from the fireball to the boy.

"Make it bigger!" he exclaimed.

"No, Tip, that's—"

"It's alright," the little boy said. His voice was soft, with an alluring, almost musical timbre. Flicking away the fireball, the little boy brought his left palm up, putting both hands slightly apart before him, and looking from Marshalla to his palms, began whispering another string of arcane words, but this time with more care, with more focus. As he spoke, a new ball of flame burst forth, only this time the ball burst forth in the space between his palms, and with each whispered word, the ball grew larger as the flames flickered higher. With each word, Tips eyes grew as he stared at the ever-growing ball. But it all very nearly ended in disaster.

"Davian, what are you doing!" a voice bellowed from the store's door. Startled, the little boy looked up at the utterer, all three did. But as Davian looked from the ball to the door, his concentration broken, the ball exploded, the roar of the explosion echoing angrily up and down the street. With a start, Marshalla and Tip leapt backwards from the little boy, Marshalla dragging Tip towards her to shield him with her body. As they stared at the exploding ball of flame however, they both watched as the flames slid off unseen walls before dissipating in the afternoon air. As one, both turned to stare at Thuridan Grovemender glaring at the little boy, his right hand outstretched. Slowly, he straightened as the heat of his glare dissipated, a slow forced smile parting his lips.

"Davian, son," he began. "I've told you a thousand times before. You mustn't practice that spell without someone around to protect you should it go awry."

Pouting, Davian dropped his gaze. "Sorry, Father."

Thuridan shook his head. "No matter, no harm done. Come, our business here is concluded."

"Yes, Father," Davian mumbled as he walked over to his father.

"Come back soon," Tip said as Davian walked past his father.

"What, to see you?" Thuridan asked incredulously. "Don't be absurd."

In response, Tip stuck his chin out defiantly at the arrogant high elf while Marshalla merely glared at him. In silence, both watched as father and son disappeared down the street.

"Come on, then," Mardaley said, breaking them from their stare. "More deliveries."

"That really Thuridan's son?" Marshalla asked as she turned to stare at Mardaley.

Mardaley nodded. "Second son. Takes after his father in more ways than I daresay the little boy is happy with."

"Oh?" Tip asked.

Again, Mardaley nodded. "His affinity with the arcane is nothing short of astonishing, just like his father's. Poor Davian's had to endure all manner of training and schooling because of it, right from near-birth. And now Thuridan's getting him ready to take his Birthing."

"What, to the Tower?" Marshalla asked.

"Yes," Mardaley said, sighing as he spoke. Marshalla frowned.

"Don't think it's a good thing? Tower takes them young, doesn't it?"

Mardaley smiled. "No, it's not that, it's… I don't think it's a good thing to rob that boy of a childhood simply because he is gifted at something. But what do I know, I'm just an old man."

Both Marshalla and Tip smiled.

"Come on, then!" And as one, all three went back inside, only for two to stare behind them at the receding pair.

Two full days went by before either Marshalla or Tip saw Davian again. This time, it was Davian who walked in on them, a hesitant smile upon his lips as he pushed the door to Mardaley's store open. Once again, it was Tip who saw him first, seated on the little stairs eating an apple larger than his fists. And as Davian stepped in, little Tip's eyes lit up as if seeing a long-lost friend.

"Davian!" he exclaimed as he rose, dashing forward to the little elven boy, stopping just before him, his eyes twinkling with excitement as a toothy grin parted his lips. As Davian stared at him, he couldn't help but chuckle.

"Hello again," he said shyly.

Both stared at each other, clearly eager to give one another a friendly hug, but both hesitating, albeit for different reasons. Abruptly, Tip turned.

"Marsha, look! It's Davian," he called out. But Marshalla was already on her way down the stairs.

"Yes, Tip," she replied with a dry smile. "Sort of guessed that when you shouted his name."

"Sorry," Tip muttered as Davian chuckled once again.

"Hello, Marsha," Davian replied as he gave her a short, polite bow.

Marshalla frowned at him. "Don't bow."

Davian smiled. "It's the polite way to greet a lady."

"You talking to a street rat, not a lady," Marshalla replied coldly. "Don't bow."

Davian's smile swiftly dissipated. "Forgive me."

"What for? You do it on purpose?"

"No!"

"Then, don't say sorry."

Davian lowered his gaze as a slow sad frown grew upon his lips. As she watched the frown grow, Marshalla felt her own guilt grow.

"Good to see you again though," she said. Davian looked back at her, and as she smiled, so did he.

"Your father send you, Davian?" Mardaley called out from behind Marshalla. Smiling still, Davian looked past her to Mardaley.

"No, sir. I'm on my play time."

"So you chose to come spend it with us, we're flattered."

Davian grinned.

"Does he know you came over though?"

Davian hesitated slightly as his grin faded.

"Yes, sir," he replied at last. A brief silence fell on all within.

"Good to know," Mardaley said after a spell. He looked over at Marshalla.

"You'd better go with them, keep them out of trouble."

Both boys grinned in unison at Mardaley's words. Marshalla looked from one to the other.

"Oh, joy," she said, a wry smile upon her lips. Chuckling, both boys pulled the door open and sped out, Marshalla hurrying after them.

"So, shall we go there?" Davian asked Tip just as Marshalla stepped out.

"Go where?" she asked. Both boys looked up at her. She liked the excited grins on both not one bit.

"Aqueduct!" Tip exclaimed. "Davian's got water spells he can show us. They're spectact...specat...they're special!" Marshalla looked from Tip to Davian, who beamed at her proudly.

"Too far to the Aqueduct," Marshalla said, shaking her head as she spoke. "Won't make it back for late day deliveries."

Davian shook his head at her. "We'll take the carriage. It'll get us there and back in plenty of time."

Marshalla and Tip exchanged glances before they both looked over to where Davian had gestured.

"Proper carriage," Tip muttered. Davian nodded as a slight frown twisted his lips. "Is…something wrong?" he asked.

"Tip doesn't get to ride in carriages," Marshalla replied.

"Or me," Tip added, his gaze firmly upon the gilded elegance before him and thus oblivious to the wry smile on Marshalla's lips or the slight shake of her head.

"Well, come on, then!" Davian exclaimed, grinning as he raced to the carriage. Without a break in his gaze, Tip raced after him.

"Hey! Wait!" Marshalla exclaimed, but it was all in futility and, before long she, too, raced after Davian. Soon, all three bundled into the carriage, Marshalla sliding in beside Tip as Davian sat across from the both of them, and once all in, they rolled on down the street.

"Woah!" Tip exclaimed suddenly, staring into the ether as he ran his fingers across the seat within. Both Davian and Marshalla exchanged glances.

"What?" Marshalla asked. Tip looked at her.

"So soft," he whispered. "Like feathers."

"It's velvet," Davian replied, grinning. Tip looked at him quizzically.

"What's a velvet?"

"I… oh, I don't know. It's what my brother calls it."

"What, your brother's carriage?" Marshalla asked.

"Hm," Davian nodded in response. "Father thinks I'm too young to have my own, so Thalas lets me use his whenever I wish."

"Nice to have money," Tip muttered.

Davian smiled guiltily as he turned to stare at Tip. "Sorry."

"What for?" Tip asked, frowning.

"I didn't mean to boast."

"You were boasting?"

"I…" Confused, Davian looked up at Marshalla, but Marshalla merely smiled at him, shaking her head slightly.

"You like it, then, Tip?" she asked as she turned her gaze to little Tip.

Grinning, he nodded in response as he began bouncing on the seat.

"How did you two meet, anyway?" Davian asked.

Marshalla's smile dimmed slightly as she looked from one little boy to the other.

"Met a while ago, almost a year now," Tip spoke up. "Was raining that day, wasn't it?" He looked over at Marshalla. Marshalla nodded at him.

"Yes, was raining really bad, too. Was trying to find a place to stay dry, place out of the rain. But everywhere, there was someone already there. But then went over to one of the small markets, don't remember which one. One of the stall places there looked empty, so went in. But Marsha was already there, that not right Marsha?"

Again, Marshalla nodded, her smile now almost completely wooden.

"Yeah, so… yeah. She was sleeping, and when she woke up, she let me stay, and we stayed together since."

"That's nice," Davian said, smiling.

"Yeah!"

Smiling still, Davian looked over at Marshalla. It was all she could do to smile back.

"So, where are you both from?" the little boy asked, his eyes drifting from Marshalla to Tip and back.

Tip shrugged. "Don't know."

Davian frowned at him. "What do you mean? You *must* know."

Tip shook his head at Davian. "Don't remember. Remember the day Marsha and me met, but don't remember before that."

Davian stared quizzically at Tip. "Nothing at all."

Shrugging, Tip shook his head.

"You don't remember your family? Your parents?"

Tip looked over at Marshalla. "Marsha's my family now."

"But—"

"Davian," Marshalla interrupted, "street rats don't want to remember, so don't ask, okay? Not nice to make us remember."

"Oh," the little boy replied. "Sorry."

"And stop doing that."

"What?"

"Saying sorry all the time."

"Oh, sorr—" Davian grinned sheepishly. "I'll try."

"Good. Now, my turn." Grinning, Marshalla sunk deeper into the lush velvet seat. "How many lovers you got, then?"

"Marsha!" Tip exclaimed as Davian instantly turned beetroot red.

"What?" Marshalla protested. "Look at him! He a looker isn't he? Must have them queuing up to love him!"

"That just… eww, Marsha! Eww!"

"Oh, shush you. So, Davian…how many?"

"Uh."

"Don't answer. Don't tell her!"

"Shush, Tip."

Shaking his head at Marshalla, Tip moved to sit beside Davian.

"Get back here, you!"

"Don't listen to her, Davian," Tip said, putting an arm about Davian as he shook his head at Marshalla.

Davian smiled, first at Tip, then at Marshalla.

"It's okay, Davian, tell me later," Marshalla continued, winking at Davian, "when Tip's not here."

"Whatever, Marsha," Tip muttered, sighing as he spoke, before turning to Davian. "So, anyway, your father teach you magic?"

"Hmm? Oh, no. I'm not ready for his tutelage yet. He's been sending me to tutors in other kingdoms. Just came back from Aderelas, in fact. Father sent me there to learn the secrets of wind magic."

"Where's that?"

"Aderelas?"

"Yeah."

"Oh, it's the capital city of the highland elves."

"Oh, it's a big city like Merethia, then?"

Davian nodded. "Yes, though not as nice."

Tip grinned. "Don't think anywhere's as nice as Merethia."

"Heh, you're probably right."

"So, they teach you a lot?"

Davian frowned as he shook his head distractedly. "No. I honestly don't know why Father bothered to send me there. It was so *boring*!"

"Boring?" Marshalla asked.

Davian turned to Marshalla nodding as he did so. "Yes. I learnt everything they had to teach me in the first couple of weeks. And they're not that good either."

"How long you there for?" Tip asked.

"Four months."

"Woah!" Tip and Marshalla said in unison

"Precisely."

"What they make you do?" Tip asked.

"Ugh! They made me do these stupid exercises. They made me lift things with nothing but air, that's all. Oh, sure, they made me use different spells, except it was more or less the same thing; the harder the spell, the bigger the thing I had to lift. It was so silly."

Marshalla chuckled at Davian's words. She couldn't help it.

"No, truly. I mean, can you imagine the things you can do with air magic? You can stop a fireball in mid-flight with the right gust, or turn a tidal wave right back to source with a strong enough current, or maybe even split it in two with a large enough wind blade. But did they let me do any of that? No, I just lifted things, over and over and over."

"Sounds like you miss them," Marshalla replied with a cheeky grin. Davian cocked his head to the side.

"Yes, of course I do." His words elicited a chuckle from Marshalla.

"So, what one you like the most?"

Davian looked at Tip. "Which one what?"

"Magic thing. Like air."

"Like…oh I see. Water's my favorite."

"Oh?" Marshalla asked. Davian nodded at her.

"Why?" asked Tip.

"Because… I don't know, there's something… nice about water. The spells… they calm me."

"Is it the strongest?" Tip probed.

"Oh, gods, no. The most destructive is fire, by far."

"So, water's the weakest?"

"Hrm, no. It's the most… I don't know. It's definitely not the most protective, that's earth. Water is… it's in the middle between the two."

"Is it easy to learn?"

"Why, you wish to learn?"

Tip nodded simply, an act that called forth a curious frown from Davian, and a worried stare from Marshalla.

"You wish me to teach you?"

Again, Tip nodded.

"Well… I can try, if that's what you truly wish."

Once more, Tip nodded, this time more emphatically.

"Very well, I'll teach you what I can, but it's not easy to learn."

Tip grinned. "Still going to learn."

Grinning, Davian looked over at Marshalla.

"Shall I teach you too?"

"Marsha hates magic." Tip snickered.

Curious, Davian looked from Tip to Marshalla. "Why?"

Marshalla smiled politely. "Have my reasons."

"Oh, alright," Davian replied with a deep frown. Just then, the carriage began to slow.

"Ah, we're there!"

"About time!" Marshalla exclaimed as she turned to reach for the door. "Didn't think it would take this long."

"Oh, it's because we went to its source."

"Source?"

A slow delicious grin spread across Davian's lips. "You've never been to the Aqueduct's source?"

"Well… we seen it," Marshalla replied. "Can't go anywhere in Merethia without seeing it sticking out like that. Just… never gone to it before."

"Oh, in that case, you are in for a treat."

Angling past Marshalla, Davian swung the door open, clambering out while Marshalla and Tip stared at each other.

"Come on, then."

Before long, both clambered out to stand beside Davian, but the sight they beheld stole their breaths. The carriage had stopped alongside the Aqueduct itself, and towering before them lay, just as Davian had said, its source. Except its source was none other than the very heavens themselves, for standing before them was a magnificent bridge, one which carried Merethia's Aqueduct skywards, reaching higher and higher until it touched the very clouds of the air, Merethia's city walls running about its final pillar. The water that flowed down it was of crystal purity, rushing forth like a flood and giving a roar akin to a waterfall. It was truly a majestic sight to behold.

"Gods above," Marshalla whispered while Tip merely stared, open-mouthed. Davian simply chuckled at them.

"Come," he said. "I'll show you the way up." Coming to their senses, both followed Davian as he headed towards the levelled part of the bridge.

Straightening in his chair, Thuridan placed the little smooth stone he'd been holding against his ear on the reading table beside him as he raised his goblet to his lips.

"Now, isn't that interesting?" he muttered as he took a sip. "The little boy wishes to learn magic, but the girl hates magic. Why, I wonder?"

But as he raised his goblet to his lips for another sip, a curious thought wormed its way to the fore of his mind, and with it came a most delicious smile.

"Now, wouldn't that be something?"

Draining his goblet, the scheming mage sprang to his feet. This was a thought simply too good to ignore.

*****

As the carriage arrived back at Mardaley's, its door flew open as Marshalla and Tip stumbled out, drenched and exhausted.

"But truly, Tip, you did rather well today."

"Stop saying that, his head'll swell again."

In response, Tip made a face at Marshalla as Davian chuckled.

"Sorry you got wet," Tip mumbled as he looked from Marshalla to Davian.

Davian grinned in response. "I don't mind."

"Well, best get inside," Marshalla said. "Take care, Davian, today was nice."

"That it was, yes!" Davian replied with a grin.

"Coming tomorrow?"

Davian nodded. "If Father will let me out."

Tip grinned. "Okay, see you tomorrow maybe."

Davian's grin widened in response.

"See you tomorrow maybe," he echoed as he closed the door. And with that, the carriage rolled down the street with both Marshalla and Tip watching it go.

"That was fun," Marshalla said at last as she watched the carriage disappear round a corner.

"Mhm," Tip replied, nodding in agreement as he spoke.

Smiling, Marshalla turned to Tip. "You like him."

Grinning, Tip turned to return Marshalla's gaze.

"Yeah," he replied. "He's funny," Marshalla's smile grew at his words, "and he's good at teaching things." Marshalla's grin shrunk greatly at this.

"You don't have to do this, Tip," she said.

Frowning, Tip shook his head.

"No, Marsha," he replied resolutely, "need to. We look out for each other, you said. You always said we look out for each other, no matter what. And you don't like magic, so has to be me. Have to be strong so can protect you. And got to protect you, Marsha, got to. We look out for each other, no matter what." The fire in Tip's words burned deep into Marshalla's heart. Forcing a smile, she reached out and ruffled Tip's hair, eliciting a chuckle from the little elf.

"Thank you," she managed to say.

Tip grinned at her in response.

"What time do you call this, then?" a voice called out to them.

Startled, both turned to face an angry Mardaley as he stood outside his store, a delivery sack in his hand.

"Sorry, Mardaley!" Marshalla shouted back as she hurried over.

"Yeah, sorry!" Tip added as he followed.

"Sorry, nothing," Mardaley replied. "You were supposed to… What in the world happened to the both of you?"

Smiling guiltily, both looked at each other.

"On second thoughts, never mind. Tell me when you return. These are past due!" Frowning deeply, he shoved the delivery sack into Marshalla's right hand and a list into her left as he glared at the both of them.

"Well?" he demanded as they stared at him.

Turning, both headed down the street away from their irate employer.

"Wrong way!" Mardaley thundered.

Stopping, both turned and headed the other way.

"Sorry," Marshalla mumbled as she hurried past him.

"Sorry," Tip repeated in much the same manner.

"He's mad at us, isn't he?" Tip whispered at Marshalla once out of Mardaley's earshot.

"Just a little," she replied.

Sharing a guilty grimace, both quickened their steps as they hurried to their first delivery.

As the carriage neared his home, little Davian couldn't stop a contented sigh escaping his lips. It had been a far more pleasant day than he'd imagined. All his life, he'd wondered what it would be like to play with someone his age. No competitions, no scrutiny, no false laughter or empty praises, but simple happy play. And now he knew, but not only that, it was every bit as glorious as he'd imagined. More than that, it was so wonderfully liberating.

Sighing once again, he leant back into the plush velvet seats and savored the memories once more, closing his eyes as a smile parted his lips. As he relived the events at the Aqueduct, the odd giggle escaping, he was blissfully unaware as the carriage finally pulled up.

"Master Davian?" a voice intoned from outside the carriage. Opening his eyes, Davian looked at the door. "Your tutor's waiting."

Almost immediately, the smile on Davian's lips dissipated as he glared at the door.

"Master Davian?"

Frowning deeply, Davian took a deep breath as he shuffled towards the door. "Coming."

The reprieve was over.

"Atchoo!" Tip cried as his almighty sneeze echoed all about them.

Grinning, Marshalla stared at him.

"Sorry," he mumbled the moment he noticed Marshalla's stare.

Shaking her head, Marshalla adjusted the delivery sack across her shoulder and continued on.

"Not my fault," he muttered glumly once he'd reached her side. " Got to sneeze."

"No, Tip," Marshalla replied, "it's very your fault. You pushed Davian into the water, and then jumped on him. You sat in the water giggling and playing with him, even after me telling you to get out of it. It's very your fault."

Tip pouted briefly before breaking into a wide grin. "It was fun though."

Marshalla grinned in response.

"Aaatchooo!" Tip sneezed again, his whole body shaking from the effort. Chuckling, Marshalla stared at him as he wiped his nose on the back of his sleeve. Even after all this time, she still hadn't gotten used to how something so loud could come from someone so small.

"Sorry," Tip mumbled.

Thankfully, they'd reached Mardaley's.

"Best ask Mardaley to do something about that, come," Marshalla said as she swung the door open.

"Took you long enough," Mardaley called out at them as they walked in. Both smiled sheepishly as they looked to where he sat. Frowning, the elderly storekeeper rose.

"Well, I hope you've both learnt your lesson."

Tip and Marshalla stared briefly at each other before turning to stare at Mardaley.

"Yes, Mardaley," they replied in unison.

"Good," he muttered. After a brief silence, he sighed, waving them both towards him.

"I'm closing the store early today," he said as they climbed up the short stairs, "but I've got a fresh change of clothes for the both of you in the washroom."

Both stared at each other briefly in silence before staring back at him.

"Tip's got a cold," Marshalla noted.

Mardaley nodded. "Yes, I expected one of you to by now. The clothing will draw the cold out of him."

Both stared at each other once again.

"What?"

"You made us clothes," Marshalla said as they both looked at him once more.

"Yes, so?"

"Just like that."

"So?"

"No question, no nothing."

"*So?*"

Marshalla smiled cheekily at him. "Feeling guilty, then?"

"Don't be silly," Mardaley replied haughtily. "Guilt has nothing to do with it. This is practicality."

"Uh-huh."

"Yes."

"Really."

"Yes, Marsha. You're no good to me dead."

"You're saying sorry!" Tip declared suddenly, laughter not far from his voice.

"I am not!" Mardaley protested. But Tip's smile only grew as he chuckled.

"You said you'd learnt your lesson."

"Yeah, lied," Marshalla replied, shrugging briefly as she spoke.

Mardaley's gaze darkened, but his anger did not last, sighing soon after as he sank back into his chair. "You two are impossible sometimes."

"Only sometimes?"

"Just go get changed, will you?"

Laughing, Marshalla led Tip to the back room as Mardaley rose once more, taking the delivery sack from Marshalla as she walked past him.

Before long, both appeared once again, though neither smiled. Stopping, Mardaley turned from the shelves he was restocking to stare at them, a satisfied smile upon his lips.

"Now that's much better."

"They look just like our old clothes," Marshalla glowered.

"Of course they do; I made them that way."

"So, what's the point?"

"Oh, don't be so ungrateful. Come, help me."

Glumly, the pair shuffled to him.

"So, how was it anyway?" Mardaley asked as they reached the shelves.

In an instant, Tip's face lit up as he grinned at Mardaley. "It was the best!"

Mardaley chuckled. "Was it now?"

Tip nodded eagerly. "We played all these games, Davian knows lots of them! Kept trying to push me into the water—"

"Because you pushed him in and held him in," Marshalla added.

"Hee hee, yeah! That was funny."

"Funny?" Mardaley exclaimed in mock horror. "You could've drowned him!"

Giggling, Tip shook his head. "Don't think so. He's very good with water magic."

"Is he now?"

Tip nodded emphatically. "Yes! He's teaching me!"

The smile on Mardaley's lips dimmed. "Is he now?"

Eagerly, Tip nodded, unaware of the change in Mardaley's demeanor.

"You want to learn magic, do you?"

"Mhm. I want to be strong, like you!"

Mardaley stared at Marshalla. Her eyes told him all he needed to know.

"And like Davian," Tip continued, his gaze on the harpy talons he was restocking. "He's very good, Mardaley. Made a water thing come out of the water."

"Water thing?"

"Falimiar."

"What?"

"Familiar," Marshalla corrected. "Called it a kelpie."

Mardaley frowned at Marshalla, but before he could speak, Tip continued.

"Yeah. Very pretty. He let me pet it too."

"Did you ride it?" Mardaley asked, the barest traces of worry in his words.

Tip laughed. "No, silly! Too small."

Mardaley forced a smile as he nodded at Tip.

"But you enjoyed yourself."

Eagerly, the little elf nodded. "He said he'll come back maybe."

"You like him."

Tip nodded without any hesitation. "He's nice."

Nodding himself, Mardaley turned to Marshalla.

"And you?"

Marshalla looked at Tip briefly before looking back at Mardaley.

"He and Tip like each other."

"But do you like him?"

"Think he needs a friend. He seems… lonely… sort of."

"So, you feel for him."

"Yeah."

Mardaley stared at Marshalla in silence. But there was something in his gaze, an unnatural intensity that put Marshalla on edge. Abruptly, Mardaley broke gaze with her, reaching into his pocket as he smiled.

"Well, that's enough for one day. You two get going, I'll finish up here and lock up."

"But…" Marshalla began, but fell silent when Mardaley pulled out their coin for the day. Smiling, she swiped the small pouch from his hand, stuffing it into her pocket in one deft motion.

"Now, go on."

"See you tomorrow!"

"Yeah, see you tomorrow."

Mardaley grinned as they left. "Just take care of those clothes, alright?"

But the moment they were out of sight, his grin faded.

"You would use your own son, wouldn't you?" he muttered darkly moments later. Shaking his head and uttering a string of incantations, the elderly storekeeper flew out of the door himself, the shelves and counters tidying up of their own accord as he hurried down the street.

Stifling a yawn, Davian willed himself to stay awake as he stared at his tutor.

"… but even so, you still need to countenance the ether flow of these manifestations with a flow of opposing elemental affinity…"

Groggily, he stared at his mentor as she blathered on, nodding distractedly at her. Her words flew past him, their meaning utterly lost to him. Sleep, that's all he wished for. It was all he cared for.

"… which is not too dissimilar to your familiar's residual imprint. Or do you not agree?"

"I do," he replied without hesitation.

"Good, because…" his tutor began, but as she looked over at him, she fell silent, a disapproving frown twisting her lips.

"Elaborate, Davian," she added.

"Hunh?"

"Elaborate. You say you agree; in what manner do you agree? To what level are we in accord?"

"I… that Kel's ether… countenance is the same as an opposing affinity's—"

"You see? This is why I demand you are on time for all our lessons! You're half asleep! You haven't listened to anything I've said! Do you not appreciate the importance of what I'm tasked to prepare you for? Or do you think the Birthing is some mere child's play?"

"No, Mistress Dunmore."

"No, precisely! And yet here you are, your mind elsewhere instead of in the here and now. Your tiredness, Davian, is due to your showing up late! You hear me? Late!"

"Sorry, Mistress Dunmore," Davian muttered.

"Sorry is not good enough. I must insist you begin taking these lessons far more seriously, else I will have to have words with your father, and you do not want that, do you?"

"No, Mistress Dunmore."

"I should hope not." Frowning deeply, Elena Dunmore rose, her burning gaze burrowing into Davian.

"I see no point in continuing tonight, you're clearly in no fit state for tutoring."

"Thank you, Mistress Dunmore."

"I'm not done with you, Davian. We may be ending the session early today, but I'm going to have to give you double home assignments to make up for it." Elena glared down at Davian, daring him to protest, but he was too tired to care.

"Of course, Mistress Dunmore."

"Good."

After a few more tortuous moments, Davian was finally free. With a deep sigh of relief, he shuffled off his seat and made his way out of the tutoring room.

"And don't be late again!" Mistress Dunmore shouted at him as he left, but Davian chose not to reply.

"You look like death warmed up," a voice called out to him as he walked across the hallway to the stairs.

Stopping, he turned to see his father coming out of the reading room. Davian grinned sheepishly. "Just a bit tired."

"Hrm," Thuridan replied, nodding at his son. "I hear you showed up late for afternoon study."

Almost at once, Davian's grin dissipated, replaced by a guilty frown.

"I didn't mean to," he mumbled. "I just got carried away at the Aqueduct."

"Son, you've been there plenty of times before. This is the first time I'm hearing of you returning so late. I hear your tutor was all set to leave."

Davian dropped his gaze as he shuffled uncomfortably.

"Son, look at me," Thuridan pleaded. Pouting, Davian did as he was bid.

"What happened today? I need to understand why you were so late."

Biting down on his lower lip, Davian looked about him as he tried to come up with a suitable lie.

"Were you alone?"

Davian nodded in response.

"Are you sure?"

Again, he nodded.

"Then, why did Thalas tell me parts of the seats in his carriage were soaked from top to bottom. You're not tall enough to soak them that much."

Davian dropped his gaze once more, his cheeks reddening. Thuridan sighed before walking towards his son. Worried, Davian took a few steps back until his back was right up against the wall. At last, his father stood right before him.

"Davian, look at me."

Davian didn't move.

"Son, please. Look at me."

A brief silence followed but at last, Davian did as he was bid.

"I need you to be honest with me, alright?"

Davian stared at his father for a spell, but finally nodded.

"Were you alone?"

This time, he shook his head.

"Who were you with?"

"Tip and Marsha," he mumbled.

Thuridan frowned at him. "Who?"

"Tip and Marsha," Davian replied, a little louder.

Cocking his head slightly to the side, Thuridan stared at his son. "Who are they?"

"The people from Mardaley's."

Frowning still, Thuridan raised his gaze as he seemed to try to recall who his son meant. Eventually, his eyes lit up with surprise.

"The street rats!" he exclaimed, looking down at his son.

Mutely, Davian nodded.

Thuridan stared, open-mouthed, at his son. "Why?"

Guiltily, Davian shrugged as he dropped his gaze. Sighing, Thuridan went on one knee, placing a hand on Davian's shoulder as he did so.

"Son, look at me."

Grudgingly, Davian did as he was bid. The pain he saw in his father's eyes bore deep into him.

"Why in the world would you want to mix with them? They're street rats, they live in the gutter! They're beneath you!"

Again, Davian shrugged, averting his gaze from his father's.

"Davian, you need to answer me, please. What is this truly about? Why spend so much time with them? What is it you're looking for?"

"They're nice."

"So are Thalas and his friends. You used to enjoy being with them. What changed?"

"They're older than I am. They never want to do what I wish to do. And every time they want to play a game and I ask to join, they say I'm too young. I don't have anyone to play with."

"So, you want to play with street rats?"

"I don't have anyone to play with," Davian repeated as a single tear rolled down his cheek. Thuridan sighed as he stared at his son. Sighing, he wiped his son's tear away.

"Davian, I am not saying this to be cruel, but you are a Grovemender, and as such, there are certain things expected of you. Mixing with street rats goes against all of these things."

"But they're nice, Father," Davian protested.

"Be that as it may, they are street rats. You cannot be seen mixing with them. This is truly quite important, Davian."

"But you let me mix with the servants."

"That's different."

"How?"

"Servants have a much higher standing than street rats."

"But... but aren't they also servants? They work for Mardaley don't they?"

Thuridan shook his head at his son. "They still sleep on the streets, Davian. Mardaley doesn't offer them room and board."

"But..." Davian began, then a thought forced its way to the fore, and with it, his eyes lit up wide and clear. "But you do."

Thuridan frowned. "Pardon?"

"You do. You offer all your servants room and board."

"Davian..."

"And you have an opening, don't you? You let Elise go this afternoon for stealing."

Slowly, Thuridan rose.

"Davian," he repeated.

"Why not? And, if they work here, they can also make sure I'm back in time!"

"Davian, no."

"But why?"

"They're street rats."

"But they no longer will be if they work here!"

Thuridan stared intently at his son, his lips twisted in a deeply disapproving frown. But his son stared up at him hopefully, his eyes pleading. At last, Thuridan relented.

"Very well." He sighed. "But only if they both agree. Alright?"

Squealing, Davian lunged at his father, hugging his legs tightly. Grinning, he looked up at his father's warm gaze before racing up the stairs, stopping not once before his room. Thuridan watched his son, a hugely satisfied smirk on his lips.

"Sometimes I forget how heartless you can be, Father," a voice called out from further down the hall.

Straightening, Thuridan stared at the shadows from whence the voice came. "Hiding in shadows again, Thalas."

"He's your favorite," Thalas continued as he stepped out into the light. "Your great legacy. Yet, you use him like you would one of your Tower peons."

Thuridan sneered at his older son before turning to head to the reading room.

"You know, it would be a shame if Davian ever found out about what you're doing."

Thuridan's hand froze as he reached for the door's handle.

"Wouldn't it, Father? I'm sure you'd be open to discussing how best to—"

Without warning, Thuridan spun to face his son, and with but a single flick of his wrist, blew a sharp gust hard against his son's legs, knocking them out from under him with such vicious strength as to send him crashing, face first, into the cold marble floor. But as Thalas struggled to rise, an unseen force grasped him by the back of his head, smashing his face against the marble floor.

"Listen to me very carefully, Thalas," Thuridan snarled, his tone as cold as his gaze. "Never, *never* in your life are you to even *think* about extorting anything from me. Do you understand? Son or not, I will destroy you should you ever try such nonsense with me. Is that clear?"

In response, Thalas tried to raise his head, only for the unseen hand to smash his face against the marble floor once more, this time eliciting a pained gasp from the frightened elf.

"Is that clear?"

"Yes!"

All at once, Thalas was freed. Rising to sitting, he stared at his father, his eyes wide with fear as blood flowed freely from his nose.

"Go clean yourself. You're to dine with Neremi and her parents tonight, and a girl of that standing is not to be kept waiting." Spinning on his heels, Thuridan marched back to the reading room.

"And clean my floor!" he barked before slamming the door shut behind him.

Leaning into the shadows, Mardaley lowered the pearl he held by his ear, placing it in his tunic pocket as his eyes stared unmoving at the Grovemender's home across the street from him. Lowering his head, he stepped out of the shadows and headed down the street, his face set and his mind awhirl.

TRUE LOYALTIES

Lying on the inner wall of the Aqueduct, Marshalla gently massaged the mane of Davian's familiar. A curious little creature, the glimmer of its silvery scales at complete odds with its equine head, it neighed softly beside Marshalla as it swirled its tail under the water's surface. All at once, an almighty splash startled both elf and familiar, and as one, both looked up the Aqueduct to see Tip and Davian sitting within the waters, staring at each other.

"Ugh," Marshalla muttered as she settled back down, little Kel beside her snorting at the boys before shaking its head at them. As Marshalla settled down, however, the little creature swam under her hand, nudging it. Smiling, Marshalla stared briefly at the creature before willingly obliging. That was, until another big splash startled them both. Sighing, Marshalla looked down at the creature.

"Think they had enough fun, don't you?"

Snorting in response, the little kelpie swam up towards its master while Marshalla rose and headed up toward the boys.

"Come, out you get," she ordered as she reached them. "Both of you. Practiced enough for one day."

"Aww!" Tip protested.

"But he's almost mastered it," Davian pleaded. "Just a few more tries."

"He's soaked through. And you too!" She looked over at Tip. "Remember what Mardaley made us do last time?"

"But we not late though, we still got time."

"Yes, time enough for you two to dry off a bit."

Both boys looked at her with such heartbreaking forlorn. But Marshalla was having none of it.

"Come on!"

Admitting defeat, both clambered out of the Aqueduct before sitting on its wall. Sighing, Marshalla sat down beside them.

"Stop sulking. Both of you."

Both boys looked at each other before staring at her.

"Well, fine, then." she muttered before lying back down onto the Aqueduct's edge, her left hand going into the waters once again.

"So, did you reconsider my offer?" Davian asked after a moment's silence. Slowly, Marshalla rose her head, looking first at Tip, then at Davian.

"Yeah, did," she replied at last.

"And?" he asked, grimacing.

"Answer's still no."

Davian dropped his gaze to his knees as he pouted. Sighing, Marshalla sat back up. She looked over at Tip once again, but Tip was now pouting too. For a moment, their eyes met, only for Tip to shrug at her before turning his gaze to Davian.

"Look, Davian," Marshalla began, turning her gaze back to little Davian. As she spoke, Davian looked up at her. "You really fun to be around, really. Been forever since Tip this happy around anyone. But your father… no."

Davian shook his head. "You're wrong, Marsha."

Marshalla smiled sadly. "Been through this already."

"My father doesn't hate you!"

"Davian, you wasn't there. Tip almost fell over, and your father didn't even stop to say sorry or nothing. And, when we gave his purse back, should've seen how he was staring at us. As if we was going to give him a sickness standing so close to him. And then, there's the day when we first met. Remember what he said? Remember what he called us?"

"But—"

"He hates us," Tip said softly. "He really hates us."

"If we take the offer," Marshalla continued, "time will come when he'll do something to Tip or me that'll make me yell at him. He'll yell at me, and we'll be yelling and yelling until he kicks us out and Tip and me end up with nothing. At least now we got coin coming in. Not as much as if we came to work for your father, yeah, but we got almost enough for our own place."

"You've been saying that since we first met," Davian protested. Marshalla smiled at him, but kept her peace.

"And besides," Davian continued. "If you take my offer, you can use your money for something else."

Marshalla shook her head at him. "No, Davian. Sorry."

"It's not fair, Marsha," Davian mumbled. "It's just not fair."

"No, it's not."

"Doesn't matter anyway, does it?" Tip asked. "We're happy, you're happy. Right?"

Marshalla looked at Tip, a knowing smile on her lips. "We're street rats, Tip. People don't like seeing Davian playing with us."

"But doesn't matter what people think though. You say that all the time."

Marshalla's smile widened. "Doesn't matter to us, but matters to Davian's father."

"Oh."

"At least, let me give you some money," Davian said. "You can have a place of your own sooner."

Shaking her head, Marshalla reached out and ruffled Davian's hair.

"Nothing like your father, you are. If you got coin to spare, won't say no, but doubt your father would like that."

Davian moved to speak, but then fell silent, pouting instead as he dropped his gaze to his lap.

"You know what? Enough sad talk. Let's just sit here a bit so you two can dry off, okay?"

"Okay," Tip mumbled.

"Okay," Davian echoed.

"Okay!" Marshalla exclaimed, and promptly laid back down.

*****

"And would you like to take this with you now, or delivered straight to your home?" Mardaley asked the well-dressed elf before him.

"Deliver it, please. I have quite a few places I still need to visit before the day's over."

"Of course," Mardaley replied, grinning. Just then, an elderly elf wandered into Mardaley's store. With his head bowed low, his lips buried behind the blue scarf wrapped about his neck and jaw, the elderly elf shuffled into the store, his eyes scanning Mardaley's window displays.

"I'll be right with you, sir," Mardaley said, paying the man little mind. Furtively, the man stood back while Mardaley served the other customers in the store, until at last, he and Mardaley were alone.

"I have need of your special skills, good sir," the elderly elf said as the last customer left.

Ah," Mardaley replied, smiling slightly. "A… private order?"

"Very."

"Then, step this way please." Turning, Mardaley led the elf deeper into his store, until at last they were both in the back storeroom. As they both entered, however, Mardaley whispered a few words of arcane under his breath as his guest ripped his scarf off.

"Gods, it's hot in this thing."

"Then, why wear it?"

"Oh, don't start with me, Mardaley."

Chuckling, Mardaley moved to sit in a nearby chair. His companion stared at him intently.

"From your missive, I was expecting you in a much fouler mood."

Mardaley looked up at him. "Perhaps I'm just that good at hiding it."

"Perhaps." Looking round, the elderly elf sat down on the table behind him as he regarded Mardaley once more.

"So, what's so incredibly urgent that we have to speak?"

"You should've been here two days ago."

"I know, and I'm sorry. I couldn't get away any sooner."

Mardaley frowned at his friend.

"Believe me, Mardaley, if I could've gotten here sooner, I would've."

Nodding at last, the elderly storekeeper shifted in his seat, his frown lessening somewhat.

"So, what's this all about?"

Mardaley frowned. "Thuridan is up to something."

"Thuridan's always up to something, that's what makes him so insufferable."

"This time, it involves Marshalla."

Mardaley's friend leant forward at this, his face twisted with worry. "He knows about Marshalla?"

"I… I'm not sure."

"What are you sure of?"

Mardaley sighed. "His son, Davian, he's been spending quite a bit of time with Tip and Marshalla lately."

"Tip… is that the urchin Marshalla's taken under her wing?"

Mardaley nodded.

"I'm not following. How does this concern us?"

"They're street children, Baern. You truly think Thuridan Grovemender is going to allow Davian of all people to mingle so freely with them? This is Davian we're talking about, not Thalas."

"Hrm… you do have a point," Mardaley's companion said, musing as he spoke. "But… to what end? And how in the hells did he find out about her?"

Mardaley shook his head. "I wish I knew."

Gritting his teeth, Baern rose and paced the little storeroom.

"Forgive me, old friend," he said after a brief silence, "but this isn't making any sense. We looked for that girl for years."

"I know, Baern."

"Years, Mardaley, and came away with nothing, only to find her living right here under our noses. And you're about the only person left alive outside of her own kin who could recognize her, yet it took you almost a year to finally accept it was her. If she could manage to elude us for so long, elude *you* for so long, how in the hells did Thuridan find out about her?"

"I was outside his house, Baern. I heard him twist his own son into fostering closer ties with Marshalla."

"How?"

"Davian's to try to get Marshalla to take a post in their household."

Baern raised an eyebrow at Mardaley.

"That's what I heard."

"Has he succeeded?"

Mardaley shook his head. "Thus far, Marshalla's said no. Tip, too, actually."

"I see. Why?"

Mardaley smiled proudly. "They see Thuridan for the worthless snake he is and want nothing to do with him."

Baern couldn't help but smile himself, but his smile was fleeting. "Mardaley, you're sure this isn't just a doting father relenting to the wishes of an over-indulged son?"

"Thuridan Grovemender is not a doting father."

"But—"

"No, Baern. I know what I heard, and I know what I've seen. Thuridan knows, he knows something, and he's plotting on using that knowledge. How, and for what end, I cannot fathom just yet, but plotting he is. Without a doubt."

Baern stared intently at his friend. "Are you sure you're not getting too involved here?"

Mardaley smarted visibly at this. "I know what I heard, damn it!"

"I don't doubt that, but… you're jumping to conclusions here. This isn't like you."

Fuming, Mardaley rose, shoving his hands roughly into his pockets as he turned his back to his friend.

"Are you positive you're not losing your objectivity?"

Wheeling round, Mardaley glared at Baern. "I am perfectly capable of seeing this through."

"Are you? Your actions of late have been one of a man lashing out, lashing out seeking… I don't know… redemption maybe?"

Mardaley moved to speak, but his voice died in his throat.

"Is it her mother? You never did get over how she died."

"It's not her mother, alright? Please don't bring that up."

"Then, what is it?" Baern stared hard at his friend. Mardaley stared back, but he soon felt his resolve wilting until at last, he sighed and shook his head.

"It's... we failed her, Baern," he replied. "*I* failed her. She's suffered living out there on those streets, faced horrors she had no right to face at that age. Would that you could've heard how dismissive she was of what that Toriel did to her. He ravaged her, and she talked about it as if all he did was smack her the once. And it's all something we could've stopped."

"Yes, we could've," Baern replied, nodding as he spoke, "but then we'd have had thirty other Marshallas living on those streets. We made the best decision we could in those dark times, and I stand by them, yours and mine. Besides, it wasn't your task to protect her."

"Well, it is now," Mardaley said through gritted teeth. "And I'll be damned if I let that bastard use her for one of his schemes."

Frowning, Baern cocked his head to the side before shaking it slowly. "No, Mardaley, no. This can't be it, not after all this time. I know you too well. What else is it?"

"Nothing," Mardaley replied curtly.

"Mardaley, it's me you're talking to. We've been through too much for me to fall for this. What is it?"

Mardaley glared at his friend for a spell before finally walking over and leaning onto the table beside Baern.

"The boy, Tip," he sighed.

"Yes?"

"He... he reminds me of Aldurn."

Baern's eyes grew wide as he stared at Mardaley. "Aldurn? Gods above, that was decades ago! You and I were miles away when it was destroyed! Do you truly mean to blame yourself for that too?"

Shrugging, Mardaley turned his back to his friend as he walked back to his chair.

"So...you think to protect these two to...make amends?"

Mardaley turned to stare square at Baern. "Is that so wrong?"

"Oh, goodness no. In fact, I'm surprised there's still any feeling in that shriveled old heart of yours."

"Funny, very funny."

Baern grinned, but it was fleeting. "Can you say truly that Thuridan knows about Marshalla?"

"Can you say truly he doesn't?"

"Ah..."

"And don't forget the listening stone he attuned near the door. Why go through the trouble to do that if he had no interest in her?"

"Are you sure it was him, though?"

"I told you, I make his listening stones. I'm sure."

"I… Fine. We'll have to watch him closely, uncover whatever he's plotting before it goes too far."

"That is all I ask."

Just then, the sound of the door opening reached the men. As one, both turned to stare at the door.

"I'd best let you get back to running your store," Baern said as he wrapped his scarf back about him. Mardaley nodded distractedly in response.

"Just let me know as soon as you learn anything," Mardaley replied as he headed for the door.

"Of course."

Stepping out, Mardaley returned to his store, a ready smile on his lips to welcome his new customer.

"See! Told you we'd make it!"

"All thanks to me."

Shaking his head, Mardaley watched as the pair made their way towards the short stairs.

"I'm surprised, you two are actually early for once."

At this, Tip stopped and glared hard at Marshalla.

"Oh, don't start."

"But—"

"And I see you actually kept yourselves dry this time," Mardaley continued. Marshalla turned from Tip to smile at Mardaley.

"Yeah, these new clothes dry off great!"

Mardaley grinned. "I'm glad you like them."

Just then, Baern appeared from the back room, standing beside Mardaley as he stared at the two children from above his blue scarf.

"Oh, hello," Marshalla said briefly at Baern before turning to Mardaley. "You need us gone?"

Mardaley shook his head at her. "It's okay, but you might as well start your noon deliveries early."

"Haven't filled the bag yet."

"I did."

Marshalla grinned. Hurrying over, she grabbed the bag and, throwing Baern a polite nod, turned and hurried out, Tip in tow.

"That's her?" Baern whispered once they were out of the store. Mardaley nodded, his eyes still on the door.

"You were right, she really does look nothing like her grandmother."

"Hard to imagine, isn't it?"

"Yes, very. And the little boy was Tip?"

Mardaley nodded once again.

"I see what you mean about Aldurn, the resemblance with Therese is quite striking."

"I know."

Then Baern turned to his friend, a slow smile parting his lips as he shook his head.

"What?"

But Baern merely stared, smiling.

"Whatever," Mardaley said haughtily, eliciting a chuckle from his friend. At last, Baern turned to leave. But as he turned, he stopped suddenly, as if remembering something.

"Oh, and, uh…" Baern whispered again, turning to face Mardaley once more, "was that chimera leather I saw them both wearing?"

Mardaley grinned. "Amongst other things."

"Uh-huh. And how much did it all set you back by?"

"Don't ask."

Shaking his head, the elderly high elf turned and finally headed for the door.

*****

Groaning, Thalas rolled over onto his back as he groggily opened his eyes. His mouth tasted like sawdust, and his head felt thick and heavy. Licking his cracked lips, he turned to stare at his beloved sprawled beside him. Raising his head, he cast a slow lustful gaze over her naked body, his eyes slowing at her bare behind. As he stared, he felt a familiar and most welcome stirring from down below, but with it came a most unsettling headache. Sighing, he closed his eyes as he fought down his passion, and finally opening his eyes once more, he swung his feet gingerly off the bed before rising and heading over to the nearby table.

There was a slight, cold breeze within the room, but Thalas didn't mind. In fact, he welcomed it, for the slight chill that ran all about his nude frame calmed his head somewhat. Reaching the table, he picked up the nine bottles upon it one by one to inspect their contents. Empty. Every single one.

"She drinks like a fish," he croaked. Sighing, he turned and shuffled over to his clothes, but the sounds of stirring from the bed brought him to a halt. Turning, he smiled as he watched his beloved Neremi rise to her elbow, staring at the far wall.

"Sleep well?"

Turning, Neremi stared at him with a contented smile before lowering her head back to her pillow as she nodded. "You?"

"Well enough," he replied, smiling. Turning, he made his way to his clothing once more.

"Any more drink?"

"No," Thalas replied as he began searching his pockets. "You drank it all."

"Oh, right. Mist?"

"Gone. We finished it last night."

"Oh, right."

Pulling free his purse, Thalas counted out some coins before shuffling over to a little panel on the wall near the door.

"At least we've still got one vice we can indulge in," Neremi said with an alluring smile. Shaking his head, Thalas pulled open the panel and, dropping the coins within, whispered some words into the panel before closing it and tossing his purse back onto his clothes.

"Come on, then, Thalas, don't keep a lady waiting."

Turning, Thalas stared at his beloved. The light that shone through the curtains upon her basked her in an unearthly, yet radiant glow. And with her long golden hair splayed across her pillow, her bare breasts exposed for his pleasure, Thalas couldn't help but smile at her, the stirring returning with renewed vigor. Unfortunately, so did the headache. Closing his eyes and shaking his head slowly, he shuffled back towards the bed.

"What is it?"

"I need a drink first."

"You seemed more than capable last night, and we didn't start drinking until after our third go."

"Yes, well, right now my head is threatening to explode," Thalas mumbled in response as he sat on the bed.

"I could heal you if you'd like."

Thalas looked at her. "No, thank you. I've still got the scars from the last time you tried to heal me."

Sticking her tongue out at him briefly, Neremi pouted as she turned her back to him, clearly incensed. Smiling, Thalas lay down beside her, kissing her shoulder as he did so.

"Thank you for the offer though," he said. But Neremi shook him off her.

"I expected better from a Grovemender, Thalas," she grumbled.

"Oh, don't start, Neremi," Thalas growled as his mood darkened greatly. "I get enough of that nonsense from that old fool at home, I don't need to hear it from you too."

Neremi turned to stare at her beloved, her face one of great concern. "That was in jest, Thalas."

Thalas glared at her in silence, and in response, Neremi raised a loving hand to caress his cheek.

"It was in jest, truly."

At last, Thalas relented, his face softening as he looked from her to her hand.

"I'm sorry," he muttered as he sat up on the edge of the bed.

Going onto her knees, Neremi shuffled behind Thalas, and, placing her chin on his shoulder, wrapped her arms about him and held him close. Closing his eyes, Thalas placed a hand on her arm as he savored her affection until at last a sigh escaped his lips. In response, Neremi kissed his neck before placing her chin on his shoulder once more.

"What is it, Thalas? What ails you?"

"It's nothing, it's…"

But Neremi kissed his neck once more, this time biting him lightly as well. "Thalas, my darling, what is it?"

Frowning, he turned to stare at her before staring forward once more.

"Thalas, you need to be strong; you need to not let your father get to you so. This isn't the first time he's chosen Davian over you. He's been doing it ever since the little snotspit was born. You need to be strong, my darling. Your time will come. One day soon, you will be able to stand on your own without him. You just need to be strong till—"

"It's not that, it's…"

"What?"

Thalas looked at her, then looked forward once more.

"Talk to me, what is it?"

Once more, Thalas looked at her, but this time, he did speak.

"Aren't you sick of waiting? I mean, look at us. This is all we can afford on our own, after all this time. This cheap hovel."

Sighing, Neremi let him go before shuffling to sit beside him.

"Thalas, we've spoken about this. We have to be patient. Right now, they have everything, we have nothing. We need to be patient, feather our nest with care, away from their gaze. When we started this, we both knew it would be long and arduous, but you need to be strong, my darling. We can't leave here without money. Without it, we will never be able to escape your father, or my parents for that matter. So, we need to be patient, we need to wait and—"

"I am sick of waiting; can't you hear me?" Thalas hissed through gritted teeth.

"Then, what do you propose?"

Thalas moved to speak, but shut his lips instead.

"Look, Thalas—"

"No," he said as he shook his head before turning his gaze to his beloved. "It is taking too long. We've been at this for much of the year, and we still can't afford better lodgings than this. At this rate we'll be old and grey before we are ready to depart." Thalas looked away from her. "We need a better way, a faster way."

"What do you have in mind, then?"

Thalas stared into the ether, frowning deeply. At last, he looked over at her, his face set.

"You said it yourself; they have everything, we have nothing. What we need is to have something they need, something *he* needs."

Neremi frowned. "We've tried, many times, and each time it ended badly."

"Not this time."

"What's so special about this time?"

"This time, we won't be stealing from him, not directly at least."

"Thalas, you're not making much sense."

"The gutter rats, Neremi. The little one. The secret my father wants."

Neremi stared, confused, at him for a spell, but as she finally realized what he meant, a worried frown twisted her lips.

"No, listen!" Thalas exclaimed as he sat upright, turning to face her square. "I'm going to learn that little bastard's secret, I'm going to learn it before my dear father does, then he'll have to listen to me, to us!"

"You said your father warned you against that."

"To the hells with him! I'm going to learn it and I'm going to use it to make him listen to us. He won't hurt me if I learn it, he can't risk me dying and taking the secret to my grave."

"Don't talk like that, you know I hate it."

Grinning, Thalas caressed Neremi's cheek. "Sorry."

"And besides, the boy won't just tell you, you know."

At her words, Thalas' smile took on a much darker tone. "Would be too easy if he did, wouldn't it?"

But Neremi was unmoved. Abruptly, Thalas reached out and clasped her hands. "I can handle my father, Neremi, I've lived with him all my life. In all our past schemes he's had the upper hand throughout, but this time, this time the advantage will be ours. Trust me."

Neremi looked down for a brief spell at her hands in his, then returned her gaze to Thalas' smiling face.

"Trust me," Thalas repeated as he leant in and kissed her lovingly. As they parted, a slow smile parted Neremi's lips.

"Well, the boy'll have to die, of course."

"Of course. We can't have a monopoly on the secret if he still lived."

"And the girl?"

"They're each other's shadow. She'll have to go too."

Neremi's smile grew. "And then we can have your father give us anything we wish."

Thalas' own smile grew. "Precisely."

Abruptly, Neremi leant in and kissed him deeply.

"I can taste our freedom already," she said as they parted. Thalas laughed with glee at her words, a laugh that soon infected Neremi.

"You know," Thalas said once the laughter had left them both, "it would be a shame to just kill her."

"Oh?" Neremi asked, frowning.

"Oh, yes, very."

"A shame how?"

"Well, you remember the street whore in the Gardens?"

Slowly, Neremi cast a sideways glance at her beloved, a playful smile upon her lips. "Yes…"

"Well," Thalas continued, a playful smile on his lips, "this gutter rat is just as… blessed."

"Is that so?"

Thalas nodded, his smile growing.

"It truly would be a shame to waste such a blessing, wouldn't it?"

"Hrm, wouldn't it just?" Neremi replied as Thalas chuckled.

"And speaking of wasting," Neremi continued, a slow seductive smile replacing her earlier one as she laid a hand on her beloved's temple, "we have this room till noon-chime. We wouldn't want to it to go to waste, would we?"

Thalas smiled at her in much the same manner.

"No, we wouldn't."

A brief moment's silence fell upon the pair as both closed their eyes while Neremi healed her beloved. Then, as their eyes opened once more, fair Neremi lowered herself back on the bed, her gaze on her beloved throughout. But as Thalas began to clamber upon her, there was a knock on the door. Both turned to the door.

"Your order, sir."

Thalas turned to his beloved. "Drinks first?"

Neremi grinned. "Why not?"

*****

Sighing, little Davian shuffled through the door, handing his coat over distractedly as he stared off into the ether, a sad frown on his face. Thuridan watched his son from the base of the stairs where he stood with a frown of his own. He waited patiently for his son to notice him, but so engrossed in his thoughts was Davian that he didn't so much as acknowledge his father's existence as he made his way towards the tutoring room. Thuridan looked over at his doorman, who stared back at his master with worry in his eyes. Taking one last look at the forlorn little elf, the doorman left to hang little Davian's coat. Thuridan stared back at his son.

"You're truly not going to say anything?"

Startled, Davian turned to face his father. "Sorry, Father."

Thuridan gestured his son over while he sat on the stairs. Sighing, Davian complied, and as he reached his father, the elder elf picked up his son and sat him on his lap. Davian smiled shyly at this, though his smile was fleeting.

"And what ails my dearest Davian this day?" Thuridan asked, cocking his head to the side as he spoke. Davian looked up at his father before turning his gaze to his knee.

"Well?"

"Nothing…"

"Nothing?"

Davian nodded, dejected.

"Then why do you look like you've lost your very best friend in the world?"

Davian's frown deepened.

"Did you and Tip have a fight?"

Davian shook his head.

"Then what?"

"Marsha doesn't want to live with us," he replied softly. "She keeps saying she'll end up fighting you and you will throw her and Tip out. I keep trying to tell her you're not heartless, but she won't listen. She doesn't want to listen. I don't know what else to tell her, she just won't listen."

"And what does Tip say?"

"Tip doesn't want to come either. He thinks you hate them."

Thuridan took a deep breath, then let it out slowly.

"I see," he replied at last. Davian nodded at him.

"So… the reason they're not wanting to come over is because they think Marsha and I will be at each other's throats. Is that correct?"

Davian nodded once more.

"Then, I suppose the only way to settle this is if she and I were to reach some understanding."

Davian looked up at his father, his face brightening with each passing moment. "You mean you'll go talk to her?"

Thuridan smiled. "Yes, I'll go talk to her, get this whole affair straightened out."

Grinning, Davian hugged his father with all his might. Thuridan laughed, hugging his son back.

"Thank you, Father!"

"Oh, don't thank me yet, I have yet to talk to her."

"Sorry. I know! You can go talk to her at Mardaley's now!"

Thuridan chuckled. "I'm afraid I have responsibilities to attend to, my dear son."

Davian grinned sheepishly at his father.

"Sorry. Maybe later, after work? I think Tip said they'll be bedding down at the

Priory of the Kindly Goddess tonight. Do you know where that is?"

Thuridan nodded. "Yes, I believe so. We'll see how the night goes. For now though, enough worrying. Off to your tutor with you."

Grinning once again, Davian gave his father one final hug before hopping to his feet and running to the tutoring room. Thuridan watched him go, but it was only when he disappeared from sight did his smile dissipate.

"It's not his fault…" he muttered. "He's too young. You'll have to see this through yourself."

Rising, Thuridan turned and headed up the stairs, his mind already awhirl.

*****

Humming happily to himself, High Priest Drumold Etherspire sat by his modest desk, scribbling away contentedly. It always filled him with great joy, penning letters of thanks to the benefactors of his priory, and this one letter in particular was truly well-deserved after such a bounteous and unexpected donation.

Sitting back at last, the high priest re-read the letter, checking his punctuation and turns of phrase. But as he read through his words, a soft tapping drifted to his ears. It came from behind. Frowning, he turned round. Staring at the window behind him, Drumold watched as a moth flew into his window again, and again, and again. Curious, he rose and walked over to the window, opening it as he reached it. As the window opened, the moth stopped, hovering where it was for a spell before diving to the earth. Curious still, High Priest Etherspire watched it flitter away, but as he watched, he at last noticed the figure in the shadows below, and with that came the realization of what was required of him. And there was only one person he knew who would make such a demand of him at such a time.

Gritting his teeth, High Priest Etherspire closed his window before hurrying out of the room, his letter all but forgotten. Making his way outside, the portly elf slowed his steps as he neared the spot where he'd seen the shadowy form. As he neared it, his frown deepened greatly.

"You know, most people would simply come up to my office and knock on the door," he snarled. There was no response.

"Look, Thuridan, I have a lot to do. We have yet to prepare—"

"Then cease your incessant prattling and join me," Thuridan replied from the darkness.

"Do not presume to give me orders, Thuridan."

"Very well, you stand there talking into the shadows. Let's see how long it'll take for your little peons inside to start thinking their beloved leader has gone mad."

Growling under his breath, High Priest Etherspire glowered for a spell before finally stepping into the shadows.

"What do you want?" he demanded the moment he was stood before Thuridan.

Thuridan smiled, a smile that lacked warmth of any kind. "It never ceases to amaze me just how welcoming you can be, Drumold."

"What. Do. You. Want?" Drumold repeated.

Thuridan's smile grew. "Very well, we shall skip the pleasantries. You're going to do me a favor. You—"

Drumold shook his head at Thuridan's words, a snarl twisting his lips. "No more favors, Thuridan. I told you, the last one was to be the last. That was the arrangement."

Thuridan chuckled. "Is that so?"

"Do not test me, Thuridan, our business is concluded. I owe you nothing now." Glaring at the high elf for a spell, Drumold turned and made to leave.

"And if I was to tell you I still have proof of your little antics with those young gutter rats...?"

Slowly, Drumold spun round to face Thuridan once more, but with a cold smile of his own. "And here I thought you wouldn't stoop so low. You have no such proof, Thuridan. I Compelled the truth out of you. When you said you had no other items of proof, that was no lie."

Grinning, Thuridan reached into his coat and pulled out a small, smooth stone, and, showing Drumold briefly, he tossed it at him. Frowning, the high priest caught it and placed it to his ear, and what he heard drained all blood from his face.

"But...I Compelled you!"

"Yes," Thuridan replied, nodding, "yes, you did. And yes, I truly did tell the truth then when I said I had no other forms of proof. But you see, I've been doing this sort of thing for quite some time now, so I was expecting you to Compel me. I made arrangements, old friend, for one of those little boys to pay me a visit before he left Merethia and, well, the rest I believe you just heard."

The high priest stared at Thuridan with barely suppressed rage.

"And I suppose your part in it all was forgotten?" Drumold hissed after a spell.

"Why, Drumold, you wound me. Of course we spoke about it. The little boy and I spoke at length about everything. I just decided to keep hold of the more interesting bits for later... use."

Snarling, Drumold flung the whispering stone at Thuridan, who caught it and shoved it into his pocket in one deft motion.

"What do you want?" the high priest demanded through gritted teeth.

"Two of your street rats are due to spend the night here. I want you to evict them. Permanently."

"Who?"

"They go by the names Marsha and Tip."

"Why?" Drumold asked, frowning.

"That's my business."

Drumold stared at the scheming high mage as a knot formed in the pit of his being.

"What do you mean, permanently?" he asked after a spell.

"I mean *precisely* that. From tonight, they are to receive no succor or aid from you and yours again. Ever."

"You can't be serious."

"I'm very serious. And that goes for your sister priories and hospices. I want those two shunned from every single one of them."

Drumold took a step towards Thuridan.

"Thuridan," he pleaded, "they depend on us. Why condemn them?"

"That's none of your affair."

"Is this about Davian? Does it really grate you that much that your son is mixing with—"

"I'm getting rather tired of repeating myself, Drumold. Will you do as I ask or not?"

Drumold stared with his lips slightly agape. "Thuridan, winter's coming. Without aid, they'll—"

"Will you do as I ask or not?"

A cold shiver ran down Drumold's spine as waves of revulsion washed over him. There could only be one answer.

"I will do as you ask."

Smirking, Thuridan nodded.

"I knew you would see reason, old friend. Take care." And with that, Thuridan left. The broken elf watched Thuridan leave before turning and heading back into the Priory, his shame already drowning him.

Yawning widely, Tip tried to rub the sleep away from his eyes. Marshalla stared at him with a smile, but that soon disappeared behind a yawn of her own.

"So tired," Tip muttered as they neared the entrance to the Priory.

"Yeah, me too," Marshalla replied as she reached for the door. "But Mardaley paid us extra at least, so suppose was worth it."

As Marshalla's fingers closed round the handle, however, a hand grasped her other arm, holding it in a vice-like grip before pulling her roughly away from the door.

"Wha–?" she stuttered in surprise as she stumbled backwards. It was Maline.

"Maline, what you–?"

"Hush!" Maline spat back.

It wasn't the fire in her one word that stilled Marshalla's tongue, it was the fear behind it. Regaining her balance, Marshalla rounded herself as much as she dared to better follow Maline. As she hurried on, she threw a glance at Tip. He was hurrying on behind her, his fear and worry plain in his gaze.

At last, they reached some nearby trees. It was only then that Maline let her go.

"Maline, what you–?" Marshalla began, but Maline would have none of it.

"Shut up!" she threw back, raising a hand for silence. "Just shut up and listen, please!"

Marshalla clammed up in response. Sighing, Maline looked from Marshalla to Tip, her brow furrowing deeper.

"You scaring me, Maline," Marshalla said after a brief silence. "What is it?"

Maline held her peace for a spell, but at last spoke up.

"Word's going round the Priory, and going round strong, that Tip stole the Priory's take."

"What?"

"You heard. They saying they only got enough for two more nights, then the Priory's all dry."

"Who in the hells–?"

In that instant, Maline let go of her bag and grasped Marshalla's face in her hands, both palms caressing her cheeks with the tenderness one would expect of a caring mother.

"Never mind who said what. Is it true?"

Marshalla's eyes grew wide. "You don't think–!"

"Toriel told me of Tip's blackouts."

"Wha–?"

"Please, Marsha, please! Just tell me! We can still fix this, just need to know. Did he do this?"

"Marsha…?"

Both looked down at Tip. Tears were streaming down his face as his lips twisted in a silent wail.

"Was it me? It was, wasn't it? It was me, wasn't it? Wasn't it, Marsha?"

Shaking her head, Marshalla dove to Tip's side.

"Didn't mean to take it, didn't mean to. Sorry, Marsha, didn't mean to take it."

Gritting her teeth, she pulled her dear friend close, hugging him for all she was worth. It was then that Tip truly wailed.

"Didn't mean to take it," he mumbled repeatedly, each word seeming to draw even more tears from him, till finally his whole body shook from the effort. At last, Marshalla looked up at Maline. There were tears in the elder elf's eyes.

"We not been here in a week!" Marshalla snarled. "How in the hells is he supposed to have taken anything?"

"They saying they only found out last night when looking to restock. They supposed to restock once a week."

"Not true! Drumold counts every other night! They restock next day!"

"That's not what they're saying."

"Who's *they*?"

"Everyone, Marsha, everyone. The priests got everyone hating you, hating Tip. They saying they may have to turn us all out for a few days because of it."

"Sorry," Tip sniffled.

Maline looked at Tip. "It's okay, you didn't mean to."

"He didn't do it!" Marshalla bellowed, bounding to her feet. "Tip didn't take nothing, damn it! Not taken anything from here in weeks!"

"That's not what they—"

"They, they, sick of this they!"

"Keep your voice down!"

"No! Tip didn't take it! They all lying, all of them!" With that, she spun round and, adjusting the bag on her back, Marshalla grabbed Tip's hand and began marching towards the Priory.

"Where you going?"

"To speak to Drumold."

"Marsha!"

"Tip didn't do this!"

"That's not what—!"

"He didn't do this!"

At last, the pair reached the Priory, and pulling on the door roughly, Marshalla held the door open for Tip before stepping inside herself. But as she stepped in, she finally realized the scale of the rancor. As they walked in, every single face turned to them, and each one of those faces slowly twisted in anger and disgust, priest and street rat alike. The lion's share of the ill-will was aimed at Tip, who shrank within himself under the weight of it all. But as Marshalla watched the little elf wither under the heated gazes, she felt her anger threatening to unleash. Snarling widely at all before them, she gripped Tip's hand tighter and began marching towards the high priest's office. Before long, one of the priests stepped in her path.

"And where are you going?"

"Get out of my way."

"I asked you a question."

"Going to see Drumold. Get out of my way."

"I'm afraid I cannot allow that little thief to—"

At his words, the red mist descended, and Marshalla swung her free hand into his cheek, putting behind it all the strength she could muster. The force of the slap staggered the priest as it echoed throughout the entrance hall. The silence that followed was deafening.

"Was that truly necessary?" High Priest Etherspire asked as he stepped out from behind the affronted priest.

"Tip didn't do this," Marshalla snarled in response, her ire raging still. "You know he didn't, you know that."

The high priest folder his arms about him, his face one of bitter sadness.

"And how do I know this?" he asked.

"Because we not been here in a week! No way he could've stolen your whole take and nobody noticed for a whole week!"

"We only check the Priory funds when it's time to restock the larder."

"But you check it every other day and—"

"There have been many changes since you last worked in the office. We have more responsibilities, but our numbers haven't grown. We no longer have the time to restock more than once a week."

"But he didn't—"

"I want to believe you, I truly do. But you and Tip are the only ones who know where the funds are held, other than the priests here. And each and every single priest has been subjected to a thorough and most humiliating search, and, I might add, I've had to Compel every single one of them. Do you know how insulting that is, to have to Compel a follower of Diyanis to disclose whether or not they gave into their greed? Have you any idea how that made me feel? How that made all of us feel?"

"Tip didn't do this."

"Then who? Who else has the knowledge, who has the ability? Who else?"

"He didn't do this."

The high priest fell silent as he stared sadly at Marshalla.

"The others wanted me to Compel Tip," he continued, "make him speak the truth. But he doesn't always even realize what he's doing, does he? Like that night outside at the back."

Marshalla glowered at him, but kept her peace.

"So, instead, I'll Compel you, Marshalla. If you allow it, and you truthfully say that he didn't do this, then we will believe you."

Marshalla glared at him, a ready response on her lips. But she looked behind her, looked right at Tip, and when she did, she knew she had to go through it.

"Fine."

"Good, come with me."

"No. Here, right here. Everyone hears it."

"I... very well," Drumold replied, and, bringing his right hand to bear just before Marshalla's face, closed his eyes and began chanting under his breath. As he did so, Marshalla closed her own eyes.

To be Compelled, this wasn't something new to Marshalla. So, as Drumold chanted, she cleared her mind and calmed her heart, readying herself for the prayer's call. But as Drumold chanted, Marshalla quickly realized something wasn't quite right. Opening her eyes, she glared at him.

"What you–?"

It started as a tickle at the back of her throat, nothing serious, just a light tickle, but it quickly grew, like a bursting damn, its waters crashing about in her throat, filling it and her mouth. She tried to speak, tried to form a question, a single, simple question, but her words failed her. No, Drumold wasn't Compelling her, he was binding her, and was going to force her to say whatever he wished. Then, the high priest finished his chant and lowered his hand.

"Now, Marshalla, I shall ask you one question, just one. Tell me the truth."

Marshalla glared at him. She couldn't let him succeed, she couldn't!

"Did Tip take the money?"

Marshalla's lips parted of their own accord.

"Y—"

Quivering, she gritted her teeth. She tried shaking her head, but it was no use. Her mind screamed at her, it screamed at her to tell everyone she was bound, bound and not Compelled. But her lips remain unmoved.

"Y—"

Again, she gritted her teeth. She glared at him once more, her eyes screaming her hatred. But Drumold stared at her with stoic calm.

"Do not resist, child, it's of no use. Just… relax and let the truth out."

Marshalla's lips parted once more. But she fought, she fought with all she could muster. She clenched her fists and raged at her own mind. Her heart threatened to explode within her chest, her head ached and throbbed like never before, but still she fought. Drumold must not win, Drumold *could* not win.

"Y—"

The cost of her battles within finally became clear for all to see, for as she glared at the high priest, blood began to trickle from both her nostrils. Worried gasps echoed amongst some of the gathered, while Drumold himself seemed to soften as he saw the blood.

"Marshalla, speak. Speak now and I will release you. Did Tip take the money?"

But she did not. The blood ran over her lips, down her chin, and began dripping onto the floor, and still she fought.

"Damn it all, child, just say it! Say it and I will release you!"

"Y—"

Drumold leant forward, the fear in his eyes lending Marshalla strength. "Just say it, girl! Say it and I will release you!"

But Marshalla fought on.

"Marsha…?" Tip asked worriedly.

She wanted to tell him it was okay, that she knew what she was doing. But instead, she stood where she was, her eyes on Drumold. Instead, she just fought on.

"Stop it!" Maline exclaimed. "Stop it, you hear me? Stop it!"

"She has to say it," Drumold replied.

"She already said it!"

"No, she must say it properly."

"You killing her! Drumold! You killing her damn it, stop!"

"Be quiet, woman!"

Breaking free of the crowd, Maline charged forward, but a nearby priestess grabbed hold of her and held her back.

"You're killing her! Drumold! Drumold, you're killing her! She's just a child! You're killing her!"

At last, Drumold looked from Marshalla to a flailing Maline before slowly turning and addressing the gathered.

"Does any here doubt their guilt?"

None spoke.

Drumold looked at Tip. There were tears in the little boy's eyes, and fear. He looked back at Marshalla. A small pool of her blood had formed at her feet. Taking a deep breath, he closed his eyes briefly, whispering words of arcane under his breath. As he finished, Marshalla slowly crumpled to the ground, shivering uncontrollably. Breaking free of the priestess holding her, Maline rushed to Marshalla's side, catching her just in time before sinking to the floor with her. The silence that followed was suffocating.

"I'm sorry, Marsha," Drumold muttered after a spell. "I had no choice." But Marshalla held her peace, choosing instead to glare at him. Drumold stared back at her, but he soon averted his gaze. The elderly priest stared at his feet for a spell, before raising his gaze to her once more.

"Given what has just transpired, I have to ask you both to leave. You are no longer welcome here, either here or at any of our homes. You must relinquish your bag and leave here at once."

In response, Marshalla pulled off the bag on her back, her eyes never leaving Drumold's. Even as she flung the bag at his feet, she kept her gaze locked on his.

"If, however, you chose to return what you stole, we will forgive you and welcome you back amongst us."

Marshalla said nary a word.

"As for…" Drumold continued, but his words faded away as he watched Tip kneel beside his dear friend, wailing softly as he hugged her and buried his head on her chest.

"As…" But his words failed him once again. Raising his gaze, he clenched his fist, as if fighting for strength, before closing his eyes and speaking once more.

"As for your undergarments—"

"No, mercy!" Maline exclaimed. "You can't! It's cold now. You take that from them, they won't last. Drumold, please! Mercy."

"We have a large shortfall to make up for, Maline. We need to make up as much as we can."

"Then take mine!"

"Maline—"

"No! Mercy, Drumold, please!"

"No mercy for thieving liars!" a voice cried out from the crowd. Before long, many other voices joined in the chorus, screaming obscenities and threats at both Marshalla and Tip.

"Enough!" Drumold bellowed, silencing all in an instant. He looked at Marshalla once more.

"Go, just go."

Marshalla stared defiantly at him still before finally rising, aided by both Maline and Tip. Fixing the high priest with one last hate-filled glare, she turned and shuffled out, Maline and Tip close behind, with Maline stopping to grab her own bag.

All three made their way away from the Priory in silence. It was a pained silence, one filled with hate and hurt. Before long, they were out of sight of the others. It was at this point that Maline rounded on Marshalla and, without a word, forced her bag into Marshalla's hand. Marshalla looked from the bag to Maline.

"They'll make you pay."

"Don't care."

Tears filled Marshalla's eyes, but she said nary a word. As Maline stared at Marshalla, her own eyes began to fill with tears as well. Cupping the younger elf's cheeks in both her hands, Maline leant in and gently touched her forehead to Marshalla's before turning and heading away from them and the Priory.

"We'll pay you back!" Marshalla shouted at Maline after a spell. "You'll see!"

Turning, Maline shook her head. "Don't have to, just be okay." And with that, she left them be. Both Tip and Marshalla watched her for a spell.

"Come, Tip," Marshalla said at last. Wiping her blood from her lips and chin, she slipped her hand into Tip's before they headed away from the Priory.

Smiling, Marshalla stared at a slumbering Tip. They had wandered for an age before finally settling for the night. It wasn't that they had struggled to find a good place, but rather both needed time to come to terms with what had happened, Tip more than her. And even after they'd bedded down, he'd clung to her as if for dear life, and no matter how many times she'd repeated herself, he still apologized over and over, and only truly stopped when he drifted to sleep.

Stifling a yawn, Marshalla gently smoothed out his hair before making herself more comfortable. It was past time she, too, got some sleep. But as she rolled over to sleep, it was then she noticed the figure in the shadows. With her heart in her throat, she stared at the figure, but it remained unmoving. Marshalla looked at Tip, her mind racing. The figure, whoever it was, was between them and their only exit. Gritting her teeth, Marshalla turned her gaze back at the figure. If whoever it was meant them harm, she'd have to get them away from Tip, nothing else mattered. Then, abruptly, the figure stepped out into the light, and as she saw who it was, her heart sank anew.

Marshalla watched with dread as Thuridan Grovemender stared at her in silence, their gaze locked upon one another, until at last he gestured for her to join him. Marshalla hesitated, unsure what to make of his presence. When he gestured to her a second time, however, she rose, careful not to wake Tip. If he meant them ill, there was precious little she could do to stop him, so she may as well see what he was after. But even so, there was caution in her steps, and it kept her at a safe distance from him.

"I take it you remember me, then," Thuridan said, his gaze cold and biting. Curtly, Marshalla nodded.

"Good." Abruptly, the high elf broke into a smile, though it was a humorless one. "The pair of you were rather hard to find."

"Why you looking for us?"

Thuridan's smile widened. "Why, indeed. I hear you've been met with no small misfortune."

"What's it to you?"

Thuridan tilted his head as a smirk parted his lips. "And here I thought you were the smart one."

Marshalla glowered at him in response.

"Davian's quite fond of your friend, Tip, and has been rather incessant in his pleas to allow the both of you under my roof. Much as the idea fills me with... well, let's just say, I'm not overly fond of the idea. But he *is* my son, and I vowed he would want for nothing. So, here I am to make his case for him."

This, Marshalla was not expecting, and it showed.

"Well, come, girl. Don't just stand there gawping, what say you?"

"I... uh." Marshalla tried to form her thoughts. In her confusion, she looked behind her at Tip. But as she did so, memories of their first encounter with Thuridan flashed before her eyes, and with it came her answer.

"No," she replied, turning to face him once more.

"What?"

"No. Davian's nice and all, but you not him. You hate us, and we hate you. No."

Silence fell on the pair as Thuridan stared at Marshalla, his face a picture of bewilderment.

"My, my, you truly are a fool," Thuridan said at last.

"What you—?"

"Winter is coming, you have nowhere to stay, nobody left to look after you and—"

"Mardaley looks after us."

"Ah yes, the storekeeper. Tell me, my dear gutter rat, what do you think your dear Mardaley will say once word of what happened today reaches him, hmm?"

Marshalla stared with disdain at the mage before her, but kept her peace.

"No idea? Well, let me tell you. He, like your dear friend the high priest, will throw your worthless hides right out."

"Liar! Mardaley'll never do that to us."

Thuridan laughed at Marshalla. It was a laugh that cut her deeply.

"And if someone were to tell you yesterday that your dear friend Drumold would've put you through what he put you through today, would you have believed it or would you have also called that person a liar?"

Marshalla moved to speak, but she could not.

Smirking, Thuridan took a step forward. "But you're not seeing things for what they truly are, my dear girl, you're not asking the truly important question."

"What's that, then?"

"How did I know about it?"

Frowning, Marshalla turned the question over in her mind. A simple enough question, but one she couldn't quite answer.

"How did…?" And then she saw the answer. In a moment of sickening clarity, she saw it clear as day.

"It was you!" she shrieked, her eyes going wide as she pointed an accusing finger at him. "You stole it!"

Thuridan laughed. "Oh, my dear child. So close and yet so far. The money was never stolen."

"What?"

"You heard me. The money was never stolen."

"But Drumold—"

"Drumold did as I bade him. He was following my instructions." Thuridan took another step forward. "What happened to you happened because I willed it."

Slowly, Marshalla backed away from the high elf, her face one of horror. "You… you bastard!"

"My dear, unless you wish to wake that snoring mound behind you, I suggest you keep your voice down."

"But… what we ever do to you?"

"Child, your stupidity is beginning to offend me. Did I not already say Davian is enamored with that boy? And I can't very well have that boy under my roof without having *you* under my roof, now, can I?"

"But… but you could've asked!"

"Davian did. Repeatedly. And you refused. Repeatedly. So, I took matters into my own hands."

The numbing cold within the pit of Marshalla's stomach spread all about her.

"You need to understand one thing, child," Thuridan continued. "I always get what I want, and right now that is what Davian wants. You will say yes to him, or I will destroy you utterly and completely. But, and this is truly important so do please pay attention, should Davian lose interest in you, my offer fades with that interest. And with where you are in life right now, well…"

Vehemently, Marshalla shook her head.

"No!" she exclaimed. "No, no, no, no, no! You won't own us! Rather die than go anywhere near you!"

"With winter coming, that's very likely."

Marshalla moved to speak, but stopped, gritting her teeth instead.

"Now, as for—"

"We'll leave, Tip and me, we'll leave Merethia."

Thuridan sighed as he shook his head at her. "And go where?"

"Don't know, somewhere."

"Look, you—"

"Tealan. We'll go Tealan, it's close. We'll find work there."

Thuridan shook his head, sighing once again. "So, you would swap being a gutter rat in a place like Merethia to being a gutter rat in Tealan. Truly? And this work you will find, what kind of work do you think someone like you would find in a place like Tealan? And the men there, do you think they will be as… civil… to someone with your… endowments?"

"Nothing civil about the men here," Marshalla snarled.

"If you truly think so, then you are in for a treat in Tealan," Thuridan replied, chuckling at Marshalla as he spoke.

"We not working for you, and you can't stop us leaving!" Spinning on her heels, Marshalla marched back towards Tip.

"Get back here, I'm not done with you yet."

But Marshalla ignored him and carried on walking.

"Or would you rather I make an example of your sleeping friend."

Stopping, she turned to face him. "You wouldn't dare."

"Are you sure?"

Marshalla stared at him in silence for a spell before at last doing as he bid. As she reached him though, he fixed her with a most curious stare. Unsure what to make of it, she stared back at him.

"You're a curious one," Thuridan said at last. "I know not if it's stupidity or courage that's driving you, but either way you're clearly set on refusing me, aren't you? Even if it means freezing to death, or worse."

Marshalla stuck her chin out at him in response.

"Very well," he continued. "I shall ask one favor of you, and if you succeed, I shall leave you be."

Marshalla frowned at him. "Leave us be…for good?"

"Yes."

"Ok…."

"Good." Nodding, Thuridan parted his coat, revealing his money purse. "Steal my purse."

"What?"

"You heard me. Steal my purse. Like you did the first time we met."

"Wasn't me—"

"I know, Tip did. So, come over here and do the same."

Marshalla hesitated. But his promise rang in her ears still, so at last she walked over to his side. She looked from his purse to him.

"Go on."

Frowning still, she looked back at his purse, then lunged for it. But the moment her fingers clasped round it, her eyes grew wide as a defiling blaze erupted in her hand. It was like nothing she'd ever felt, for it was corrupting and burning all at once. It shot up her arm at such an alarming pace, spreading through her body, down to her legs, and up into her head. Within moments, her entire body felt engulfed in a blazing inferno whilst drowning in a sea of vile corruption. She tried to scream, but her voice failed her. She tried to release her grasp, but her fingers failed her. All she could do was stand staring at Thuridan with her eyes wide and her mind screaming in pain and terror.

With a single word, Thuridan ended her suffering.

"Gods above!" she whispered as she cradled her hand, backing away quickly from him.

"What you felt, my dear," Thuridan said as he took a step forward, "is what that friend of yours *should've* felt the moment his fingers closed around my purse. But he didn't, did he?"

Marshalla stared Thuridan, lost for words.

"Did he?"

At last, she shook her head.

"Why?"

She shook her head once again, but this time looked over at Tip.

"Liar," she replied at last, turning to face him. "It wasn't there when Tip touched it."

"Oh, but it was. Do you remember how I turned the purse over in my hand when you returned it? I was checking the wards. They were still active, every single one of them."

"But... didn't feel anything."

"*Precisely*! Your friend over there not only stole it, but gave it to you in a manner that meant you were shielded from its effect."

"Tip?"

"Yes, my dear, Tip. So, how did he do it? How did Tip take the purse from me without suffering any of its effects? And how was he able to give it to you without you suffering any of its effects?"

Marshalla didn't have an answer.

"How well do you know him?"

"He..." Marshalla began, but her voice trailed away as she turned to stare at him once again.

"You know nothing of his past, do you?"

Still no answer.

"I mean to learn his secret, girl. I mean to learn how he was able to get past my wards so easily and so quickly. And that is why I want you and he to accept Davian's offer."

"He'll never tell you," she replied at last, turning to face him once again. "He hates you."

"You let me worry about that. All you have to do is convince him to accept Davian's offer."

"He hates you," she repeated. "Can't talk him into saying yes if he hates you."

"Of course, you can. He listens to you; he trusts you and looks up to you. And, judging from today's events, I daresay he'll do absolutely anything you ask of him."

Marshalla shook her head, looking back at Tip once more. This time, though, it was the familiar jingle of coins that drew her gaze back to Thuridan. As she looked at him, her gaze quickly settled upon the money bag in his hand, one almost as large as his whole hand. Marshalla stared, open-mouthed, at it. Then, Thuridan tossed it at her. Catching it, she looked up at him, her gaze one of puzzlement and quite some guilt.

"One more of that if you succeed in convincing him, and a final one if I get what I'm after."

Marshalla looked down at the bag in her hand.

"I will not harm him. In fact, I intend to teach him the ways of the arcane to gain his trust."

Marshalla stared at the bag in her hand, unmoved.

"You lose nothing by this, and I will not throw you both out once I have what I want. You may remain under my roof for as long as you wish. You will be fed while under my roof. And a wage, of course."

Marshalla looked up at Thuridan once more.

"Well?"

"Uhm…" she looked over at Tip, then looked back at Thuridan.

"Doing this for him, not me," she said at last.

Thuridan smirked at her. "*Of course*, you are. Oh, one more thing. We never spoke. Understood?"

Marshalla glowered at him for a spell.

"Yes," she whispered at last.

"Good." And with that, he turned and left. Marshalla watched him leave, her guilt growing with each pace he took. She looked down at the bag in her hand. It seemed to have gained in weight. Gritting her teeth, she pulled out the enchanted money purse Mardaley had gifted her to hold their coin, and carefully emptied the bag into it before shoving both the purse and the bag into her pockets. She looked over at Tip once more.

"Doing this for him…" she muttered. "For him."

Taking a deep breath, she walked over to where Tip lay, and sitting beside him, she shook him awake as gently as she could.

"Hey, Tip."

Tip looked up groggily at her. "Marsha?"

"Listen, been thinking…"

MORTAL MACHINATIONS

S tifling a yawn, Magister Meadowview rose from the bench where he sat. No
matter where he sat within the Gardens of Taith, be it by one of its many
fountains, or on one of its benches in shade, the peace and tranquility always
lulled him eventually. Shaking himself awake, he rose to his feet. It was past time he
left.

"I thought I might find you here," a voice called out to him from behind. Turning,
he watched as an unfamiliar elderly woman made her way towards him.

"Do we know each other?" he asked once she reached him, his curiosity piqued.

"Yes, I believe we do."

Frowning, the Magister stared at his new guest, trying hard to place her face.

"You have me at a disadvantage, my lady," he said at last. The lady before him
smiled.

"Good to know my illusions are good enough now to fool even you, Baern."

Magister Meadowview's eyes grew wide. He'd recognize that voice anywhere.

"Mardaley?" he whispered.

"Hmm? I'm sorry, I didn't quite hear that," the elderly lady replied in her earlier
voice.

"Oh, very funny, Mardaley," Baern growled. "So, what do I call you?"

"Emaline."

"Ema– Oh very funny indeed!"

"Thought you might like it," Mardaley replied, grinning.

"What are you doing here looking like that?"

All at once, Mardaley's grin dissipated.

"We have trouble," he muttered.

"Trouble enough that you'd go through all of this?"

Grimly, Mardaley nodded. "Sit with me."

"I can't, I need to head back."

"Then I'll walk with you."

Pausing, Baern stared at his friend in silence for a spell.

"Very well," he said at last. Turning, Magister Meadowview began walking towards the entrance with Mardaley in tow.

"So, what's happened?"

"Marshalla's accepted Thuridan's offer."

Stopping dead, Baern turned to stare at his friend, fixing him with a haunted gaze. Mardaley nodded in response, his eyes forward.

"When?" Baern whispered once he found his voice, his feet finding their rhythm as he spoke.

"They changed their minds a couple of days ago," Mardaley replied as he fell in step beside his friend. "She came in this morning, her and Tip. Both said they had something to tell me, and then just… blurted it out."

Baern stared hard at his friend. His face was set, as if chiseled in stone, but he knew Mardaley better than most, and that knowledge worried him greatly.

"They told Davian yesterday," Mardaley continued, oblivious to the strength of his friend's stare, "and he went and told his father. They told me after they told Davian, Baern. Me!"

"Mardaley—"

"Emaline, Baern."

"Whatever. Look, we need to be calm about this."

Abruptly, Mardaley turned to stare at him, the pained expression in his eyes further confirming Baern's fears.

"Calm, you say?" Mardaley asked through gritted teeth.

"Yes, calm."

"Baern, we're about to lose Marshalla to that self-serving monster, and you preach calm to me?"

"Look, Ma…Emaline, we—"

"I am calm, Baern. I am very calm."

"You… good."

Scowling, Mardaley turned his gaze forward. "Damn it all, I should've offered them room and board with their wages!"

"Emaline, no, we—"

"But if I had we wouldn't be in this mess!"

"No, we wouldn't, we would be in an even bigger mess. It would be only a matter of time before she'd stumble onto something that told her of her past before she was ready to learn of it. Your words, not mine."

Mardaley glared at his friend with gritted teeth before finally sighing.

"I'm sorry, it's just...I don't know what to do here." Stopping, Mardaley turned to stare at his friend, his gaze one of such great pain. "I don't know what to do."

"Well…" Baern began as he fought to keep his composure. Rarely did he ever see Mardaley so vulnerable, and such sights always bore into him. "When do they join his household?"

"He's meant to come over this evening to discuss the terms of their new employment. We're to discuss when best they can leave."

"That's quite… noble of him," Baern said as he resumed his earlier pace.

"Isn't it just?" Mardaley replied as he fell in step.

"Still, it doesn't give us much time to think this through."

"You don't say."

"Emaline, please. We're together in this."

Mardaley turned to glare at his friend, but even as he did so, his anger left him.

"I'm sorry," he muttered. "It's just… Gods, I can't believe I'm about to lose her to him!"

"It's not over yet."

"What do we do, then? How do we stop this? She can't just go to him."

"Is there anything at all you can do to delay this?"

"Oh, I can do a lot of things."

"Okay then, is there anything you can do to delay this that doesn't involve reducing him to ash?"

Mardaley cast an angry sideways glance at Baern, but kept his peace.

"Right, well, he's caught us off-guard, and pretty badly too. With luck, it will be a few days before they move into his home, it should at least give us some time to—"

"No, we have to stop it all now, right now."

"It's too late for that, she's accepted."

"It doesn't matter, we have to think of something. We have to stop it."

"You're not thinking this through, Emaline."

Fuming, Mardaley rounded on his friend.

"I am not losing her again!" he snarled.

"Mardaley, you need to remain calm a—"

"I *am* calm!" Mardaley bellowed, his words echoing angrily about them as lightning flashed briefly between his eyes. An unsettling silence fell upon the pair as Baern stared worriedly at his friend. At last, Mardaley brought his ire to heel, and as he did so, he cast a furtive glance about him at the many faces staring at him with a mix of worry, anger and simple curiosity.

"I'm sorry," he muttered as he quickened his pace. Shaking his head, Baern hurried to keep pace with him.

"I'm sorry," he repeated once Baern was beside him, the elderly Magister nodding at him in response.

"We have to do something."

Sighing, Baern nodded. "I know."

"Once she moves into his home, I'll be out of her life."

Baern sighed once again, but then, at that moment, he knew just what he had to do.

"Then, maybe it's time I entered it."

Frowning, Mardaley turned to stare at Baern.

"What do you mean?" he asked. Baern smiled.

"The boy wants to learn magic, correct?"

"Yes…"

"And Marshalla loves that boy, correct?"

"Yes…"

"Well, given the Tower's current policy, I think I may be able whet his appetite some. And what better way to make sure Thuridan stays on his best behavior than him knowing the Tower's taken an interest in them."

Mardaley frowned at his friend.

"What about Naeve?" he asked after a brief silence. "We can't have her meet Marshalla before they're both ready."

"We'll have to tackle that later. Right now, we have to save them from Thuridan."

Mardaley's frown remained for a spell, but soon a grateful smile parted his lips.

"Thank you."

Baern shook his head in response. "Don't thank me yet, I still need to bring it to be."

"You will; you always do."

Baern smiled at his friend. Turning, he looked up about them. People were still staring.

"Come, let's get out of here before rumors start spreading about me."

Mardaley chuckled. "Yes, I suppose we'd better."

*****

With a guilty frown, Tip stared at Mardaley. The little boy sat hugging one of the balusters of the small staircase tightly, his head resting upon the same baluster as he watched Mardaley restock his wares. When they'd told him earlier that they intended work for Thuridan Grovemender, Tip wasn't quite sure how Mardaley would react. But even if he was, the cold silence and the look of pain upon Mardaley's face were not what he'd have expected. Since then, the elderly storekeeper had been distant, and that hurt Tip, it hurt a great deal. But even more biting was the guilt. He'd been so happy, so eager to go live with Davian, he didn't once stop to think about how Mardaley would feel about them leaving. Not once.

Tip looked over at Marshalla seated at the table behind him. She, too, was staring at Mardaley. Briefly, their eyes met. She, too, was wracked with guilt. Betrayed, that's what Marshalla had called it. Mardaley was feeling betrayed. And there was nothing they could do about it. Just then, the door opened as two visitors entered the store. As they entered, the sight of one filled Tip with joy, while the other filled him with dread.

"Good evening," Thuridan said as he took in all within the store.

"Good evening, Thuridan," Mardaley replied. "Please, come in."

Tip frowned deeply as he watched Thuridan close the door behind him, but as his eyes fell back upon Davian, his frown was quickly replaced by a warm smile as Davian waved excitedly at him.

"Marsha, look after the store, would you?" Mardaley asked as he beckoned Thuridan to join him before heading for the back room.

"Okay," Marshalla replied as Tip shuffled as close to the banister as he could. But as Thuridan walked past him, Davian suddenly sprinted over and snuggled up beside Tip. Giggling, he looked over at Tip, shouldering him playfully as he did so. It was such an infectious giggle that, before Tip even realized, he too was giggling as he shouldered Davian back.

"I'm glad you said yes," Davian gushed. "We're going to have so much fun, you and I!" Then Davian turned to Marshalla. "And you too, of course." Marshalla smiled warmly at him in response. He grinned at her but the grin was fleeting.

"What changed your mind though? Did Father speak to you?"

Tip frowned. "Why would he?"

Davian turned to Tip. "I asked him to."

Tip's frown deepened at this.

"Oh, don't be angry with me," Davian pleaded. "I just asked him to talk to Marsha and you, let you see he's not such a horrible person."

"Not sure we'd believe him if he had," Marshalla said. Davian looked over at her.

"So, he never spoke to you?"

"No, made up our own minds."

Davian grinned once more. "I should've known you'd come round!"

Marshalla chuckled at him.

"But what changed your mind though?"

"We got nowhere to go now," Tip replied simply. Frowning, Davian looked at Tip. "What do you mean?"

"Drumold said we took his coin, but we never. Then he said we could never go there again. Or any of the hopsices."

"Hospices," Marshalla corrected.

"Who's Drumold?" Davian asked, frowning.

"High Priest of the Priory," Marshalla replied. "We go there for meals and bed once a week. They give us blankets and things so we can manage on our own. And when it gets really bad out, they let us sleep in the hall if it's not our time."

"And they said you stole their money?"

Marshalla nodded. "Yeah. Said we can't ever go back too. And winter's coming. We got nowhere left to go when it gets bad, so... we said yes."

Without warning, pangs of guilt struck at Tip as he stared at Davian.

"We using you," he said.

Davian looked at him, grinning. "Of course you are! But think nothing of it. You said yes, and that's all that matters, right?" He looked over at Marshalla. "Right?"

Both Marshalla and Tip looked at each other before sharing a smile.

"Right," they replied in unison.

"Right! But what Drumold did wasn't very nice. I'll speak to Father, see if there's anything he can do to teach him a lesson."

"Don't have—" Marshalla began, but at that moment, the door opened once more. As one, all three looked over at their new guest.

"Maline! You came!" Tip exclaimed once he saw who it was.

"Hello, Maline," Marshalla added, smiling.

"Hey, you two," Maline replied nervously as she looked from one to the other, before finally resting her gaze upon Davian.

"Good evening, miss," Davian said, bowing slightly at Maline.

Maline smiled at him as she cocked her head to the side.

"Evening," she replied at last.

"This is Davian," Tip said with quite some excitement. "Me and Marsha going to live with him."

Surprised, Maline turned to Marshalla.

"Live-in servants," Marshalla replied. "New job."

"Wait, really?" Maline asked.

Marshalla nodded.

"That what the new clothes are for, then?"

Marshalla stared down at the dress she wore. "Yeah, just got them." Then she smiled as she looked back at the older elf. "Glad you came, Maline."

"Yeah, really glad!" Tip exclaimed as he rose. Walking up to her, he stood before her as he grinned at her. "You going to like working for Mardaley. He's very nice."

Maline frowned. "Working for Mardaley?"

Tip nodded as his grin widened. "He pays well too. We saved *loads*, and all we did was deliver things. But you're older, so you know loads more than us, so loads more ways to help him. Think how quick you'll save up!"

Maline looked up at Marshalla, her gaze one of confusion and wonder.

"Mardaley asked us if we knew anyone to take over when we leave," Marshalla said. "Told you we'd pay you back somehow."

"Yeah," Tip added, chuckling as he spoke.

Through it all, Davian sat perfectly still and silent, staring from one to the other as he tried to discern the meanings behind their words. At last, Maline looked at him, and for some inexplicable reason, she shrugged at him before looking over at first, Tip, then Marshalla.

"Thank you," she said as tears stung her eyes.

"See!" Tip giggled. "Told you she'd like it!"

Laughing, Maline fell to her knees and held the little elf in a tight embrace.

"Ah, you must be Maline," Mardaley called out as he stepped into view, Thuridan close behind. All four turned to stare at him.

"Yes," Maline squeaked as she rose. Mardaley smiled warmly at her.

"They told me what you did for them at the Priory. You have my thanks."

Maline blushed as she dropped her gaze to her feet briefly.

"Had to," she replied softly. "Wasn't right what Drumold did."

"No, it most certainly wasn't. I take it they've told you they put your name forward as their replacement?"

Maline nodded.

"And I take it you accept?"

Maline smiled shyly, dropping her gaze to her feet once more before once again nodding.

"Excellent!" Thuridan exclaimed as he darted forward, hurrying down the stairs, but stopping at their base to spin round and regard his son.

"And you, my dear son, will be glad to know that Mardaley's agreed to allow your two friends return with us this very evening!"

Davian's eyes lit up.

"But only if they are both permitted to return every noon-chime to show Maline what needs to be done," Mardaley added. "And go with her on her noon rounds. For one full week." He looked at Marshalla, then Tip. "If that's acceptable with you two, of course."

Tip and Marshalla looked at each other before shrugging.

"Don't mind," Tip said.

"Same," Marshalla added.

"Good!" Thuridan exclaimed. "Then we have an accord."

"May I go with them, Father?" Davian asked. "It can be my noon break."

"Whatever for?"

Davian shrugged as he lowered his gaze.

"Oh, very well, then."

Looking up at his father, Davian grinned.

Grinning back, Thuridan turned to Mardaley. "And now I believe our business is concluded."

Mardaley nodded at the Archmage. "I believe it is, yes."

"Good." Thuridan looked down at the others. "Well, shall we?"

And with that, all four left. Two stared back guiltily at Mardaley as they left. But none saw the pain in the elderly storekeeper's eyes, save Maline.

*****

Grimacing, Thalas opened the bottle beside him and raised it to his lips before taking a deep gulp, coughing and spluttering soon after as the firewine burned its way down his throat. Sighing, he shuffled slightly across the windowsill upon which he sat, his gaze upon the city below, his feet dangling freely beneath him. Most of Merethia was asleep, and so, too, should he be. But sleep was the last thing on his mind. Once again, he raised the bottle to his lips, this time taking a more measured gulp. As he sighed once again, there was a gentle knock on the door.

"Thalas?" Neremi called out.

With his brows furrowed in concentration, Thalas traced intricate patterns in the air as he called forth a hand of pure air before commanding it to unlock and open the door. As the door swung open, his beloved walked in, her eyes quickly resting upon him.

"Thalas, my darling, is all well?"

Thalas did not reply.

Frowning, Neremi closed and locked the door behind her before, taking off her coat and, tossing it onto a nearby chair, she walked over to the window where he sat.

"Thalas, you know it frightens me when you sit like that. Come inside so we can talk."

In response, Thalas stared at the street far below his feet, but said nary a word.

"Thalas, what's happened? Your father called the house, asking after you. He tried to hide it, but I could hear his anger. What did you do?"

Thalas scoffed at her before raising the bottle to his lips once more. As he lowered the bottle, however, Neremi took it from him before taking a deep gulp herself. Coughing, she put it on a nearby table before resting her face on the wall as she stared worriedly at Thalas.

"Thalas?"

At last, he turned to her, but even in the weak light, Neremi could quite clearly see the large bruise down the side of her beloved's face.

"Thalas!" she exclaimed, reaching for him. "What did he do to you?"

"He brought them home today," Thalas replied, "those two gutter rats. He actually paraded them about like they were nobility. The little one's bedding down with Davian. Can you imagine it? My little brother sharing the same room, the same *bed*, with a street rat. And the slut, he's given her one of the guest rooms. But not just any old guest room, no, it's the one he said I could use for *my* guests."

"Thalas, I—"

"And why, you ask? Because it's close to Davian's room. He wants that harlot mothering my brother. That old fool's lost his mind, I tell you."

"And he did this to you because you told him as much?"

"Of course, I told him!" Thalas bellowed. "To his face! But that's not why he did this. Oh no. He wants *me* to treat them as my equal. Me! Thalas Grovemender! I am a mage of the Shimmering Tower! I will not have them as my equal! They are not, and will *never* be my equal!"

Not knowing what else to do, Neremi threw her arms around her beloved, hugging him close.

At last, she looked at him once again. "Come inside, please. Come inside and let's talk."

Thalas glared at her for a spell before finally relenting and clambering back inside.

"How long do you have this room for?" Neremi asked as Thalas stepped inside.

"Till the noon-chime."

"You're spending the night here?"

Thalas nodded sulkily as he walked over to the bed. "I'm not sleeping under the same roof as those two."

"Wish me to keep you company?"

Thalas stared at her in silence for a spell. "I'd like that."

Neremi smiled at him as she walked over and sat beside him.

"Will your parents not mind, though?" Thalas added. "You've been sleeping out of their home quite a lot of late."

Neremi shrugged, smiling still. Thalas couldn't help but smile at her.

"All will be well, my love," Neremi said softly. "You'll see."

Thalas' grin faded as he stared before him, his gaze darkening greatly.

"I can't go back to that house, Neremi," he muttered. "I will never accept them as my equal. Never."

"You must, for the time being."

Gritting his teeth, Thalas turned to glare at her. "They are *not* my equal."

"Well, do you see any other way? Or are you all set to put your plan into action this very moment?"

Thalas held his peace.

"Well, then, you must."

Huffing, Thalas walked over to his bottle. Neremi watched him for a spell, her worry for him growing.

"How close are you to enacting your plan anyway?"

"I... I'm still to work out a few details."

"Like what?"

Thalas drank deeply from the bottle before coughing once more. Turning, he headed over to Neremi, offering her the bottle as he sat back down beside her.

"Like what?" Neremi repeated as she took the bottle and drank deeply herself.

"Well, I'll need to get him on his own, and often, but father's going to be watching him like a hawk now, and if I show too much interest, he'll begin to wonder."

"Oh," Neremi muttered.

"Yes," Thalas said, sighing. "I need a reason, some ruse, to need to be in his presence regularly."

"It would be so much easier if we could just snatch him and make him talk," Neremi muttered bitterly before taking another deep gulp. As she turned to offer the bottle to Thalas though, he was staring at her with a most unsettling gaze.

"What...?" Neremi asked.

"Neremi, that might actually work."

"What would?"

"Maybe I'm trying to be too clever. It really would be easier to just snatch him, wouldn't it?"

Neremi shook her head at her beloved. "But it's too late now, isn't it? He's in your father's clutches now."

A slow grin parted Thalas' lips. "Father's taking them to the Tower on its next open doors."

Neremi stared, confused, at Thalas for a spell, but as the meaning of his words sank in, the blood slowly drained from her face.

"Have you gone mad? In the Tower?"

Thalas gave a slow, deliberate nod.

"We can't! We'll never succeed!"

"Yes, we will. I need to think, but in the morning, we call the others together, talk through it all. We can do this, Neremi, we can."

"If we fail, Thalas, we'll be banished from the Tower!"

"But what if we succeed? If we succeed, we win our freedom! To the hells with the morning. Send word for the others, have them come over now! I need to think, think this through."

Standing, Thalas began pacing around the rented abode. Neremi, for her part, rose and headed for the door. Taking one last look at Thalas, she left to do as he'd bid.

*****

As the noon-chime struck its twelfth chime, Tip walked into Mardaley's store. With him were Marshalla and Davian, Davian being the last to enter. None were sure what kind of reception they would receive, so as they entered, trepidation hung about them like a heavy winter's coat.

"Hello, Mardaley," Marshalla called out. Seated round the table past the small stairs was indeed Mardaley, and Maline.

"Ah, just in time!" Mardaley exclaimed, grinning as he rose. "I've been instructing Maline on the details of the deliveries. But, now that you're here, perhaps you can complete the lesson for me while I see to some things in the back."

"You didn't send her on the morning deliveries?" Marshalla asked worriedly as she hurried up the steps to Maline's side.

"No," he replied. "No more morning deliveries. Maline's helping me with a few other things besides deliveries, so her mornings are better spent here."

"See, Maline!" Tip exclaimed, grinning. "Told you!"

"Hmm? Told her what?"

"Nothing," Maline replied quickly as she fixed Tip with a silencing glare, but one which lacked any venom.

"You're keeping secrets from your employer?" Mardaley asked in his most solemn tone.

"Lady's got to have her secrets, Mardaley," Marshalla replied on Maline's behalf.

"You're supposed to be on my side, not hers!"

Smiling, Marshalla walked over to sit beside Maline, then proceeded to tutor her on the routes, clients and, most importantly, how to wrap and label the deliveries themselves. As she spoke, Mardaley turned his attention to Tip and Davian, who had both climbed up the stairs. He stared last at Tip with a slight, almost forced smile, before turning and heading for the back room. Tip stared as he left, before turning and looking sadly at Davian, then at Marshalla.

"Don't be like that, Tip," Maline said as he stared at Marshalla. "He really missed you both."

"If you say so," Tip mumbled. Smiling, Maline reached out and ruffled the little elf's hair before turning her attention back to Marshalla. Tip stared sullenly at her for a spell before staring at the back door once more.

"Tip," Marshalla called out to him.

"Hmm?"

"Go show Davian the things Mardaley sells, eh?"

Tip turned to Davian, but as he pondered Marshalla's request, a cheeky grin parted his lips.

"You're going to love these," he said to Davian as he raced down the stairs, chuckling. Giggling, Davian followed. Before long, both boys were engrossed in tales of wonder and adventure as they made up tale after daring tale about Mardaley and how he retrieved the items he sold, with each tale being more wondrous than the last.

"Right, you two, let's go," Marshalla called out to them suddenly as she and Maline headed for the door, the delivery sack slung over Maline's shoulder.

"Already?" Davian exclaimed.

"What you mean *already*? Come on!"

Exchanging brief glances, both raced out of the open door, but as Tip stepped through, he stopped and spun about.

"Bye, Mardaley!" he yelled, then waited for Mardaley's response. None came. At last, he looked up at Marshalla, his eyes filled with sadness. Without a word, he left to join Davian outside. As he did so, Marshalla and Maline looked at each other before Marshalla turned to the door through which Mardaley had disappeared.

"Come," Maline said. "Boys are waiting."

With a grim frown, Marshalla looked at Maline before doing as she bid her.

"He hates us, doesn't he?" Tip asked once Marshalla and Maline were with them.

"It's okay, Tip," Marshalla replied as she began walking away from the store, the others falling in step about her. "Don't need him anymore, we got Davian now."

"That a cold thing to say," Maline said.

Frowning. Marshalla turned to her, shrugging. "No colder than him ignoring Tip."

"He doesn't hate you," Maline replied as she looked from Marshalla to Tip. "He doesn't."

"Then why ignore Tip?"

"Some men have difficulty expressing their pain," Davian replied, his voice soft and barely above a whisper. All three turned to him.

"Davian's right," Maline said before any of the others spoke, looking at each of them in turn. "Mardaley does care, just too proud and stubborn to show it." Then rested her gaze upon little Davian once more. "But how come you know all this?"

Davian shrugged. "My father's a proud man. We weren't always this close."

"Oh…"

"But that's just silly, though!" Tip exclaimed. "Why pretend you don't care?"

Davian grinned. "Some people are silly like that."

"Well, Mardaley wasn't pretending," Marshalla noted stubbornly. "Not the type."

"You didn't see how he was after you left yesterday," Maline said.

"Oh?"

"Yeah, went all broody and silent; couldn't rid of me fast enough. That man's in pain, Marsha. It's as if he saw you two as his."

"I'm not surprised," Davian added.

"What you mean?" Tip asked.

"Well, did you not see how he was staring at Father that first time we met, after Father insinuated you weren't worth being around me? Thought he was going to strike Father down."

Marshalla and Tip exchanged glances, but their moods had decidedly improved.

"What's insinuated?" Tip asked after a brief spell.

"Suggest," Marshalla replied.

"Don't know what to suggest, don't know what it means."

"No, Tip, it means suggest."

"Ah."

"So, anyway," Maline said, "what's it like living with Davian?"

"It's horrible!" Tip exclaimed.

"Hey!" Davian cried in response.

"Ha, tricked you!"

The others giggled as Davian glowered at Tip.

"It's nice," Tip conceded soon after. "His father likes us now. He used to call us gutter rats and everything, but this morning he almost sent his head houseperson away because she called Marsha a street whore."

"She what?" Maline frowned at the little elf.

"It was spoken in the heat of the moment," Davian added hurriedly.

"Yeah, she was really angry." Tip nodded.

"Angry about what?" Maline pressed.

Tip paused and frowned at Davian for a spell.

"Don't know," he said at last. "She's always angry when she sees Marsha and me."

"But everyone else likes you, right?"

Tip grinned at Maline. "Most of them, yeah. Marsha and me are going with Davian to the Tower at the end of the week too!"

Frowning, Maline looked at Davian.

"The Tower has been running an open-door event of late. On the last day of the week, every week, they throw their doors open for the whole day to any who would like to see what it would be like to be a mage of the Tower."

"Oh! Anyone?"

Davian nodded. "Well, elves only, of course."

Maline looked at Marshalla. "But you hate magic."

Marshalla shrugged. "Only going to keep an eye on those two, make sure they don't break nothing."

"We won't!" both boys echoed in unison.

"Yeah, going be there to make sure."

"Going to be a mage though," Tip said grinning. "That why he taking me."

"He wants you to join the Tower?"

"No!" he exclaimed, giggling. "Davian's joining. But Davian needs someone to practice with to be good, so he's going to teach me so Davian can practice with me."

"Teach you himself?"

"Oh, yes!"

Maline looked at Davian, who was smiling proudly at her.

"I told Father about Tip's desire to be a powerful mage. Father can be quite generous, you know."

Maline couldn't help but smile as she shook her head at Tip. "Well, so long as you both happy, that's all that matters."

"Oh, we are!"

Just then, they reached the first delivery stop. The others waited patiently as Maline completed the delivery. As the patron's door closed, Maline turned to Marshalla and Tip both, her right palm open for all to see.

"You never told me about this!" she exclaimed.

Grinning, both Marshalla and Tip stared at the coins in her hand.

"About what?" Davian asked.

"The coin," Marshalla replied as Maline showed them to him.

"That the best bit!" Tip added. "What Marsha and me did was, we go to the ones that give us the most first! They started giving us even more when we did that! Don't tell Mardaley though."

Maline laughed. "So, which are those, then?"

"Thought you'd never ask!" Marshalla exclaimed. And as they walked, Marshalla proceeded to give Maline the tutoring that truly mattered - which deliveries would gain her the most coin, and which customers responded best to flattery. As they walked, though, Marshalla couldn't help but throw the odd glance at Tip, her guilt hidden perfectly behind her warm smile.

*****

Sighing, Thuridan stared down at the mass of activity below him. His lips twisted in a disdainful frown, he stood silent as he watched elves from all walks and stations meandering and mingling below.

"I didn't expect to see you in today, Thuridan," a voice called out from the doorway behind him. Spinning, Thuridan stared at his new guest.

"Baern," he said, nodding.

"Does this mean you'll be taking a more prominent role in our open-door event today?"

Thuridan glowered at Baern from where he stood. The Archmage simply smiled back.

"That was in jest, Thuridan," Baern added after a moment's uncomfortable silence.

"Funny."

"Oh, come now," Baern replied as he walked into Thuridan's office, "I'd have expected even you to have warmed to the event by now."

"Why in the world would I have done that?" Thuridan replied testily. "My opinion of this farce hasn't changed. It's only a matter of time before I am proven right."

Sighing, Baern shook his head as he leant on a nearby chair.

"My dear Thuridan, this event has been running for weeks now, and we have yet to see anyone rampaging through our halls looking to steal our artifacts and our knowledge."

"And you think because it hasn't happened yet, it's not going to happen?"

"Well... yes. If anything, I'd say given the increased interest we've had of those wishing to join us, this event has been a resounding success."

"Increased numbers of simpletons and imbeciles... Yes, that does sound like a resounding success."

"Thuridan..."

"Did you actually come in here to talk about something of note, or is this a social visit?"

"Neither, actually, I was walking by and happened to notice your door open."

"Walking by...? And what, pray tell, would you be doing on this floor on a day like today?"

"Now, that would be telling," he replied as he sat on the chair nearest him, smiling. Thuridan watched him with cold regard.

"But, now that I'm here, you're right, we don't really get to talk much," Baern added once seated.

"And what would we have to talk about?"

"Thuridan, my old friend, you and I have been at each other's throats since my appointment to the Matriarch's side. Isn't it time we buried this rancor between us? We are both working for the good of the Tower, are we not?"

Thuridan stared at Baern in silence for a spell.

"Forgive me if I find your words a bit..."

"Hollow?"

"Yes."

Baern smiled. "I don't blame you. But I do mean it, and this open-door event is prime example of our need to join ranks. I must admit, when the Matriarch first voiced it, I agreed with your dissension. The Tower has managed through millennia by closely guarding its secrets and ways. To throw so much caution to the wind would be madness. However, it does seem to be getting some form of result, and gods know our numbers have been dwindling quite noticeably the past few decades."

At last, Thuridan smiled, but there was no mirth in it.

"I see…" he replied as he too sat. "So, you're here to have a friendly little chat, and also see if you can sway my mind on this insult, is that right?"

"Thuridan…" Baern replied, sighing as he shook his head. "Perhaps we shouldn't talk Tower politics for now."

"If you insist…"

"How's the family?"

"They are well."

"And Davian? I hear you're preparing him to partake of the Birthing this year."

"Yes, he'll be old enough."

"It's amazing how quickly they grow up, isn't it?"

Thuridan sighed as he frowned at Baern. "What are you truly after?"

"Like I said, I merely wish to quell the rancor between us."

"To what purpose?"

"Must there be a hidden agenda to everything?"

Thuridan kept his peace for a spell as he held the smiling high elf before him in a cold gaze. At last, he rose.

"Davian is fine. His studies are progressing as well as can be expected. Thalas is also fine. Now, is there anything else? I do have a lot to get done today."

"I hear you have some new additions to the family. Is that true?"

Slowly, Thuridan sat back into his chair and smirked at Baern.

"A young boy, I hear," Baern continued. "About Davian's age, is he? And a girl, too, older from what I hear."

Thuridan shook his head as his smirk grew. "The truth finally comes out. I never thought you would be one to indulge in gossip, but I suppose we all have our vices."

Baern frowned at Thuridan, his face one of pure innocence. "Whatever do you mean?"

"I've heard the rumors. '*Old Thuridan has gotten soft, allowing his son mix and mingle with the dredges of society.*' Well, I will tell you this - my business is my own. What I allow for my family is my choice, mine and no other's."

"Thuridan," Baern replied, looking visibly hurt, "you wound me. I did not come here to gossip. If anything, I was looking to commend you on this. Too many of us have turned a blind eye to the sufferings of the less fortunate among us. Too many have pretended not to have noticed the daily struggles of the penniless and homeless about us. In truth, it is because of these rumors that I have come here now. You have shown yourself to be far nobler than I ever thought of you. If anything, you've put me and many like me to shame, for while we have spent far too long talking about what could be done to alleviate the suffering of the many, you have actually gone out of your way to make a difference."

Thuridan stared at Baern with no small measure of suspicion, but it was clear this was an answer he was not expecting.

"In fact," Baern continued, "I would like nothing more than to meet them, and also urge you to allow them come to the Tower often."

"Why?"

"Guilt, why else? The more often the others here see them, the more they are reminded that mere words are not enough."

Thuridan stared in absolute silence at Baern as he pondered the elderly mage's words carefully.

"The younger one, Tip," he replied at last, "he's shown quite some interest in becoming a mage himself. I daresay he's obsessed with it."

"Truly?"

Thuridan nodded. "Davian suggested they both take advantage of today's event to see what that life would entail."

"Ha! Imagine that!"

Thuridan smiled, but this time it was a smile with much more warmth. "Yes, the irony is not lost on me, Baern."

Baern grinned at him. "So, when will they be arriving? I would very much like to meet this Tip."

"They should be here shortly. They had some… errands to run at noon-chime, so they'll be coming in with the first of the afternoon visitors. I'll send word and make sure you are at least introduced."

"That would be wonderful!"

Thuridan nodded politely at Baern in response.

"Well, I'd best get going," Baern said as he rose. "I shall see you later, then?"

Once again, Thuridan nodded. "Indeed, you shall."

Nodding himself, Baern spun round and left, a self-satisfied smirk on his lips as he walked out.

*****

Tip stood, stunned, before the entrance of the Shimmering Tower. With his mouth agape, he stared skyward at the tower itself, the single largest structure in the compound where they now stood. Grinning, Davian looked at his friend.

"Impressed?"

"Hunh?" Tip looked at him.

Davian chuckled. "Believe me, I was every bit as awestruck as you when I first stood this close to it."

Grinning, Tip looked back at the tower. The first thing about it that stole his breath was its sheer size. Craning his neck as far back as he possibly could, he still could not see its peak. In truth, this should not have surprised him, for the

Shimmering Tower was one of only two structures that could be seen from any part of Merethia, so to expect to see its zenith when this close would be an impossibility. And then there was its girth. At its base, the tower itself was wider than a fair few streets in Merethia, Tip was sure.

"How in the hells did they build something like that?" Marshalla whispered behind them.

Chuckling, Davian turned to her. "You think this is impressive? Wait till the sun comes out from behind those clouds."

Both turned to Davian.

"What happens then?" Marshalla asked.

Davian grinned. "You will get to see why it's called the Shimmering Tower."

Tip and Marshalla glanced at each other before looking at the tower once again just as the sun shone upon it. Both gasped at what they saw.

"How do they make it do that?" Marshalla asked.

"They won't tell me. I asked the first time I came, but Father said to stop asking, that when I join the Tower, such secrets would be revealed to me."

"Tell me when they tell you, please," Tip pleaded, his eyes still on the Tower.

"Of course."

Tip looked over at Davian, grinning. "Thank you."

"Best get moving," Marshalla said. "Someone's at the door."

Nodding, the boys began walking towards the entrance, but even as he walked, Tip couldn't take his eyes off the Tower's walls, for the little light that touched those pure white walls left them mesmerizing to behold.

"Ah, young master Davian, you're early."

Standing by the entrance was a kindly-looking elf, a warm smile upon his lips as he beheld the three of them.

"My apologies. My friends were eager to see the Tower." Turning, Davian stared at Tip and Marshalla both.

"This is Archmage Tarman Rocksplitter, the head attendant here."

Smiling, both Marshalla and Tip bowed graciously at him, even though neither knew what a head attendant was.

"Welcome to the Shimmering Tower, my young friends," the Archmage said. "We've heard tales of Davian's new friends, and I'm glad to have finally made your acquaintance."

"What stories?" Tip asked.

Smiling, the Archmage looked at Tip. "Nothing untoward, I assure you. Please, come in." Turning, he headed in. The others fell in behind him.

"I'm afraid there's still a fair amount of preparation left to do before the afternoon's open door," he said as they walked, "so I must leave you both in Davian's capable hands."

"Don't worry, Master Rocksplitter, I'll take good care of them," Davian replied.

"Oh, I know you will," the elderly elf replied, smiling. "Your father wants to see you before the event starts though. Why not go see him first before showing your friends around?"

Davian nodded. "I'll do that."

"Splendid!" Stopping, the elderly elf turned and bowed regally at both Tip and Marshalla before hurrying off down the grand corridor they stood within. Smiling, Davian turned to his friends, but once his gaze fell upon Tip, his smile faded.

"Tip."

"Hmm?"

"Pockets."

"What?" Marshalla stared at Tip, then Davian, before casting a furtive glance about them.

"It's okay, Marsha," Tip replied. "Told him yesterday."

"You not supposed to tell anyone!" Marshalla hissed, throwing a guilty glance at Davian as she spoke.

"He had no choice, Marsha," Davian replied. "Thalas lost his purse yesterday. Tip had it in his pocket, so he told me about it so I'd help give it back. I admit, it does sound a bit... odd, but it's alright."

Marshalla stared at him, perplexed. "You not mad? Tip stole your brother's purse, and you not mad at him?"

Davian grinned. "When he told me, I immediately remembered all those times I'd lose things - my purse, my ring, my keys - but always found them in the carriage. It was Tip stealing them, wasn't it? If he was truly stealing them to keep, he would've taken them with him, and not drop them in the carriage."

A slow smile parted Marshalla's lips as she stared at Davian before reaching out and ruffling his hair. Then she turned back to Tip. "Well?"

"Oh," Tip said before shoving his hands in his pockets. As he did so, his eyes grew wide.

"What is it?" Marshalla asked, a worried frown on her lips.

In response, Tip pulled out a medallion affixed to a short chain from his right pocket. It was clearly a special medallion, one with glowing symbols etched onto both sides. Frowning, he handed it to Davian, but his frown was quickly replaced with a grimace when he saw the fear in Davian's gaze.

"What is it?" Marshalla repeated as Davian took the medallion from Tip.

"It's Master Rocksplitter's runic key."

"His what?"

"Parts of the Tower are off-limits to some. Those permitted to enter need to have one of these upon their person to be able to walk past the runic wards."

"Oh dear," Marshalla muttered.

"Sorry," Tip mumbled.

Davian forced a smile as he shoved it into his pocket. "Master Rocksplitter dropped it. We saw it, and we will return it, nothing more."

Abruptly, he reached for Tip's left hand. He looked at Marshalla. Marshalla stared quizzically at him for a spell before smiling and reaching for Tip's right hand. Both looked at Tip. He smiled guiltily at each.

"Let's go to Father, then. We'll go the long way."

And thus did they make their way down the grand corridor of the Shimmering Tower, their shoes sinking deep into the red carpet that ran the length and breadth of the vast corridor, a corridor whose height seemed to stretch to eternity. As they walked, Davian spoke of the different rooms they walked past. From the greeting rooms to the meditation chambers and guest rooms, he spoke of each at length, giving insights into each room, and what great events had transpired within. At last, they came to the end of the corridor, and into the central hall.

"Woah!" Tip exclaimed as he came to a sudden halt, his eyes going wide with wonder at the great expanse before him. Chuckling, Davian shouldered him playfully. Tip looked over at him.

"It took my breath away the first time I saw it too."

Shaking his head in amazement, Tip turned his gaze back before him. It wasn't just the breadth of the hall that left Tip speechless, its height was just as astounding, and the more he stared, the more reasons he found to be awestruck. From the busts of past Tower patrons and members, whose lifelike appearance made them every bit as unsettling as they were impressive, to the murals and paintings that lined the walls as high as he could see, murals and paintings that seemed to depict everything from famous battles to creatures Tip couldn't always recognize, Tip was spellbound.

"Can't even see the ceiling too well," Marshalla whispered.

"Father said the central hall was built as a place where patrons who couldn't be welcomed in other rooms could be properly welcomed."

Both turned to stare at him.

"Who in the world would they need a place this big to welcome?" Marshalla demanded.

"Dragons, mostly."

"Dragons?" Tip and Marshalla exclaimed in unison.

"Oh, yes. Or rather, dragons who do not wish to take on human form. And then there are the giants that sometimes make the journey to the Tower.

"Dragons can fit in here," Tip whispered, staring at Marshalla. "Dragons, Marsha, *dragons*."

"Well, gold dragons definitely, and silver dragons. But red dragons, after a certain age, and even black dragons, they won't be able to fit in here at all."

"Wait," Marshalla said, looking down the corridor. "How they get through the front door?"

"Oh, that's no problem, all attendants are wood singers."

"Wood singers?"

"Know this one!" Tip exclaimed excitedly. "They sing to trees! Their songs make a tree grow big and tall, and can sing to the trees to make them grow small too!"

"But... it's a door, not a tree."

"Oh yeah..."

"It's a *living* door," Davian corrected. "The enchantments on it make it akin to an actual growing tree, so the wood singers can command it to grow and shrink at will."

"But what happens to the walls after?" Marshalla asked.

"What do you mean?" Davian asked, frowning.

"Well, if they make it grow, what happens to the wall that it grows into? And when they shrink it back, that not leave a big hole in the wall?"

"I... don't know. Let's ask my father when we see him."

"It's magic, Marsha," Tip intoned sagely. "Magic fixes the wall."

Marshalla smiled. "Probably."

"Of course!"

In response, Marshalla ruffled Tip's hair, an act that earned her a mock glare from the little elf.

"Well, where to now?" Marshalla asked as she looked at Davian.

"My father's office is up there," Davian replied, pointing to one of the windows high above them.

"Up there?"

"Mhm."

Both Tip and Marshalla glanced at one another, but it was Marshalla who spoke. "Not taking any stairs, are we?"

"Hmm? Oh, goodness, no! I'd die of exhaustion before we even get halfway!"

Both Marshalla and Tip grinned at him.

"No, we're using that portal stone there," he continued, pointing to a rather large circular stone in the near corner of the central hall. All three headed over to it. As Tip neared it, he soon realized the strange markings he's noticed on it from afar were actually symbols similar to those etched on Master Rocksplitter's runic key, and these glowed as well.

"What's that?" he asked.

"A portal stone," Davian repeated.

"But what's it do?" Marshalla asked.

"It allows you passage to anywhere in the Tower. You stand within the circle and speak the area you wish to go, and you will be ported to the portal stone nearest to the place. Provided you are permitted there in the first place, of course."

"Oh," Marshalla and Tip said in unison.

"Yes!" Hurrying on, Davian beckoned the others to him.

Exchanging glances once more, they did as he bid them.

"Now, do what I do," he said once they were near, and, taking a deep breath, he walked onto the stone, cleared his throat and uttered his destination.

"Thuridan Grovemender's office!"

In an instant, he was gone.

"Woah!" Tip exclaimed, looking at Marshalla. But before Marshalla could speak, he darted into the circle and did as Davian had.

"Thuridan Grovemender's office!"

And he too was gone.

"Tip…" Marshalla muttered, shaking her head. Sighing, she too wandered into the circle, and clearing her throat, uttered her destination.

"Thuridan Grovemender's office!"

And barely had she spoken those words than Tip and Davian were standing directly before her once more.

"That's it?"

Davian grinned. "I know, it's so fast it's almost underwhelming. But my father's office is down at the end."

The corridor they now found themselves in was nothing like the central corridor, for this was much smaller, with a much lower ceiling and far fewer etchings on both wall and ceiling. As one, all three hurried over to Thuridan's office, and on reaching it, stopped and waited patiently while Davian knocked.

"Enter," Thuridan called from within. Without hesitation, Davian did as his father bid, swinging the door open as he and the others walked in.

"Ah, there you are!" Thuridan exclaimed as he rose from his desk. "I was beginning to think you'd gone sight-seeing."

A sheepish grin parted Davian's lips. "We used the portal stone in the central hall instead of the one near the main door."

"There was one near the main door?" Marshalla asked, looking from Davian to Tip.

"Didn't see one," Tip said as he shrugged.

"No matter," Thuridan said. "What matters is you're here now. And since you're here, Master Rocksplitter was here earlier. Did you happen to see his runic key perchance?"

"Ah, yes!" Davian exclaimed, reaching into his pocket. "It dropped out of his pocket when he came to meet us."

Thuridan grinned. "I told him as much. Stubborn man that he is, he was insistent it couldn't simply have fallen out."

Grinning, Davian walked over and placed the runic key on his father's desk, the others trying to appear nonchalant.

"Father…" Davian said as he placed the key on the desk.

"Yes?"

"Why did Master Rocksplitter come to greet us? He's the head attendant, he doesn't tend to the door unless it's a noble attending."

Thuridan beamed with pride at his son. "I knew you'd see through that, my boy, but I think I'll let Baern explain that one."

"Who?" Tip asked. Both father and son turned to stare at Tip, but it was Davian who spoke.

"Master Meadowview. He's the Matriarch's right hand, and second most important person in the Shimmering Tower."

"Oh."

"Yes," Davian replied, before grinning. "And he happens to be a close friend of my father."

Thuridan leant back in his chair, laughing at Davian's words. But before he could respond, a voice spoke from the doorway.

"I hope I'm not interrupting."

All four stared at the door.

"Ah, Baern, impeccable timing. Do come in."

"Good afternoon, Master Meadowview," Davian said as the elderly elf took a seat near Thuridan's desk.

"Davian, my boy. How are you today?"

"I'm well, thank you."

"Good to hear it," Baern replied, then turned his attention to Tip and Marshalla. "And these must be the dear friends of yours I've heard so much about?"

"Pardon?" Davian said as Tip stared curiously at the Magister.

"Your friends are somewhat famous, Davian," Thuridan replied.

"We are?" Tip asked.

Thuridan nodded at him. "Oh, yes."

"I'm afraid I'm to blame for that…" Baern said. "Tip, isn't it?"

"Yeah."

"I've been telling everyone how kind-hearted Davian and Thuridan have been taking the two of you into their home without charge. And now, well, pretty much everyone wants to catch a glimpse of the two of you."

"Master Rocksplitter!" Davian exclaimed, grinning.

"Hmm? Ah, yes, I told him, too. Did he come find you?"

"He welcomed us!"

"Ah, trust old Tarman to be first in the queue," Baern said, smiling. He turned to regard Marshalla and Tip once more. "I do hope to see much more of you both, if Davian and his father permit it of course."

"I'm sure we can arrange something," Thuridan replied, smiling.

Through it all, though, Marshalla stared at Baern with her brows furrowed deep. It was an expression that had been hers ever since Baern had walked in.

"Is something the matter, Marsha?" Thuridan asked.

"Hmm?"

"You look unwell."

She smiled. "Sorry. Just a lot to get used to."

Thuridan smiled at her. "Yes, this place can be a bit overwhelming the first time you come here."

"Yes, that it can be," Baern added.

"Well, you'd all best get going," Thuridan continued. "The open-door event should be starting soon. You know where you're going, right, Davian?"

Davian nodded at his father.

"Good. Well, off you go, then."

Smiling, all three left Thuridan's office and headed back towards the portal stone.

"Are you sure you're alright, Marsha?" Tip asked, his worry plain in his voice.

"Tip…" Marsha replied, frowning once again, "you seen Baern before?"

Tip frowned as he pondered Marshalla's words.

"No."

"You've met him before?" Davian asked, his curiosity piqued.

"Don't know," Marshalla muttered, "but can't shake the feeling seen him somewhere before."

"Maybe you've seen him around Merethia?"

Marshalla shook her head. "No, not that. It's… never mind," She turned to stare at Davian, forcing a smile.

"Where to?"

"We're going back to the central hall."

"Okay. But me first this time."

"Race you!" Tip yelled suddenly and broke into a dead sprint.

"Hey!" she exclaimed before grabbing the hem of her dress and racing after him, Davian bringing up the rear. But just as she reached the portal stone, Tip leapt into the middle before yelling at the top of his lungs.

"Central hall!"

And was gone from their sight.

"Hey!" Marshalla repeated.

"I guess he won."

"Oh, shush you!" she snapped, eliciting a chuckle from Davian.

"You go next, then," Davian offered.

Pouting, Marshalla walked into the center of the portal stone, and as she disappeared from sight, Davian followed her. Before long, all three made their way to the middle of the central hall. There had been a small gathering in the middle when they'd first arrived, but the gathering had since grown, and as they headed for it, an elf floated above the gathering, beckoning for silence.

"Welcome, all of you, to the Shimmering Tower. I am glad to see so many of you would consider joining us in our pursuit of knowledge." With a warm smile, the elf swept her gaze about the gathered, who responded with nods and smiles of their own.

"I am Archmage Arenya Drakesong," she continued, "and I will be your guide. We will begin with a tour through the Shimmering Tower, and I will explain along the way what we do and why. The tour will bring us back here, where you will be free to wander through our halls as you choose, and speak to any you see. The only request I would make is that you take due care when viewing the artifacts on display. They have been placed there for your pleasure, but I ask that you respect the power that dwells within them. I will talk about them as we pass." Tip looked at the others briefly, his eyes bright and his grin wide.

"But above all, please do not attempt to touch the artifacts. If you do, the protective wards about them will harm you."

"Aww," Tip muttered.

"Oh, don't fret, Tip," Davian whispered. "You'll still be able to get a good look at them."

"If any of you have a question, please do ask. You may ask during the tour, or when you are left to yourselves."

The room fell silent as the Archmage looked over the sea of faces.

"Very well, let us begin!"

Leaning against the entrance, Thalas stared sullenly at Marshalla and Tip, his lips twisted in a hateful scowl.

"Is that them?" Neremi asked as she walked up behind him. Grimly, he nodded.

"Are the others in place?" he asked.

"Yes."

Thalas turned to face her, and as his eyes fell upon her, he realized the fear he thought he heard in her voice was real. Smiling, he took her hands.

"All will be well, you'll see."

"Thalas, I'm afraid," Neremi whispered in response. "If this goes badly, we will be banished from the Tower, and if that happens my parents will disown me."

Shaking his head, Thalas clasped her face in his hands.

"All will be well, Neremi. We've planned this down to the very last detail. As soon as Arenya gives the signal, we'll move in, grab them both, and the void sphere, and be out of here before anyone even realizes what's happened."

But the fear in Neremi's gaze remained. Smiling, Thalas leant in and kissed her softly.

"Go, go get ready."

Neremi remained unmoving.

"Go," Thalas said, pushing her gently. Swallowing hard, Neremi finally turned and did as she was bid. As she left, Thalas turned his gaze back to Tip, his hate returning.

With eyes bright and wide, Tip rubbed his hands as he grinned at Davian, who grinned in response, his own eyes bright with the same expectation.

"Now, do please remember, necromancy is not for everyone, so if you do feel a bit unwell, there is no shame in stepping out to join those waiting outside," Archmage Drakesong explained. Tip glanced at Marshalla, who was looking decidedly pale. As their eyes met, Tip pretended he was about to throw up himself, a gesture that earned him a heartfelt glare.

"Are you all ready?"

Murmurs drifted from those gathered before the door.

"Very well, let us proceed." And with that, the doors flew open and the gathering made their way inside. As one, both Tip and Davian took in a deep breath, but each then looked at the other, their gazes full of disappointment. However, their disappointment was fleeting as they soon laid eyes on jars of floating eyeballs, severed hands and creature entrails placed between the tomes that lined the many shelves about the room.

"As you will all understand," Archmage Drakesong continued as she walked into the Undead Halls, "undeath magic is the least popular of all arcane mysteries. What many of you will not know, however, is that it is also the least understood. Throughout the ages, those who have studied this particular discipline have, on many occasions, been forced to carry out their studies in secret, lest they face the wrath of the misunderstanding masses."

"Misunderstanding?" a voice bellowed from the crowd. It was an elven woman, her eyes ablaze with furious scorn while her daughter stood beside her, her own gaze directed at her feet.

Archmage Drakesong turned, smiling. "Yes, misunderstanding. Necromancy in itself is neither good nor evil. It is a discipline like all others, like fire magic, or even illusions."

"They bring the dead back to life! It's because of necromancers we have all these undead abominations walking amongst us."

Archmage Drakesong shook her head briefly before responding. "Yes, in the past, necromancy has been abused, and abused greatly. But would it surprise you to learn that there have been more lives lost throughout recorded history to fire magic, than there have been to necromancy? At least ninety to one."

There were gasps in the crowd at the Archmage's words.

"And I mean innocent life. Admittedly, this is not an exact science, but the figures are roughly correct. However, as I mentioned before, necromancy is the least understood to date, and here at the Shimmering Tower, we are striving to change that, a charge we have placed upon those within the Undead Halls."

"I don't care if it's a hundred to one, my daughter will not dabble in this... filth!"

"Mother!"

The Archmage stared at the glowering lady and her embarrassed daughter.

"In that case, I'm afraid your daughter cannot join us," she said at last, her smile now gone.

"What?"

"Should she be accepted within our number, what disciplines she follows will be decided by her and the Tower, Lady Runestone. You will have no say in it whatsoever. If that is unacceptable, she cannot join us."

A tense silence fell on all within.

"What's that over there?" Marshalla piped up.

The Archmage turned to where Marshalla pointed, then smiled once again.

"This," she replied, walking briskly towards the table in the center of the chamber, and the mask that floated eerily above it, "is prime example of the trials and tribulations necromancers often face."

Soon, all were gathered about the table, staring at the mask as they murmured and pointed. But even as they surrounded the table, each kept their distance, for they all felt the corrupting magic pulsing from it.

"This is the Face of the Witch Queen," Archmage Drakesong announced once the murmurs subsided. The mask itself was a disgusting thing to behold, with pulsing brown tendrils snaking every which way across its face. It bore the semblance of a fair human lady in the midst of an angry scream.

"It was made roughly four centuries ago, by a powerful necromancer called Ariel the Blackhearted. A descendant of necromancers herself, she excelled in the craft more than her own kin. However, she and her whole family were reviled by the townsfolk, and lived apart from them, until the day when war came upon their kingdom. You see, one of the neighboring kingdoms had taken up arms in a bid to subjugate them. They fought back, of course, but their enemies proved the stronger."

Silence fell on all within as each hung on Archmage Drakesong's every word.

"But they fought on regardless. Defeat after crushing defeat, they fought on, until Ariel's town was the last free town of the kingdom. It was the seat of the kingdom, you see, and the neighboring kingdom had taken each and every single town around it, cutting it off and slowly bleeding it dry. In desperation, the prince went to Ariel, and promised her marriage were she to aid them."

"Did she agree?" a voice asked.

Archmage Drakesong shook her head. "Not at first. She wanted nothing to do with them, for she bore great hate against the king and his family. She blamed him and all in his household for the suffering of her family. But her mother, her mother saw a way for her daughter to have a better life, a life where her skill and prowess would be lauded and accepted rather than reviled and ignored. And so, she changed Ariel's mind. The records of what Ariel did to the invading armies are scarce, but the end result was clear. With her aiding her people, they were able to take their towns back one by one. It was by no means an easy feat, and it took two more years of fighting before the invaders were finally driven back. But driven back they were, and they owed it all to her."

"The prince betrayed her, didn't he?" Marshalla asked.

Archmage Drakesong looked at her, shaking her head as she did so. "Records say he tried to honor his word, but his father forbade it. The king refused to listen to his son, and was insistent that having a necromancer in his house would defile his name. Needless to say, Ariel would have been less than pleased."

"What did she do?" another voice asked.

Archmage Drakesong smiled sadly. "It's not what she did that you should be asking, it's what the king did."

"What did he do?"

"Well, he knew firsthand what Ariel was capable of, so rather than simply telling her he would not allow his son honor his word, he dispatched a great many assassins to kill her and her family in the dead of night."

Murmurs of disbelief floated amongst those gathered.

"Did they kill her?" Tip asked, his heart in his mouth.

Archmage Drakesong looked at him. "They succeeded in killing all but her youngest brother before she finally killed them all. As for her, they managed to wound her mortally. Knowing she had not long left to live, and, perhaps more importantly, knowing who'd sent the assassins, she charged her brother with vengeance. Vengeance for her and their family. And to aid him, she forged this." Archmage Drakesong pointed at the artifact.

"She poured all her power into it, all her rage, all her hate, then gave it to her brother. Four months later, the king's entire household was slain, but he was spared, spared to watch his kingdom fall to ruin within a year, never to rise again."

"What was the kingdom called?" one of the gathered asked.

"Farnham. It was a human kingdom."

"So, Ariel was human."

"Yes."

"That's rather sad," Davian muttered.

Archmage Drakesong smiled sadly at him. "Yes, it is. But it's also the reality of a great many necromancers over the centuries."

The Archmage let her eyes wander about the gathering.

"Let's continue, shall we?" she said after a brief silence.

Slowly, the gathered began heading towards the door, the sadness in the air almost palpable.

"Interesting name for it," another voice said. "Why not call it a mask, why face?"

"Ah, yes, well…" Archmage Drakesong replied, "it's… made from the skin on her face."

At those words, the gathered began exiting the room much faster.

Once out of the room, Marshalla looked at Tip and Davian.

"That was scary."

"Wasn't scared!" Tip exclaimed, chuckling.

"Me neither," Davian added. "But it was a rather sad tale, though."

"Yeah." Tip nodded. "Not nice what that king did."

"Hello, Davian," a voice called out from behind them.

Turning, all three looked up at the smiling face of Archmage Drakesong.

"Hello, Mistress Drakesong," Davian replied.

"I take it these are your two young friends that I've heard so much about."

Marshalla and Tip looked at each other while Davian grinned at the Archmage.

"Yes, they are."

The Archmage looked at Marshalla, then Tip.

"I hope you're enjoying the tour so far."

"We are," Marshalla replied.

"Yeah," Tip added.

"Good, glad I am to hear it. I'm sure you'll be happy to know we're almost at the end. Just one more visit, then you will be free to wander as you see fit. Perhaps even come back to the Undead Halls."

"Can we?" Tip exclaimed.

"No," Marshalla glowered.

Laughing, the Archmage patted Davian on the shoulder before making her way to the front of the group to lead them on. It was not long before they were standing at the library's entrance.

"And here we are, at the final part of our tour," Archmage Drakesong called out as the gathered surrounded her at the entrance. Grinning, she walked in, gesturing for the others to follow, but to do so quietly. Stopping at the center of the library, she gestured for the others to cluster before her.

"And this," she began once all were gathered, raising her voice for all to hear, "is the most important place in all of the Shimmering Tower. For this is where all our knowledge is kept, and where much of our research is conducted and confirmed. This hallowed room contains the thoughts and recordings of every single high elf to have ever called the Shimmering Tower home. Each piece of knowledge, each breakthrough, noted here for posterity."

But Marshalla and Tip heard not one word of what was said as they stared open-mouthed at the room itself. From floor to ceiling, each wall was covered with tomes, tomes of various shapes and sizes, colors, and forms. If that was not enough, on the far wall stood rows of shelves, each filled to overflowing with tomes. And from where they stood, both could see corridors on both sides of the far wall, corridors both were convinced led to rooms filled with even more tomes.

"How do you find anything in this place?" a voice from the crowd asked.

"It does look a bit overwhelming, doesn't it. Well, allow me to show you." Smiling, she looked at Tip, who had made his way towards the front along with Marshalla and Davian.

"Tip, isn't it?"

"Yes," Tip replied, his voice soft and subdued.

"Come."

Tip hesitated, looking at Marshalla.

"It's alright, I won't bite," Archmage Drakesong said. "Unless you wish me to, of course."

Ripples of laughter drifted through the crowd, but this merely served to confuse Tip, and it showed.

"Come, Tip. Please."

Once more, he looked at Marshalla, who finally nodded at him. Taking a deep breath, he walked over to the Archmage. Clasping him by the shoulders, Archmage Drakesong spun him round to face the gathered, holding him close as she did so.

"Now, Tip. I would like you to look upwards."

He did, and so did everyone else. As they all did, Archmage Drakesong whispered a single word in a tongue he did not know, and as they all stared, a creature leapt off one of the shelves and hung briefly in the air before slowly flying down towards Tip. To Tip, it looked like a butterfly, or some such winged insect.

"Now, isn't this interesting," a voice whispered to Tip.

"Hunh?" Tip asked, looking from the descending creature to Archmage Drakesong. The Archmage looked down at Tip.

"Look up, Tip. You don't want to miss this."

"Oh, do look up...Tip, is it? We don't want that stupid cow to become suspicious, do we?"

The voice, it was in his mind. The hairs on the back of Tip's neck stood rigid as a knot formed in the very pit of his stomach. Looking briefly at Marshalla, he at last directed his gaze upwards, his heart threatening to burst out of his chest.

"Who are you?" he thought.

"The name is Anieszirel, but you may call me Ani."

Gasps from the crowd broke Tip from his thoughts, and as he stared upwards, he soon realized that the creature was no insect, for it looked much like an elf, though vastly smaller, and with wings.

"What's that?" Tip asked.

"*Why, it's a sprite, Tip!*"

"That, Tip, is a sprite!" Archmage Drakesong exclaimed.

"*Told you.*"

"She, along with her kin, are charged with the safe-keeping of our tomes. Each and every tome in here is known to them, and all you have to do is ask them for one and they will bring it to you." Gently, Archmage Drakesong held out Tip's left hand, and the sprite soon landed on his open palm. Hugging Tip closer, the Archmage looked from Tip to the sprite as it stared expectantly at Tip, its wings beating lazily behind it.

"Now Tip…" Archmage Drakesong continued.

"*She's going to tell you to ask about me.*"

"…you're going to ask her for a specific tome…"

"*She does this every single time.*"

"…it's a very special tome…"

"*You'd think she'd be bored of this parlor trick by now.*"

"…a tome about our most prized relic. Ask her for a tome on Anieszirel, Kin-Slayer."

"Ani," Tip said distractedly. As he did so, the sprite took flight and flew towards the west wall.

"What did you say?" the Archmage asked.

"*Careful, Tip.*"

"How did you know she's called Ani?"

"*You don't want her to know you can hear me, trust me.*"

"Uh…" Tip said as he forced a smile, his mind racing. "Lucky guess."

The Archmage stared hard at Tip in silence for a spell.

"Who is Ani?" a voice from the crowd asked.

"*That was close.*"

Breaking her gaze from Tip's face, Archmage Drakesong turned to the crowd. But as she spoke, Tip turned his attention inwards.

"Where are you?" he thought.

"*I'm behind you. Well, behind her and you.*"

Tip moved to look behind the Archmage.

"*Don't!*" the voice exclaimed, forcing Tip to stand rigid. "*If you look, she'll definitely know you can hear me.*"

"You're not supposed to talk to me?"

"*No, I'm not. Arenya sealed the runic circle, and I'm supposed to be able to speak through it to only those possessing an attuned runic key.*"

"So, how come you can talk to me?" But even as he asked, a cold chill filled Tip's heart as he snuck his fingers into his pockets. What his fingers found in there sent the chill spreading all over him.

"*I wish I knew,*" Anieszirel continued. "*Though I'm glad I can. You have no idea how good it is to be able to talk to someone other than these self-righteous bastards.*"

Just then, the sprite returned, several tomes of varying thickness and size floating behind it. Archmage Drakesong turned to Tip. "Hold out your hand."

Tip did as she bid, and as he did so, the sprite flew into Tip's open palm, the tomes floating behind her.

Smiling, the Archmage turned her gaze to the crowd. "And that is how we are able to find anything in here."

Returning her gaze to the sprite, she bowed to the fair creature before whispering another word in the same tongue as earlier, and in response, the sprite bowed and flew away, all the tomes in tow.

"And as for the Kin-Slayer herself, behold!" With a flurry, the Archmage stepped aside, pulling Tip with her, revealing a stepped podium unlike anything Tip had ever seen. Circular in nature, its base was wide enough to allow most present to stand side-by-side about it with ease, while its topmost step was higher than Tip was tall. But it was the orb that hung eerily above it that drew Tip's gaze. It was of a deep violet hue and roughly the size of a newborn ogre child, its surface reflecting the runes etched into the stone upon which it floated, runes pulsing in rhythm to the runes in the circle drawn upon the lowest step of the podium. Though, while the runes themselves clearly held great power within, the power emanating from the orb itself was far greater.

"Now, unlike the other artifacts, I must ask you to keep your distance from this one. The runic circle you see below it will hurt any who get too close, and the runic stone above which the void sphere floats will, unfortunately, kill any who get really close to it and are not permitted to."

An uncomfortable silence fell on the group as all eyes went on the orb.

"What's a void sphere?" Tip asked.

"*It's my prison.*"

"It's a prison, created to trap the souls and essences of any creature. Given the power involved in creating one, we only ever use them to trap creatures that are too hard or too important to do away with, but too dangerous to be left free."

"And Ani is too dangerous?"

"Were you not listening?" Archmage Drakesong asked, frowning.

"*She lies! Don't listen to the stupid bitch! They've held me here against my will all these millennia for no other reason than to gawp and gawk, to poke and prod! I'm no more dangerous than a wolf!*"

"There are very few recorded uses of void spheres," Archmage Drakesong continued, "and with good reason, for those trapped within are unable to free themselves. And if someone were to try and free them, void spheres are designed to collapse in on themselves, destroying the souls of those trapped within."

"That's horrible!" one of the gathered exclaimed.

"You've forgotten what she did?" another asked.

Shaking her head, Archmage Drakesong raised her hands for calm, but as she did so, she stared at the door, and staring right into the eyes of the young elven male standing at the doorway, she nodded once, then returned her gaze to the crowd.

"Now that we are at the end of our tour, for those of you who would like to learn more about the Kin-Slayer, do feel free to remain. I will return here after a short spell, and will be happy then to retrieve tomes on her for you."

She looked at Tip and Marshalla. "You two can stay if you wish. Davian knows his way around, so there's no need for you to return with the rest of us."

Turning, the Archmage made her way towards the door, the rest of the gathered going with her.

"Well, shall we stay?" Davian asked as he and Marshalla walked over to Tip.

"Might as well," Marshalla replied, nodding. "Looks really nice here."

But Tip was far less pleased with the idea.

"Let's leave," he begged. "Please."

"*You can't leave!*"

"You okay, Tip?" Marshalla asked. But before he could respond, an ear-splitting crash reverberated about the room, and shrieking, all three turned to the doorway, only to see the door had slammed shut.

"Everybody on their knees!"

There was a fair number of those on the tour still within the library along with Tip, Davian and Marshalla, but there were now six others there too. The six were all masked, with the one standing at the fore shouting.

"I said everybody on your knees!" he bellowed.

The three friends looked at each other, their fear rising rapidly.

"What is the meaning of this?" Lady Runestone demanded.

The masked intruder stormed over to the noble, lightning dancing between his fingers. But as he reached her, one of the gathered stepped into his path, swinging a fist at his temple. Only the fist never found home, for in an instant, the ringleader touched the man before him, and as he did so, the unmistakable crack of lightning filled the air as the poor man was flung across the library. At this, the room erupted in a cacophony of screams and cries.

"Everybody on their knees!" the ringleader bellowed once again. This time, all obeyed, including Lady Runestone, and as they fell to their knees, the other five began swiftly going through the kneeling crowd robbing them all. As for the ringleader, he hurried over to Tip, pulling the poor frightened little boy to his feet before rifling through his pockets.

"Leave him alone!" Marshalla yelled.

"Shut up, whore!" he spat back as he searched Tip.

Snarling, Marshalla jumped to her feet and shoved him off Tip.

"Leave him al—" But that was as far as she went, for the ringleader spun round and crashed a fist into Marshalla's stomach before sweeping her feet out from underneath her. And as she fell, he kicked her in the stomach again and again and again.

"Leave her alone!" Tip shrieked.

Stopping, the ringleader glared at Tip, before turning and kicking Marshalla in the face, her blood spraying across the carpeted floor. Tip screamed, racing over to where Marshalla lay. Unrepentant, the ringleader grabbed him once within reach, pulling him away from Marshalla before resuming his rifling through Tip's pockets.

"Hurry up!" one of the invaders yelled at their ringleader.

"What does it look like I'm doing? The stupid whore got in the way!"

But Marshalla was never one to give up so easily, and as he yelled, she crawled up to him, wrapped her arms about his legs and bit into the back of his right leg just above his heel. With the roar of an injured lion, the ringleader looked down at Marshalla wrapped around his legs and, raising his hand to her, unleashed a lightning bolt of quite some venom at her, catching her square in her shoulder. Shrieking in pain, Marshalla let go of his legs and squirmed away from him.

"You stupid little whore!" he shrieked as he limped after her before finally sitting astride her even as she squirmed still.

"*He's going to kill her,*" the voice whispered in Tip's mind.

"Marsha!" Tip called out in tears.

"*He's going to kill her, Tip.*"

"No!" he cried as the ringleader placed his right hand on her bosom. As he did so, the smell of burnt flesh quickly filled the air as Marshalla screamed for all she was worth.

"Stop it!" Tip yelled. "Stop it, please!"

"*I can stop him.*"

"Leave her alone!"

"*I can stop him, Tip.*"

"Leave her alone!"

"*Release me. Release me and I'll stop him. I'll stop them all.*"

"Leave her alone!"

"*Touch the sphere. Touch the sphere and release me.*"

"Damn it, just get the blasted key and let's go!" one of the invaders yelled. But the ringleader refused to listen. Instead, he raised both his hands, and as lightning flashed between them, he slowly lowered them towards Marshalla, his hands wide enough to fit aside her head. It was then that Tip turned and, hurrying over to the podium, began scrambling up its steps.

"Tip, what are you doing?" Davian called out.

At his words, all within stopped to stare at him, including the ringleader. Emboldened, Tip continued his scramble.

"Tip!"

Tip ignored his friend. Once near the top, he raised his right hand. But then, another lightning bolt ripped through the air, this time striking Tip's outstretched hand. Screaming in pain, Tip looked over at the ringleader as he stood glaring at Tip. Glaring briefly back at the brigand, Tip returned his gaze to the void sphere, before lunging at it just as the ringleader brought his hand up to strike Tip once more. But he was too late, for as the lightning danced between his fingers, Tip slammed his left palm upon the void sphere.

"*Thank you.*"

As all within stared, the void sphere sank slowly into the runic stone.

"What have you done?" Davian whispered once the sphere was gone from sight.

Tip turned to his friend, his mouth agape, but no words came. There was an energy about him, a force that seemed to still his tongue and bind him where he was. Shaking his head, he turned his gaze back to the runic stone, not knowing what to expect. Then, all at once, a roar like nothing Tip had ever heard echoed thunderously about the library, deafening all within as a mighty wind blew forth from the runes upon the lowest step of the podium, its raging currents forcing away all that was near as it circled the podium, leaving Tip cowering in wide-eyed terror.

"Marsha!" he cried as he stared at his dear friend, his eyes pleading.

"Tip," Marshalla whispered, scrambling to her knees, her terror raw and palpable.

Then, the howling winds began to climb the podium, their ascent steady and sure.

"Marsha!" Tip shrieked as he clambered up to the top of the podium, his gaze now upon the encroaching winds.

"Tip," Marshalla gasped. To stand was beyond her, for her legs were not her own, but every fiber of her being willed her to race over to Tip, to vault up the podium and snatch her dear friend from the clutches of… whatever now held him captive. And so, in her desperation, she sought to crawl to him. But then, as the winds touched the runic stone upon which poor Tip now stood, it all suddenly collapsed in onto him, sending the little boy to his knees.

"Tip!" Marshalla screamed.

As she reached out to him, Marshalla watched as Tip threw his head back and, clenching his fists tightly near his chest, roared at the heavens. But it was not this that stopped Marshalla and forced her blood to run cold. No, it was the sight of the great ghostly azure dragon that rose above him. With its wings stretched up to their highest, its own great maw raised skyward, it too roared at the heavens, a single heartfelt roar that shook the room to its very foundations, before finally falling into Tip just as the little boy crumpled upon the stone. Then, there was silence.

"Tip?" Marshalla called out.

There was no response.

With her heart in her mouth, Marshalla sat where she was, waiting with bated breath for some sign, anything. Then, with a smirk upon his lips, little Tip rose, his eyes azure and without pupils. He stared at the ringleader, who stood behind Marshalla.

"Now, where were we?" he said as he floated down from the podium.

Swallowing hard, the ringleader backed away from Tip. But Tip wouldn't let him, closing the gap between them as quickly as it opened. Before long, the ringleader was amongst his own people, the rest of those within scattered to the sides of the library. Abruptly, one of the invaders pulled forth a blade, and, with a blood-curdling scream, lunged at Tip. But as he sailed through the air, an ice lance of such biting cold formed out of the very air itself, and with a flick of his wrist, Tip plunged the ice lance deep into the intruder's chest, and with a force great enough slam him against the door behind them, pinning his now lifeless body against it.

"No!" one of the intruders shrieked.

Tip's smirk grew. "So, who dies next?"

Just then, the door itself exploded, showering Tip and the intruders with fragments great and small.

"Look! The void sphere!" came a voice from the doorway. "It's gone!"

"The boy!" screamed another. "She's in the boy!"

"Stop him, she mustn't escape!"

"Everyone, get down!"

Diving for cover, the intruders scattered before the charging mages. Hastily forming an arc before Tip, the mages all raised their hands and unleashed all they had at the little boy.

"Tip!" Marshalla screamed, even as Davian and some of the others near her held onto her. But she needn't have worried, for as the mages flung fireballs, ice lances and even lightning bolt after lightning bolt at Tip, he stood strong, encased in an enchanted barrier that protected him from all that they flung at him. And yet, the mages persisted, throwing ever grander and more lethal spells at him. The onslaught lasted until the azure dragon rose above Tip once more, and eyeing the mages briefly, unleashed an azure flame from its maw upon them. As the dragon breathed its fire upon them, one by one, the mages cowered and crumpled, screaming and hollering, till all that could be heard was their senseless gibbering.

Sighing, Tip turned and walked over to Davian and Marshalla, the azure dragon already receded.

"Time we were away. No telling how many more are coming."

Davian and Marshalla stared terrified, at Tip.

"Oh, don't look at me like that, Tip's fine! He's still in here. Come, let's get out of here and you can talk to him to your heart's content."

He offered his hands to them. Sharing a worried glance, both Davian and Marshalla slowly reached out to take his hand. Grabbing their hands, the little elf closed his eyes, and with a flicker, all three disappeared from sight.

THE HUNT BEGINS

This is bad," Thuridan muttered, staring at the carnage wrought in the Tower Library.

"I know," Baern replied.

"We have to do something."

"I know," Baern repeated, sighing.

They'd both been in Thuridan's office when they heard the roar, a sound that froze their hearts as it rattled the windows of the office. At the time, they had no idea what had made such a sound, but one thing was undeniable, it came from within the Tower. But it was not until they'd reached the central hall and saw Archmage Drakesong standing guard over some of those that had taken part in her tour, it wasn't until she had looked up at them and told them where the roar had come from that they realized just how precarious the situation was. Or at least, they thought they did. It was that thought that had spurred Thuridan to race over to lend what aid he could to the mages that had been the first to respond, while Baern marshalled the other mages within the hall for a second offensive.

"Of all things to steal, it had to be that," Thuridan muttered through gritted teeth before sighing deeply.

"When is the Matriarch back?" he asked, turning to Baern.

Baern looked over once more at the now empty runic circle. "She should be on her way back now. I sent word that she was needed immediately."

"You didn't tell her why?"

Baern shook his head. "I couldn't risk the wrong people overhearing."

"Of course," Thuridan replied, nodding. "But you have to wonder about her sense of timing, choosing today of all days to dine with the woodland nobles."

Frowning, Baern turned to the Archmage. "She can't very well see the future, can she? How is she to know someone would try to steal the Kin-Slayer today?"

"She didn't?"

"Oh, don't start, Thuridan," Baern replied, a tired sigh escaping his lips. "Now's not the time for this."

"Very well…" Thuridan replied as he wandered over to Archmage Drakesong, who'd followed Magister Meadowview in.

Shaking his head, Baern made his way over to the survivors. Huddled in a corner, some of the mages he'd led into the room had shepherded them all together before forming a protective circle about them. Reaching them, he smiled and waved the closest mages to stand aside as he let his gaze sweep over them all. His gaze soon fell upon Lady Runestone.

"Lady Runestone," he said, with a slight bow.

"Magister Meadowview," the noble replied in much the same manner.

"I'm glad to see you're safe." It was then he noticed the noble lady's hands were quivering.

"I very nearly wasn't."

Baern smiled at her. "Thank the gods for your safety, then. Would you mind telling me what—"

At that moment, an angry yell boomed from behind him and, startled, he turned round to see an irate Thuridan Grovemender bearing down upon a cowering Arenya Drakesong.

"Please excuse me," he said as he hurried over, reaching them just as Thuridan grasped Archmage Drakesong roughly by her tunic.

"Thuridan!" he yelled, clasping a hand upon Thuridan's and stopping him from shaking the very life out of the terrified mage. "What is the meaning of this?"

"My son was here!" Thuridan exclaimed, his face whiter than Baern had ever seen it. "My son was in here, and now he's gone!"

"Thalas?" Baern asked, turning to Arenya.

"No, Davian!" Thuridan replied. "He was here, Baern, he was here! And now he's gone!"

Quickly, Baern scanned the room. "Where is he now?"

"I don't know," Arenya replied.

"What do you mean, you don't know?"

"The boy took him," Lady Runestone called out.

The two men turned to the noble.

"Boy… what boy?" Baern asked.

"The boy he came in here with. He took Davian and the young girl that was with them."

"Tip," Thuridan whispered.

"Took them where?" Baern demanded. "Took them how?"

"*I* don't know, *you're* the mage! He grabbed their hands, lowered his gaze, and then they simply vanished."

Baern frowned for a spell, but as he stared, he soon realized what had happened, and that realization chilled him to the core.

"Lady Runestone," he said, his face now ashen, "the loud noise we heard earlier, was that also from the boy?"

Lady Runestone nodded. "Of course it was! Damndest thing I've ever heard. Had a great blue dragon above him when he shouted too, scared the very life out of me. He's the one who drove your people mad, you know."

Baern looked over at Thuridan, but it was clear he'd already reached the same conclusion.

"But… that's impossible!" Baern whispered, his gaze shifting from Thuridan to Arenya. "Nobody should've been able to release her. The void sphere should've collapsed in on itself!"

"My runic key is gone, Magister," Arenya said. "It's been stolen."

Baern looked over at Thuridan.

"This isn't making sense," he said at last. "Even with the key, it would take a *very* skilled mage to breach the surface of a void sphere and survive, never mind prevent its implosion, and the time he would need, this—"

"We'll have to worry about how later, Baern, I need to go find my son."

Baern nodded. "Of course. Go. I'll send you all the aid I can spare." Then he turned to Arenya. "Now, from the beginning. Leave nothing out."

Frowning, Thalas massaged his palm with his thumb as he stared at the door.

"You just couldn't leave it alone, could you?" Neremi spat at him, her voice trembling greatly. Biting his lower lip in shame, he lowered his gaze to his hands.

"Answer me, damn you!"

"Quiet, Neremi, please," a voice called out from behind her.

"Quiet? Quiet?" Fuming, she turned to face the one who'd spoken. "It was your brother who got hung up like some worthless piece of meat!"

"Yes, and if you don't stay quiet, we are liable to join him, or worse."

"Someone comes," Thalas said suddenly as he fell against the wall. In an instant, the others hid themselves, including Neremi, tears not far away. Before long, the sound of shuffling feet reached them. It stopped right before the door.

"It's me," a voice whispered.

Sighing, Thalas undid the latch. As he did so, the door swung open as the last of their group dove in, shutting the door quickly but silently behind him.

"How is it?" Thalas asked.

The new arrival glared at him, his breath labored and his eyes ablaze.

"Thane," Neremi pleaded, "don't make us beg. How are things out there?"

Thane glared at Thalas for a moment longer before facing the others. "They've found Fallon's body. That old hag, Runestone, told them about us, all of us. Her and that bitch daughter of hers."

"What did they say?"

"They spoke of what we did, how it all unfolded. They even gave descriptions of all of us."

"Oh, dear gods," Neremi whispered as tears swelled in her eyes.

"Oh, no, no. They still don't know it's us. All they have is what we wore, our heights, and suchlike."

"And Fallon?" Thalas asked softly.

Thane glared at him once more. "They know he was involved, Alisae and her mother left no room for doubt."

Thalas swallowed hard as he broke his gaze from Thane.

"They're looking for you, Durlin," Thane continued, turning briefly to nod to the one who'd spoken earlier. "They're assuming you were involved too, given how close you two are... were."

"Dear gods," Durlin whispered as he sank into a nearby seat.

"There's more," Thane said, turning his gaze back on Thalas. "Your father's on the rampage. He knows Davian was there in the library, and now that he's missing, he's gone off to find him."

"I can handle my father."

"Can you truly?"

Thalas moved to speak, but no words came.

"What else, Thane?" asked Eldred, the last of the six.

"That's all. Baern's losing his head, screaming at everyone. I've never seen him so frightened."

"What of Arenya?"

"Oh, for goodness sake, Eldred, not now!"

"Damn it, Thane! What of Arenya?"

"Ugh! Baern has her confined to quarters for the time being. He's been questioning her about what happened. I'm not sure if he believes her, but she's kept her story clean thus far."

"Can we trust her?" Neremi asked worriedly.

"Of course we can!" Eldred exclaimed.

"Stop thinking with your manhood, Eldred," Thane growled.

"We can trust her," Thalas said.

"What makes you so sure?" Neremi asked.

"Because she stands to lose a great deal more than we do should the truth come out."

"Oh…"

"So, what now?" Durlin asked.

"Now…" Thalas muttered, his mind awhirl. Abruptly, he looked up at Durlin, his face set and his gaze hardening.

"Now, you go home."

"Are you mad?" Durlin exclaimed, springing to his feet.

"Have you lost your hearing, Thalas?" Thane added. "I said they are looking for him!"

"And they will find him eventually. The only thing he can do is pretend all is well."

"But they know I was part of it."

Thalas shook his head. "They think you are, nothing more. You're going to give them a reason to no longer suspect you."

"And how do I do that?"

Thalas took a step forward. "This is important, Durlin. You have to make them believe Fallon acted on his own. This was something he kept from you, kept from all of us."

Durlin shook his head in disbelief.

"He's my brother!" he exclaimed. "We have no secrets, everybody knows that!"

"You do now."

"But—"

"He did it for coin. Or love. Perhaps even both! Tell them… tell them you've noticed he's been getting more and more broody whenever he saw Neremi and I together."

"What?" Durlin and Neremi exclaimed in unison.

"You heard me. If you play it right, their imagination will do the rest."

"But that's—" Durlin began.

"Wait… it could work," said Neremi. "It could quite possibly work. I've known you both from childhood, and our parents did try on many occasions to bring Fallon and I together."

"You're not seriously considering—"

Neremi grasped Durlin's hands, squeezing them tightly.

"What choice do we have? They have him, and they know he was involved. We cannot salvage that, no matter what we do. The best we can do is limit the damage, stop the spread at him."

Durlin looked from her to Thalas before finally relenting.

"Good," Thalas nodded.

"Don't think this means we have forgiven you, Thalas," Thane growled. Thalas looked over at him. "You're the reason Fallon is dead. You. Nobody else, just you. Had you simply taken the runic key like you were supposed to, that boy would never have been able to release the Kin-Slayer, and we would've been gone by now. Instead, you just had to go try for the girl's life. Be grateful I don't rip your blasted head off."

Thalas looked at the others. Their thoughts were the same.

"Look, I'm sorry, alright? I'm sorry I lost my temper. I truly am. And yes, I'm so very sorry Fallon is dead. But we can still salvage this."

"Wait, you mean to continue?" Eldred asked, smiling at the incredulity of it all.

"No, I've had enough," Thane said as he turned to the door. "I'm going home now."

Gritting his teeth, Thalas barred the way as he stared at his friends.

"Get out of the way, Thalas," Thane warned.

As the elf glared at him, Thalas was more acutely aware than ever of just how much larger than him Thane was.

"We know Merethia better than they do," he said. "We know it better than Baern and my father. We can find them first."

"And what makes you think they're in Merethia?"

"Because that's all they know. And the Kin-Slayer won't have full control of the boy yet. It's too soon."

Thane glared at him, but Thalas could see he was seeing the truth in his words. Nodding, he looked at the others.

"We can get to them first, then we can—"

"Do what, Thalas?" Neremi demanded. "Do you honestly believe you'll be able to control that boy now? Do you think there is a place we, the five of us, can put him, that he won't simply walk out of?"

"Then... maybe we don't control him."

"What?"

"Chronomancy has been dead for aeons. Perhaps it's time the art was re-learnt."

"Thalas—"

"Why not? We help her, she helps us. It's a deal she's made before. Nothing's stopping her from making it again."

"But if we learn it, they'll know we helped her, and they will banish us without a doubt."

Thalas grinned as he wandered his gaze about his friends.

"If even half the stories of chronomancy are true, do you truly think we will need the Tower anymore? We will be our own lords; we will make our own rules! Wherever we go, whatever we do, we will be the masters! Us! Not the Tower, not our parents, us!"

Silence fell upon them as Thalas stared at his friends. Slowly, one by one, he watched as the gazes of the others changed. One by one, the anger and disgust in their gazes faded away, replaced with simple desire. At last, Thalas nodded.

"We have work to do."

And with that, he swung open the door and marched out.

*****

Kneeling between Marshalla and Davian, Tip wept softly as the cooling waters of Merethia's Aqueduct ran behind his dear friends. With his tears running freely down his face, Tip stared at Marshalla and Davian both as they sat leaning against the Aqueduct's wall. He was waiting, praying for some sign of life, be it a twitch, a groan, anything. Dear gods, anything.

"I said I was sorry, didn't I?"

Tip held his peace.

"How many times do you wish me say it? I am sorry. I am sorry. I. Am. Sorry!"

Sniffling, Tip wiped his nose on his sleeve, but his tears fell still.

"Oh gods, Tip, do stop that! I told you, a thousand times already, I had no choice. The paling around the Tower is immensely strong, stronger than you can comprehend. I had to put a lot of power behind my portal spell, especially since it was three I was porting rather than just you. If anything, you should be thanking me! With the power I put into the spell, there was only a one-in-five chance of death! From certain death to one in five, you have to admit that's quite something, right?"

But still, Tip didn't answer.

"It will wear off, Tip, upon my honor. Just, please, stop the weeping!"

But Tip ignored her still.

"Ugh! Fine, be that way!"

Just then, Marshalla stirred as a pained groan escaped her lips.

"See? Told you."

"Marsha?"

Slowly, Marshalla turned to squint at Tip. "Tip?"

In an instant, Tip flung his arms about her and hugged her, burying his head in her bosom.

Smiling, Marshalla looked down at him. "Glad to see you too."

Looking up at her, Tip wiped his nose on his sleeve again as he grinned at her. It was then that Davian groaned. Both turned to watch as the young elf stirred and slowly straightened himself before finally looking over at his friends.

"Where are we?"

"The Aqueduct, looks like," Marshalla replied, taking in her surroundings.

"Why here?"

"*Because it was the first place you thought of.*"

"Was the first place could think of," Tip said.

"She brought us here?" Davian asked. Tip nodded.

"Is she still there?" Marshalla asked. Again, Tip nodded. Straightening, Marshalla lowered her head slightly as she stared at Tip with quite some concern.

"Is she hurting you?" she whispered.

"*I can hear you, you know!*"

Tip smiled before shaking his head. Marshalla smiled, relaxing visibly.

"How long have we been here for?" Davian asked as he stared at the setting sun.

"A while," Tip replied. Davian looked at him, frowning.

"Why? What happened?"

"Ani said you had alaric poisoning."

Davian and Marshalla looked at each other, visibly alarmed.

"*Etheric poisoning, Tip, etheric.*"

"Sorry, etheric poisoning."

"Oh," Davian replied, relaxing somewhat.

"What's that?" Marshalla asked.

"It's mostly harmless," Davian replied, turning to Marshalla. "Our etheric signatures were compromised by being in the center of a spell whose power was beyond that which our bodies could safely withstand. It's most common during teleportation or illusion spells directed at the self."

"You mean, Tip's porting."

"Right. The power of it must've been immense. Which is to be expected, actually, given the paling about the Tower."

"*Thank you!*"

"So, we'll be fine?" Marshalla asked.

Davian nodded. "We just needed time for the excess ether our bodies absorbed to be lost."

Marshalla smiled at last. "Good, one less thing to worry about." Then she turned to Tip. "You scared?"

Tip's smile slowly faded as he nodded.

"Me too."

"*You don't have to be afraid, Tip, I'm here.*"

"Listen," Marshalla continued. I need to talk to Ani. Can she hear me?"

Once more, Tip nodded.

"Good, uhm…"

"*Actually, let me talk to them.*"

"She wants to talk to you too, wait," Tip said, then stared off into the ether.

"*Give me control, Tip. It'll be easier that way.*"

"How to do that?" Tip asked aloud.

"Do what?"

Tip stared at Marshalla. "Sorry, talking to Ani."

"Clear your mind, and count to three."

Confused, Davian and Marshalla watched as Tip slowly nodded once, again, and again, before suddenly looking straight at Marshalla.

"Greetings," he said, his piercing gaze boring deep into her.

"Hello," Marshalla replied nervously. "You Ani?"

"Who else?"

"Right. Now, look, don't mean to sound ungrateful, but we out now, we all safe, so why don't you just be on your way, and we be on ours, eh?"

Anieszirel smiled at her. "I'm afraid it's not that simple."

"Why not? You climbed into Tip, now climb out and be on your way."

"My dear, do you honestly think if I were able to take corporeal form, I wouldn't have by now? I don't have one. Tip is my host, and here I shall remain until I find a new host."

"But...but he's just a boy!"

"Yes, I noticed."

"Now, look—"

"No, you look. You're worried for him, I understand. You're worried I might hurt him, do something horrible to his mind. Well, I won't. My hatred is not for Tip. If anything, I owe him a great deal. He freed me, saved me from that horrible existence, and the very last thing on my mind is to hurt him. I am no monster, my dear, no matter what those retarded fools at the Tower tell you."

Marshalla stared at Anieszirel for a spell, before finally relaxing somewhat.

"How did Tip save you anyway? He only knows water spells. Hearing that Drakesong go on about the void orb—"

"Void sphere."

"Right, that thing. From what that Drakesong woman was saying, Tip shouldn't have been able to go anywhere near it."

"Ah, yes, well… it would appear our young friend is rather… light-fingered."

Marshalla stared at Anieszirel, confused. In response, Anieszirel nodded towards something further away from them. Curious, both she and Davian turned, though it was Davian who rose and walked over to it.

"What is it?" Marshalla asked when Davian came to a halt.

He stared down at it, and finally bending, he picked up the runic key Tip had tossed the moment they'd appeared.

"It appears to be a runic key," Davian said. "I think it's Archmage Drakesong's."

"Oh Tip," Marshalla said. "You didn't."

"Sorry, Marsha. Really sorry."

"Tip truly is quite sorry he stole it, but I for one am glad he did. With the key in his possession, he was able to reach the void sphere and breach its surface enough to allow me escape."

"But since he stole it, everyone'll think he wanted you out from the start! And then there's those six that tried to rob us all. They'll be looking for us too since you killed one of them."

"You make it sound like I did a horrible thing."

"Well—"

"Do not finish that sentence, young lady."

Marshalla fell quiet, glaring instead at Anieszirel.

"What are we going to do, Marsha?" Davian asked.

Marshalla moved to speak, but she genuinely didn't know what to say.

"The safest thing right now, is to find somewhere safe and stay out of sight," Anieszirel said. "At least till the pressure has waned somewhat. Preferably somewhere outside Merethia."

"Outside Merethia?" Marshalla exclaimed.

"Of course! The Tower'll be looking for you, looking for *me*. And if they were to find our friend, Tip, they won't be gentle, or nice."

The hairs on the back of Marshalla's neck slowly stood tall. "Meaning what?"

"Well," Anieszirel replied, avoiding Marshalla's gaze as she spoke, "rather than risk me escaping to a new host, they will most likely trap Tip as he is in a void sphere."

"No!" Marshalla exclaimed.

"That's horrible!" Davian added.

Anieszirel nodded sadly. "Yes, that it is. That's what they did to my last host. His essence only lasted just over a decade before the forces within the void sphere pulled him apart completely. With a mind as young as Tip's, he wouldn't last anywhere near as long."

Placing a gentle hand on Marshalla's leg, Anieszirel looked deep into her eyes. "Get out of Merethia while you still can. Go far away from here. Wait a year, maybe three, then return. I know it's a lot to ask, but if you stay here, it'll only be a matter of time before they find you."

Marshalla stared at her, but the more she stared, the more she felt the truth in her words. At last, she nodded.

"Fine."

"Good!" Anieszirel exclaimed. "Though you'd want to hurry. They'll be closing the gates out of town, if they haven't already."

"Can't you port us somewhere?" Marshalla asked, frowning.

"Ah, I wish it was that simple."

"Why not?"

"Well, to teleport somewhere, you need to see the place clearly in your mind's eye, focus on it. The only places I can focus on are in the Tower. I've been their prisoner for too long to clearly recall anywhere else. And Tip only has clear memories of Merethia. I'm afraid we'll have to make our way out of here the old-fashioned way."

"Maybe we should go to my father," Davian offered. Both looked at him. "He'll know what to do. He always knows what to do."

Marshalla shrugged after a spell. "It wouldn't hurt."

Davian nodded, smiling as he rose. "We just have to get to him when Thalas isn't there."

At this, Marshalla frowned.

"Why?" she asked.

"Why what?"

"Why don't you want Thalas to be there?"

Davian stared for a spell with a blank gaze, but then as he moved to speak, no words came forth. He looked from one to the other, slowly cowering away from them.

"Davian…" Marshalla began, leaning towards him. "What is it? Not nice to keep secrets."

Davian pouted as he dropped his gaze to the runic key in his hands.

"The one who hurt you," he replied after a brief spell, "it was Thalas."

With the blood draining from her face, Marshalla raised her hand to her bosom, where he'd seared her flesh. But the skin there was smooth.

"I healed you while you were unconscious," Anieszirel said. "You're welcome."

Marshalla stared at her a spell, then turned to Davian. "You sure?"

Davian smiled sadly as he looked up at her. "He's my brother, Marsha. I'd recognize his gait anywhere."

"But wasn't his voice."

"It was him, Marsha, it was him. He must've woven a spell to hide his voice, but I'd recognize his gait anywhere."

Marshalla frowned, staring off into the ether as she tried to make sense of what she'd just heard.

"Why?" she asked at last.

Davian shrugged then frowned as he dropped his gaze back to the runic key in his hands.

"He and Father never really liked each other," he replied after another brief silence. "Father's always seen him as a…failure. He's always coming up with these schemes and plots to make himself rich so he and Neremi can leave. I hear them sometimes. They think I don't hear them, but I do."

"So, they were thinking of stealing me, then selling me off," Anieszirel mused. "Well, they certainly wouldn't have wanted for money had they succeeded."

"Dear gods," Marshalla whispered, turning to the chronodragon. "The Drakesong woman must be with them! She made Tip steal the key, must've! Thought it was weird the way she kept pulling Tip close. She wanted him to steal the key!"

"That makes no sense," Davian said. "Why not just give them the key?"

"The keys are attuned to their owners," Anieszirel replied. "Without retuning them first, giving them away will deaden them. And any retuning is etched onto the key, visible for all to see."

"But if it's stolen, it doesn't stop working?" Marshalla asked. "A bit stupid that, isn't it?"

"Not necessarily. Each key comes with a binding chain, which keeps the key upon the owner's person at all times. The magic in the chain needs to be recast every few weeks, though, else it is spent. Arenya must not have recast hers so Tip could take it."

"That bitch."

"Language!" Anieszirel exclaimed at Marshalla, who made a face at her in response before turning her gaze to Davian.

"We'll do it your way, then. Know how we can get in quietly?"

"I can teleport you there," Anieszirel offered. Both looked at her. "Right into your room. Tip just showed it to me."

"Okay, take us to their room. We sneak down, see Davian's father and decide what to do then."

"Right!" Anieszirel exclaimed as she leapt to her feet. As she did so, the others rose.

"So, uh…what next?" Marshalla asked.

"Well, for this to work you must both hug me as tightly as you possibly can, then you must both kiss me."

Frowning, both stared at each other before turning to the chronodragon. Neither moved. After a moment's silence, Anieszirel rolled her eyes at them, sighing heavily as she did so.

"You're no fun, you know that," she muttered, and teleported them to Davian's room.

"Woah!" Davian exclaimed as they reappeared. He looked at Anieszirel, his eyes wide and his mouth agape.

"Just like that?"

Anieszirel shrugged, grinning. "When you're this skilled, you don't need any silly gestures or incantations."

"No, you just show off instead," Marshalla muttered drily as she headed for the door.

"Jealous, are we?" Anieszirel replied with a smug smile as Marshalla walked over to the door.

Opening the door a crack, she checked the hallway. Satisfied, she nodded to the others. Gently, carefully, they crept out of Davian's room, making their way towards the stairs.

"We should check Thalas' room," Davian whispered, "make sure he's not in."

"Where's his room?" Anieszirel asked, whispering also.

"At the end of the corridor," Marshalla whispered, nodding to the far end before them.

"Then, he's not in."

Marshalla and Davian both looked at Anieszirel.

"Sure?" Marshalla asked.

Anieszirel nodded. "Positive. I sense no other presence upstairs."

"Good," Marshalla replied as Davian relaxed visibly.

"But why are we whispering?" Anieszirel asked as they crept forward.

"So nobody will hear us, silly!"

"Even though I've cast a sound barrier about us?"

"Why didn't you say something before?" Marshalla exclaimed, raising her voice to near shouting.

Anieszirel shrugged. "You didn't ask."

Marshalla and Davian stared at her with mouths agape.

"What?"

"Ugh!" Marshalla cried. "Come on."

"They can still see us though, so, do be careful."

"Well, can you do something about that?" Davian asked.

"Yes."

An uncomfortable chill ran down both Marshalla and Davian's spines as they stared on at Anieszirel, but it did not last long.

"All done?" Marshalla asked.

Anieszirel nodded.

"Good, come on, then."

As one, they hurried down the stairs towards the reading room, the one place Thuridan was sure to be found.

"Anyone in there?" Marshalla asked.

Anieszirel nodded. "One."

"Good," Marshalla replied as she reached for the handle. Just then, the doorbell rang. As it did so, the door to the reading room sprang open as Thalas hurried out.

"Who is it, Albrecht?" he asked their butler as he closed the study door behind him just as Anieszirel placed a calming hand on both Marshalla and Davian's arms.

"It's the master," Albrecht replied, opening the door as he spoke.

"Welcome home, Father," Thalas said as Thuridan Grovemender flew into the house. He eyed Thalas with a fiery gaze as he peeled off his coat.

"Where have you been?"

"I was out with Neremi. We'd had our fill of the open-door event, so we went about Merethia for a spell. Then I came home. Albrecht told me what happened, so I waited around in case Davian or one of the others came back."

"Did you now?" Thuridan replied as he handed his coat and hat to Albrecht. The venom in his words bore into all who heard.

"Is all well, Father?" Thalas asked.

"Where's Fallon?" Thuridan asked, his arms crossed behind him as he slowly walked towards Thalas.

Thalas frowned in apparent confusion. "I'd imagine he's up to no good with Durlin again. Did something happen to him?"

"He's dead."

"*Dead?*"

"Yes, Thalas, dead. Do you know anything about that?"

"I... now hold a moment, Father, I didn't kill him! I haven't even seen him today!"

"Is that right?"

"Yes!"

"You haven't asked me how he died. I take it you already know, then?"

"Upon my honor, Father, I have no—"

By this time, Thalas was within arm's reach of his father, and as he spoke, the Grovemender patriarch reached out and clasped his hand about his son's throat. It was a light touch, but Thalas' eyes grew wide nonetheless as, slowly, he was lifted off his feet.

"Now you listen to me very carefully, boy, very, *very* carefully. I will give you this one chance, this one sole chance to come clean. If you come clean now, I may forgive you. But if you do not, and I find out you are as involved as I think you are, Thalas, my boy, you will rue the day you were born."

"Upon... my honor..." Thalas stuttered as his face reddened more and more.

Abruptly, Thuridan let his son go, with Thalas crumpling to the floor.

"Very well." Thuridan muttered before marching past his son towards his reading room.

"How did Fallon die?" Thalas asked as he rose.

Stopping, Thuridan turned to his son. "He was killed trying to steal the Kin-Slayer."

"What?"

"You heard me. He and five others. One of them, a girl, long blonde hair. Does that sound like anyone you know?"

"Neremi?" Thalas asked, frowning. Thuridan stared in response. At last, Thalas shook his head.

"She was with me the whole afternoon. It couldn't have been her."

"If you say so."

"Father, I have done nothing wrong."

"Is that so?"

"Yes!"

"Did you know Tip was there?"

Thalas nodded. "He and the other one went with Davian to the Tower."

"And did you know the thieves used him to steal Arenya's runic key?"

Thalas frowned. "She say as much?"

Thuridan laughed. "No, my dear son, she's keeping quiet. It's the witnesses who spoke. One moment, she was hugging the little thiefling close, the next, the raiders are searching his pockets for something." Thuridan took a menacing step closer to his son.

"You and I are the only ones who know of his gift," Thuridan continued, "so explain to me how these raiders knew to use him to take her runic key."

Thalas swallowed hard at this. "Mardaley knew."

"Mardaley? Mardaley's a lot of things, but he would never do something like this. So, that leaves who precisely?"

"Father, I swear to you, upon my hon—"

"You have no honor, be quiet!" Thuridan snapped, then he took a few more menacing steps forward.

"But do you know what's most irksome about all this?" he continued. "The Kin-Slayer should be a Grovemender artifact. Our family crafted her void sphere prison in the first place, and it was one of your ancestors who paid the ultimate price in entrapping her. I've been planning for years, decades, to finally make her mine. And you, you and your stupid, brainless, idiotic friends go in and not only ruin my plans, but actually release her! Of all the stupid things to do! That boy was the final key, the final piece! And now that creature has infested him! How could you be so stupid!"

"Father, upon my—"

"You have no honor!" Thuridan bellowed, his face a hair's breadth from his son's. Sweating profusely, Thalas stood cowering before his father.

"How did he release her anyway?" Thuridan asked.

"Pardon?"

"They said the boy simply touched the sphere and the Kin-Slayer was free. Is that true? That's all that happened? No spells, no incantations?"

Eagerly, Thalas nodded, but as he did so, his eyes grew wide as he realized what he had just admitted to. In an instant, he dropped to his knees, his forehead touching the stone floor.

"Forgive me, Father! Please forgive me!" he pleaded, his voice quivering.

"You insignificant—"

"Father, please! Please forgive me! We only meant to take the boy and the girl, that was all. The void sphere was meant to be a diversion. We never planned to leave with it, but we knew if we took it, the Tower would be too busy looking for it to give chase! That was all, I swear! We were going to leave it in one of the training rooms and make good our escape. We never meant to release her! Please, Father, I beg of you, forgive me!"

Thuridan stared at his son in disgust. "Would that you understood how much you've cost me today."

Thalas looked up at his father. "Then allow me salvage this."

Thuridan crossed his arms as he glowered at his son.

"And how do you plan on doing that?"

"We'll find her for you."

Thuridan scoffed. "Do you honestly believe I will entrust you with finding her?"

"We know Merethia better than anyone. We'll find her."

"What makes you so sure they're still in Merethia?"

"I spoke to Eldred earlier. He overheard his father saying the Matriarch had told the king, and all the roads leading into and out of Merethia are being watched. The same holds true for the other cities nearby. If they didn't leave immediately, they're still here."

Thuridan stared at his son in silence for a spell.

"They haven't left. The teleport spell the Kin-Slayer cast would've given Davian and that Marsha girl etheric poisoning. They would've needed time to allow the excess ether dissipate."

Eagerly, Thalas nodded. "Then let us find her for you, before the king or the Tower does."

Thuridan glowered at his son for a spell.

"That was your plan already," he said at last.

"Father I—"

"And, unless I miss my guess, you were going to offer her aid in exchange for her teaching you chronomancy."

"Upon my honor, I—"

"Shut up, boy, just shut up."

A deafening silence fell upon the pair as the father glowered furiously at the son. At last, he went on one knee, but only to grab his son's chin, forcing Thalas' gaze to his.

"You will find her, but you will find her for me. Betray me, and I will not banish you, I will not disown you, I will simply kill you. Do you understand?"

Once again, Thalas nodded eagerly.

"No, I don't think you do. It will take you years to master chronomancy to any real effect, maybe even decades. Within that time, I will find you, Thalas. Do you understand?"

Slowly, Thalas nodded.

"Good." Letting go of his son's chin, Thuridan rose. "And bring your brother back alive. He must still be with them."

"What will you do once I find her? How do you intend to control her?"

"You let me worry about that," Thuridan replied as he turned away from his son.

Thalas moved to speak, but the tone in his father's voice forced a thought to the fore of his mind, one that was both ridiculous and patent in equal measure.

"You have a void sphere, don't you?"

Thuridan turned to glower at his son anew.

"And the girl?" Thalas asked after a moment's charged silence.

"I couldn't care less about her," Thuridan said, sighing as he walked towards the door of the reading room. "Once the Kin-Slayer's taken care of, she'll have outlived her usefulness."

Hurriedly, Marshalla shuffled away from the door, and as Thuridan disappeared into the reading room, all three watched Thalas grab his coat and leave. Quivering, Marshalla gestured for them to return upstairs, and all three returned in silence. None spoke till they were in Davian's room.

"That was unpleasant," Anieszirel said at last.

Both looked at her.

"Get changed," Marshalla said at last.

"What?"

"Tip's old clothes, get changed." With that, she hurried out of the room.

Confused, Anieszirel looked at Davian. Smiling sadly, Davian walked over to a nearby cupboard and opening it, pulled out a neatly folded bundle and threw it at her.

"Ah," she said, and duly changed into them.

Before long, Marshalla returned, herself changed into different clothes, and with a bag slung behind her.

"What are you doing?" Davian asked, his worry plain in his words.

"Leaving. Now."

"Good," Anieszirel said. "With luck, we'll still be able to slip past the gate guards."

"Didn't you hear Thalas?" Davian asked, frowning. "They'll be watching the gates."

"Doesn't matter," Marshalla replied, shaking her head. "She'll hide us again, and we'll slip past."

"But it's just an illusion of vision," Davian replied, "not an illusion complete. If anyone bumps into you, they will feel it."

"Worth a try," Marshalla replied stubbornly, Anieszirel nodding in agreement.

"But it's you who'll die, Marsha, and Tip. Ani'll just find a new host."

With an exasperated sigh, Marshalla glared at the little boy. "Got any better ideas?"

"I…"

"Hold, Tip wishes to speak," Anieszirel said.

An awkward silence fell upon them as Anieszirel stared into the ether. Then, Tip turned to Marshalla, his eyes wide with excitement. "Mardaley! He'll know what to do!"

Marshalla's gaze softened at the mention of that name.

"Mardaley hates us," she replied at last. "Better we do this on our own."

At her words, the excitement drained from Tip's features as he pouted at her.

"I'm coming with you," Davian said suddenly.

"What? Why?" Marshalla demanded as she spun to face him.

"I'm not staying here."

Smiling, Marshalla walked over and held his face in her hands. "Davian, you live here, your family—"

"My father is a monster; you were right from the beginning. He was using Tip, using you. And now he intends to entrap Tip in a void sphere of his own. He knows what that'll do to Tip, he must know, but he doesn't even care. My brother's no better either. I can't stay with them. I won't. If you don't let me come with you, I'll simply run away."

Marshalla looked at Tip, who looked from Davian to her.

"Ani says to let him come," he said. "She says his father won't do anything stupid if Davian's with us."

"Precisely!" Davian exclaimed. But Marshalla was not convinced.

"Let him come, Marsha. Please."

Marshalla stared into the pleading eyes of Tip, and felt her resolve slowly crumble. She looked at Davian once more, then sighed.

"Pack light, take all the coin you can. Hurry."

Grinning, Davian flung his arms about her, hugging her close, then turned to do as she'd bid. Marshalla and Tip watched as Davian darted all about the room, one with a happy smile, the other with a guilty frown.

"Uh-oh," Tip said suddenly.

"What is it?" Marshalla asked, turning to him.

"He's coming upstairs."

"Who?"

"Thalas."

Eyes going wide, Marshalla turned to Davian, who had stopped and was staring at Tip. But as he looked at Marshalla, he resumed his gathering, only this time at twice the pace.

"Get Ani, Tip, quick."

"Okay."

Nodding, Marshalla looked over at Davian. He had a bag of his own, and was busy stuffing it with clothes and some other belongings.

"Light, Davian, light."

"This is light!"

"He's up the stairs."

Marshalla looked at Tip.

"Ani?" she whispered.

"Who else?" Anieszirel replied. "Oh wait, he's heading to his room."

Smiling, Marshalla sighed.

"Oh no, no he's changed his mind and is now heading over here."

"Davian!"

"Almost ready!"

"We have to go, now!"

"I need to get Kel's things!"

"He's at the door."

"We have to go!"

"Money, the money!"

"He's turning the handle."

"Forget the coin!"

"But we need money!"

"The door is opening."

"Got it!"

"Now, Ani, now!"

Carefully, Thalas pushed the door open. No, there was no Davian. Instead, the room was a complete mess.

"Wishful thinking," he muttered, surveying the room.

"The little lickspittle couldn't even tidy up," he growled before slamming the door shut and marching over to his room.

Closing the door firmly behind him, he latched it before marching over to his bed. Once seated, he reached under and pulled out a small box. Opening, he took a deep breath and pulled out a smooth round stone roughly the size of a large fist. Holding it in both hands, he cleared his mind and stared at the stone. He stared till it began to glow a soft blue. Satisfied, he looked up and waited until a ghostly image of Neremi swam into view.

"Did you find anything?"

Thalas nodded. "Let's wait for the others first."

They did not have long to wait, and before long the other four were standing about his bed.

"So, did you find anything?" Neremi asked the moment an apparition of Eldred swam into view. Setting the stone back in its box, Thalas sat further back as the others also sat.

"My father still knows nothing of what happened. And neither does the Tower."

"Are you sure?" Thane asked.

Thalas nodded. "I'm positive. He has some theories, but I managed to convince him we're not involved."

"So, we're safe?"

"For now, yes." As he stared at the smiling faces of his friends, a great relief washed over him. He'd felt sure Neremi at the very least would've seen through his lie.

"So, we stick to the plan?"

Thalas nodded. "Yes. We find them before the Tower, or the king."

"But where do we even begin?" Durlin asked. "It's all well and good to say we know Merethia better than them, but that knowledge doesn't really serve us that well unless you wish to search street by street."

"We don't have to," Thalas replied. "When they left Mardaley's employ, they asked him to take on one of their gutter-rat friends. She's our key. By now, they'll have made contact, get her to aid them. We watch her, follow her and have her lead us to them."

"Brilliant!" Neremi exclaimed.

"It could work," Eldred added.

"Why not just watch Mardaley?" Thane asked.

Thalas shook his head. "There's something about that old human, something... I don't know. Father had me watch him some time ago, and he more or less found me out within moments. No, we're better off watching their gutter-rat friend away from that storekeeper."

"If you say so," Thane replied coldly. "We do have a complication though."

"What?"

"I heard the Tower's having doubts about Arenya's innocence."

"In what way?" Eldred asked.

"Has she spilled the truth?" asked Neremi.

Thane shook his head. "Not yet, but there are inconsistencies in her tale. Little ones, here and there. They're making Baern question her whole tale."

Thalas frowned. "We'll need to do something about her."

"I'll take care of it," Eldred replied.

"And how will you bedding her again fix this?" Durlin asked.

"It worked before, didn't it?" Neremi quipped, prompting mocking chuckles from the others.

"I'll take care of it," Eldred repeated.

"Very well," Thalas replied at last. "You take care of your beloved. But know that should you fail, Thane and I will be paying her a visit."

Both Thane and Eldred smiled, but one was a smile of evil delight, while the other was of mocking condescension.

"You do remember she is an Archmage, right?"

Thalas smirked. "Yes, but she is no battle-mage. Thane and I can handle her."

"I'll take care of it," Eldred snarled after a brief moment's charged silence.

"See that you do."

"I do have one thought, though," Eldred continued, "about your brilliant plan."

"What?"

"What's to stop the Kin-Slayer simply killing us all once she's gotten to safety? Or simply vanishing?"

An uncomfortable silence fell upon the group.

"He's right," Durlin muttered. "We have no hold over her."

"And once she's regained all her powers, nobody will," Neremi added.

"Then we must stop that. We use her powers as our hold on her," Thalas replied.

"And just how do you propose we do that?" Eldred asked.

Thalas held Eldred in a blank stare as his mind spun.

"Precisely."

"Why don't we just bash the boy's head in?" Thane asked. "I heard tell if you do this to the host of a spirit, it traps them in their host. Perhaps it'll work with her."

"And if we don't hit the boy hard enough?" Neremi asked in response. "I don't know about you, but I have no wish to have the Kin-Slayer for an enemy."

"If she betrays us, we betray her," Thane replied firmly.

"And if she chooses to vanish, what then?" Eldred asked, folding his arms as he spoke.

"If only we can entrap her somehow," Durlin muttered.

"You have a spare void sphere lying around somewhere?" Eldred mocked.

"My father does," Thalas said, a huge grin on his face. All four fell silent.

"How in the hells did he manage that?" Durlin asked.

Thalas shrugged. "I stopped wondering about my father's ways a long time ago."

"I… think I know," Eldred muttered. "Mother told me a tale about your father some time ago. It was one of her annoying tales to show me how poor your company is, Thalas."

"Oh, one of those, is it?" Neremi asked, grinning. "Both my parents tell me those regularly, about all of you."

"I can imagine," Eldred replied, smiling. "But, anyway, she said about a year or so after she became Archmage, your father tried to convince the Matriarch to sanction research into the forging of void spheres, claiming he knew a much faster and less time-consuming way to forge them. The Matriarch didn't believe a word of it, and rejected his requests. He defied her, though, and went ahead with his research. Some lives were lost, quite a few actually, and he very nearly got stripped of his Archmage status over it."

"So…he failed?" Neremi asked.

"In a manner of speaking, yes," Eldred nodded. "He did forge one, but it was very unstable, and when it collapsed, the energy released from it was what killed all those mages."

"And you want us to use that?" Thane demanded, glaring at Thalas.

"My father is nothing if not tenacious," Thalas replied. "He wouldn't have given up so easily. He would've been working on it since."

"That sly bastard," Neremi muttered.

"He is, yes. But, more importantly, he'd have perfected it by now."

"Do you know where it is?" Thane asked.

"Not yet, but I will."

"Are you sure?"

"Yes, Thane, I'm sure."

"So, we do that, then," Neremi said. "We find her, Thalas uses his father's void sphere on her, and we take the sphere and leave."

"That's if Thalas finds the damn thing."

"He'll come through, Thane."

"And the blasted thing doesn't kill us all."

"It'll be fine."

"If you say so."

Through it all, Thalas glowered at the elf.

"I'll head over to the Priory," Thalas said after a brief spell. "Each of you head over to the other hospices. Do you know who we're looking for?"

Some nodded, others shook their heads.

"I'll send you all an image of her. Let the rest know if you see her. Remember, we are to follow her, that's all. Alright?"

One by one, the others nodded.

"Good."

"Shall we use viewing stones or seeking stones?"

"Seeking stones, Durlin," Neremi said. "Last time we took our viewing stones out on a hunt, Fallon lost… his."

"Get going, all of you," Thalas said.

One by one, his friends faded from view. When the last left, Thalas touched his viewing stone once more, and its blue hue soon faded. Closing the box, he slid it back under his bed. But as he looked at the door, his mood soured greatly. Gritting his teeth, he pulled out the dagger he'd stolen from his father's reading room. Staring at it, he found himself feeling more and more convinced stealing it was a good idea. Thane's behavior was getting worse, and the sooner he dealt with Thane the better for him.

"Pity," Thalas muttered, "we used to be such good friends."

Rising, he attached the dagger to his belt, and pulling his tunic over it, headed for the door.

J.B. Drake

FLIGHT OF DESPAIR

Glowering furiously at the battle-mage rifling through her bag, Maline stood silent as the cold air sent a shiver down her spine.

"We will be done soon," the ranger beside her whispered, the fairy on his shoulder staring at Maline as his wings fluttered lazily behind him.

But Maline refused to reply.

"We do not enjoy this any more than you do," he continued, "but we have a duty to perform."

As Maline turned to glare at him, the weak light caught the unsightly bruise on her right cheek.

"Duty?" she hissed. "Your friend kicked me in the face!"

Guiltily, the ranger looked at their commander, who stood brooding, his hands on the hilts of the blades on either side of him.

"There's nothing here," the battle-mage said at last.

Maline turned to the commander, a smug smile upon her lips, but the commander met her mocking smile with a cold stare before turning his gaze to his mage companion.

"Are you sure?"

"Everything here is worthless garbage," the battle-mage replied with biting bluntness. "Nothing here belongs to our quarry."

Maline turned a darkened gaze upon him, but bit back her words.

"You done, then?" she asked instead.

The commander sneered at her a spell, then turned to the others.

"Come," he said, "let us meet up with the others. Perhaps they've had better luck."

Angry still, Maline watched the mage and the commander depart, but as the ranger turned to leave, he pressed something soft and damp into her hand before he, too, departed. None met her gaze as they left, an act that merely served to stoke her rage. Gritting her teeth, she at last stared down at that which lay in her hand. It was damp, soft and green. Moss. Healing moss, perhaps? As she stared at it, the bruise on her face began to throb most painfully. Staring at it for a moment longer, she pressed it against her cheek, and almost at once, a smile broke across her lips as a grateful sigh escaped from them.

"Thank you, ranger," she whispered, then knelt and went about placing her meagre belongings back in her bag with her free hand before preparing for bed.

"Hello, Maline."

With a startled cry, the terrified elf sprang to her feet, darting back into the wall behind her. But as she did so, she let go of the healing moss, and could only watch as it fell into a heap.

"Sorry, sorry!" Marshalla exclaimed as she swam into view before Maline, bending down to pick up the fallen moss. "Didn't mean to scare you."

"Don't do that!" Maline exclaimed, snatching the moss from Marshalla's outstretched hand.

"Sorry," Marshalla repeated, grimacing as Tip and Davian swam into view near her. As Maline's gaze fell on the others, Marshalla placed what was left of her friend's strewn belongings into Maline's bag, and as Maline finally touched the moss to her bruise, Marshalla rose, handing her the bag.

"Thank you," Maline said. Marshalla smiled in response.

"Sorry about what they did to you," Tip mumbled.

Maline frowned. "You saw?"

Davian nodded. "Just turned into the alleyway when the commander kicked you in the face. Marsha thought best to hide till they left."

Frowning still, Maline kept the moss against her bruise, but at last, she shook her head, her worry plain in her gaze.

"Marsha, what you do?" she demanded. "Army's looking for you! Tower too! They say you killed someone!"

Marshalla looked over at Tip, but kept her peace.

"Tell me you didn't. You tell me right now, tell me you didn't! Look at me!"

Mutely, Marshalla obliged.

"Tell me that's not you."

"Didn't kill nobody," Marshalla replied softly.

"Then why they looking for you? And why they keep calling you Kin-Slayer?"

"She didn't do it, Maline," Tip replied in much the same manner. "It was me."

Stunned, Maline turned to stare at Tip. "You?"

Tip nodded as his face fell. "Took something, and it killed someone."

"But…" replied Maline, her confusion apparent. "… they kept calling this Kin-Slayer a she."

Again, Tip nodded. "She's inside me, and when she took over, she… killed someone."

"Oh, dear gods…" Maline whispered.

"But Tip's okay though," Marshalla replied quickly. "It's just a spirit that sort of—"

"Essence," Tip mumbled.

"Yeah, essence. She's not hurting Tip, she just lives in him now."

Maline looked from Marshalla to Tip before her face finally fell as her heart broke for the little elf.

"Oh, Tip," she sighed.

"They were going to hurt us, though! They hurt Marsha, and she made them stop! She made them all stop."

Maline stared at Tip as he started back at her with stubborn defiance. Sinking to her knees, her eyes on Tip, Maline reached out for him with her free hand and pulled him closer to her.

"She inside you still?"

Tip nodded, his gaze to the ground.

"But she had no choice, right?"

Again, Tip nodded. It was then Maline noticed the tears in his eyes. Gritting her teeth, she pulled him closer and hugged him as tenderly as she could.

"We were hoping you could help us get out of Merethia," Davian said after a brief moment's silence. Maline looked at him.

"You going with them?" she asked.

Davian nodded in response, but Maline shook her head at him as a worried frown twisted her lips.

"No, your father's tearing up the city looking for you."

"If he goes home, he'll get in trouble," Tip said.

"What kind of trouble?"

"I'm not going back," Davian said firmly.

Maline stared hard at him, her frown deepening.

"Will you help us?"

Staring at him for a moment longer, Maline finally nodded, rising as she did so. "Will try at least. What you need?"

Marshalla moved to speak, but her voice failed her. She looked at Tip, who nudged her.

"How's Mardaley?" she asked Maline at last. Maline smiled sadly.

"Losing his mind."

"Oh?"

Maline nodded. "Every time the doorbell chimes, he looks up, then he looks sad that it's not one of you."

"Told you he'd miss us," Tip said with a smug smile.

"Can you get him to meet us?" Marshalla asked, ignoring Tip completely.

Maline looked from her to Tip before looking back at her. "Not sure that's a good thing."

"Why?"

"They watching Mardaley, army and Tower. Watching the store and his house."

All three faces fell at this, but Maline smiled at them.

"But he's smart. Maybe he can trick them, sneak away. If not, will come see you myself, bring what he gives me to give you."

Marshalla smiled gratefully. "Thank you, Maline."

Maline shook her head in response. "We look out for each other, always have, always will. Got somewhere safe to stay tonight?"

Marshalla nodded.

"Good. Stay away from the others though, okay?"

"Why?" Marshalla asked, frowning.

"Tower's offering coin for you and Tip, lots. Stay away from them all, hear?"

Tip and Marshalla exchanged worried glances.

"We will," Marshalla replied at last. "Meet us tomorrow, at the place where you and me first met?"

Maline nodded at this. "This time?"

Marshalla nodded in turn.

"Okay. Stay safe till then, hear?"

Grinning, Marshalla nodded once more. Sighing, Maline hugged her dear friend close before gently pushing her away.

"Now, go. Those bastards might come back."

Nodding, Marshalla stepped away from Maline, and as she did so, she and the others slowly faded from view.

"And stay safe, hear?" Maline whispered. With nothing else for it, she pulled out her blanket and began to bed down for the night.

Dawn found Maline awake and alert. Her slumber had been fitful, and her head throbbed. Sighing, she looked over at the rising sun. There was no point closing her eyes now, she may as well get up. Sighing once again, she rose and, putting her blanket back into her bag, began making her way over to Mardaley's.

As she walked, however, her mind turned to the short tale Tip and Marshalla had told her the night before. Tip was possessed, there was no other word for it. That the spirit bore no ill-will for poor Tip did lessen the blow somewhat, but it was still such a heartbreaking thought. They were right to wish to leave though. With the bounty on their heads, Merethia was no longer safe for them, they had too few friends left.

It was not long before the welcome sight of Mardaley's store came into view, but as she neared it, she couldn't help but look across the street to the small contingent camped there. They were dressed like ordinary folk, but Mardaley saw right through their disguise the very first day they appeared. It made Maline sick just looking at them. Forcing her gaze forward, she headed over to the door. But she could feel their gaze upon her. Frowning deeply, she reached for the door, whispering the words of unbinding that Mardaley had taught her. As she touched the handle however, she realized the door was already open. Stopping, she looked over across the street, her anger building.

"Ah, Maline," came a voice from within.

Surprised, she turned to find Mardaley staring at her from the other side of the door.

"Open already?" she asked as she walked in.

Mardaley smiled and shrugged. "I couldn't sleep, so I came in early. I see you couldn't sleep either."

Maline shook her head.

"Well, now that you're here, you may as well help me with some stock taking."

"Why not?" Maline replied, grinning as she stowed away her bag.

Grinning still, she followed Mardaley into the storage room. But as she entered behind him, she quickly closed the door behind her.

"Maline?" Mardaley asked as he stared frowning at her.

Maline turned to face him. Her grin was gone, but there was a fire in her eyes, one that clearly put him on edge. Forcing a grin, Maline walked closer to him.

"Saw them last night," she whispered.

"Saw who?" Mardaley asked in response, but as the words left his lips, his eyes lit up as he reached for her elbow.

"You saw them!" he whispered.

Eagerly, Maline nodded.

"Where? When? How are they?"

Maline laughed. "They came to find me. They all well."

But Maline's grin soon faded.

"What is it?" Mardaley asked, letting go of her elbow.

"This Kin-Slayer thing, it's in Tip."

153

Mardaley took a deep breath and let it out slowly as he nodded. "I heard."

"It's not hurting him," Maline continued, "but don't like it one bit. Nothing good'll come of it."

You're right on that point, my dear."

"Yes," Maline replied as she nodded, hugging herself for comfort.

"So, what did they say? And why are they still in Merethia?"

Maline shrugged. "They can't get out, they need help. It's what they said anyway."

"Well, they won't *now*." Mardaley sighed, shoving his hands into his pockets. "The gates are heavily guarded now, and the city walls are being patrolled near constantly."

Maline's face fell. "So, they're stuck here?"

Mardaley sighed once again as he reached for her once more, this time placing a comforting hand on her upper arm.

"We'll think of something," he said. "Where are they now?"

Maline shrugged. "No idea. Know where they'll be tonight though."

"Oh?"

Maline nodded. "Marsha asked me to bring you to them tonight."

Mardaley frowned in response.

"Tricky," he muttered as he crossed his arms about him before stroking his beard, deep in thought.

"Yes, won't be that easy with your new friends."

"Quite," Mardaley replied distractedly. Turning, he began pacing the storage room. But as he paced, his eyes soon chanced upon an unopened box of arachne webbing.

"Maline…" he said as he turned to face her, a most mischievous smile upon his lips.

"What…?" Maline said cautiously as she cast a sideways glance at him.

"You're not afraid of spiders, are you?"

"Depends how big…"

Mardaley's smile grew. "Let's head back outside. Our dear friends will be beginning to wonder where we went."

"Mardaley, what you planning?"

"You'll see," Mardaley replied as he headed for the door.

"Mardaley…"

"You'll see."

"You turning me into a spider?"

Mardaley turned to stare at her as he opened the door.

"You'll see," he replied, smiling sweetly as he headed back to the store. Shaking her head, Maline followed, muttering several dark oaths under her breath as she did so.

It wasn't long before Maline forgot about Mardaley's ominous words. With the royal curfew still in effect, and no word when it would be lifted, many of Mardaley's customers seemed to decide all at once that the best thing would be to stock up on all their essentials while they could. At the same time.

So, when it finally came time to close shop, Maline couldn't be any more grateful. Yawning, she shuffled out of the door. To any who saw her, it was plain this was a woman in dire need of sleep. Just as she was about to close the door, however, Maline turned and stared within.

"You sure you don't need me to stay?"

"No, no, I'll finish up here. You go and get some rest," Mardaley's voice called back. Nodding, Maline closed the door and, throwing her customary glare at the contingent across the street, shuffled away.

"Are they staring at us or the store?" the spider perched in Maline's hair whispered. As casually as she could, Maline threw a glance over her shoulder at the contingent.

"The store."

Mardaley chuckled. "I can't believe I didn't think of this sooner."

Maline smiled, but it was brief. "How long you think it'll take them to know it's not you in there?"

"Oh, it should be a good long while, I expect," Mardaley replied. "Not that I'm boasting, mind."

Maline smiled. "Of course not."

"Good. Now, where are we going?"

"You'll see."

"Hrm…quite."

"And stop moving, please. Making my head itch."

"Sorry, your hair's getting in my eyes."

Close your eyes, then."

"I would if spiders had eyelids."

"Well…manage!"

Fighting back the urge to scratch her scalp, Maline made her way through the city to the agreed meeting place. Bowing her head low and clutching the straps of her bag, she trundled through the near-empty streets, her eyes to the ground before her. On a few occasions, she was accosted and indeed searched by a passing patrol, but not a single one of them became aware of Mardaley's presence.

At last, the imposing building that was Merethia's Halls of Justice loomed in the distance. Grinning, Maline quickened her pace.

"We're almost there?"

"Yes," Maline whispered in response.

Soon, she reached its steps, and racing up them, stood by the door, staring about them.

"We're here," she muttered.

"Good, find somewhere in the shadows to sit."

Nodding distractedly, Maline did as Mardaley bid, and finding a nice, darkened corner, pulled off her bag and made herself comfortable.

Smirking, Thane pulled out his seeking stone and seeked out to the others.

"I found the woman," he said as the stone in his hand pulsed softly.

"Good," Thalas said. "Which hospice?"

"None. I went to Mardaley's."

"Didn't we agree that was too dangerous?" Neremi asked.

"No, Thalas said it was too dangerous. I never said I agreed."

"Thane—"

"What does it matter?" Durlin said. "He's found her."

"Precisely," Thane said, his smug smile growing.

"Where is she now, then?" Thalas asked.

"The Halls of Justice."

"What is she doing there? No rats are permitted to spend the night on its steps."

"She appears to be waiting for someone. Care to guess who?"

"Excellent!" Eldred exclaimed. "I'm on my way."

"Yes, let's all head over," Thalas added.

"Yes," Thane growled. "And bring the void sphere with you, or do you not yet have it?"

"It's not so straightforward. I'll explain when I get there."

"Why am I not surprised?" Rather than waiting for a response, Thane willed the seeking stone to silence and, placing it back in his pocket, settled down and prepared for the wait.

"You sure you don't want to get out of my hair?" Maline pleaded. "Nobody here, promise."

"Much as I'd love to, and believe me, I'd like nothing better than to be myself again, we are at the Halls of Justice. Sooner or later some patrol will chance by, and we stand a much better chance of avoiding conflict if they think you're simply bedding down here for the night on your own."

"Fine. But, please, stop moving!"

"Sorry. Spider forms aren't really my favorite."

Maline frowned. "You mean you done others before?"

"Oh, yes. Quite a few."

Maline shook her head as she smiled. "And here thought you were just a shopkeeper."

"Even shopkeepers have past lives, my dear."

Slowly, Maline's face fell as she stared down the street.

"Yes, suppose they do," she replied softly.

"Maline…?"

Taking a deep breath, Maline forced a smile.

"Nothing it's…something a friend used to say, every street rat used to be somebody."

"I…" Mardaley began, but his voice failed him. Just then, Maline sat up as she stared deep into the shadows.

"What is it?" Mardaley asked.

But Maline kept her peace, her gaze piercing the darkness. Finally, she smiled.

"They're here."

"Is there anyone else around?"

"Uh… don't see anyone else."

"Good," Mardaley replied, and began crawling out of Maline's hair.

"You see? I told you she can't see us," Thane whispered smugly.

"You weren't saying that when she was staring this way," Neremi whispered in response.

"Quiet, you two!" hissed Durlin. "They'll hear us!"

"And our glorious leader is to be nowhere to be seen," Thane growled.

"He said he'll be here," whispered Eldred, "so he'll be here."

"Of course, he will."

"Yes, Thane," Thalas whispered in response as he swam to view behind his friends. "I will."

"Thalas!" Neremi exclaimed. "What kept you?"

"Father," he replied simply. "What do we have?"

"We have the child, the girl, your brother and their gutter rat friend," Thane replied before turning to sneer at Thalas. "And I still do not see a void sphere."

Thalas stared cooly at Thane for a brief spell before staring past him to the Halls of Justice, his ire straining on its leash.

"I don't have it with me."

"I can see that."

"Oh, for the love of the gods, Thane, enough!" Neremi demanded. "You're angry with him, yes, we're aware of that, but your constant sniping and sneering isn't helping anyone!"

"It's alright, Neremi," Thalas said, smiling softly at her before staring calmly at Thane.

"This is a heavily patrolled area. I myself had to get past two separate patrols to get here, and I take it you all had to navigate your way around one or two yourselves. So, do you truly think it will be a good idea to lug a void sphere all the way here?

Where a patrol can walk by at any time and sound the alarm? Truly?"

Thane held his peace, but it was clear Thalas' words had struck home.

"The void sphere is close, but we will not be carrying it to the Kin-Slayer, we will lead her to it."

Thane glared at Thalas for a spell longer before turning his gaze to their quarry.

"So, what's the plan, then?" he asked at last.

"The girl is the key. With her as bait, we…"

But his words died in his throat as, before their very eyes, Mardaley Templeton appeared as if from the ether.

"Where'd *he* come from?" Eldred whispered, his confusion mirrored perfectly in the gaze of his friends.

"No matter," Durlin replied, his gaze as cold as his words. "He interferes, he dies."

"No," Thane replied, his smile matching Durlin's mood. "He dies anyway. Can't have him telling on us, can we?"

As one, both turned to Thalas, expecting him to be in accord.

"Thalas?" Durlin asked after a short spell.

"What is it now?" Thane demanded.

At their words, Neremi and Eldred turned to Thalas. He stared at them all in turn. There was fear in his eyes.

"We will not do this tonight."

"What?" Thane demanded.

"What do you mean, not tonight?" Neremi asked, throwing a heated glare at Thane as she spoke.

"There's more to that human than meets the eye. Any plan we decide on will be fraught enough as it is. With him here, it'll end badly for us."

Shaking his head, Thane laughed at Thalas.

"He's one human," Durlin said, "we're five Mage Adepts trained in the Shimmering Tower. And you truly wish to walk away?"

Thalas stared at Durlin. "Durlin, to go out there now will be folly."

"Do you truly mean to tell me you're afraid of some decrepit human storekeeper?" Thane asked in a most condescending tone. "Truly, Thalas?"

Thalas glared at the large elf, his anger straining greatly on its leash. "My father is one of the Shimmering Tower's foremost battle-mages. His arcane skill in battle is unquestioned."

"It's not your fath—"

"And yet, that decrepit human storekeeper gives him pause. He gives my father pause, Thane. But if you somehow think your training in the Tower makes you a much better battle-mage than my father, please, by all means, go out there and challenge him. When he's done with you, we'll be sure to give you a proper burial."

Frowning, Thane looked from Thalas to Mardaley and back again.

"Him?"

"Yes, him."

Thane looked once more at Mardaley.

"And another thing," Thalas continued. "I have had quite enough of you. I am sorry Fallon died. But dear gods, man, he was my friend before he was yours! And *I* got him killed! Do you not think I feel his loss? Or do you somehow think you are the only one here who cares for his loss?"

"He was my brother before he was your friend," Durlin added as he held Thalas in cold regard. Thalas looked from Durlin to Thane. What he saw unnerved and angered him in equal measure.

"If any here feel I no longer deserve to lead, speak now," he said after a spell.

In response, Durlin looked expectantly at Thane, but Thane merely stared at Thalas. None else moved.

"You lead, Thalas," Thane said. "For now."

"And what is that supposed to mean?" Neremi demanded.

"It means precisely what it sounds like," Thane snarled.

"Are we done fighting?" Eldred asked in disgust. "Can we go back to why we're here?"

Thalas looked from him to their quarry. "What are they saying?"

"And we've been wandering the city since," Marshalla said as both Maline and Mardaley stared at her.

"That's quite a tale," Mardaley said after a spell. "You three have had quite an adventure."

All three smiled.

"Adventure is putting it mildly," Davian replied.

Laughing, Mardaley patted the little boy on the shoulder.

"I'm sure it is." He smiled before lifting his gaze to Marshalla's, his smile fading as he did so.

"But now you must leave," he continued, the sadness in his words heavy upon all who heard.

"Going to come back," Tip said cheerily.

Forcing a grin, Mardaley reached out and ruffled little Tip's hair before turning his gaze back at Marshalla. Through it all, she'd stared at him with saddened eyes.

"Going to miss you, Mardaley," she said softly.

With a deep breath, Mardaley stared at her. They gazed at each other for a brief moment with eyes that spoke volumes, far more than mere words could convey. It was a moment that ended when Mardaley gently caressed her cheek, an act that brought a smile to Marshalla's lips. Then, Mardaley looked at the others before sitting on the ground and crossing his legs.

"Now, what do you need? What's stopping you from leaving?"

Sighing, Marshalla too sat down, the others following suit.

"Well," she began, "gates all bad now. Tried the north and west ones, same thing."

"Bad how?" Maline asked.

"Guards, lots of them. Never seen so many in one place before. Half of them mages, the other half anything from rangers to proper soldiers. And then there's the fairies. Saw seven at both gates."

"Hrm, that *is* bad," Mardaley muttered as he stroked his beard distractedly.

"Bad how?"

Mardaley looked over at Maline. "Fairies are natural scryers. They can see past almost any illusion or transformation spell. It takes a truly powerful one to fool a fairy, and the older the fairy, the more powerful a spell you will need."

Marshalla nodded. "Same thing Ani said. Said she couldn't sneak us past without the fairies seeing, she was too weak."

"But," Maline said, frowning, "how come the ones in those patrols didn't see you?"

Mardaley smiled. "I was inside your hair, Maline, not in plain sight."

"That would stop them?" Davian asked.

Smiling still, Mardaley turned to Davian. "Of course, but we digress," he said, and before the little boy could reply, he turned to Marshalla.

"You were saying?"

"Right… uh… thought about flying over the wall, but that won't work either."

"Why?" Maline asked. "More fairies?"

Marshalla nodded. "And archers, and mages, lots of them. No way we'd go very high before they saw us, and once they did, Ani didn't fancy our chances before one of us got shot down dead."

"Oh," Maline said.

"This is a conundrum, isn't it?" Mardaley muttered, stroking his beard once more.

"That it is." Davian nodded, the others staring expectantly at Mardaley.

At last, he stared at Marshalla.

"The fairies are the problem. With them in tow, you won't be able to get past any of the guards with any form of illusion. But at the same time, they're your answer."

"Oh?"

Mardaley nodded. "The guards will be too reliant on them. If we can find a way to blind them, or separate them from the guards, you should be able to slip past."

"How do we do that?" Davian asked. "You don't expect us to kill them, do you?"

"What?" Tip exclaimed. "No!"

Mardaley chuckled. "No, no killing. No, what we need is to contrive a situation where the fairies will be reluctant or unable to accompany the guards." Mardaley fell silent once more, the others staring intently at him.

"What we need," he said once again, "is cold iron, lots of it. The purer the better."

"Oh, of course!" Davian exclaimed, before immediately frowning at Mardaley. "Wait, you just said no killing."

"There won't be. But if we can get cold iron, truly pure cold iron, and lots of it, get it into a…"

All at once, Mardaley's eyes lit up. He looked up at Marshalla once more. "Where are you staying?"

Marshalla shrugged at him. "Anywhere. Need to keep moving."

"Right, of course…" Mardaley muttered. "Can you get to the Oaken Square market?"

Marshalla frowned at him. "By when…?"

"Noon-chime tomorrow."

"Noon-chime?" Marshalla exclaimed.

"Yes, noon-chime."

"But that down by the south gate!"

"Can you get there by noon-chime though?"

"But…" Marshalla stared at the others. "… suppose so, yes. Will have to travel most of the night."

Mardaley smiled. "Good. By noon-chime tomorrow, look for a single cart carrying items of cold iron. Pans, kettles, and the like. The cart will be driven by a human. He'll have a green cloak, long black hair and a scar about his neck. Let him see you. He will hide you within, under the cold iron. Once inside, cloak yourselves with the best illusions you can. The cold iron above you should keep the fairies away, and your illusions should do the rest. Ride with him till the end of his journey. He'll take you somewhere safe. You must stay there until we send word that you can return, but you must do everything he tells you, always. Do you understand?"

Silently, all three stared at Mardaley with a mix of wonder and bewilderment.

"Do you understand?"

Smiling, Marshalla nodded.

"Father always said you were more than just a storekeeper," Davian said.

Mardaley smiled, but it was Maline who answered him.

"Even storekeepers have past lives."

Smiling still, Mardaley stared at her briefly.

"Now, go," he continued as he rose. "We've been here far too long. A patrol should be about here soon. Go, and be safe."

"Yes, we'd better," Davian replied, while the others simply nodded. But as they turned to leave, Mardaley reached out to Marshalla.

"Marsha…" he began.

"Yes?"

Mardaley looked at the boys, then back at Marshalla. Reading his gaze, Marshalla turned to the others.

"Go wait for me at the bottom."

Nodding, the two made their way down the stairs as Marshalla stared back at Mardaley.

"What?"

"Here," Mardaley said, reaching into his tunic and pulling out a purse.

"Got coin already," Marshalla said, shaking her head as she spoke.

"Take it, you can never have too much."

Pouting, Marshalla took it from him. As she did so, Mardaley stared briefly over her shoulder before staring back at her.

"There's a small pouch in there," he whispered. "It contains sleeping powder. In Anieszirel's current state, she cannot make Tip do anything without his consent. If you feel she is forcing him towards doing something he mustn't, use the powder on him. It will send him into a deep slumber even she won't be able to rouse him from. But it must be while he is in control."

Marshalla looked up at him. He held her in a fierce gaze.

"Use it with care," he continued. "You don't want that creature turning Tip against you."

Looking down at the purse, she slowly clasped her fingers tighter about it before putting it away. She looked up once again at Mardaley, and without warning, threw her arms about him, hugging him with all her strength before turning and racing down the steps. Mardaley watched them leave in silence.

"They'll be fine, won't they?" Maline asked, wincing as she spoke.

Mardaley sighed. "I pray so." Finally, he turned to her, smiling. "Time you, too, were away."

Maline smiled, nodding. "Yes, suppose."

"Do you have a place for the night?"

Maline shrugged. "Not yet."

"I have a spare bed."

Maline slowly cocked her head at him.

"Thank you," she said softly. Nodding, Mardaley crooked his arm for her, and hand in arm, both left the Halls of Justice.

"Are you sure that's what he said?" Thane growled at Eldred.

"When have you ever known Eldred to read lips wrong?" Neremi glowered at Thane.

"I'm just asking," Thane muttered.

"I am sure, Thane," Eldred replied with no small hint of injured pride.

"So, what do we do about it?" Durlin asked, staring at Thalas.

Frowning, Thalas stared at Mardaley and Maline as they disappeared into the distance before turning to his companions.

"We go home, all of us. I need time to think, form a plan. When I get home, I'll seek out to you all." Then he shook his head, smiling to himself.

"Sleeping powder... I can't believe we didn't think of that."

"Yes," Neremi replied, chuckling. "Such a simple idea too."

"Yes," he replied, staring at her as he nodded. Then he turned to the others.

"Head home, we'll talk later." And without pause, Thalas spun round and began making his own way home, his mind awhirl.

*****

It was the unmistakable sound of metal upon stone that roused Anieszirel. It was faint, distant, but it was getting louder.

"*Tip.*"

No answer.

"*Tip, wake up.*"

Still no answer.

"*Come, Tip, wake up!*"

Snorting slightly, Tip stirred and mumbled.

"*We have to go! Now!*"

"Just a little bit more, Marsha. Just a little."

"*No, Tip, we have to go! Now!*"

Moaning angrily, Tip raised his head, rubbing his eyes with the back of his hand. But just as he was about to yawn, voices drifted to his ears, banishing all vestiges of sleep from them. Rising to his knees, he shook Marshalla to waking, then Davian.

"Someone's coming," he whispered.

Rising to her knees, Marshalla looked at the stable doors before glancing back at Tip.

"Time to go," she whispered before hurrying over to the stack of hay behind them.

"Help me," Marshalla whispered, gesturing to the pair.

Before long, they'd moved the stack far enough away from the wall to allow them squeeze behind it and out of the hole Anieszirel had made in the stone wall the night before. As Marshalla shuffled back from the stack though, the stable door creaked open.

"Hurry!" Marshalla exclaimed, but she needn't have bothered, for Davian was already scurrying out of the hole, Tip close behind, and by the time the stable owner and the patrol guards had all entered the stables, Marshalla too was out of the hole, bag in hand, pulling the hay stack back to as it was.

"Quick, this way," Marshalla whispered once they were outside, and with great care, all three snuck away from the stable. Once far enough away, Marshalla pulled them into the shadow of a nearby doorway.

"Think they saw us?" Tip whispered nervously.

Shaking her head, Marshalla smiled at him before going on one knee, opening the bag in her hand.

"At least we got some sleep this time," Davian said as he too opened his bag. As he did so, Marshalla rose, pulling out two hooded cloaks. Checking their sizes, she offered one to Tip before donning hers. She looked over at Davian. He'd already donned his, along with his bag.

"Wish we didn't have to steal all of this," Tip muttered miserably as he did up the clasp of his cloak.

Marshalla stared at him as a sad smile parted her lips.

"Come," she said, pulling Tip's hood up. "Still have a long way to go."

Pulling on her bag and pulling up her own hood, she slipped her hands into Tip's and Davian's and with them in tow, set forth once more. It was still quite early, dawn was only just breaking, but they were still quite some way away from the Oaken Square, and gods only knew what path the patrols would force them take. They travelled in silence, each lost in their own thoughts, each worried that the next corner would spell their end. It was a fear they'd all carried since their escape from the Grovemender home. It was a fear all wished to be done away with. And it was a fear that had taken its greatest toll on the tiniest of the three.

"Will you stop fretting? We're safe now."

"Not fretting," Tip thought in response.

"You're fretting, and I tell you we are safe."

"You okay, Tip?"

Tip looked up at Marshalla.

"Fine," he mumbled before dropping his gaze.

"I do wish you didn't do things like that. She truly will think I'm turning you against her."

Frowning, Tip kept his head down as he bit his lower lip. The kinship that had formed between he and Anieszirel was one that filled him with shame and guilt, but was one he welcomed, nonetheless.

"Just easier to talk to you than to Marsha sometimes."

"I appreciate that, Tip, but she is your friend. She's been looking after you far longer than I have."

"Marsha still my friend."

"Not if you keep being rude to her like that."

"Was not!"

"Tip, you were, it's—hold, someone comes."

"Someone's coming," Tip whispered as he came to a dead stop, pulling Marshalla gently back as he did so.

Darting back into the shadows, Marshalla pulled Davian and Tip with her as they waited in silence. A group of merchants walked past, laden with wares.

"Merchants," she whispered, breathing a sigh of relief as she spoke.

"*Not them.*"

"Not them," Tip whispered.

But it was too late, for Marshalla had already stepped out of the shadows. And it was at that moment that a ranger appeared, a fairy perched upon his shoulder. At the sight of him, all three froze, their hearts in their throats.

"Hello, kind sirs!" the ranger called out to the merchants, his back to them as he took a few paces towards the merchants.

"What do we do?" Davian hissed.

"Might I trouble you for a moment?"

"We got to go back!" Tip whispered.

"Can't!" Marshalla whispered. "It'll take too long to go around."

The ranger had stopped walking.

"We hide in the shadows till they leave, then," Davian whispered. But Marshalla shook her head.

"No time," she whispered. "Come."

"No!" Davian and Tip cried in unison.

"Come! Hurry!"

Dragging the others, Marshalla hurried towards the ranger.

"*What in the hells is she doing?*"

Slowing to a crawl, all three snuck round behind the ranger before turning round the corner he'd appeared from. But as they did so, the silhouette of the ranger's companions came into view a few paces before them, and began heading towards them. At their sight, both Tip and Davian came to a sudden halt as their fear held them rigid. Except, Marshalla refused to be cowed, even by her own fear, and with her head bowed low, she dragged the two boys behind her, pulling them round a nearby corner. But it was not until they'd made three more turnings before Marshalla finally slowed her pace and loosened her grip. Leaning on a nearby wall, she looked down at the pair.

"You two okay?" she asked.

Both boys nodded.

"I thought we were done for," Davian muttered, his voice trembling greatly.

"Me too," Marshalla replied. Taking a deep breath, she looked about them, as if trying to get her bearings.

"Come," she said at last, slipping her hands into theirs before setting off once more.

"*I'll give her this, your friend has courage.*"

"She's crazy," Tip thought, smiling.

"Ha! Crazy in a good way!"

"Yeah!"

"Ask her how much farther."

"How much farther, Marsha?" Tip asked.

Marshalla looked down at Tip. "Still a bit of a trek, but think we'll make it by noon-chime. So long as no more surprises on the way."

"We'll make it, won't we, Marsha?" Davian piped up.

Marshalla turned to him.

"We'll get out, won't we?"

Marshalla smiled at Davian, but Tip could see it was forced. "Yeah! Mardaley's friend already waiting for us. Be there and gone before you know it."

Davian smiled, nodding as he did so, but his smile was just as wooden.

"We will make it, Tip. You just watch."

"Marsha doesn't think so."

"She does, she's just scared. Like you."

"Scared, Marsha?" Tip asked.

Marshalla looked down at Tip, a ready answer on her lips, but as she stared into his eyes, she paused.

"Yeah," she said. "Very."

"Told you."

"But Mardaley's always looked out for us, he's always helped us. His friend'll get us out, Tip, he will. He's got to."

Tip stared at his dear friend for a spell.

"We'll make it," he said at last, his face set.

"Yes." Davian nodded, his voice resolute. "We *will* make it."

"Yeah," Marshalla said, smiling warmly as she breathed deep. "Yeah, we will." She turned to Davian, picking up the pace as she did so.

"So, what you doing first when we safe?"

"A bath!" the little elf exclaimed. "I haven't had one in five days!"

"Ha!" Marshalla exclaimed. "Yeah, a bath would... wait, what you mean, five? We only been hiding three days."

"Uh..."

Marshalla looked from him to Tip, who was glaring at Davian.

"Tip...?"

Tip looked at her with a sheepish grin before turning his gaze forward.

"Unbelievable! And all that splashing noise?"

Neither boy spoke.

"Unbelievable!"

Abruptly, little Davian giggled, casting a cheeky sideways glance at her as he did so.

"Not funny," she snarled, but Davian's laughter soon spread to Tip.

"Said it's not funny!"

Neither boy paid her any heed, and before long, their infectious laughter spread to Marshalla herself, and with their mood lightened, they hastened their steps. As they walked, they soon fell into banter in hushed tones, one punctuated by the odd warning from Anieszirel. It was banter that had the boys so engrossed that that when Marshalla abruptly stopped, both boys very nearly pulled her off her feet.

"What is it, Marsha?" Davian whispered as he stared in the direction of Marshalla's gaze.

"Think that the South Gate Tavern," she said, gesturing at the building at the entrance of the alley they were in. She looked down at the boys. Their confusion was plain.

"It's at the edge of Oaken Square market."

All at once, both Davian and Tip's eyes widened as her words sunk in.

"We're almost there!" Davian whispered.

"Come on, then!" Tip exclaimed as he tugged at Marshalla's hand. Laughing, Marshalla obliged, and soon all three were racing for the alley's entrance. But as they reached it, all three stopped. Marshalla and Davian looked at Tip. Nodding, Tip stared into the ether.

"Ani?" he thought.

"There's a lot of people out there, Tip. I can't tell how many are guards."

Tip looked at the others. "Lots of people out there. Ani can't tell how many guards."

Frowning, Marshalla stared skywards.

"Not surprised," she muttered, "it'll be noon soon."

Gesturing for the others to move deeper into the alley's shadows, Marshalla rested against the tavern wall and carefully peered out.

"Well?" Davian whispered after a spell.

Marshalla turned to them. Her eyes were aflame as she struggled to keep a smile from her lips.

"Well, got good news and bad news. Which one first?"

"Bad news," Davian said.

"Good news," said Tip. Davian looked at Tip, his eyes speaking volumes.

"Bad news," Tip corrected.

"I see two patrols out there."

As one, both faces fell.

"Good news," Marshalla continued, "they're on the other side of the market now, and Mardaley's friend is here."

As one, both faces lit up as they hopped with barely contained joy.

"But first," Marshalla hurriedly added, reaching out to calm the boys, "got to get past the market people, get past without any of them seeing us and calling the guards."

"Ani can hide us easy!" Tip exclaimed.

Marshalla shook her head. "The fairies, Tip, remember what we said. Easier for us to dodge if they see three people in plain sight than three people hiding. No, we got to do this stealth-like."

"Stealth-like?" Davian asked.

"Yeah, stealth-like."

"Is that even a word?"

Marshalla shrugged. "Know what it means?"

"Well, yes, but—"

"Then it's a word."

"No, but... ugh, fine."

"So, this is what we do. Saw lots there with hoods up, so we won't look funny with ours up." As she spoke, Marshalla raised the hood of her cloak over her head. Nodding, both boys did the same.

"Good. Now, keep your heads down, walk normal and don't look at nobody. We go round this side and get to Mardaley's friend. We go close to him, let him see us. Okay?"

Meekly, both nodded. Marshalla could sense their fear. Smiling, she knelt and pulled both boys closer.

"Almost there. Okay? Almost there."

Both boys looked at each other, before nodding once again at her.

"Okay," Marshalla sighed and, rising, slipped her hands into theirs. With a deep breath she finally stepped out of the alleyway, her head bowed slightly.

They walked on in silence, the three. With his head bowed, Tip couldn't see much, save what lay before his feet.

"*It's alright Tip, it's quite alright.*"

"Scared, Ani," he thought.

"*It's alright. Just breathe, breathe and trust in Marsha. We're almost free.*"

It felt like an eternity, but Tip kept his head resolutely bowed and focused his mind on his feet, on his walking. One foot after the other, one after the other. At last, Marshalla stopped. With his heart in his mouth, Tip dared to raise his head just a smidgeon. They were standing before a cart, before a man whose back was to them. Before him was a basket filled with odds and ends made of iron. And he wore a green cloak.

"It's him!" he thought excitedly.

"*Yes, I do believe it is!*"

With the greatest of care, Tip looked up at Marshalla. She was staring intently at the man. Tip looked back at him. He seemed not to have noticed them. As he stared,

Marshalla took a few measured steps forward till they stood right behind him. Stopping, she coughed politely. As she did so, the man straightened. But as he spun round, a white haze blurred Tip's vision as he breathed deep of the powder that had been flung in his face. Groggily, he looked up at Marshalla.

"Marsha?" he said softly before crumpling to the earth as he fell into a deep sleep, his hood slipping off his head.

"Tip!" Marshalla shrieked as she grabbed hold of Tip.

"Quiet!" Thane snarled as he jabbed a dagger at Marshalla's side.

Marshalla stood stock still as she stared down at the blade, Tip hanging awkwardly from her hands. With mounting rage, she watched as four of the merchants milling around came over to them. Most of the faces she did not recognize, but one was unmistakable. She looked over at Davian. His eyes burned with the same rage coursing through her.

"Nicely done," Durlin said as he reached them, nodding at Thane as he spoke.

"Of course," Thane replied, a smug smile upon his lips.

"Ever the humble one, eh, Thane?" Neremi asked smiling.

"Just being honest."

All eyes fell upon the last to join. His eyes in turn were upon Davian.

"Hello, Davian," Thalas said at last. "You gave us quite the fright, I must say, running off with scum like that. Whatever were you thinking?"

"They're not scum, you are," Davian snarled in response. Thalas laughed.

"You won't be laughing once I tell everyone you were the one who attacked us in the library."

Thalas' laughter died in his throat as he stared at his brother.

"Davian," Thalas began, his tone as cold as his gaze, "we were nowhere near the library, and if you so much as—"

"I know your gait, Thalas, I know it! And yours, Neremi! It was you! It was you, Thalas, who tried to kill Ma—"

With a string of incantations, Thalas called forth a void within Davian's throat, silencing him.

"The little bastard knows it was us," Eldred said, his fear apparent. "You think he'll tell?"

"Look at him," Durlin said. "You think he won't?"

"He's your brother, Thalas," Thane said, an evil smile upon his lips. "You'll have to take care of him."

Thalas stared from brother to friend, his tongue stilled.

"You wish to borrow my blade to do it?"

"No!" Marshalla exclaimed, an act that earned her a curt blow to the back of her head. Furtively, the others looked about them. Some of the other merchants were staring at them.

"Let's move," Thalas said. "We have what we came for." Grabbing Davian's arm, Thalas turned to head deeper into Merethia.

"Don't change the sub—"

"People are staring at us, Thane!" Neremi hissed as she followed Thalas.

Angrily, Thane looked at Marshalla.

"Pick him up and let's go,"

Holding Thane in a heartfelt glare, Marshalla did as she was bid, wrapping Tip's limp arms about her neck as she carried him, and, with the blade at her side still, fell in behind the others, Thane and Durlin coming up behind her, the latter pulling Tip's hood back down over his head. They walked on in silence till they were clear of the market place, then without warning, Thalas slammed Davian into a nearby wall, pinning him to it. As he held his little brother in place, Thalas undid the void, granting Davian speech once more.

"Now, I need you to listen very carefully, Davian," Thalas said in a deceptively calm voice. "Whatever it is you think you know, you are going to forget it, and forget it right now. Do you know why?"

"I'm not—"

"Because you and Tip are the only ones we need. Do you know what that means?"

"Don't threaten m—"

"It means, my dear brother, that I will kill your dear friend Marsha over there, should you tell anyone anything about what happened in the library. Do you understand? And I won't kill her quickly, oh no. We're going to enjoy her first. We are going to take turns on her, Davian, all of us. And when we've had our fill, we will set her aflame. And through it all, she will be aware, Davian, she will experience it all with all her senses heightened."

Davian looked guiltily at Marshalla.

"So, if you care for her," Thalas continued, "you will keep your little mouth shut. Do you understand?"

Davian stared at her still, tears stinging his eyes. Marshalla smiled back at him.

"It's okay," she mouthed.

Thalas shook him abruptly forcing the boy's gaze back upon him. "Do you understand?"

Meekly, Davian nodded.

"I did not give you back your voice so you can nod at me," Thalas snarled. "Do. You. Understand?"

"Yes."

"Good."

"That's going to keep him quiet?"

Thalas looked over at Thane. "He's a Grovemender, Thane. If he dies, half of Merethia will hunt you down."

"Not if he dies by your hand."

Thalas smiled at his friend. It was a smile with no warmth within it. "Do you truly believe my dear father will let the world think one of his sons killed the other?"

Thane stared at Thalas for a spell, his gaze darkening with each passing moment. Smirking, Thalas turned and continued walking, the others eventually falling in step. They walked on in silence, but Marshalla's mind was awhirl. This couldn't be the end, there must be a way out of this. But what? What could she do? Marshalla chanced a glance behind her. Were she without Tip, she might've been able to dash between Thane and Durlin. But she couldn't leave Tip, she could never do that. But still, she had to do something, anything, and do it fast before—

Stopping, Marshalla's heart sank as the noon-chime rang loudly out about them.

"Keep moving," Thane ordered gruffly, shoving her hard as he spoke.

"Oh, don't be so hard on her, Thane," Neremi said with a smug smile, "she's merely thinking of her human friend."

"You mean the one we had the peacekeepers move away from the marketplace?" Eldred asked, his tone mirroring Neremi's perfectly.

"The very same," Durlin added. "Though by now they've probably sent him on his merry way out of Merethia." At this, all five friends burst into laughter.

Marshalla glared at them with all she could muster. She glared at them with all her anger, all her hate and frustration. She glared at them with all her strength. But in the end, she could do nothing save glare. And at last, when she had no strength left for even that, she relented and continued her march to her doom, her head bowed low and her heart broken.

They walked on in silence, for how long Marshalla neither knew nor cared, but they soon came across a patrol. At their sight, tears stung her eyes. Fighting back the tears, she turned to glare at Thalas, but as she stared at him, she watched him throw a furtive glance at Davian.

"Remember, your friend dies if you speak ill of us," Thalas snarled before pulling Davian's hood even lower.

Frowning, Marshalla stared hard at him. Why would he not want to hand them over? Was the reward not worth it? As the questions echoed in her mind, she chanced to look upon Davian. It was then she noticed his slouch had begun to fade, and as she stared, she watched as he slowly began walking taller and taller till he walked with his back ramrod straight. A slow smile parted Marshalla's lips at this. She knew him, she knew what that simple gesture meant. He was about to do something naughty, something incredibly naughty. Taking a deep breath, she adjusted her grip on Tip. Whatever Davian was planning, she had to be ready.

It was not until the patrol was indeed close enough to see them clearly that Davian put his plan in motion. As the patrol captain nodded a greeting at Thalas, Davian suddenly called forth a ball of flame in either hand, hurling one into his brother's face and the other into Eldred's before barreling into Neremi as she stood on the other side of him, forcing her off her feet.

"Halt!" the patrol captain barked.

Grinning, Marshalla spun round ready to charge into the two behind her, but as she did so, she felt Thane's heavy hand upon her shoulder, and as she looked up at him she saw his blade from the corner of her eye, and could only watch as he rammed the blade with all his might into her side. Marshalla winced the moment she felt the blade's tip touch her tunic, but that was as far as it went. Confused, both Thane and Marshalla stared at each other for a moment, but before Thane could try again, Marshalla sprang up at him, slamming her head against his nose with all she had. The sound of crushing cartilage was such sweet music to her ears, as was his pained howl. Before she could do more, however, a small hand gripped her elbow tightly, pulling her away from Thane, and as one, both Marshalla and Davian charged down the street, a chorus of angry shouts following close behind them as Davian hurriedly cast a haste spell on the both of them.

"This way!" Marshalla yelled as she dove into a nearby alleyway.

"Are you sure?" Davian exclaimed as he raced on behind her.

"Yes! Don't know, maybe."

"*Maybe?*"

"Yes, maybe!"

"We had a straight run back to the market place back there!"

"Yes, and the blasted patrols in there too! Come on!"

They raced desperately on, but even as they ran, their pace gradually slowed. It was Marshalla, her arms were getting tired, and her lungs burned with an unquenchable fire.

"Marsha, come on!" Davian exclaimed when their pace slowed to a near crawl.

"Trying, but…Tip's heavy."

"What? Oh!" Grabbing Marshalla's arms, and closing his eyes, Davian whispered words of arcane under his breath. As he finished, Marshalla felt Tip's weight drop to little more than a feather. She looked down at Davian, who smiled cheekily at her.

"One of my tutors taught me that, so I could carry all my study books with me."

Marshalla smiled at him, but before she could speak, angry voices drifted to their ears.

"Come on," she said instead, and raced on.

"Where are we going though?" Davian asked as he raced on behind her.

"South gate," she replied, darting between the people in their path.

"Oh. Oh!"

"Yes! Now, hurry!"

They raced on in silence. Their lungs burned and their hearts drummed loudly in their ears, but they raced on. Even as those about them stared and pointed, even as those they darted past muttered and glowered, they raced on, oblivious to all things save one. And at last, as they turned yet another corner, both stopped and laughed euphorically as before them lay a queue of merchants. It could mean only one thing.

"Quick," Marshalla said hoarsely, and together they hurried to the end of the side street they were in. Staying in the shadows, Marshalla peered out into the main street as Davian cancelled his haste spell. As she expected, the south gate lay at the end of it, and with her heart in her mouth, she scanned the merchants' queue. It was not long before her gaze fell upon Mardaley's friend, and while the sight of him filled her heart with joy, the joy was short-lived. She slid back into the shadows, looking at Davian.

"What is it?" Davian asked worriedly.

"He's already at the gate," Marshalla said. Davian's eyes grew wide. "They're checking his cart next."

"We have to do something!"

Marshalla tried to speak, but no words came forth.

"Don't know what to do here," she said at last. The fear in Davian's eyes broke her heart.

"We need to distract them somehow," Marshalla added hurriedly. "But there's lots of them there, and we got nobody we can call or shout at and—"

At that moment, the voices of their pursuers drifted to their ears.

"Gods, they're almost here."

Driven by sheer desperation, Davian peered out into the street. The gate guards were waving the merchant before Mardaley's friend through.

"It can't end like this," he said as the voices got louder.

"It can't end like this!" he repeated as he scanned for something, anything.

"Wait!" Marshalla whispered fiercely as she pulled him back. "Look! Over there!"

Davian turned to what Marshala was pointing at. It was a large cart further behind in the merchants' queue, laden with bales of tightly packed hay. He looked at her.

"Burn it!"

"What?"

"Look, look! It's between that wine merchant and that oil merchant. Burn the hay, they'll have to come put the fire out if they want to stop the whole place going up!"

Davian looked from her to the cart. "It's far though. Never thrown one that far before."

The voices were getting louder, their pursuers were almost upon them.

"Davian, please, try."

"They won't all come."

"Just try!"

"But—"

"We don't have time! Please, just try!"

Swallowing hard, Davian wiped his hands on his cloak before, parting his hands slightly, called forth a ball of flame. Anxious, Marshalla stared at the ball as it slowly grew before staring behind them once more. As she stared back at Davian though, he hurled the flame at the cart. With a gasp, Marshalla watched as the ball charted a beautiful arc through the air before landing upon the bales, bursting as it landed, and in one moment, much of the hay came aflame at once, the cries from the merchants about the burning cart filling the air rapidly.

"You did it!" Marshalla exclaimed.

"I did it!" Davian exclaimed in disbelief.

"They did that!" shouted those about them.

Marshalla winced, then turned to Davian.

"Go! Quick!" she exclaimed. "Go!"

As one, both hurried out into the main street, into the gathering crowd, hugging the merchants' queue as tightly as they dared as they snaked their way towards their salvation. But as they neared the front of the queue, both soon realized Davian had been right. Not all the guards had left to douse the flames, and from where the remaining three stood, there was no way they would be able to get any closer without being seen. Davian looked at Marshalla, but as she looked down at him, his eyes lit up.

"I know!" he whispered. "Kel!"

Confused, Marshalla watched as Davian summoned his familiar, and as the kelpie answered the call, he hurriedly pointed at the large water barrel that stood near the guardhouse at the side of the south gate.

"Kel, go swim."

The little hippocampus stared at its master in confusion.

"Go swim, Kel."

Again, the little kelpie looked at the water barrel, then back at its master, but stayed where it was.

"Where did they go?" came a cry from behind them.

Marshalla and Davian looked at each other as their faces whitened. Davian looked at his familiar.

"Kel, please, I beg you. Go swim in that barrel. Do it now, please!"

Confused still, the little creature looked at its master before finally breaking into a canter to do as was bid.

"Why would that–" Marshalla began.

"Just watch."

"Whose familiar is that?" one of the south gate guards said as Kel hurried to the barrel. As both Marsha and Davian stared, they watched the guard head over towards the little kelpie. They watched as little Kel stopped right by the water barrel, stare at the top of it, and leap in just as the guard reached it.

"Get out of there! We drink that!"

The other guards were now staring at the barrel.

"Hurry!" Davian whispered, and together both hurried over to the human merchant in the green cloak. As one of the remaining gate guards hurried to the barrel, Marshalla tugged at his cloak. Turning, he took one look at the three of them before quickly opening a side panel in his cart. Words could not describe the elation that washed over Marshalla as she saw the dark opening, and without pause, rolled Tip inside.

"Hurry," she whispered to Davian, helping him in before slipping in herself, with the merchant closing the panel just as the remaining guard at the south gate stared back at him.

"Well?" the merchant demanded.

"Well, what?" the distracted guard snarled before returning his gaze to his comrades.

"Well, can I go now?"

"Not until you've been inspected. Get that damn thing out of the water now! It's going to pollute it, damn it!"

"You've already searched me."

"What? No, we haven't!"

"Yes, you have. Your people back there sent their fairy friends to sniff around my cart when they ran to the fire."

"Nice try. Just grab it by the tail, how hard can that be? Pull it out! Pull. It. Out!"

"Look, I truly must be on my way. If you need to search me again, fine, just hurry up and do it."

"Hurry up, damn you! What did you say?"

"Can't you search me and let me go?"

"I'm not searching you on my own it's—why are you climbing in there? Why in the world do you need to climb in there? How will you climbing in there keep the water pure?"

"Please, just let me—"

"Alright, alright, just go! Just shut up and go!"

And with that, Marshalla, Davian and Tip were finally free.

THE BITE OF BETRAYAL

A nd give my regards to your sons," Mardaley called out as another satisfied customer left his store. Smiling, he turned to Maline.

"Well, I think—" As he spoke, the door opened once more.

"Good afternoon, Master Templeton. May I have a word in private?"

Frowning, Mardaley turned to the utterer.

"Magister Meadowview, good afternoon to you. I don't often see you away from the Tower, is there something you would like procured for the Tower?"

"I'm afraid I'm here in an official capacity. May we talk in private?"

Mardaley looked over at Maline, who was staring at him with a worried frown.

"Mind the store for me please, Maline."

Nodding in response, Maline turned her gaze to the Magister, her frown deepening. Mardaley turned to face him also.

"This way, please," he said as he headed for the back room. Nodding, the Magister followed. It wasn't until both were in the room and Mardaley had completed casting his wards that either one spoke.

"I haven't seen you come in looking this serious in ages, Baern," Mardaley said as he turned to regard his friend. "Is all well?"

Baern stared at Mardaley. "They've fled Merethia."

"Who have?"

"Mardaley," Baern begged, "don't do this, please."

"Do what?"

"This! Whatever you may think of that boy, you can't possibly think helping him escape is a good thing."

Mardaley stared unmoving at Baern for a spell before finally walking over to a nearby chair.

"Baern," he said as he sat, "what precisely is it that makes you think I would allow the Kin-Slayer flee Merethia?"

"There was an incident at the south gate earlier today," Baern replied, his gaze unwavering. "It would appear someone set fire to a merchant's hay cart as it stood in the queue. From local witnesses' testimonies, that someone was none other than little Davian Grovemender."

"Truly?"

"Yes. And with him was Marshalla, carrying your Tip."

"Truly?"

"Yes. They were lost in the crowd, in the commotion that followed, only for Davian's familiar to be seen prancing towards the south gate guards' water barrel and dive straight in."

"Truly?"

"Yes. And as one would expect, the guards at the gate had their hands full dealing with a burning merchant cart and a feisty familiar who was refusing to leave their water supply alone. So much so, in fact, that they would be forgiven for dropping their guard momentarily."

"I don't see how this has anything to do with me."

Baern took a step forward. "At the head of the merchant's queue, when all this happened, was your ranger friend, the one with a scar around his neck from that hanging incident last year. Remember? I forget his name."

"Oh, he was in town, was he?"

"Yes, Mardaley, he was. And what's more, he seemed to have taken up trading in cold iron utensils."

"Has he now? I never would've guessed."

Baern shook his head in exasperation. "Mardaley, it's me you're talking to here. Please, just stop this."

Mardaley stared at Baern in silence for a spell before sighing and, crossing his arms about him, lowered his gaze to his feet.

"Very well," he said at last, looking up at his friend, his words dispelling the charged silence between them. "You have the right of it, I did help them."

"Why?" Baern demanded. "What in the world were you thinking?"

"I was thinking how unfair it would be to end Tip's life over something that wasn't even his fault."

"It would've been for the greater good!"

"Whose greater good, Baern?"

"Everyone's!" Baern exclaimed, staring at his friend with visible frustration. "Or have you forgotten just how vindictive and dangerous Anieszirel is?"

"No, Baern, I haven't forgotten," Mardaley replied with an air of indignation. "But *you* have obviously forgotten how long she was trapped for. In her current state, it'll be months before she can force her will on Tip, and years before she can mount a successful campaign against the Tower. And she'll know that. She won't do anything to lead you or your people to her, so she'll behave herself."

"You think so, do you?"

"I know so. And in that time, I'll have learnt how to separate her from Tip."

"Mardaley, you are not thinking rationally."

"No, Baern, I *am* thinking rationally. What I am *not* doing is thinking coldly. What I am not doing is refusing to accept his life is worth something. I will not do that anymore, and certainly not to Tip."

Baern held Mardaley in a sad, heavy gaze. "I told you this would happen. I told you, you were getting too attached to those two, I warned you. Now look at you."

Mardaley shrugged. "I'm not complaining. I'm going to sleep with a clear conscience after this."

"Is that so?"

Mardaley nodded. "Yes, without a doubt."

"Well, let me tell you something about your darling Tip, something you need to know now more than ever."

Frowning, Mardaley slowly rose, crossing his arms about him.

"Which is?" he asked, his gaze hard upon his friend.

"When he and the others came to the Tower the other day, they managed to steal not one, but *two* runic keys right off their owners."

Mardaley shrugged as he sat back down. "I already told you he was sticky-fingered. Those two obviously forgot to empower their keys' binding chains."

Magister Meadowview shook his head. "No, Mardaley, one of those chains was fully empowered. I inspected it myself."

Mardaley held Baern in a slight sideways glance. "What do you mean?"

"I mean precisely what you heard, my friend. Your Tip stole two runic keys off their owners without breaking or otherwise disturbing the keys' binding chains."

Mardaley's frown deepened. "That's impossible."

"Is it?"

"Baern, he's just a boy."

"Is he now?" Baern took another step forward. "Answer me this as well, old friend. Anieszirel was freed by Tip simply touching the void sphere. Given her weakened state, there was no way she would've been able to release herself without significant aid. So, care to explain precisely how she could have been freed by your little boy simply touching the sphere?"

Mardaley stared at Baern. He couldn't.

"I didn't think so. I know not what's afoot here, Mardaley, but there is something about that boy, an immense power within him, that even *he* is unaware of, I wager. And now that power is within the Kin-Slayer's reach. Do you still think you will be able to sleep well tonight?"

Still, Mardaley kept his silence. Shaking his head, Baern turned on his heels and left. Mardaley watched him leave before staring into the ether. Some moments later, Maline entered. As she entered, Mardaley rose quickly undid his wards, smiling at her throughout.

"What he want?" Maline asked with some trepidation.

"To frighten me."

Maline frowned in confusion.

"They made it, Maline."

"They... Oh!" Maline exclaimed as her hands flew to her lips.

Mardaley's smile grew as he nodded.

"He knows I was involved," Mardaley continued, "but he can't prove it, so he came to scare me, rattle me, see what he could learn."

"What you tell him?"

"Nothing."

"Oh, thank the gods. And thank the gods they made it!"

Just then, the front door chimed as it was opened.

"You'd best get back out there." Mardaley said.

"Yes," Maline replied as she nodded, "yes, okay."

"I'll be out shortly."

"Okay."

But as she turned to leave, she didn't see Mardaley's smile become replaced by a deep worried frown.

Glaring furiously at his companions, Thalas nursed his cheek. Though the unsightly burn upon it had long since been healed, he felt a throb from it nonetheless. But that ache was nothing compared to his anger, an anger that burned brightest whenever his gaze fell upon Thane.

"Half your size, Thane," he muttered at last.

"I'm getting sick of hearing you carry on about her size, Thalas," Eldred glowered.

In response, Thalas turned to fix him with a most heated glare, before turning his gaze back to Thane.

"And still you sit there, staring, pretending not to hear me," Thalas continued.

Thane remained unmoved, his lips twisted into an angry frown.

At last, Thalas shook his head in disgust. "Half your—"

"Why don't you come over here and say that to my face?" Thane snarled abruptly.

"Given how easy it clearly is to put you on your arse, are you sure you should be saying such things?"

As Thane rose to lunge at Thalas, the door swung roughly open as Thuridan marched into his office, slamming the door behind him as he went. As he reached his desk, he looked at Thane.

"Did I give you leave to stand?"

Thane looked from Thuridan to Thalas and back again before finally settling back into his seat.

"Half your size."

In that instant, the red mist descended upon Thane and he lunged at Thalas anew, his chair flying away from him as he did so. But as he sailed towards Thalas, an unseen force slammed into him, one with such great strength as to send him crashing into the nearby wall. A stunned silence fell upon all the others as they stared at Thane lying in a crumpled heap.

"Get off my floor and sit down." Thuridan's tone was calm, but it chilled the hearts of all within nonetheless.

Gingerly, Thane did as he was bid, the fear in his eyes as he stared at Thuridan marched perfectly with the hate in the gaze he held Thalas in once he was sat.

"Now," Thuridan began once Thane was seated. "I would like to know how one street rat, carrying another street rat, who happened to be deep in slumber I might add, was able to best no less than five Shimmering Tower Mage Adepts to this degree."

"Davian aided them," Eldred offered weakly.

In response, Thuridan turned to the cowering elf.

"So… you're claiming the core reason for your defeat was a boy who is considered to be less skilled than a Novice. Is that right?"

"Well…" Eldred began, but faltered. Turning, he looked over at Thalas for strength, only to see Thalas already staring at him, his eyes screaming a clear warning. Swallowing, he looked back at Thuridan.

"No, sir."

"That is not what you're saying."

"No, sir," Eldred repeated, shaking his head.

"Then, what are you saying?"

Again, Eldred looked at Thalas for aid.

"Father, I—" Thalas began, coming to his friend's aid. But Thuridan held up his hand.

"Eldred, I am expecting an answer from you."

"It was my fault, Father."

Thuridan turned a cold gaze at his son. "Your fault."

Gritting his teeth, Thalas nodded.

"So, you're saying it's your fault you friends are less than worthless?"

"Now, hold a moment!" Neremi barked, and though her anger deflated greatly the moment Thuridan turned to her, there was still enough of it to carry her forth.

"They got the better of us, that is true. We made a grave error, we're not disputing that. But you cannot talk to us like this! Our parents are people of import!"

Thuridan chuckled at her. "Truly?"

"Yes!"

"So, tell me, Neremi, if your parents are people of such import, why are you all still in my office? Why have they been unable to bend enough ears to ensure your release?"

Neremi moved to speak, but no words came forth.

"Hmm?"

Silence still. Thuridan leant forward, his gaze fixed on Neremi.

"I'll tell you why. They are all ashamed and afraid. Ashamed to have such worthless failures for children, and afraid of the stain your actions these past few days will have upon their names."

"What actions?" Durlin asked, the barest traces of fear in his voice. Thuridan looked at him.

"You wish to play this game? Truly? Very well. I know it was you, all of you, who went with Fallon to steal the void sphere."

All at once, the others turned to glare at Thalas. Thuridan sighed as he shook his head at them, a smirk dancing on his lips.

"It's truly quite amazing how quickly you turn on each other. No, Thalas didn't tell me. He didn't need to. In fact, had you not all turned to glare at him, I would still be lacking the proof of it."

At his words, all color drained from their faces, all save Thalas.

"But your actions today are the most alarming," Thuridan continued. "You all knew full well we were hunting those two, that the *king's soldiers* were hunting those two, and yet you captured them yourselves and were dragging them to gods only know where. Because of that clear and flagrant disregard for the king's authority, your parents have been forced to plead with him directly for clemency for you."

"You're not pleading for Thalas, though, are you?" Thane growled. "Why does he get pardoned and we don't."

Thuridan stared at him. "Who said he was pardoned?" Then he carried his gaze across them all. "You have all been granted temporary clemency. That you were able to subdue the boy is the only reason you are here, and not rotting in a dungeon somewhere. There are many who believe such resourcefulness should be exploited rather than discarded."

Thalas and Thuridan both watched as the others visibly relaxed.

"And so, now you answer to me," Thuridan continued. "In truth, I highly doubt it was you who put the boy to sleep, but the two eye-witnesses at the market were quite adamant he fell into the girl's hands after one of you threw something in his face. But, be that as it may, we are where we are."

Sighing, Thuridan leant back into his chair. "You are going to tell me all that you know, all that you have learnt, and you will leave nothing out. And when you are done, I will tell you what you are going to do to rectify things. Do you understand?"

Slowly, one by one, they nodded at Thuridan.

"Good. So, who speaks first."

As one, the others stared at Thalas.

Smirking, Thuridan looked at his son. "Begin."

*****

Yawning, Marshalla stretched her arms upwards as sleep faded from her eyes. But as it faded, her memories returned, and, with a start, she sprang to sitting as her eyes scanned her surrounds.

"Tip?" she whispered as she stared at the simple furnishings about her. No Tip. She was all alone.

"Tip?" she called out a little louder. No response.

"Davian?"

Still no response. Frowning, Marshalla swung her feet off the bed and slowly rose. She was still wearing her old clothing, and as she looked down, she noticed her boots placed neatly beside her bed. Frowning, she reached into one of her pockets. No, she hadn't been robbed. Frowning still, Marshalla sat back down and slipped on her boots before making her way to the door. Gingerly, she listened at the door. She could just about make out the sound of laughter, but it was faint. Taking a deep breath, she opened the door and stepped out. Before her was a staircase that wound downwards.

"Tip?" she called out again. Still no response. Taking another deep breath, she descended the stairs, but with such great care, and with each sound she made seeming a thousand times louder.

"Tip?" she called out as she reached the bottom of the stairs. "Davian?"

To her left was a kitchen of sorts, and as the stared, a shadow flittered across the entrance. From the size of the shadow, it was clear something small was hiding within. Shaking her head, Marshalla sighed as she marched towards the kitchen.

"Not in the mood, you two," she said as she reached the door. "You could at least have said some—" But as she swung around the door, her voice died in her throat

183

as her eyes fell upon three little panther cubs seated in their litter, staring up at her.

"Oh," Marshalla said, gazing at the cubs, her curiosity piqued. Going down to her knees, she smiled.

"And what might you three cute little things be?"

"Panther cubs," a voice replied behind her. Yelping, Marshalla fell backwards before scrambling to look behind her. It was the merchant who had gotten them to safety.

"Awake at last, I see."

Marshalla stared mutely at him for a spell before finally nodding.

"Good. I wouldn't…" But his voice trailed away as he stared behind Marshalla.

"No, Kasha. That's just mean."

Curious, Marshalla turned her gaze to what lay behind her, and as she did so, her gaze fell upon a most fearsome creature. With a head the color of darkest night, eyes of deepest blue, and a maw twisted into a snarl, Marshalla took just one look at the creature before her fear overcame her, forcing from her one long, ear-splitting scream. So piercing was the scream that the poor night panther was soon cowering from her, ears pinned as far back as they could go, wincing in pain all the while. At last, Marshalla fell silent, her lungs fully spent.

"I see you have a good pair of lungs on you," the merchant muttered.

Marshalla tried to turn, to face the merchant, but her fear held her rigid. Just then, the sound of running drifted to her.

"See, told you it was Marsha!" Tip exclaimed as he burst into the kitchen.

"I didn't think Marsha could make that kind of sound," Davian replied as he stumbled in behind Tip. At last, Marshalla turned round, but again it was her fear that drove her on.

"Stay back!" she exclaimed, waving at the boys to keep their distance.

"Why?" Tip asked, frowning.

"She's afraid of Kasha," Davian said, grinning, and as Marshalla stared at him, he walked over and hugged the large cat sat by the kitchen's other door. Chuckling, Tip raced over and hugged Kasha too.

"I think it's best you all go play outside," the merchant said, "let Marsha recover some."

"Aww, okay," Tip said before heading out of the open door behind Kasha.

"Come, Kasha!" Davian said as he raced past Tip. In but a moment, the big cat was gone, racing after the little elf.

"Wait for me!" Tip yelled as he hurried after them. Marshalla watched all three with wonder and worry.

"Is it really—"

"He may be big, but Kasha's quite gentle."

"Oh," was all Marshalla could manage.

A gentle nudge brought her gaze down to her knees. One of the panther cubs was seated before her, staring up at her.

"You gave them quite the fright with that scream."

Smiling guiltily, Marshalla rubbed the cub behind the ear, an act that elicited a gentle chuff from it, and brought its siblings scrambling towards her. Chuckling, Marshalla willingly obliged, alternating between each cub as she rubbed and petted them.

"You seem to have a way with animals."

Marshalla grinned, nodding. "Suppose, yeah. Easier to be around than people sometimes."

"Yes… yes, I think I know what you mean."

Sitting cross-legged on the kitchen floor, Marshalla turned to her guest.

"What they call you?" she asked.

"Drake," he replied as he turned his back to her and his attention to the kitchen's work top.

"Just Drake?" she asked as the three clubs began clambering up her crossed legs.

"What's wrong with that?"

"Never met a human with only one name."

"I've never met an elf with just one name either."

"Street rat, not elf," Marshalla replied mater-of-factly as she picked up and cradled one of the cubs. "Don't need more than one name."

"You look like an elf to me."

"Yeah, well…doesn't make me one."

"I see… Well I don't need more than one name either."

"Why? You a street rat too?"

Drake laughed. "Some might say so."

"Oh?"

"I'm a ranger, Marsha. Titles and names, they're not for me. They won't get me fed or keep me warm."

Smiling, Marshalla looked down at the other two cubs. They were amusing themselves by play-fighting within her crossed legs.

"Thank you for helping us," she said suddenly.

"Don't thank me, thank Mardaley," Drake replied. "It was his idea."

Marshalla smiled. "Yeah, he—" But her words were cut short by a rather loud and angry growl. Stopping, all three cubs stared at Marshalla's stomach. Grimacing, she looked from her stomach to the cubs before looking up at Drake. As she looked up, she caught sight of a luscious red apple sailing through the air towards her. With a start, she caught it with her free hand, just.

"That should keep things quiet in there till I'm done here."

Grinning, Marshalla took a large bite from her apple, but as she chewed, the two play-fighting cubs stopped and stared at her intently, while the one in her arm reached for the apple.

"Uh..." she began as she looked up at Drake once more.

He was staring at her, a smile dancing on his lips. Sighing, he pulled forth another apple, and pulling forth a blade, sliced the apple in three before walking over and handing the pieces to the cubs.

"Thank you," Marshalla said as he returned to what Marshalla could now see was a large cooking pot.

"No trouble."

A moment's silence followed as the three cubs and Marshalla chewed, chomped and slurped their apples.

"How long we here for?" Marshalla asked after a spell.

"Why? You're sick of my company already?"

Marshalla smiled. "No, not that, it's—"

"I jest, girl, I know what you mean."

Marshalla's smile widened.

"Things are bad in Merethia right now. Too many people want your Tip dead, or worse."

Those words made the hairs on the back of Marshalla's neck stand tall and rigid.

"How long will you be here..." Drake continued. "I honestly do not know, but I do know the longer you're here, the easier it'll be for your friend."

Marshalla nodded as her face fell. "Yeah, Mardaley said we had to stay away for a while."

Drake nodded. "Yes, and the longer you are away with no disturbance anywhere, the harder it'll be for the Tower to keep Merethia afraid of Tip."

But there was something in his tone. It was faint, subtle, but ever so slightly unnerving.

"You don't want us here," Marshalla said as she realized what it was.

At her words, Drake's back went straight and rigid, just for a fraction of a spell, but it was enough. Frowning darkly at him, Marshalla made to rise, but as she did so, Drake turned to face her square.

"What do you know of Anieszirel's past?"

Marshalla stared at him with an air of disgust. "They don't call her Kin-Slayer for fun. Not stupid, you know."

"No, not stupid, just naïve."

Marshalla glared at him in response.

"And easily offended." Grabbing a nearby napkin, the ranger wiped his hands before placing it beside him, clearly forming his thoughts as he did so. In spite of her rising anger, Marshalla waited to hear what he had to say. She needn't wait long.

"Right now, your friend Tip thinks Anieszirel is the greatest being in this world, save you."

Marshalla shrugged at him, even as a warming wave of pride washed over her.

"So?" she asked as nonchalantly as she could.

"He has known her for only a few days, and already he trusts her more than he trusts Davian. Or even Mardaley."

Marshalla frowned.

"So?" she asked with the same calm air, an air that belied the rising disquiet within her.

"That is what she is good at, my girl. She is *very* good at worming her way into people's trust, into their hearts. She's spent aeons perfecting it. And as sure as the sun rises and sets, she is right now doing her very damnedest to make Tip love her more than you."

"So…?"

"Once she has him, my girl, she will begin to isolate him. She will take him away from you, both of you. You will wake up one morning and he will be gone. She will take him away from everyone and everything he knows, make him completely reliant on her. And once she has him under her thumb, once she has him completely and wholly subservient to her, she will simply ask him to let her be in control, full control, and he will say yes. And do you know what comes next?"

Marshalla shook her head, her heart in her mouth.

"Then you will see the real Anieszirel. Then you will see why she is so feared." Drake took a step forward, his gaze piercing deep into Marshalla.

"Right now, our two saving graces are Tip's love for you, and the fact that she is too weak to force her will upon him. The latter will take months to rectify, even with a host as young as Tip, so she will be working on redressing the former."

Marshalla broke her gaze with the ranger. The discomfort was too great.

"I don't want you here, my girl," he continued, "because I'd hate to do what I'd have to do should she succeed in supplanting you in his heart."

"She won't!" Marshalla exclaimed, gritting her teeth in defiance as she stared at him once more. "Tip loves me!"

Drake smiled at her.

"Make sure he never forgets that, for all our sakes." And without another word, Drake turned back to his cooking.

"*Mardaley* believes in us," Marshalla muttered, her defiance burning bright as she lifted what was left of her apple to her lips.

"Ha!" Drake exclaimed as he stared over his shoulder at Marshalla. "The Mardaley I know would've handed Tip over to the Tower by now!"

Icy tendrils clawed at Marshalla's insides as she stared at the ranger before her.

"Don't believe you," she managed.

"Oh, it's true, my girl," he replied, turning back to the pot before him. "The

Mardaley I know only cared for the greater good. Nothing was too great a sacrifice for The Greater Good!"

He looked over his shoulder once more at Marshalla. "But, for reasons I cannot fathom, you and that little boy have softened his shriveled old heart. Hells, he's even looking into how he can separate Anieszirel from Tip! Did you know that?"

A proud, grateful smile parted Marshalla's lips.

"You didn't, did you? Well, he is, old fool that he is. Never mind that countless mages and suchlike have tried gods know how many ways over the centuries, old Mardaley's convinced he can do it, for Tip's sake. And that's his great plan. For once, he's sacrificing the greater good to save someone." Drake shook his head. "You and that little boy are going to have to tell me how you got to that old goat."

Marshalla grinned. "It'll cost you."

"Oh? Bartering, are we?"

"Of course. A street rat's always got to be thinking of the future."

"Ha! I'll make a ranger of you yet." He looked over at Marshalla once more.

"Go on, go look after those boys. You go make sure Kasha hasn't gnawed their legs off or somesuch."

Marshalla's eyes grew wide before darting to the open door.

"I jest, girl, I jest."

Sighing, she turned back to Drake, shaking her head. But the smile upon her lips faded as his did.

"But remember my words."

Slowly, she nodded as an uncomfortable silence fell upon them both. Nodding himself, he turned back to the pot. Nodding once again, Marshalla rose and headed for the door, the three cubs in tow. It did not take her long to find them, their laughter drawing her straight to them. They were playing battle-mages, firing off spells and swinging mighty staves of twig at an invisible army of epic proportions. Shaking her head, Marshalla headed for them. It was Davian who spotted her first, the sounds of her coming clearly breaking him from his play.

"Hey, Marsha!" Davian yelled, turning to wave at her. Grinning, Tip stopped and waved too. Smiling, Marshalla waved back as she hurried her steps. But as she neared them, the hulking head that was Kasha's rose from the grass not far from the pair to stare straight at her. As Marshalla stared into his eyes, she felt herself slow to a crawl. As if reading her discomfort, the night panther lowered his head back to the grass.

"Oh, don't be like that, Marsha," Davian said. "He really is quite harmless."

"And big," Marshalla replied. "Don't forget big."

Davian smiled. "Yes, he *is* rather big for a panther. Drake called him a night panther. Never really heard of that kind before."

"Marsha's never seen a panther before though," Tip said. "Can't blame her for being scared."

"Like you, you mean?" Davian asked with a mischievous grin on his lips.

"Wasn't scared!" Tip cried in response.

"Truly? So you screaming and crying when he snuck up behind you, that wasn't—"

"Shut up!"

"Okay, okay, enough." Marshalla stared at a pouting Tip, smiling at him before levelling a scolding gaze at Davian, who remained unrepentant. Shaking her head, she looked about her till her eyes fell upon a cluster of little trees nearby.

"Come, let's go sit," she said as she headed for the trees. Before long, all three were seated under the trees and within their shade. They watched in silence as Kasha played with the three cubs.

"Glad you finally awake, Marsha," Tip said as he pulled at the grass before him. Frowning, she looked at him.

"What you mean?"

"You were sleeping for quite a long time," Davian replied.

"What you mean?" she repeated, turning to stare at Davian. "Sun's still up."

"We got here yesterday, Marsha."

Surprised, Marshalla looked at Tip. "And you didn't wake me?"

Tip shrugged. "After all that pretend sleeping you were doing, Davian and me thought we should let you sleep proper. Just didn't think you'd sleep this long."

"Pretend sleep?" Marshalla asked, frowning.

"You were often the last to sleep and the first to wake," Davian replied with a smug smile. "We knew you weren't always sleeping."

"Oh, did you now?"

"Yes," Davian replied as his smile grew.

"Yes," Tip added, grinning as well. "Can't fool us."

"Must remember that for next time, then."

Chuckling, the two boys looked at each other before staring at Kasha and the cubs once more.

"I'm glad we made it out though," Davian said as he too began pulling at the grass before him.

"Me too," Tip added.

"How long are you planning to stay here for?" Davian asked

"Ani says at least a year."

"A whole year?"

"Uh-huh. She says going to take that long before people forget about us. Start to forget about us."

"What do you think, Marsha?"

Marshalla tore her gaze from Tip to stare at Davian. "Hoping we can go back sooner, a year's really long."

"Yes, it is, isn't it?" Davian replied.

"Yeah," Tip said, nodding as he spoke. "But Ani says we shouldn't count our kitchens just yet."

"Don't have any kitchens," Marshalla replied, frowning.

"Chickens."

"You don't have any chickens either," Davian said.

"Oh, yeah."

"I…think she means we shouldn't get ahead of ourselves," Davian offered. "I've heard that phrase used by humans before."

"Oh. Funny thing to say," Marshalla mused.

"Hehe, yeah," Tip added.

Then, Marshalla looked at Tip. "You and Ani been talking a lot."

"Yeah," Tip nodded, but as he answered, he dropped his gaze to the grass before him, and Marshalla couldn't help but feel it was because he couldn't look her in the eye when he spoke, a feeling that made Drake's words ring all the truer.

"So, how long do you think we should stay for then, Davian?" Marshalla asked as she tore her gaze away from Tip once more.

"Me?"

Marshalla nodded.

"Well, I don't know… Left to me we won't go back."

Marshalla frowned. "But Merethia's your home."

Davian smiled sadly as he lowered his gaze to the grass in his hands.

"Not anymore, it's not," he muttered. "I can't condone what my father tried to do, what my brother did. And if I can't condone that, how can I go back?"

An uncomfortable silence fell upon them all as both Marshalla and Tip stared at the forlorn Davian.

"He still loves you, Davian," Marshalla said at last. Davian laughed as he looked at her.

"Oh, he loves me, but not like you think. He loves me like… like a shepherd loves a prized sheep dog." Shaking his head, he dropped his gaze to the grass once more.

"I guess I've known all my life," he continued, pulling at the grass one more. "Guess I've always known just how much he cared, but I… I wanted to believe I could make him care more." He looked up at them. "Do you know what I mean?"

Marshalla nodded in response. Smiling, Davian dropped his gaze once more.

"And Thalas," he continued, "well, it wasn't hard to see why he was always so angry, always so hateful. Father never hid his displeasure of Thalas from anyone, not from me, or his friends, or even the help." Gritting his teeth, Davian pulled angrily at the grass.

"Do you know what the stupidest thing was though?" he asked, raising his gaze to Marshalla as he tugged away at the grass. "I thought… I truly thought… if I could make Father love me like my friends' fathers loved them, and make Thalas like me, maybe then, Father would like Thalas and Thalas wouldn't be so angry and miserable. Such a stupid notion if there ever was one."

Marshalla shook her head. "No, it's not."

But Davian shook his own head, dropping his gaze once more. The silence that followed was deafening.

"So, what you both been doing all day, then, eh?" Marshalla asked, eager to lighten the mood. Before either could answer though, Kasha rose suddenly, his gaze going to the house. Taking a step forward, he stopped and turned his gaze towards Marshalla and the boys.

"What ails him?" Davian asked, frowning. Marshalla stared at the great panther for a spell before smiling.

"Think...Drake's called him. Food's ready."

With eyes wide with excitement, both boys looked at each other before scrambling to their feet and racing off towards the house.

"Hey!" Marshalla exclaimed, but it was too late. Sighing, she too rose and followed, the great panther already heading back himself, the three cubs in tow.

*****

With his hands behind him, Thuridan stared out of the window in his reading room, his features twisted in a frustrated frown.

"You're certain?"

Behind him, Thalas nodded as he glanced briefly at the others. "I'm certain, Father."

But Thuridan remained unconvinced. "He matched the eye-witness descriptions perfectly, and he's well acquainted with Mardaley. Do you truly mean to tell me it wasn't him? You have failed me in the past, Thalas, so I shall ask you just once more, are you certain?"

Thalas sighed through gritted teeth. "We made him watch us have our fun with his wife, then we made him watch Durlin extinguish the life out of her. Then, we told him if he gave us what we wanted, we would spare his daughters. He wasn't lying, Father, I am certain."

At last, Thuridan turned, his displeasure plain. "I take it you cleaned up after yourselves."

Thalas nodded in response.

"I have that to be thankful for, at least," he muttered, just loud enough to be heard by all.

"What other avenues are there, sir?" Neremi asked, stifling a scowl.

"Avenues?" Thuridan snarled. "My dear Neremi, do you think I would be standing here wasting breath with you if there were others?"

"Sir, it's been almost two months now," Eldred replied. "Surely, there must be—"

"Did you hear me stutter, young man?"

"No, sir," Eldred replied, visibly smarting.

"So, you did not understand my words?"

"No, sir."

"No?"

"I mean, yes sir."

"Yes?"

"I mean—"

"Father, what do we do now?" Thalas asked, coming to his friend's aid.

Thuridan turned his piercing gaze onto his son. "*We? You* do nothing, save whatever nonsense you do to waste your lives away. *I*, on the other hand, have the unenviable task of salvaging this mess you've brought me." Frowning still, he turned his gaze on the others.

"Go, get out of my sight," he growled, and without another word, turned back to the window.

"Come," Thalas said before turning and heading for the door.

Before long, all five were walking down the darkened streets away from the Grovemender residence.

"I swear, your father gets more insufferable the longer this drags on," Neremi snarled once they were a safe distance away.

"Can you blame him?" Eldred asked.

"Yes!" Neremi exclaimed.

"No, I mean, it's been almost two months, and still nothing. No great rampage, no threatening missives, nothing. The king's long since abandoned the search for the Kin-Slayer and regularly belittles the Matriarch over how she handled the escape, even calls her a scaremonger. He's feeling the pressure from the Matriarch to show she was right. I heard she's practically sitting upon his neck, demanding daily updates."

"Well, I hope she chokes him."

Thalas chuckled at this.

"I do! And I hope I'm there to watch."

"Much as I would love to see the old bastard die myself," Thane said somberly, "we're still suspended from the Tower, and until he releases us, suspended we will remain."

"I know," Neremi said, sighing as she spoke.

"And if he is proven to be incapable of resolving this," Durlin said, "do you truly think we will be allowed back?"

None spoke.

"So, what do we do?" Neremi asked, staring at Thalas as she spoke. He looked at her before sighing and shrugging.

"We hope, and we pray."

"That's it?" Thane asked, sneering.

"You have a better idea?"

"You're our glorious leader, and that's the best you can come up with?"

"Do you have a better idea?" Thalas asked, his ire straining on its leash.

Thane glared before turning and walking away. As he walked away, Thalas turned his gaze to Durlin, who was staring intently at him. No words passed between the two, but soon Durlin turned and hurried after Thane.

"I'd... best go with them," Eldred said. "Keep them out of trouble."

"Yes, good idea," Neremi replied.

"Yes." But as he began walking away, he suddenly stopped and turned to Thalas.

"You'll find away." He smiled. "You always do." And without waiting for a response, he hurried after the others.

"That Thane is becoming more and more of a handful," Neremi muttered.

His eyes still on the receding figures, Thalas nodded. "That he is."

"I'm surprised he hasn't challenged you yet."

"He will, once this is over."

"I... yes, he will, won't he?"

"And then, there's Durlin," Thalas said, a worried frown twisting his lips. "He and I used to be so close."

"Yes..." Neremi muttered sadly. "It used to be as if he was your counsel."

"Yes. But now... the way he stares at me sometimes, it's almost as if he can barely contain his hate."

Neremi looked from him to the distant figures before staring back at him. "Well, you *did* get Fallon killed."

Thalas moved to speak, but no words came. Smiling guiltily, Neremi slipped her hands into his.

"I know a quaint little inn not far from here. Perhaps you and I can find something... naughty we can do to pass the time."

Thalas looked down at her hands, then shook his head.

"It was not my intent for Fallon to die, Neremi," he said, his voice heavy.

"I know, Thalas," Neremi replied as her smile faded.

"I know my anger cost us our prize, and not a day has gone by that I haven't berated myself for it."

Raising a gentle hand to her lover's cheek, Neremi sighed. "I know."

Sighing himself, Thalas closed his eyes as he savored her touch.

"Come," she said, a mischievous smile dancing on her lips. "The inn isn't far."

Thalas said nary a word, and instead allowed Neremi to drag him down the path of her choosing. As they walked, however, Neremi stopped suddenly as a disgusted gasp escaped her lips.

"What is it?" Thalas asked, following her gaze, only to lock eyes with the tiniest mouse he'd ever seen staring up at them from within the shadows nearby.

"Ugh," he muttered in disgust. "What is this city coming to?" Shaking his head, he raised his right hand at the little creature. But as he did so, the mouse walked forward into the light before stopping and staring up at them once more, and as Thalas was about to begin casting his spell, the mouse stood on its hind legs and stared calmly at them both as its eyes glowed a hue of purest azure.

Slowly, Thalas lowered his hand as he turned to Neremi, who stared nervously back.

"Greetings," the little mouse squeaked at the stunned pair.

*****

Groaning, Marshalla stirred in her bed, the light of the morning sun bathing her room in a warm golden hue. Yawning, Marshalla rose to sitting, stretching as she did so, and with a deep sigh, swung her feet off her bed, narrowly missing the panther cub resting beside her bed.

"Oh, sorry, Gray," she said, wincing. "Didn't see you there."

The startled panther stared at her with indignation before nestling down once more.

"Said sorry," she muttered as she rose, stretching once more as she headed for the door, little Gray hurrying after her.

"There you are!" Drake exclaimed the moment Marshalla reached the bottom of the stairs. "What time do you call this, my girl?"

Marshalla pulled a face at him in response.

"Warned you, didn't I?" Drake continued with a smug grin. "Warned you the washing up would take forever, didn't I?"

Marshalla frowned, but kept her peace.

"Exactly. So next time I tell you to best get started, you'd best get started."

Marshalla growled under her breath as she glared at Drake. It was then she noticed the bow in his hand. "Going hunting already?"

"It's almost noon!" Drake replied, laughing.

"What?"

Shaking his head, Drake picked up his hunting bag from the hook where it rested beside the stairs just as Davian and Tip wandered into the corridor.

"Morning, Marsha!" Davian beamed.

Marshalla looked at the pair, and couldn't help but smile, for they were dressed similar to Drake, complete with their very own bows.

"All dressed already."

As one, both nodded, grinning.

"And running late, too," Drake growled as he marched towards the kitchen.

Marshalla pulled a face at him once more before turning to the pair.

"You take care, both of you. Do what Drake tells you."

The boys exchanged glances before giving Marshalla a knowing smile.

"This isn't exactly the first time we're going hunting with him, Marsha, " Davian replied. "You do realize that."

"Yeah," Tip added. "And you still tell us the same thing every time."

Marshalla frowned at them as she crossed her arms about her. "Just do it, okay?"

"Okay," both intoned.

"Okay," Marshalla replied, then headed after Drake. He was petting Kasha as she walked in.

"Right, you know what to do," Drake said, turning to her.

Marshalla nodded in response.

"Good. And don't go wandering off, you hear? Kasha can't watch you, the house *and* the cubs all at once if you go wandering off."

At his words, Marshalla's gaze darkened greatly.

"That *one* time…" she glowered.

"We won't be gone long," Drake continued, ignoring her glare. "Be sure to get the pot ready."

Marshalla said nary a word.

"Good. Boys!"

"Coming!" Tip and Davian yelled as they raced into the kitchen. With her heart in her throat, Marshalla watched as they sped past her and followed Drake out of the kitchen. With her hands folded under her bosom, she walked out after them, Kasha behind her. Leaning against the kitchen door's frame, she watched them till they disappeared within the trees. Sighing, she turned at last to Kasha. He was staring at her.

"Don't say it, okay? Don't," she muttered, before looking to where they'd disappeared, a worried frown on her lips. "Can't help it."

As she stared, Marshalla felt a gentle nudge against the back of her leg. Looking down, she smiled as little Gray stared up at her. Crouching, she tickled her beloved little companion on the diamond-shaped patch of gray fur just below her neck, an act that elicited a playful swipe from the little cub, followed swiftly by a deft lick of Marshalla's hand. Chuckling, Marshalla rose and made her way back into the kitchen.

"What a mess," she sighed as she carried her gaze about the kitchen.

Shaking her head, she rolled up her sleeves and began clearing the place, making it ready for the game that would be brought back. Whistling to herself as she went,

Marshalla worked her way through the piles of pots and plates, tossing the odd leftover morsel to Gray and her two brothers, who all watched her with some interest as they lay in their beds, while Kasha lay by the door, soaking up the warming sun.

How long she worked, Marshalla did not know, nor did she care in truth. So focused was she in her task that she did not notice when Kasha slowly rose from where he lay, turning to stare outside, his ears pricked to their fullest. Neither did she notice Gray and her brothers join Kasha by the door, one by one. In fact, it wasn't until Kasha growled that Marshalla finally took note. Frowning, she looked at the panthers.

"What is it?"

Kasha fell silent as he lowered himself into a crouch.

"Kasha?" Marshalla said.

Then she realized the birds had fallen silent. Swallowing hard, Marshalla felt her heart climb up her throat.

"Kasha?" she whispered.

In response, the great panther turned to her, and as she stared at him, she watched as he faded from view. Gasping, she fell into a crouch.

"Oh, gods," she whispered, her mind racing.

With eyes wide with fear, Marshalla crawled over to the cubs, pulling them into the kitchen and away from the door. Huddling in a corner, she stared intently out of the door, looking for some sign, any sign, of the night panther. An eternity went by and nothing. Finding her courage, Marshalla made her way towards the door. As she reached it, she pressed herself by the doorway, daring to peek outside of it. As she did so, she felt a soft bundle press up against her. Turning, she looked down by her side. It was Gray and her brothers. Smiling, she motioned for them to go back. But at that moment, Marshalla suddenly found herself being lifted clean off the floor as an arm wrapped itself about her chest while a gloved hand covered her mouth.

"I have her!" a voice cried behind her.

Screaming into the glove, Marshalla struggled, scrambling and fighting with all she had.

"I have– Argh!"

As suddenly as she'd been grabbed, Marshalla felt herself being let go of as she fell into an undignified heap. Turning, she stared at her assailant as he staggered backwards, cradling his arm, blood gushing from between his fingertips. Scrambling to her feet, Marshalla steadied herself, bringing her fists to bear before her, but she needn't have bothered, for just then, Kasha swam back into view, swiping a large paw across the intruder's throat as he did so and showering Marshalla with the man's blood. Stunned, Marshalla could only watch as the battle-mage fell backwards, a death gargle escaping from his lips. She looked over at the night panther. The battle runes etched deep into his skin pulsed furiously beneath his fur.

"It came from over here!"

Startled back to life, Marshalla turned to the other door. As she did so, Kasha bounded into the kitchen, fading from view as he went, all except his eyes. As he reached the door, he turned to Marshalla before his eyes too faded away. Marshalla stared at the door for a scant few moments, till her courage returned. Shivering greatly, she grabbed a nearby cloth, wiping the blood off her face before hurrying over to the door Kasha had bounded out of. It was clear what she had to do, but her terror made it no easy task. She waited in silence, her breath coming in snatches. Then, another scream punctured the silence, swiftly followed by another death gargle. Rising, Marshalla swung the door open just in time to see another battle-mage fall lifeless to the ground. She turned to the cubs. They could sense her fear, and she theirs.

"This way," she whispered before hurrying to the stairs.

But rather than climb, she moved the little rug beneath the stairs aside, revealing an iron ring. Grasping the ring with both hands, she lifted up the trap door as quietly as she could, and, ushering the cubs inside, she clambered in, taking great pains to ensure the rug fell smoothly back in place as she closed the door. Sitting in the darkness, Marshalla hugged the cubs tightly as her mind raced. How had they found them? How many were there? Would Kasha be able to fend them all off? Her thoughts were punctuated by the screams of the battle-mages that fell to the night panther, and by the cries and bellows of those that remained, their voices becoming more and more shrill as Kasha thinned their number. How long the game of hunter-hunted went on for, Marshalla could not say, but with each cry, her heart warmed, with each scream, her courage grew. That was until a fierce roar rang out. Hearing it stopped Marshalla's heart.

"Kasha…" she whispered. "No."

The pain was unmistakable. They had him; they had him and they'd hurt him. Then, he roared again, this time louder, more distraught.

"No," she whispered, tears stinging her eyes.

The silence that followed was deafening. Then, after what seemed like an eternity, Marshalla heard hurried footsteps from above, followed soon after by more measured steps.

"Did you find her?"

"No. But she has to be here somewhere!"

"Did you check under the stairs?"

Marshalla's hand flew to her lips.

"Yes, just an old rug there."

"Are you sure? Thuridan was quite specific."

"Damn it, I'm sure."

"What about under the rug?"

With her heart in her throat, Marshalla could only stare into the dark as she heard the rug being pulled back, then the iron ring being grasped roughly, before finally the trap door being pulled open.

"There you are!"

With a communal growl, the three cubs launched themselves at the battle-mage peering down at them. With a startled cry, the battle-mage staggered backwards, the three cubs mauling him for all they were worth. But their efforts were in futility, for though they managed to score some deep wounds, the second battle-mage ended their attempts with three well aimed lightning bolts. At last, the two battle-mages stared back down at Marshalla.

"Come out, or be carried."

"To the hells with you!" she spat at them through tears.

In response, the older of the battle-mages chanted words of arcane at Marshalla, then darkness claimed her.

"You think Marsha will like it?" Tip asked as he looked from the rabbits hanging from the rod on Drake's shoulder to Drake himself.

"Aye," Drake replied, turning to stare at Tip, a proud smile upon his lips. "But I dare say she'd be real proud of you both given you managed to kill one each without my help, and without any of your fancy spells either."

Beaming, the two boys looked at each other as they adjusted their bows proudly.

"It was a rather rewarding experience, I must say," Davian said. "Especially with all that stalking and sneaking. Even the…"

But his voice died in his throat, for at that moment, Drake dropped to a crouch before placing the rabbits on the grassy earth.

"What is it?" Davian whispered.

For a time, Drake didn't answer, he didn't even look at either of them. But just as Tip was about to repeat the question, he turned to them, though his gaze sent their fear into a near panic.

"I need you both to stay here," he whispered as he freed his bow.

"What is it?"

"Stay here. And if you hear me yell at you to run, run, don't stop. Don't stop and don't look back."

"Drake—"

"Stay here." And without another word, the ranger turned and moved soundlessly through the woods.

Both boys looked at each other.

"*Don't worry, Tip, I'm here.*"

"Scared, Ani."

"*Don't be, I'm here. I'll protect you.*"

Moments ticked by, but no sign of Drake. Without realizing, Tip slipped his hand into Davian's, the latter keeping a fireball primed in his free hand. They waited in silence, their fears filling their heads with all manner of horrors, until at last, Drake returned. The relief that washed over both boys as they saw him however, soon turned to fear anew once they saw the blood upon him. But when Tip saw the tears in his eyes, his heart broke.

"Marsha…" he whispered in disbelief.

"Dear gods, no," Davian whispered, his fireball fading away to nothing.

Tip looked from Drake to the woods behind him, and losing all control, broke into a dead sprint. As he raced past Drake, a firm hand gripped him by the shoulder, stopping him dead in his tracks.

"Let me go!" he yelled, tears stinging his eyes. "Marsha!"

"Wait."

"Let me go!"

"Wait, damn you!"

Forcing him about, Drake went on one knee. But Tip fought his grip.

"Marsha!" he shrieked, desperate to break free of Drake as tears rolled down his cheeks.

"Damn it, boy, I said wait!"

But it was hopeless, and realizing there was nothing he could say to reach Tip, Drake let him be. And the moment his grasp loosened, Tip raced on to the house.

"Tip, slow down!"

But Tip was past reasoning. He had to reach his friend, he had to see her.

"Tip, please! Stop!"

Breaking free of the woods, Tip soon came to a screeching halt. It was the stench that hit him first, but it was the sight before him that turned his stomach. Never had he seen so many fallen in one place before. But, as he stared, he soon realized one calming fact. Marshalla was not amongst them. Finding his feet again, Tip raced on.

"Tip! Stop!"

Reaching the kitchen door, he vaulted over the body slumped across it, only to slip on the blood of the other fallen battle-mage within.

"Careful!"

With arms flailing wildly, he managed to regain his balance before racing on once again.

"Marsha!" he yelled as he swung round the door at the other end, but the sight that greeted him finally stopped him cold. Gray and her brothers were lying unmoving near the open trap door. With his heart in his throat, Tip neared the opened hole.

"Marsha?"

No reply.

Finally reaching the trap door, Tip peered in.

Empty.

Just then, a low, barely audible whimper reached his ears. Turning, he looked once again at the unmoving cubs. Then the whimper came again. Hurrying over, he felt the three cubs, one by one, and as his hands touched Gray's snout, she whimpered once more.

"Is she alright?"

Startled, Tip looked up. It was Davian.

"Don't know, but someone hurt her bad."

Nodding, Davian went over to Tip. Tip looked up at his friend.

"Don't know what to do."

"I…" Davian began, but his voice failed him as he looked from Tip to the little cub. That she was near death was plain for both to see.

"*I know what to do, Tip.*"

With a grateful nod, Tip gazed into the ether.

"Tip?" Davian said, staring at him.

"Fetch me some water," Anieszirel said in response as she carefully began clearing the clumps of fur that had stuck to Gray's wound.

Nodding, Davian rose to do as he was bid, and as he returned, both dragon and elf did what they could to bring the little cub from death's door. At last, Anieszirel sat back as a satisfied sigh escaped her lips. Davian looked at her worriedly.

"Will she be alright now?"

With her eyes on the cub, Anieszirel nodded.

"Gray's alive?"

Anieszirel turned to stare at Drake as he walked up behind them. His sleeves were rolled up and his hands were covered with blood.

"Someone hit her with a lightning bolt. It went through her, seared her heart in the process. It's a miracle she survived it." She looked back at the weak cub. "But she's past the worst now."

"And the others?"

Sadly, Anieszirel shook her head as she glanced over Gray's brothers. Then she turned her gaze back to Drake.

"Marsha's?" Anieszirel frowned, nodding at the blood on his hands.

Drake looked down at his hands before looking up at her.

"Kasha's," he replied.

"Oh gods, I'm so sorry."

At her words, Drake shook his head, grinning.

"He'll pull through. He's one tough bastard, that cat. He'll pull through."

"So, where's Marsha?"

"Not here. They must've taken her."

"Who?"

"The Tower," Davian spat.

Both looked at him. He stared at each in turn.

"I recognize their attire. They're Shimmering Tower battle-mages."

"Then we go get her back!" Tip exclaimed as Anieszirel relinquished control to him. "Let's go!"

"No," Drake said firmly.

"But…!"

"If we go now, Gray will die, and so will Kasha. No, we tend to our friends, then we go get Marsha back."

"But they'll kill her!"

Drake shook his head at the screaming little boy. "No, they won't. She is bait, Tip, bait for you. They want you back in Merethia, and this wish we will grant. Except you won't be going alone."

He looked at Davian. "Come help me with Kasha. Ani and Tip can take care of Gray." And without waiting for an answer, he turned and hurried back to Kasha's side.

THE BEGGAR'S POWER

Thalas stared, seething, at the waters rolling down the Aqueduct. His nose had stopped bleeding, a fact he was thankful for, but it still felt swollen and clogged. He looked at Neremi beside him as they sat on the inner wall of the Aqueduct. As she stared into the ether, the anger etched on her face matched his own square. After a spell, he moved to speak, to say some words of comfort, but his rage was too great, and instead he simply returned his gaze to the waters. It wasn't till the sound of footsteps drifted towards the pair before either stirred again.

"Why in the world are we meeting *here?*" Eldred asked as he neared them. "We haven't met here since... Thalas, what happened?"

Without waiting for a response, Eldred glared at Neremi. "Truly, Neremi?"

"Oh, don't be an idiot, Eldred!" Neremi snarled as she hopped down to her feet.

"Where are the others?" Thalas asked.

"Right here," Thane replied as he and Durlin stepped into view.

"What happened?" Thane asked the moment he got a good look at Thalas' face.

"My father happened."

"Is this your reward for betraying us, then?"

"Thane, if you have nothing useful to say—"

"We heard, Thalas, we heard. Your father has the girl. And do you know what else we heard?"

Straightening, Thalas stared at Thane, his hand going to his belt as his anger climbed ever higher.

"No, do tell," he replied with a calmness he did not feel. Sneering,

Thane took a menacing step forward. "We heard you told him where the girl was. We heard you found out and went running to your darling father."

"Is that all you heard?" Thalas asked, his hands clasped tightly around the hilt of his blade as he leant forward, ready to spring off the wall.

Thane laughed mockingly at him.

"Look at him, just look at him." Thane said in a tone of utter contempt. "Pathetic."

Without warning, Neremi marched over to Thane, and as she reached him, she slapped him with all her might, an act that stunned all gathered, Thalas included.

"You—!"

But before he could speak further, Neremi shoved a single smooth pebble under his nose.

"Thuridan slipped this in my pocket, Thane," she snarled. "He was listening when Thalas and I learnt where the gutter rats were hiding!" Her anger burning still, she flung the listening stone into the Aqueduct's waters. "Thalas didn't tell his father anything!"

"So, that's why we're meeting here," Eldred said, nodding in understanding. "The waters would make it hard for him to hear us."

"Yes," Thalas replied. "Neremi and I have already scryed ourselves, that's the only listening stone upon us. Scry yourselves."

An awkward silence followed as the others did as was asked.

"Well?" Thalas said once they had finished.

Shaking his head in disgust, Eldred held up a listening stone, but he was not the only one.

"You have nothing to say, Thane?" Neremi sneered as he too held up a listening stone.

Glaring in silence, Thane flung the listening stone into the Aqueduct before turning to Thalas.

"So, what happened?"

Sighing, Thalas hopped off his perch and rested upon the Aqueduct. His nose had started throbbing again.

"The Kin-Slayer sent an… emissary to find us, tell us where they were. She offered us knowledge and a promise to take us as her students if we killed the girl and left her for the boy to find. Naturally, we agreed, but Neremi and I tried to find you all last night with no luck. So, we spent the night together and went back to my house in the morning. We were going to tell you right after the morning briefing, but when we got there, he was waiting for us, standing there with that stupid smug smile of his. He tried playing one of his games with us, asking us if we had anything to tell him. And then when he saw we weren't going to play, he told us he'd been listening in on us last night, that he'd heard everything, and that he'd already dispatched teams to return the girl."

"Thalas was livid," Neremi continued, staring at her beloved with a worried frown. "I've never seen him so incensed. I thought he was going to try for his father's life. Old Thuridan must've thought the same."

"He did that to you," Eldred said.

Glumly, Thalas nodded.

"Well, at least it's over," Eldred said, sighing as he spoke. "Thuridan has the girl, and we get to return to our studies. Not the best of endings, but at least it is an ending of sorts."

Both Thalas and Neremi looked at him before sharing an uncomfortable gaze.

"What?"

"Our suspension stays," Neremi said.

"What?" all three exclaimed.

"You heard her. My father, in his infinite wisdom, is going to keep our suspension firmly in place until such a time as he deems fit that we have paid our debt to the Tower."

"You cannot be serious!" Thane yelled.

"Oh, I am *very* serious. That old fool is keeping us under thumb, turning us into his slaves. That bastard is crushing our future for his amusement and petty games."

"So, what do we do now?" Durlin asked.

"We—" Thalas began, but caught himself as he stared at Eldred once more. "The listening stone."

"I flung it into the Aqueduct."

"Good. Good." He turned his gaze back to Durlin. "We go back to our earlier plan."

"Which is?"

"We take the Kin-Slayer for ourselves."

"And how do you propose we do that?" Thane asked, bemused.

"The girl, Thane."

"The girl? The same girl your father now has in his custody? The same girl he will undoubtedly have under heavy guard by now? The same girl who, if we do manage to somehow get near, and that's a big *if*, and we so much as fart, we will be incinerated in an instant? That girl?"

"Yes, Thane, that girl."

"Right…"

"She's the key. Without her, we'll never get to the boy."

"Do you even know where she is being held?"

"As a matter of fact, I do."

"Oh, you do, do you? So, what, you intend for us to break in, take her and use her as bait ourselves? The five of us?"

"If you have lost your nerve, Thane, leave now," Neremi muttered, glowering.

"Thane is no coward," Durlin replied in Thane's defense, "but he is right. A tad overly dramatic, but right nonetheless. From what I've heard, he has somewhere between thirty and fifty battle-mages guarding the girl. The five of us will not get anywhere near her."

"That is where you're both wrong," Thalas said, a smug smile upon his lips. "My father always thinks of himself first, and there's nothing he hates more than being outmaneuvered. The lengths he'll go to, to avoid that can be... extreme."

"How does that help us?" Thane asked, frowning.

Thalas' smile grew. "He's holding her in one of his larger storehouses. He's moved all items of import out of it, naturally, but the place contains a few secret entrances hidden from the naked eye, and from most common scrying spells."

"Will they not be guarded though?" Eldred asked.

Thalas shook his head at this. "He thinks nobody knows about them, not even me. If he did, he would've caught me sneaking in there years ago."

"So, we sneak in through one of these entrances, grab the girl and leave," Durlin muttered, deep in thought.

With his smile turning into a smirk, Thalas shook his head. "No."

"What do you mean, no?"

"I mean precisely that, no. I know these secret entrances and tunnels, but I'm not the only one. Davian also knows."

"Oh? How?"

"I showed him."

"How does that help us?" Eldred asked, confused.

"If Davian knows, it's a safe bet he will be telling the boy about them. And if you were him, what would you do with that knowledge?"

"I would use it to free my friend," Eldred said, smiling.

"Precisely. We won't free her, we let the boy do that. No, what we will do is use it to acquire the void sphere."

"The void sphere is there?" Thane exclaimed.

Thalas nodded at him. "Not my father's, the Tower's. They finally completed one two days ago. We're going to steal it, and we're going to use it on the boy. If we do this well, the Tower, and my father, will think Anieszirel destroyed the void sphere before making good her escape."

"And if they think that, they will have no reason to look for us!" Eldred exclaimed. "It's brilliant!"

"Thank you." Thalas grinned.

"Do you truly think she will teach us anything if we trap her in there?" Durlin asked skeptically.

Thalas shook his head at Durlin. "No, nor do I care. No, we sell her, and with the money we make, we shall live the life we deserve."

With a proud grin, Neremi threw her arm about her beloved's neck before smiling smugly at the others.

"So, who's with us?"

*****

Nervously, Maline paced up and down the hallway.

"Should be back by now," she muttered, wringing her hands as she paced.

Stopping at the door, she peered through the peephole before turning and continuing her pacing. At last, the sound of keys jangling on a chain reached her ears, and with a grateful sigh, Maline darted to the door, and, as Mardaley unlocked it, she swung it open, nearly pulling the elderly storekeeper off his feet.

"Well?" she asked, staring expectantly at Mardaley.

"I thought I told you to calm yourself."

"Is it her?"

Shaking his head, Mardaley cast a quick eye about him before hurrying inside and closing the door behind him.

"You truly should calm yourself," he said as he locked the door.

"Mardaley, please, is it her?"

Sighing, Mardaley stared at her for a brief spell before taking off his coat and hanging it by the door.

"It's her."

Those two words were like poison to Maline's ears, and upon hearing them, she staggered backwards till she fell upon the nearby stairs.

"Dear gods," she whispered as tears stung her eyes.

"Now, don't start with the tears again."

Angrily, Maline looked up at him. "But they have her! Gods, they have her! She's supposed to be safe! She's supposed to be gone, and now they have her!"

Sighing once again, Mardaley walked over and sat beside a distraught Maline.

"Look…" he began, taking pains to choose his words with care. "It's not the end, it's not. Yes, they have her, but she is alive. Alive and unhurt."

"How do you know she's unhurt?"

"Because there are too many witnesses around for Thuridan to dirty his hands right now."

But that did little to assuage Maline's pain. "You said they'd never find them."

Mardaley sighed. "I know."

"You said they'd be safe."

"I know."

"They have her, Mardaley."

Sighing once more, Mardaley placed Maline's head upon his shoulder before holding her close to him.

"I know."

They sat in silence for what felt like an eternity before a knock at the door broke both from their thoughts.

"Expecting someone?" Maline asked, her brows furrowed.

Nodding, Mardaley rose and headed for the door. As he opened it, a hooded figure flew into the house while Mardaley quickly shut the door behind him. The figure turned to Maline, who slowly rose as she stared intently at him. She could not see the man' face, but the deep scowl upon his lips was setting her teeth on edge.

"What did you find out?" Mardaley asked, turning to his guest.

"Is it safe to speak?" his guest asked in response, nodding at Maline as he spoke. Mardaley looked at Maline before turning his gaze to his guest.

"She'll keep quiet."

"Very well," Magister Meadowview said after a spell, then pulled the hood from his face.

"You!" Maline exclaimed.

"Yes, me," Baern replied drily.

Confused, Maline looked at Mardaley.

"He's a friend. He's helping me with Marsha."

"Oh... oh!"

"Yes, although I'm finding myself questioning the rationale behind it all."

"What do you mean?" Mardaley asked as Maline frowned at Baern, her dread returning.

"How about we sit down first?"

"Yes, of course," Mardaley replied before leading Baern into the sitting room, Maline close behind.

"Well?" Mardaley asked anxiously as Baern sat. Gritting his teeth, he looked from Mardaley to Maline, who had made her way to the shopkeeper's side, before turning his gaze to his friend.

"The situation is dire, my friend. I'm not sure how much aid I can give you on this one."

"What do you mean?"

"The Matriarch's involved."

Mardaley's brows furrowed, his confusion apparent. "Of course she's involved, she wants Anieszirel back."

Baern shook his head at his friend. "She's *personally* involved, Mardaley. It was her, not Thuridan, who gave the order to have Marshalla brought back to Merethia, and she personally gave the order to Thuridan to use Marshalla as bait."

"I see…" Mardaley muttered as he sat back in his seat, his confusion turned to worry.

"There's more. They finished the void sphere two days ago. It's there with Marshalla, in that house."

"Dear gods," Mardaley whispered.

"If your Tip goes anywhere near that place, they'll have him. As sure as the sun rises and sets."

"How many are they?"

"Fifty."

"Fifty?" Mardaley and Maline exclaimed in unison.

"Yes, fifty."

"Why so many?" Mardaley asked.

"Blame your ranger friend. Three teams were dispatched to bring her back, but only three battle-mages returned."

In spite of himself, Mardaley couldn't suppress a proud smile.

"You find that amusing, do you?"

"No, of course not," Mardaley said hurriedly.

"Well, those losses are why you have many guarding Marshalla now, and why each and every one of them have been chosen because they have proven themselves on the battlefield. They have orders to capture Tip by any means necessary, and to kill any who aid him, if need be."

"Can you help her?" Maline pleaded.

"No," Baern replied, shaking his head as he spoke, his voice as heavy as his gaze.

"Oh, come now, Baern," Mardaley said, "surely you can do something."

"Mardaley, you don't understand. The Matriarch has taken a very personal role in this. Thuridan is answering to her and her alone. He's outmaneuvered me, and she's excluded me. I can't do anything."

"Damn it all."

"But that's not the worst of it."

The hairs on the back of Mardaley's neck stood tall at those words. "What, then?"

Baern paused as he licked his lips. "You know what I said about Thuridan and his battle-mages having clear orders to kill any who aid Tip, should they need to?"

"Yes…"

"That order mentions the both of you by name. If you aid him in any way and are found out, Thuridan's been given free rein to hunt you down, and given the many grudges he carries against you, I'm sure you can appreciate his sentiment on the matter."

"Then I'd best make sure I'm not found out, then, hadn't I?" Mardaley said as he smiled warmly at Baern.

Baern's frown deepened at his words. "This is serious."

"I know."

"Look, Mardaley—"

"It's too late, Baern. By now, Tip'll be on his way here."

"What?" Baern asked.

"Tip's coming here?" Maline demanded.

"When?" both cried in unison.

"When he can," Mardaley replied, raising his hands as if to fend the pair off. "I helped him escape, so it stands to reason he will come here to seek my aid in freeing Marsha."

"So, you haven't heard from him?" Baern asked. Mardaley shook his head in response.

"In truth?"

"In truth."

"What do you intend, then?"

"The only thing I *can* do. The Tower won't stop hunting Tip, that much is plain, and that they found him where I kept him shows nowhere is safe. The only way out of this is to make them stop the hunt."

"And just how do you intend to convince the Shimmering Tower to stop hunting Anieszirel?"

Mardaley smiled sweetly at his friend. "Wait a while, you'll see."

"But…" Baern began, but he knew his friend all too well.

"You'd better be right about this one, Mardaley," he said instead.

Mardaley's smile widened. "When have I ever gotten it wrong?"

Sitting back in his seat, Baern chose not to answer.

*****

With his heart in his mouth, Tip hurried along beside Drake as they made their way through the streets of Merethia.

"You're doing fine, Tip, you're doing brilliantly. We're almost there, I'm sure."

But Tip paid her nary a mind, nodding distractedly as he stole glimpses of those about them. He was afraid, but his fear was not for himself.

"They will save her, Tip, you'll see. Soon, you and Marsha will leave Merethia together, hand in hand! And if not, at least you still have me."

It wasn't the first time Anieszirel had hinted at such an abhorrent notion, and, like all other times previous, it filled him with dread. A life without Marshalla… no, it was not worth contemplating. But then again, they had left so late, she'd been in those horrible people's hands for four whole days. Was she well? Was she even alive?

There was a strong chill in the night's air, one Tip was grateful for.

"We won't look out of place with our hoods up in this, too cold out," Drake had said to him when they'd first arrived in the city, and as they wandered through the evening's masses, he found himself more and more grateful none could see his face, let alone look him in the eye. Shivering slightly, Tip stole another glance at Davian as he hurried on, on the other side of Drake. Like him, he too hurried along with his head bowed. Like him, he too struggled to keep pace with Drake. And, like him, he too was afraid. But his fear was not just for Marshalla. No, he was also afraid for himself. Not that Tip could blame him, he may be returning home to a family he loathed, to a father he'd betrayed.

Lowering his gaze, Tip brought his mind to his own fear, and fought to bring it and his breathing under greater control. At last, Drake began to slow his pace.

"*I think we're here.*"

With a grateful sigh, Tip raised his head.

"Head down!" Drake hissed.

Instantly, Tip obliged. Before long, they were standing before an unfamiliar house on whose door Drake knocked quickly and quietly. For a tense few moments, all three stood silent. Tip stole a glance up at Drake. He was staring with increasing irritation at the door. With his own worry growing, Tip looked at the door once more.

"Do you think he's in?" he thought to Anieszirel.

"*Gods, I hope so.*"

Then the door finally swung open. All at once, Drake darted in, dragging Tip and Davian behind him just as the door swung shut.

"What in the world took you so long?" Mardaley demanded, glaring at Drake. Though it wasn't directed at him, Tip couldn't help but cower from Mardaley under the heat of his glare, backing into the door as he did so.

"Nice to see you too," Drake replied drily as he lowered his hood.

"This is serious, Drake. They've held that girl for four days now! Gods only know what she's had to endure!"

At those words, the now-familiar pangs of guilt struck Tip once again. Mardaley was right, they should've left sooner.

"*Now, don't start this again, Tip. We came as soon as we could. You have nothing to be ashamed of.*"

"I almost lost Kasha to your Tower friends, Mardaley," Drake snarled in response after a brief moment's silence. "I know how serious this is."

At those words, Mardaley's anger dissipated, replaced with worry. "That bad?"

Grimly, Drake nodded.

"His battle runes?"

"Only reason he's still alive."

"Dear gods. I'm sorry."

Nodding once more, Drake looked at the others.

"Bet you're glad to be here now, eh?" he said, smiling.

Mardaley dropped his gaze at them also. "Hello, you two."

"Hello, Mardaley," Tip and Davian said in unison as they both lowered their hoods. Mardaley smiled at them as he saw their faces, a gesture that drew a smile to their own lips.

"How have you been keeping?"

The two boys looked at each other.

"We've been—" Davian began, but a shrill cry cut him short. It was long and piercing, boring into Tip's brain as it threatened to deafen him completely. Then, as abrupt as it started, it stopped.

"Dear gods above, what was that?"

Cowering still from the onslaught, Tip's eyes darted up the stairs to the figure standing at their apex as blissful silence fell upon them all.

"Gods, woman!" Mardaley exclaimed, placing a hand on his chest as he fought to calm his nerves.

Ignoring him, Maline thundered down the stairs, her skirt hitched up in her hands, before dropping to her knees once at Tip and flinging her arms about him.

"Hello, Maline," Tip replied once they parted, the little elf smiling at her.

"My little darling," she said, her voice heavy with emotion.

"Missed you too."

Laughing, Maline hugged him once more, a hug Tip returned.

"She actually doesn't smell so bad now."

At last, they parted, and as they did so, Maline rose as she turned her gaze to Davian.

"Hello." She smiled.

Smiling, Davian bowed. "Nice to meet you again, Maline."

Maline nodded in response before turning to Drake. "Thank you for looking after them."

Drake frowned at her. "Didn't do a good job of it, did I?"

"Now, now, Drake," Mardaley said soothingly. "It's as much my fault as it is yours. And besides, you're here to get her back, are you not?"

Taking a deep breath, Drake nodded. "That I am."

"Come, then," Mardaley said as he headed for the sitting room. "This way."

"Will get supper started," Maline said as she turned and headed for the kitchen.

Tip watched Maline leave, then hurried after Mardaley and the others.

"About time you had a woman look after you," Drake said as Tip entered.

"Yeah, Maline's very good at looking after people," Tip said proudly.

"*That's not quite what he meant, Tip,*" Anieszirel noted as Drake stared at the little elf, an unmistakable glint in his eye.

"We don't have time for this, Drake," Mardaley growled as he sat.

"Oh?" Drake asked, smirking as he too sat. "Don't worry, old man, I'm not stealing this one."

"Drake…"

"Not a bad looker, though."

"Drake."

"I bet she can cook too."

"Drake!"

Smiling, Drake sat back in his seat as Mardaley glared at him, his cheeks taking on a slight reddish hue as he kept his gaze on Drake.

"Well, I for one think it's noble of you to take her in," Davian said.

Sitting tall, Mardaley looked at the stately young elf, nodding as he did so. "Thank you for saying that, young man, though it was something that had to be done. I did have a spare room after all."

Drake's smirk grew at Mardaley's words. "I know a few lords who met their courtesans in that manner."

"What's a courtesan?" Tip asked. As one, all three looked at him.

"Oh, I'm not touching that one," Drake said, shaking his head.

"*You truly don't know?*"

"No," Tip thought in response. "Asked Marsha lots, but she kept saying she'll tell me later."

"Tell you what, Tip, how about you ask Marsha when we get her out, eh?" Mardaley said.

At first, Tip moved to repeat what he'd told Anieszirel, but something in Mardaley's tone convinced him it would be pointless, and instead he simply nodded and sat back.

"I'll explain later, Tip," Davian said.

"You?" Drake asked, arching a brow at Davian.

Davian shrugged. "With a brother like mine, there are few things of that nature I don't already know."

"Is that right…?" Drake said, smiling evilly as he leant forward.

"Drake…"

"What?"

"Look, we're getting nowhere, and the night isn't getting any younger. Shall we at least focus on the task at hand?"

Sighing, Drake sat back once more.

"Thank you." Mardaley sighed, and casting one last sideways glance at Davian, he began.

"Now, before I begin, I must mention that this is a most delicate matter, not just because of the precarious situation Marsha is in, but also once this is all over, we need to ensure the Tower no longer has any reason to hunt Tip."

"But they want Ani back," Tip said, confused.

Mardaley looked at him, smiling. "And they shall have her back."

"*What?*"

"And before that harridan in your head starts screaming, I intend for the Tower to merely *think* they have her, nothing more."

"*There'd better not be!*"

Mardaley turned to Drake, the smile on his face fading to nothing.

"What that *does* mean though, is no Tower blood must be spilt this night."

Drake stared at Mardaley as a dark cloud fell upon him.

A tense silence filled the room as the men held each other's gazes.

"I cannot give the Tower any more reasons to hunt Tip and Marshalla," Mardaley continued after a spell. "For this to succeed, for them both to be safe once this is all done, no Tower mage can die. None. Do I have your word on this?"

"They nearly killed Kasha."

"Do I have your word on this, Drake?"

The tense silence returned as shopkeeper and ranger stared at one another.

"Yes," Drake said at last.

"Good," Mardaley said, relaxing visibly as he spoke. "Now, to the plan. There are tasks that must be performed by each of us. Except you, Tip."

"Wait, no!" Tip exclaimed, sitting bolt upright.

"I'm sorry, Tip, but they have a void sphere. We simply cannot risk you getting caught."

"But—"

"No, Tip. I give you my word, we will free Marshalla, but you must remain here while we do."

"*He's right, my darling. If we get caught in that thing, even I can't save you. Better we stay here.*"

The young boy's face fell greatly, but at last he nodded.

"Good."

"So, what's this great plan of yours?" Drake demanded.

"Well, Marshalla's being held in a storehouse in the Eastern Quarter, owned by Thuridan. The storehouse is guarded and patrolled by a total of fifty battle-mages, and—"

"Fifty!" Davian exclaimed.

Mardaley nodded. "I'm afraid so. After what happened to those sent to get her, the Tower's taking no chances."

"How are we going to get past so many?"

"Simple, the Matriarch is going to let us past."

"You've lost your mind," Drake said, Mardaley's words clearly unnerving him. "That heartless harpy would sooner carve out our hearts!"

Mardaley shook his head. "No, she won't, and do you want to know why?"

"No, I don't. But you're going to tell me anyway, and I'm not going to like it either."

Shaking his head in exasperation, Mardaley continued. "I have a friend in the Tower, a dear friend, who's close to the Matriarch. Thuridan's outmaneuvered him and kept him frozen out of the hunt for Tip, so we're going to help him outmaneuvere Thuridan in return."

"How do you propose we do that?"

Turning, Mardaley looked at Davian, a slight frown upon his lips.

"Davian is going to convince her."

"Me?" Davian said, frowning.

Mardaley nodded.

"How?"

Taking a deep breath, Mardaley turned to face Davian square before leaning towards the little elf.

"Understand, Davian, that I take no pleasure in asking this of you, but we are desperately short on time, and I see no other way."

Davian swallowed hard as he looked from Mardaley to his friends before turning his gaze back to the elderly storekeeper.

"What am I to do?"

"You're going to tell the Matriarch the truth, or at least our version of the truth."

"What truth?"

"That your father was behind the theft of Anieszirel."

"What?" Davian said, stunned.

"Was he?" Tip added in wonder.

Mardaley shook his head before shrugging briefly. "I don't know, maybe. The important thing is that she believes Davian."

"Why me?" Davian asked.

"Because it'll be more believable coming from you. You were there when Anieszirel was set free, but the whole scene seemed staged. And after you were whisked away, you woke up in some house you've never been in, bound in enchanted restraints. You managed to break yourself and Marshalla free, and you both decided to split up and make your way home, just in case you were still being hunted. Then, you arrived home just in time to hear your father berating your brother for not properly taking advantage of Fallon's death, like they'd planned."

Davian stared at Mardaley, his face a mask of horror. But Mardaley was far from done.

"But, and this is truly important, you need to say you overheard your brother plead with your father to teach him the mind domination magic he used to control Tip like he did. And when you realized what they were talking about, you confronted them."

"Dear gods," Davian whispered as all blood drained from his face.

"I know it's a lot to ask, but—"

"The Matriarch will think my father's a monster!"

"No," Mardaley replied firmly. "She will think you, Marshalla and Tip were nothing more than pawns."

"What if she asks me where I've been? What if she asks me why I didn't come forward sooner?"

Mardaley nodded. "We need her to ask you that, and when she does, you tell her you ran away from home, went out to find Marshalla and Tip. Then you three came to find me, and I helped you escape Merethia."

"Wait," Drake said as he sat forward, "won't she ask Marshalla what happened to her? Are you sure she will mention anything about enchanted chains."

Mardaley turned to the ranger, smiling. "She won't, but we can explain that away. Mental domination magic, remember? Thuridan would clearly not want her remembering anything that looks even remotely like he had a hand in any of the unpleasantries."

Drake pondered Mardaley's words for a spell. "But you'll still be giving that old bitch something to hang over you, having Davian admit you helped them escape."

Mardaley shrugged, turning his gaze back to Davian. "She already suspects, and before you say it, she's already using it against me."

Drake moved to speak, but instead sat back into his seat.

"If we play this right," Mardaley continued, "my friend will do the rest. He'll be there with us, Davian. He'll be the one to take us to her. After Marshalla's capture, you came to me with Drake, and Drake and I escorted you to him. He will suggest confronting Thuridan and Thalas together, so we will all go to Thuridan, and he in turn will send word for Thalas to join us."

Then Mardaley turned to Drake. "The next bit is for you."

"Go on." Drake replied, leaning forward.

"I'm going to suggest Anieszirel has been hiding in plain sight from the beginning, that she was never in Tip, but in one of Thalas' friends."

"What? No!" Davian exclaimed.

Mardaley looked back at Davian. "It's for the best, Davian. You of all people know the many evils they've committed. Would you choose one of them over Tip? Over Marshalla?"

"But…" Davian began, but his voice faltered.

"It's for the greater good, Davian. I wish there was another way, but we don't have the luxury of time."

"So, where do I come in?" Drake asked after a moment's uncomfortable silence.

Mardaley turned back to him. "You, my friend, have possibly the most important task of all. When I suggest one of them harbored Anieszirel, they will, of course, deny it. I will then suggest the void sphere be brought forth. When it is, and when the void sphere is passed near the biggest of them, a lad named Thane, I'm going to make him seem nervous, nervous enough for the Matriarch to see. She will naturally demand an answer from him, and when one is not forthcoming, she will press him. At that point, he will attack her, and when he raises his hands to cast a spell at her, I need you to put an arrow though him, but just graze his heart."

"*Clever.*"

"The timing is crucial, Drake. It *must* be when he prepares to cast his spell, and it *must* be before anyone else reacts. You must be the first."

"Why?"

"Because the others will try to contain him. If they do, they will then try to scry his mind, and should they do that, they will realize Anieszirel isn't in him."

"So what will putting an arrow through him do."

"*Panic.*"

"Panic, my friend. Anieszirel's reputation is such that none gathered will want her lodging within them if they can help it. That panic, I will feed. I will feed it and use it to make them trap the boy in the void sphere. And then, they will think they finally have Anieszirel."

"But why Thane?" asked Davian. "Why not one of the fifty mages?"

Mardaley turned to smile sadly at Davian. "Because he was there, Davian, and of all of your brother's friends, his parents have the least influence in Merethia. Which means they are least likely to have the Matriarch confirm the contents of the void sphere anytime soon."

"Are you sure this Thane will attack the Matriarch?" Drake asked.

"Oh, I'm sure. As sure as I am of him seeming nervous near the void sphere."

"Ah…"

"Won't they just look inside the sphere and see Ani's not in there?" Tip asked.

Mardaley turned to Tip, smiling. "You can't see what's inside it with your eyes, my boy. And the last time your friend was trapped in that thing, it was almost seventy years before she spoke to anyone from within it."

"*That long? I never realized.*"

"So, where is Marsha, then?" Drake asked.

"Thuridan's storehouse is in Wyvern District over in the Eastern Quarter. She's there."

"I see."

"I can't go through with this," Davian whispered, his gaze haunted. Mardaley turned to him. He stared at the little boy in silence for a spell, staring at him as he cowered in his seat before finally rising and, walking over to little Davian, squeezed beside him.

"I know what I ask is a lot, my boy, but without it, without you, Marshalla will never leave that place alive, and Tip will be running for the rest of his life. I need you to find the courage within you to see this through."

Davian looked away, but Mardaley reached out and gently turned his face to his.

"I know he's your father, and I know you still care for him, so what I ask is quite possibly the hardest thing anyone will ever ask of you. And, yes, I know the shame that will follow will be hard for him to swallow. But believe me when I say it won't be forever."

"It will destroy him."

"No, it w—"

"It will destroy all of us! The Grovemender name will be forever sullied. I can't—"

Mardaley clasped the little boy's face in his hands. "Two weeks from now, one of your father's apprentices will make a rather uncomfortable discovery. They will discover a trace of fennel mist in his office."

"Fennel mist? Where in the world would he be getting that from?"

"Do you know what that is?"

Frowning, Davian shook his head. Mardaley looked over at Drake, who was staring at him.

"I take it you know what it is?"

"Aye, but it hasn't been seen on these shores in decades."

"More like a century."

"What does it do?" Davian asked.

Drake looked at the worried little boy. "When its petals are ground into a paste, then treated and fed to someone, it allows that person's thoughts to be… influenced, without him knowing or realizing."

Davian's eyes widened in alarm as he pulled Mardaley's hands roughly off his face. "You can't feed that to my father!"

Mardaley laughed. "My dear boy, I have no plan to. It will, however, give your father the excuse he will need to free himself. It will allow him claim that someone must've influenced his thoughts, made him do what he did."

But Davian shook his head. "Nobody will believe that."

"Oh, they will have to, or risk being accused of being the ones to feed the fennel mist to him."

Davian remained unconvinced.

"It will work, Davian. It will set your father free. My friend will make sure of it, and he will make sure there's no word of dissent loud enough to cause you or your family any ill."

Davian stared at Mardaley for a spell, before staring into the ether as he pondered his words. But, at last, he shook his head.

"No. No, I can't—"

"Yes, you can. You can because you must. Your father will suffer shame, yes. He will suffer humiliation, yes. But he will recover, he will survive it. My friend in the Tower will make sure of it. When all this is over, your father will not have lost much. But your friends, your friends will have gained their freedom. Is that not a worthy trade?"

The guilt in Davian's eyes was almost heartbreaking as he stared at Tip.

"I…" But his voice failed him. Just then, Maline came back in. In a glance, she took in all present.

"Supper's ready," she said, her gaze matching the mood of the room perfectly.

Forcing a smile, Mardaley rose. "Come, let's eat. We'll talk more afterwards. Then we'll talk sleeping arrangements." And without waiting for any response, he followed Maline into the dining room.

"You think Davian will do it?" Tip asked Anieszirel as he rose.

"*I don't know. Mardaley's asking a lot of that little boy.*"

"But want him to do it. Does that make me bad?"

"*No, Tip, not in the slightest.*"

Casting one last guilt-filled glance at Davian, Tip hurried after Mardaley.

"*Tip, my darling, wake up.*"

"Urgf…"

"*Wake up, Tip.*"

"Just a bit more, Marsha."

"*No Tip, it's Ani. You need to wake up now.*"

As he came to his senses, Tip realized someone was rocking him gently, if a bit firmly. Muttering, he opened his eyes.

"Davi—" he began, but little Davian covered Tip's lips as he looked over at the softly snoring Drake lying not far from them. As the sleep lifted from his eyes, Tip looked quizzically at Davian, who simply gestured for Tip to follow as he rose. But when Tip stayed on his pallet, little Davian knelt back down, glancing at Drake once more before turning his gaze back to Tip.

"What say you and I go rescue Marsha?" Davian whispered, with a smile that was plainly forced. "Just us, together."

"But Mardaley said you go see the Matriarch lady day after tomorrow."

"I know, I know. But what if we save Marsha now, tonight? Just us."

"But… you told Mardaley you going to stay and practice what to say."

Davian sat back on his heels, his eyes screaming his exasperation at Tip. "But what if we save her, Tip? If we save her, we can all be free now, tonight. Isn't that what you and Ani wanted from the beginning? Just think, Tip, you, Marsha and I going wherever we please! Just us!"

"But Mardaley—"

"I can't go through with it, don't you understand?" Davian hissed. "I can't do as he asks! I can't damn my family like that. He's my father, for gods' sake!"

"But... but you promised—"

"I lied, alright? I lied. He just wouldn't shut up about it. But I can't do it, do you understand? I can't!"

"But how can you and me save Marsha by ourselves? Mardaley said there's fifty of them. That's a lot."

Davian grinned as he visibly relaxed. "I know the storehouse Mardaley mentioned. There are secret tunnels, hidden passages in! We can sneak in behind them all, rescue Marsha, and sneak out before any of them notice!"

At the mention of secret tunnels, little Tip had sat bolt upright as his eyes shone with excitement.

"We can sneak in like shadows!" he whispered.

"Yes, yes, just like shadows! But we'll have to go now, before they wake up."

All at once, Tip's excitement left him as he thought of Mardaley.

"Go, Tip."

"But he promised Mardaley," he thought in response.

"If you don't go, I think Davian's going to go without you. At least this way we can keep an eye on him."

"But what about that void thing?"

"The void sphere?"

"Yes."

"They can't use it on us if they can't see us, can they?"

Tip looked at Davian once more. He was staring at Tip with an air of expectation and worry.

"What did Ani say?"

"To go with you."

"There, you see?" He beamed. "Come."

Rising to his feet, Davian treaded carefully towards the front door. Tip rose and followed him.

"Wait, need to put my shoes on," he whispered once at Davian's side.

"Wear them outside, come," Davian whispered as he knocked both his and Tip's coats off their hanging pegs before pulling the key off the hook nearby and carefully unlocking the door. Then, with great care, both boys pulled back the bolt before stepping outside, closing the door as quietly as they could behind them.

"Go on," Davian whispered once outside, "wear your shoes."

Nodding, Tip did as Davian mentioned, and as he wore them, he heard the bolt slip softly into place behind the door and the key turn in the lock. Frowning, he looked up at a smiling Davian.

"How you do that from outside?"

"A little trick my brother taught me," he replied with a smug smile. "Come, we have a long way to go, and the sooner we get there the better."

Pulling Tip to his feet, Davian handed him his coat, and they both wore their coats as they hurried down the street. Then they heard a coach approach.

"This'll do nicely," Davian said, smiling as he waved at the coach.

"Got coin for it?"

"Mardaley did," Davian said with a mischievous grin as the coach stopped before them.

"No!" Tip exclaimed as Davian clambered in.

"Ani, Davian stole Mardaley's coin!" he thought.

"Yes, it would appear so. But he did it so you can go save Marsha, so that makes it alright, doesn't it?"

"Guess so…"

"Good. Now hurry up, Davian is waiting."

Looking up at his friend, Tip sighed and clambered in after him.

"Wyvern District please, Southern Keepers' Sector," Davian said once Tip had closed the coach door, and sitting back comfortably, both boys stared out of the window nearest them as the coach carried them forth.

The boys rode on in silence, each lost in their own thoughts, until at last, the coach came to a halt.

"We're here," Davian said with a cheer that was plainly forced as he clambered out.

"Okay," Tip said, the dread he felt lowering his voice.

Shivering, though not from the cold, he waited in silence as Davian paid the coach driver, and before long, they found themselves all alone on a deathly quiet corner.

"This way," Davian said and began walking.

They walked on in silence, side by side. As Tip walked on beside Davian, though, his mind was awhirl. He shouldn't be there, he was betraying Mardaley. Yes, they were going to save Marsha, yes, they intended to free her, but he'd given Mardaley his word, he'd sworn to stay behind. But then again, they were going to *save Marsha*. And besides, Davian was his friend, and Ani was right, having Davian go on his own would've been folly. But still, he was betraying Mardaley.

"Mardaley'll understand, Tip."

"But… feels wrong, Ani."

"Would you rather Davian went on his own and died?"

"No…"

"Neither would I. And neither would Mardaley, given the choice."

"But gave my word though. Marsha always said always keep your word, no matter what."

"And she's right. But sometimes we have to do things, or say things, that we don't like to do or even want to do. Sometimes we have to do some difficult things so we can help the ones we love. Or don't you agree?"

"Guess so…"

"Yes. And you do want to help Davian, don't you?"

"Yes…"

"And you do want to free Marsha, don't you?"

"Yes…"

"Then, just this once at least, it's okay to not keep your word."

But his guilt remained unmoved.

"It's for the best, Tip. Trust me."

Sighing, he looked at Davian beside him. Davian was staring worriedly at him.

"Is all well, Tip?"

Forcing a smile, Tip nodded.

"Thank you for coming."

"You should be thanking him."

Tip smiled. "Ani says should be thanking you."

Davian grinned at his words. "Did she now?"

"Yes," Tip replied, nodding. "But not going to."

"How rude!"

"Not rude! You was going to go on your own and leave me behind."

Davian stared at Tip with mock indignation.

"Well, maybe I'll do just that!" he exclaimed and quickened his pace.

Laughing, Tip hurried to his side, to which Davian simply quickened his pace even more. Except Tip matched him once again. It was at this point that little Davian broke into a dead sprint, laughing as he ran.

"Hey, wait!" Tip exclaimed as he raced after his friend.

The pair raced through the near-empty streets, laughing as they ran, until at last, Davian stopped before a moss-covered wall. Panting, he looked about him as Tip caught up to him.

"What… what is it?" Tip asked.

Davian nodded at the wall in response.

"We're here," he said as he scanned about him once more.

All at once, Tip's smile dissipated as fresh dread filled him. Davian looked over at him. Tip saw the same dread in Davian's eyes.

"Ready?"

Mutely, Tip nodded.

"Alright." Davian said as he placed a hesitant hand on the wall. Tip watched in silence as his friend undid the seals upon the wall, until at last the wall opened inwards. Taking a deep breath, little Davian called forth a small ball of flame above his outstretched palm and, looking at Tip briefly, stepped into the void before them. Tip watched him for a spell, but soon he too stepped within. Though, as he did so, an unnerving shiver ran down his spine. Stopping just inside, he spun round, looking about him.

"Ani, what was that?" he thought.

"What was what, my darling?"

"That… thing that touched me."

"What thing?"

"Something… don't know, something… touched me and—"

"You need to focus, Tip. Davian's waiting for you to get clear so he can close the wall… door…. thing,"

Tip looked behind him at Davian.

"Sorry," he said with a sheepish grin as he hurried past Davian.

Once both were clear, Davian returned the wall to as it was, before, side by side, they ventured deeper into the passage.

"Where we going?" Tip asked after a spell.

"Well," said Davian, "if I know my father, he will most likely be holding Marsha in one of the annex rooms. Easiest rooms to defend, hardest rooms to get to. This tunnel will take us straight to them."

The tunnel itself was long and winding, and alternated between taking the two boys downhill and forcing them uphill.

"How long is it?" Tip asked after another spell.

"Uhm…" Davian replied, "not altogether sure now. I don't recall it being this long. But then again, it's been some time since I was here."

Tip frowned as he turned to stare at Davian. "We lost?"

"Oh, don't be silly, Tip, we can't get lost! It's a single passage, how can anyone get lost following a single…"

But Davian's words died in his throat as the passage led them to a crossroad, with three paths forked out before them. Tip looked at Davian, but Davian kept his gaze ahead.

"Which one?" Tip asked after a brief moment's silence.

"Just a moment," Davian said hurriedly. "I'm trying to remember."

They stood in silence for another spell as Davian stared from one passage to the other. But, as time wore on, Tip's impatience grew.

"Which way?" Tip said at last.

"Uhm…" Davian said, staring frantically from one corridor to the other.

"This one!" he exclaimed and hurried towards the leftmost one.

"You sure?"

"Positive."

"*He's lying.*"

"Ani thinks you lying,"

"*Hey!*"

"Hey!" Davian echoed as he spun round to glare at him.

"Well, she does," Tip said softly.

"*You didn't have to tell him that.*"

Davian glared at Tip a spell, an act that fueled Tip's discomfort.

"For your information," he said at last, "the annex rooms are on the leftmost side of the storehouse. So, we are going left!" And without waiting for an answer, little Davian spun round and hurried on, leaving Tip in encroaching darkness.

Tip pouted at his friend a spell before finally racing after him.

"Ani says sorry," he lied once beside Davian.

Davian stared at him sideways.

"She's forgiven," he said at last, the stiffness of his gait dissipating as he spoke.

Smiling, Tip nodded before turning his gaze forward, the tension between them now gone.

"*And this from the boy who says lying is bad.*"

Tip chuckled in response, but kept his gaze forward.

"How long this one?" he asked.

"Uhm… not sure. But it's shorter, I think."

"Good," Tip replied, "feet are killing me."

Both boys walked on in silence, the light from Davian's little ball of flame casting a bright, if uneven light about them. Though not as winding as the path earlier, there were still a fair few turns the two boys had to navigate. But they carried on, their spirits lifted and their hearts set. Then, after quite some time, voices began drifting towards them. Slowing to a halt, Tip looked at Davian, who motioned for silence. Nodding, Tip obeyed as he stared at Davian, who seemed to be listening to the voices as if trying to determine their source.

"*Tip, allow me take over.*"

"Why, what's wrong?" he thought in response.

"*Davian's flame, it's too bright. Quickly, Tip.*"

Nodding, Tip did as he was bid.

"What is it?" Davian asked as he watched Tip nod.

Abruptly, Anieszirel looked up at him.

"The light is too bright," she whispered, gesturing to Davian's fireball.

"What?"

Shaking her head, she leant over and, clasping a hand over Davian's, extinguished the little ball.

"Hey!" Davian hissed as they were plunged into darkness. But it was only for a moment, for almost at once, a soft, unearthly glow encased them both, providing just enough light for them to see. Confused, Davian looked down at the glow about him.

"Ani?" he asked as he looked up.

Nodding, Anieszirel carried on. Smiling, Davian fell in step beside her. But his smile soon faded for, as they walked, the voices got louder. None spoke as they walked, but they all had the same one question on their minds – would Marsha be alone? At last, they reached the end of the tunnel. Standing before a solid wall of stone, Ani looked over at Davian, but her apprehension was mirrored in his eyes. The voices, they were coming from the other side.

"What now?" she whispered. Davian looked back at her, his apprehension already turning to fear.

"I…" he began, but his voice failed him.

"Does it open inwards or outwards?" Anieszirel asked.

"Inwards."

"Good," she nodded. "What's on the other side?"

"It opens up into a small corridor just outside the annex rooms," Davian replied.

Anieszirel winced. "Let's hope they're only checking on something. Maybe they'll leave soon,"

"Alright," Davian said, nodding as he spoke.

Both fell into silence as they stared at the wall before them, their ears pricked to hurting. Thankfully, they didn't have long to wait, for soon the voices were accompanied by the sound of footfall on stone, before both sounds began fading away.

"They're leaving," Davian whispered with a grin.

Smiling, Anieszirel nodded. "Seems like it."

Stepping aside, Anieszirel turned to Davian. "Go on, then."

"Right," he replied and reached out to touch the wall.

Closing his eyes, he whispered words of arcane as Anieszirel watched him intently, until at last the wall itself groaned and swung inwards.

"You didn't tell me it was this loud!" Anieszirel exclaimed as she hurried through.

"Sorry!"

Just then, the footfalls returned, and they were getting louder.

"Quick, close it!" Anieszirel hissed as she gestured first with her left hand, then with her right. As she did so, Davian turned to the wall, doing as he was bid. As the wall swung closed, however, it did so in complete silence, and it did so just in time as the moment it closed, three battle-mages came into view. Each battle-mage had one hand outstretched, with each hand surrounded by a pulsing aura.

"This way," Anieszirel whispered as she hurried over to the shadows nearby. Davian, however, stood where he was, staring mutely at the battle-mage.

"Davian!"

But little Davian remained unmoved, his eyes wide as he stared at the advancing battle-mages.

"Dear gods, Davian! Move!"

But it was too late, for now the battle-mages were standing directly before him.

"I don't see anything," one said, his eyes darting every which way.

"Me neither," a second replied, his tone much calmer.

"That doesn't mean nothing happened," said the oldest. "Let's check the wall, make sure it's true,"

All three spread apart as they walked over to the wall, with the first and second battle-mages walking on either side of a rigid Davian. As they passed him, the little elf finally came to his senses, and, breathing hard, he looked over at Anieszirel, who stared, dumbfounded, at him. Fighting back his tears, he hurried over to her as the three battle-mages began scrying about them for any illusions.

"Nothing," the first battle-mage said, his relief plain.

"Then, what did we hear?" the second asked.

"Perhaps it came from elsewhere?" the first offered.

"No," the third battle-mage said, "it came from here."

"It might've come from directly above here," the second said.

The third battle-mage looked at his comrades.

"Hurry," he said before breaking into a sprint.

In but a moment, the other two followed. Once their footfalls could no longer be heard, Anieszirel stepped out of the shadows, a shamed Davian following her.

"I'm sorry," he muttered once clear of the shadows.

Anieszirel looked at him a spell, then placed a reassuring hand upon his shoulder.

"You are young, Davian. The battlefield is no place for you, not yet at least, so what you felt is understandable. Just… try not to let it happen again, alright?"

Guiltily, Davian nodded.

"Good. Now, which way?"

"They didn't see me, did they?"

"Hmm? No, I hid us both."

"How did you make them walk past me?"

Anieszirel smiled. "I didn't. For that, you need to thank the gods. And while you're at it, thank them for making you come to your senses when you did."

"Oh?"

Anieszirel nodded. "The strength of their scrying spell would've unveiled you had you remained where you were."

"Oh."

"Yes. Now, which way?" Davian looked about him, but as he did so, his face fell.

"What is it?" Anieszirel asked, but before Davian could reply, the footfalls returned.

"Davian!" Anieszirel hissed.

"This way," Davian said and hurried down the passage before them. It was a passage that led to a set of large twin wooden doors.

"Where's that?" Anieszirel asked as they hurried down the passage. As if in response, the doors began creaking open. Grabbing Davian, the chronodragon leapt to the wall beside her as she hid the both of them from sight. As she finished her spell, the door opened wide and several battle-mages spilled into the passage. With eyes wide, she looked at Davian, whose eyes had grown in size. Pulling the little boy to his knees, Anieszirel dropped to hers, then motioned for them both to begin crawling forward. Hugging the wall as tightly as they could, both made their way forward.

At last, they reached the door. Stopping just behind it, both waited with bated breath for their chance to slip past. Once or twice, Anieszirel tried to do just that when there appeared a gap between the line of battle-mages, only for her to almost come face to shin with yet another battle-mage.

Then the line stopped. Nervously, Davian looked behind them, but Anieszirel paid the mages little mind, so intent was she on the door before her. As voices drifted towards them, the second door swung open and another battle-mage stepped out, the first door left open behind him. Seeing her chance, Anieszirel grabbed Davian, and snuck behind the battle-mage standing before the first door before sticking to the walls as soon as they entered the room.

As she entered, however, Anieszirel finally realized why so many battle-mages had stepped forth. This was their resting quarters. As this realization dawned on her, she turned to place a heartfelt glare upon little Davian, who cowered and wilted beneath it.

"You said it would take us straight to the annex rooms!" she hissed.

"I'm sorry."

"Where are we, Davian?"

Davian began to speak, but then began gesturing at something behind Anieszirel. Turning, she saw a battle-mage coming towards them. Grabbing Davian once more, the chronodragon hurried them over to a nearby corner.

"Well?" she demanded once they were safe.

"Well," Davian began, pointing to the twin doors at the far end of the room. "those doors should lead to some stairs. The annex rooms are at the bottom of the stairs."

Anieszirel looked from Davian to the twin doors and back again.

"Those doors."

"Yes."

"The ones on the other side of the room."

"Yes."

"A room filled with people looking to stick me in a void sphere."

"Yes…"

"Are you out of your mind?"

"Yes… I mean, no, no!"

"Urgh!" she exclaimed and turned to scan her surroundings.

"I'm sorry," Davian said softly.

Spinning, she glared at him, a sharp retort on her lips, but as her eyes beheld the dejection in his, her rage dissipated. Sighing, she ruffled his hair instead, then turned to survey their surroundings once more. Staring in silence, she watched the battle-mages intently, till at last, confident that she knew a way past them all, she turned to Davian.

"Now, I need you to follow me closely. You must move precisely when I move, and stop precisely when I stop. The illusion upon us is not an illusion complete, so we cannot so much as touch any of them. Do you understand?"

Davian nodded.

"Good." She turned her gaze forward. "Good." Taking a deep breath, she began crawling forward.

With their hearts in their mouths, the pair made their way towards their destination. With the many beds and furnishings in the room, their pace was hampered greatly, and with so many mages ambling through the few narrow pathways available, many a time the pair were forced to rapidly retreat, or even follow a long and painful detour to avoid being cornered by a battle-mage or two. It was a slow journey, one every bit as nerve-wracking as it was painstaking. But Davian did just as Anieszirel had asked, halting the moment she halted, and moving the moment she did, until at last, they reached the twin doors. But as they did so, the chronodragon paused, staring intently at the doors.

"Go on, then," Davian whispered after a spell, "open them."

Frowning, Anieszirel turned to him. "And how would you explain these doors opening of their own accord?"

"I…" Davian began, but fell silent.

Shaking her head, Anieszirel looked at the doors once more. She needed a ruse, any ruse. But she could think of none. Biting her lower lip, she looked about the room.

"There must be something…" she muttered as her mind raced.

"We can't stay here," Davian whispered, staring at the battle-mages nearby.

"I'm aware of that!" she snapped.

"*He's scared, Ani.*"

Anieszirel looked at Davian. "Sorry."

Mutely, Davian nodded, but as he looked away from her, his eyes lit up as he pointed, smiling. Frowning, Anieszirel turned to that which he pointed to, and as she beheld it, she too smiled.

"Quick, this way," she whispered and scrambled to a safe distance from the doors. As one, both watched a lone battle-mage approach with a tray of food. As one, both watched as the battle-mage opened one of the doors before carrying on, balancing the tray carefully as she did so.

"Go!" Anieszirel exclaimed, scrambling towards the door as it swung back into place. Both squeezed past just in time, and as the door slammed shut, both stared euphorically at each other.

"This way," Davian whispered, a huge grin on his face as he headed down the passage.

"Wait," Anieszirel called out and she hurried to him. "Best I go first, there *is* a battle-mage down there after all."

"Oh, right."

Cautiously, Anieszirel made her way down the passage, Davian hurrying behind her. Before long, they reached the stairs.

"Are you sure you don't want something more?"

It was the battle-mage.

"We're not your enemy. We just want Anieszirel, we have no wish to harm you."

Before long, they reached the bottom of the stairs. The battle-mage was standing before the middle of the three annex rooms, its door ajar. Turning, Anieszirel gestured to Davian to follow.

"I know it's a horrible thing we shall do to your young friend, but it is not something we relish. And I know it doesn't seem like it now, but you will heal. You will move on."

With the greatest of care, both made their way past the battle-mage.

"*Marsha!*" Tip exclaimed as Marshalla came into view behind the opened door. But she had her back to the mage, and to them.

"Very well, I shall return later for the tray. And I am sorry for this."

"Saying sorry so many times won't magically make it true," Marshalla growled.

"But if I say it often enough, perhaps you will believe it."

Marshalla held her peace. With a sad sigh, the battle-mage closed Marshalla's prison door and, whispering a word of arcane, turned and headed back the way she came. Huddled in the dark, Anieszirel waited till she heard the twin doors close before stepping out and undoing her cloaking spell. Walking over to the door, Davian close behind, she reached out and, placing a hand upon its handle, whispered the same word the mage had whispered, before swinging the door open. Marshalla had her back to them, but the tray was no longer to be seen.

"I see you decided to take the tray, then," Anieszirel said, her voice unnervingly similar to the battle-mage's.

"You come to gloat now?"

"No, but perhaps you will give an old friend the pleasure of seeing your face again?" she replied with a smile.

"Go on, Tip, go to her," Anieszirel thought to Tip as she allowed him take control once more.

"Hello, Marsha."

With a gasp, Marshalla spun round, her eyes going wide with surprise.

"Tip!" she exclaimed as her eyes fell upon the grinning little boy. "Davian! Dear gods, you came! How in the world did you get here?"

"Surprise!" Tip exclaimed, grinning widely as he threw his arms wide. Laughing, he turned to look over at Davian, who was chuckling behind him. But as he turned, something caught his eye, and as he focused upon it, his face turned from one of pure joviality to one of sheer terror. Then, in that one split moment, a thunderous crack filled the air as a lightning bolt of superior arcane brilliance struck Tip squarely in the chest, flinging him hard against the far wall.

"Tip!" Marshalla cried as she rushed to the edge of the room.

"No!" Davian whispered as he moved to run to his friend.

"Stay where you are!" a voice bellowed. "Do not move! Do not think for one moment that you being Thuridan's son will save you from my wrath. Do. Not. Move!"

Quivering with rage, Davian looked up at the battle-mage who had unleashed the spell at Tip. It was the elder mage from earlier, and he was not alone.

"You see?" the mage said, casting a sideways glance at the mage behind him. "I told you those etheric residuals couldn't possibly be from any elven spell. Now, do you believe me?"

"That I do," his companion said. "But do you truly think killing the boy was a sound tactic with Thuridan's son being so close to him?"

"I…"

"We shall discuss your battle tactics later," the leading battle-mage continued before turning to the others about him. "All eyes on the boy. I do not see any signs of Anieszirel leaving his body, so he yet lives. But should he so much as twitch, end him."

As one, the others raised their arms at Tip, pulsing auras surrounding their hands.

"If you end him, Anieszirel will be free to possess me," Davian warned.

The lead battle-mage nodded somberly at Davian. "Which is why I now advise you to hurry over to us, and do so immediately. You will not get another chance."

Davian tarried where he stood. "She might possess you instead."

"Yes, but we are trained to resist her, and have each sworn to give our lives and our existence to her capture. We will contain her till the void sphere is brought forth. Now, to us, young man."

But Davian remained where he stood.

"As you wish," the lead battle-mage said before abruptly turning.

"You," he continued, looking over at the mage nearest him. "Go upstairs, give word to the others that I need two more teams down here, and the rest to seal the entrance until further notice."

Nodding, he moved to obey, but, just then, Tip groaned.

"Careful, he stirs!" one of the other mages cried.

As one, all eyes turned to the little elf as Tip pulled himself to his feet, his hand using the wall behind him for support.

"You would strike down a little boy with no hesitation or warning," Anieszirel said through gritted teeth.

"Stay where you are, creature!" the lead battle-mage barked. "We will destroy you if we have to!"

"Oh, I fear you are going to have to." Slowly, she straightened, her eyes narrowing into slits as she snarled at the mages.

"Ready yourselves!" the lead battle-mage roared.

"Davian, please join Marsha in the room," Anieszirel said in a deceptively calm tone.

"There's a ward—" Marshalla began.

"Not anymore. Davian, now please."

"Release!" the lead battle-mage bellowed.

With a scream, Davian dove to the ground as all seven battle-mages unleashed their most lethal spells at Anieszirel. But none found their mark, each spell reflecting harmlessly off the shielding Anieszirel had erected about her, all save a lightning bolt, which slammed against the cold stone floor inches from Davian's head, erupting with such a roar as to startle the little elf, forcing him to scramble screaming into Marshalla's room.

"Go! Now!" the lead battle-mage barked at the one beside him.

Nodding, the younger high elf turned to do as he was bid. Anieszirel watched him as he turned. She watched him as he raced towards the steps. She watched as the others prepared another onslaught, and as she watched, she took one step forward, then a second, and by the third, she whispered a single word of arcane. As she exhaled the word, time itself slowed to a crawl. As she exhaled, she watched as Davian's desperate scramble slowed to a profoundly lethargic crawl. As she exhaled, she watched as the magic between the battle-mages' fingers sizzled, fizzled and danced. As she exhaled, she watched the retreating battle-mage's pace slow to a deeply lazy amble.

With an evil smile, the chronodragon then turned her focus to within, closing her eyes as she did so. And as she breathed deep, she supped of the power within, drinking deep of its splendor, gorging of it till it filled her with unbridled arcane brilliance. Then, when she'd supped enough, she opened her eyes.

"Now, you die," she snarled, before racing towards her prey.

With a single vault, leapt over those who had struck her before landing in a roll. As she came out of the roll, Anieszirel sprung to her feet, slamming both her knees into the back of the retreating battle-mage before clasping his shoulders with her hands, using her weight and her momentum to topple him, and as he landed face-first, the force of the blow to his head forced a darkness upon him. Smirking, Anieszirel placed a hand on the back of his head just as time began returning to as it was.

Turning, Anieszirel breathed at the remaining mages, her breath painting a mesmerizing pattern in the air as it encased the mages, only to dissipate just as a thunderous roar filled the passage, the stonework where she once stood reduced to smoldering rubble.

"What?" the lead battle-mage gasped when he realized Anieszirel was no longer there.

"Looking for me?"

Startled, they all turned, and as they laid eyes on her resting upon their companion, their surprise turned to fear. As they stared at her, though, they watched as a familiar flicker surrounded the hand she had placed upon the young battle-mage's head.

"No!" the lead mage exclaimed, reaching out to her, but his words were for naught, for Anieszirel then unleashed her spell into her captive's head, the lightning bolt searing a hole straight through him before blowing the step beneath his head asunder.

"You monster!" he cried as the remaining mages stared at her in horror.

Rising, Anieszirel walked towards them, rage and menace emanating from her in pulsing waves. It was then that the mages all realized; their spells of protection and defense, they were all gone, and it was then that their horror turned to panic. As their panic grew, they scrambled to form a wall between Anieszirel and their leader as they recast their protections. In response, Anieszirel whispered another word of arcane, one that, rather than slow time, sped time about her.

"Hold—" the lead mage began, but before he could complete his words, Anieszirel lunged through the still-forming wall and at him, slamming her head into his gut with such ferocity as to slam him hard against the wall behind him. The impact reverberated about all within as the man crumpled to the floor.

"Get—" began another, but before she could complete her words, Anieszirel barreled into her, slamming an elbow into her gut and throwing her off her feet before flinging her through the wooden door behind her.

Then, before the others could react, the seething chronodragon leapt briefly into the air before burying her left heel deep into the chest of the mage that had attacked Tip, the sound of breaking bones sweet music to her ears as he flew backwards from the others.

But she was far from finished, and as she landed, Anieszirel dropped into a crouch before sweeping the last three off their feet, and, as they sailed into the air, she rose briefly before dropping into a crouch once more, this time slamming her right palm onto the stone floor, releasing from it earthen magic of such dark designs as to call forth from the stone floor three stone spikes upon which all three mages were impaled by the skull.

Slowly, she rose, her eyes fixed upon the battle-mage cowering at the far end of the passage. She walked towards him, her ire burning bright and fierce.

"Mercy," he mumbled, clutching his chest in pain.

"Mercy?" she asked, undoing her spell as she walked. "Did you show Tip any mercy? Or me? Hrm?"

"Please," he begged, wincing as he spoke. "I was only—"

But his voice died in his throat as loud voices drifted toward them. More mages coming down the stairs. Anieszirel looked from the stairs behind her to the now smirking mage.

"No matter what you do to me, creature," he snickered, "you will not leave here."

Anieszirel stared at the smirking face of the battle-mage before her, and as she stared, and as she listened to the clamoring behind her, her blood began to boil.

"She's over here!" the mage bellowed with all the strength he could muster.

Roaring with rage, Anieszirel darted over to him, and, clasping his tunic in her hand, pulled him towards her. Staring at the stairs, she took a step, a second, and a third before leaping up into the air, mage in hand, her eyes firmly fixed on the base of the stairs. As she hovered in the air, she raised her hand, complete with flailing mage. As she hovered there in the air, she called forth arcane power in its rawest form into her hand. As she hovered there in the air, she filled her hand with the power she would need to save herself and her friends, and when she'd called forth enough power, she lunged at the stairs just as the first mage appeared, slamming her hand, complete with flailing mage, onto its base. The explosion that ensued flung the mage on the stairs back upwards before shattering the stairs themselves, every single one of them, a shattering that brought the entire alcove within which the stairs were crumbling down.

As the rumble subsided, Anieszirel rose. She looked at the mage that was in her hand. There was precious little left of him. She looked up at the pile of rubble where the stairs once were.

"Did they have to die, Ani?"

"They tried to kill you, Tip. They tried to hurt Davian."

"But did they have to die?"

"Only way to stop them,"

"Wish they didn't have to die."

Not knowing what to say, she turned and headed towards the middle room. As she passed the first room, a pained groan drifted to her ears. Turning, she saw one of the battle-mages huddled in the darkness, and with a snarl, she stormed forward.

"Please, please!"

Ignoring her pleas, Anieszirel grabbed her tunic, pulling her to her knees.

"Aah!" she exclaimed as she cradled her right arm.

"*She doesn't have to die, Ani, she won't hurt us. Please.*"

Anieszirel glared at the woman before pulling her close, so close she could hear the mage's beating heart.

"Thank Tip."

"Who?"

"Tip!" Anieszirel barked, shaking her roughly as she spoke, an act that elicited a very loud yelp.

"Thank him! He just saved your life!"

"Thank you, Tip!" the battle-mage exclaimed. "Thank you! Thank you!"

Snarling still, Anieszirel flung her backwards.

"Pathetic," she growled, then marched out and over to Marshalla and Davian. "Time we were away."

"What happened out there?" Marshalla asked, her voice quivering.

"Do not ask me something you do not wish answered. We need to leave. Now."

"Can you not teleport us out of here?" Davian asked.

Anieszirel turned to the boy. "They've erected a strong paling about this place. You will both get etheric poisoning if I do, and I doubt either one of you wishes to be afflicted with that while we're running for our lives, now do you?"

"No," Davian replied as Marshalla shook her head.

"Good. Now, tell me there's a way out of here."

"Yes," Davian said, heading out of the room. "This way." But he soon came to a halt when the carnage Anieszirel had wrought came to view.

"Gods…" he whispered as his eyes grew wide.

"You killed them," Marshalla whispered.

"You would rather I had let Tip and Davian die?"

Marshalla said nary a word.

"Precisely!"

"*Ani, please.*"

Stopping, Anieszirel closed her eyes before bringing her ire to heel.

"And you're welcome, by the way," she said in a much calmer voice, forcing a smile as she spoke.

Marshalla looked from the carnage to Anieszirel before smiling gratefully at her. As one, both turned to Davian.

"Well?" they said in unison.

"Oh, right," he said and hurried to the wall.

"And speaking of surviving," Anieszirel said. "Where did Tip get these clothes from?"

"*Mardaley.*"

"Mardaley," Marshalla replied. "Gave me some too, but left them over at Drake's."

"Remind me to thank Mardaley next we meet," she said as the sound of groaning stone filled the room.

"Wait..." Anieszirel said, a slow smile parting her lips. "This is the entrance we were supposed to come out of, isn't it?"

Davian turned to Anieszirel as a sheepish smile parted his lips.

"So we should've gone... right?"

"Yes..."

Rolling her eyes, she stepped into the darkness, followed closely by the others. And with that, all three left the massacre behind and made good their escape, Davian closing the passage behind them as they left.

Irritated, Thuridan stepped out of his reading room.

"What is the meaning of this?" he demanded as a nervous battle-mage walked over to him.

"Archmage Grovemender." The mage bowed as he reached Thuridan.

"Spit it out, I'm busy!"

The young battle-mage licked his lips. "Archmage, we... we were attacked a few moments ago..."

Thuridan's irritation drained at those words, chased away by his rising panic.

"... by... by the Kin-Slayer, and—"

"What did you say?"

Instantly, the battle-mage dropped his gaze.

"And why aren't you there stopping her?"

"We have her trapped, Archmage," the young mage replied, raising his gaze. "We—"

"Where?"

"Down by the annex rooms. Some of us corn—"

Thuridan raised a hand for silence. "She managed to fight her way all the way down there, and only *now* you come to inform me?"

Thuridan's voice was barely above a whisper, but the battle-mage before him cowered as if it were a thundering bellow.

"N-no, Archmage," the poor elf stammered, "we didn't realize she was inside the compound till one of our patrols chanced upon her near the annex rooms, and—"

Once again, Thuridan raised a hand, a deep frown twisted his brow.

"What do you mean, she was inside without being noticed? Do you mean to tell me—" As he spoke, however, Thuridan suddenly stood ramrod straight as his eyes widened greatly.

"Was Davian with her?" he gasped.

"Archmage?"

"My son! Was my son with her?"

"I—"

"There's a secret passage into the annex rooms, you fool! Davian must've shown her. I didn't think he knew of it."

"Archmage, we didn't know! We—"

"Shut up, just shut up! Get back there, now. I want a full contingent down in the annex rooms immediately! I want that creature imprisoned in the void sphere by the time I arrive!"

"There's a complication, Archmage."

"Complication, what complication?"

"The void sphere, it's down there with her."

At those simple words, all color drained from Thuridan's features, and without so much as a word, a terrified Thuridan Grovemender turned and raced out of his home, a similarly terrified elven messenger racing after him.

Turning into the shadows, the three friends cowered in the darkness. Cautiously, Anieszirel peered round the corner, her eyes scanning for signs of anyone giving chase. At last, she returned her gaze to her friends.

"I think we're safe now."

"Thank… the gods," Davian said between pants, a grateful smile upon his lips. He looked over at Marshalla, and as he did so, waves of euphoric joy washed over him.

"You're free, Marsha! You're *free!*"

Anieszirel stared from one to the other, smiling.

"Hold, someone wishes to speak to you both," she soon said, then stared into the ether. Then, without warning, Tip lunged at Marshalla, flinging his arms about her before hugging her with all his might.

Laughing, Marshalla hugged him back. "Take it you missed me, then?"

Tip looked up at her, grinning. "Only a little."

"Come," Davian said, "let's get back. With luck, we can return before Mardaley awakens."

"Oh!" Tip exclaimed, springing to his feet as he remembered the manner of their leaving.

"Tip," a voice called out from around the corner.

All at once, Tip dropped into a crouch as a frowning, Davian peered cautiously round the corner. As he turned to his friends, his frown deepened.

"It's Neremi," he whispered.

"Who?" Marshalla asked.

"My brother's beloved."

"What she want?"

Davian shrugged and peered round once again.

"Tip, I know you're there. I simply wish to talk."

None moved.

"Tip, please, I don't have much time, Thalas and the others will soon realize I've left them."

Still, none moved.

"Very well, I shall speak, and you listen. I'm sorry for what happened at the Tower. You have to believe it was not my intent for you or your friend to be harmed. That was Thalas. I know not what overcame him, but he went too far. What he did to your friend, it was wrong, it was all wrong. I know I went along with it, and that makes me guilty, but… you must understand, the reason I went along with it is because I am tired of this life. I just wanted an end to it. Is that so wrong? Tip, you have to believe all I wanted was a means to leave Merethia behind and start over, just Thalas and I."

Frowning, the three friends looked at each other.

"We were using you to steal the Kin-Slayer, yes. Thalas learnt of your… gift from his father, and we planned to use it to free the Kin-Slayer's void sphere so we may leave with it. But that was our plan, just that. We never meant to hurt you. *I* never meant to hurt you."

"Why you here, then?" Marshalla demanded.

"I… I still want to leave Merethia, but Thalas is… he's lost his mind! He scares me now. Take me with you! Please! I'll do anything you ask, anything! Just… just let me leave with you. I'm a capable mage, I truly am, and I'll do anything you ask."

"And we supposed to believe that?"

"You don't speak for Tip."

"Marsha's my friend!" Tip yelled. "If she doesn't believe you, you not coming!"

"Then perhaps you need to choose your friends with greater care."

Tip frowned. "What you mean?"

"Ask her, Tip. Ask her why she changed her mind about old Grovemender's offer. Ask her why she accepted."

Frowning still, Tip looked at Marshalla. The guilt he saw in her eyes bore into him. "Marsha…?"

"Don't listen to her, Tip," Marshalla said hurriedly. "She's lying."

"Did she tell you?" Neremi said. "Did she tell you what she did?"

"Look, Tip," Marshalla said, clasping Tip's face in her hands. "Did what was best for the both of us. That's all! Just that!"

Stubbornly, Tip pulled at her hands about his face.

"Tip, please," Marshalla begged as she held onto his face.

"She took his money, Tip. Your dear friend took Grovemender's money. He paid her to bring you under his roof. He paid her to let him use you. He paid her to help him steal your gift from you!"

It was as if time stood still between Marshalla and Tip.

"Tip, listen," Marshalla pleaded as she leant forward, tears stinging her eyes as she grasped hold of her dear Tip.

"You took his coin," Tip said, his voice heartachingly soft.

"Didn't know he was planning to—"

"You lied."

"No, Tip, please, listen to—"

"You tricked me." Slowly, Tip rose as he pulled free at last of Marshalla's grasp. "You lied."

"No, Tip, wait—"

"You said nothing was more important than us. You said—"

"Tip, please!"

"Liar!"

"Tip!"

"Liar, liar, liar! Hate you! Liar!" Yelling at the top of his voice, Tip turned on his heels and raced away from Marshalla. He cared not where his feet took him, so long as it was away from her.

"Tip!" Marshalla screamed, springing to her feet before racing after him.

Being the taller, Marshalla swiftly closed the gap between them, but as she reached out to grab him, movement at the edge of her vision caught her eye, and as she looked up, what she saw chilled her heart.

"Tip!" she screamed once more, and, lunging towards the racing boy, she shoved him roughly off his feet and out of the path of the thick tree trunk that Eldred had flung at him from the window of a nearby building. The trunk was attached by ropes to a pole protruding from another building, ropes that allowed the trunk to swing right at Tip, and by shoving him as hard as she did, Marshalla shoved him clear of it. However, in her haste to get him clear, she'd sacrificed her balance, and as she stumbled forward, she stumbled into the path of the trunk.

As Tip fell forward, he was spared the sight of the trunk crashing into Marshalla's ribs. He was spared the sight of Marshalla being launched high into the air, and was spared the sight of her falling back down to the cobbled streets. He was spared the sight of it all, but not the sound of it, and as he rose, he rose with his heart in his throat.

"Marsha...?" he said softly as he turned.

It was then he saw his beloved Marshalla lying on the stones broken and bleeding.

"Marsha!" he shrieked, racing over to her as tears welled in his eyes.

"Marsha, get up," he pleaded once by her side.

Marshalla looked at him. Smiling, she tried to speak, but her breath came in snatches.

"Marsha, get up!" he begged as he shook her.

"Tip, no!" Davian exclaimed as he reached his friend. "Her ribs are broken! We have to be gentle. We…" But his voice died in his throat as a pool of blood appeared beneath Marshalla's head and began spreading.

"No! Marsha!" Tip screamed, placing his hands on her chest as tears streamed freely down his cheeks.

Marshalla smiled at him still.

"It's okay," she mouthed at him. "It's okay, Tip."

"No! Marsha, no!"

"Didn't mean to lie, didn't… mean… to…" Then she was still.

As Tip stared at Marshalla's lifeless body, his heart broke and his soul withered as every part of his being cried out in pain.

"Marsha!" he shrieked as he shook her with all his might. "Marsha!"

Abruptly, Davian rose, glaring at something behind Tip.

"Stay back!" he yelled as he darted forward, calling forth a ball of flame as he went.

"Stay back!" he bellowed, glaring at Thalas and Thane as they approached Tip with care, the void sphere hovering eerily between them.

"Damn it, stay back!"

But they ignored him.

"Tip, run!"

But Tip could not hear him.

"Run!"

"I'm so sorry, Tip."

At last, Tip looked up, but his gaze went to Eldred.

"They killed Marsha, Ani," he thought to Anieszirel as his rage built.

"I know, Tip. I'm so sorry."

"For the love of the gods, Tip, run!" Davian pleaded.

"They killed Marsha, Ani."

"I know."

"Why did they kill her?"

"Because they are bad people, Tip."

"It's not fair."

"I know, Tip, I know."

"Tip, please!" Davian screamed.

At that moment, Thalas flung a gust at his brother, sending him tumbling safely away from Tip before casting another spell to pin Davian where he came to rest.

"*I can make them answer for this, Tip. Do you wish me to?*"

"They killed Marsha. It's not fair."

"*Do you wish me to, Tip?*"

Tip knelt where he was, staring up at Eldred as his rage grew. There could be only one answer.

"Make them pay, Ani. Make them all pay."

"*Then I need you to allow me control, allow me full control.*"

"How?"

"*I'll show you.*"

Reaching Tip, Thalas looked over at Thane. The little boy knelt, unmoving, his eyes upon Eldred. Licking his lips, Thalas nodded at Thane, and together they carefully set the void sphere on the ground. The plan had been for the trunk to knock Tip into the void sphere's reach, but the new turn of events seemed just as effective. With the void sphere in place, Thalas nodded once more at Thane, then both hurried away lest they be caught in the void sphere's grasp. Then, once safely away, Thalas began undoing the spell of shielding as Neremi and Durlin hurried over to them. But just as he began, an aura of purest azure surrounded Tip, then began pulsing.

"Thalas…" Thane said.

Thalas looked up from the void sphere and at Tip. Swallowing hard, he looked back at the void sphere as he hurried the spell. But he did not get much further, for without warning, an almighty gale blew against the four, sending them careening backwards, the void sphere tumbling past them. Slowly, Anieszirel rose, her gaze unwavering upon Eldred, and as she rose, Eldred was plucked from the window he leant out of by an unseen hand.

"Eldred!" Neremi shrieked as she raced forth, but she soon came to a screeching halt as Eldred suddenly flung his arms and feet out as wide as they could go. As his friends watched, Eldred struggled and shuddered as a great force held him.

"Let him go!" Durlin bellowed as he and the others caught up to Neremi, who had stopped only a few paces from Anieszirel.

But the chronodragon ignored them. Even when all four raised their hands at her, she paid them nary a mind. Then, Eldred screamed. It was a scream of utter pain, one as blood-curdling as it was heart-wrenching, and as his friends looked up at him, they all watched in sheer horror as his limbs were torn from his body before being flung far afield, while Eldred himself fell to the ground. The nauseating sound his body made at he landed filled all his friends with sickening disgust.

Roaring as one, they unleashed all they could at the little boy before them. Laughing, Anieszirel turned, their spells reflecting harmlessly off her shield, a shield wide enough to protect both Marshalla's body and Davian as he lay pinned a few steps behind Anieszirel. But soon, one by one, the four lowered their hands, their tears spent along with their magic.

"Is that it?" Anieszirel asked, her azure pupil-less eyes moving over each in turn. Once her gaze fell upon Thane however, she grinned.

"My turn," she said, and floating slightly above the ground, she smirked at the towering elf.

As his friends stared from her to him, a sudden gust of wind sprung up about Thane, forcing the others away from him as it encircled him.

"What– Ah!" Wincing, Thane raised his hand to his cheek where a wind blade had cut him. Looking through his cage of air at his captor, he sneered defiantly at Anieszirel, but it was a sneer that was quickly wiped from his lips as another wind blade sliced at him, this time cutting deep into his arm. And then another cut, followed by another, and another, the current in his cage getting stronger with each cut, and each growth in strength bringing about another wind blade to cut him, until at last, the roar of the wind was such that it completely drowned out Thane's cries as it hid him from view.

"Dear gods," Durlin whispered as the cage turned crimson.

But Thane had fallen silent, and as the winds finally died, Thane's blood gushed about their feet as the remains of his corpse tumbled forth.

"Your turn."

Staring at the smirking creature before them, the three friends slowly backed away.

"Oh, don't be shy, we're having so much fun."

Glancing briefly at each other once more, the three promptly turned and ran, all three casting haste spells upon themselves as they raced.

"Hide and seek it is," Anieszirel said, smirking still.

"Please," Davian pleaded where he lay.

Curious, Anieszirel turned to him.

"He's my brother."

Anieszirel stared at the pleading child for a scant few moments, a sad smile upon her lips. Then, at last, she sighed.

"He killed Marshalla, Davian. He and his friends killed her before Tip, and that young girl meant more to him than life itself. I'm sorry my dear, I truly am sorry, but... he made his choice, and now he must answer for it."

Then, she floated higher.

"Take care of yourself, my dear," she said, and with a slight bow, raced off after Thalas and his friends, the bonds holding Davian in place dissipating as she left.

Davian sat up and watched her disappear, tears welling in his eyes as his heart broke.

"Davian!"

Turning, Davian watched as Mardaley raced towards him, Drake and Magister Meadowview following close behind him.

"What in the world are you…" Mardaley began once reaching the kneeling boy, but his voice died in his throat the moment he saw who it was that lay near him.

"No…" he whispered, falling to his knees.

"What happened here…?" Baern whispered, his mouth agape as his own gaze fell upon the unholy mound not far from Davian.

"Ani's going to kill Thalas," Davian said as tears trickled down his cheeks, "and Tip's going to let her."

Mardaley looked up at him. "Which way?"

Sniffling, he pointed in the direction Anieszirel had raced. Mardaley turned to where the little boy pointed.

"Drake, stay here with him. And keep Marshalla's body safe."

"Right," Drake muttered as he knelt beside Davian.

Nodding, Mardaley looked at Baern. "Baern?"

"I'm with you, my friend."

"Then come, before it's too late."

Panting heavily, Neremi collapsed against a nearby wall. She looked over at her beloved, her terror plain in her gaze. Fighting for breath, Thalas wandered over to her, hugging her tightly once he was by her.

"We can't… stay here," Durlin said. "She'll be… hunting us."

Thalas looked over at Durlin before staring at Neremi in his arms. "He's right."

Swallowing hard, Neremi nodded as she parted from him.

"Where do we go?" she asked.

Turning, Thalas stared down the street towards a familiar storehouse.

"We head to my father. He wants his prize so badly, he can have her."

"You really think he's going to—" But as Durlin spoke, vines began growing about his feet, holding him fast and firm.

"What in the hells?" he muttered as he struggled against them.

With his heart in his throat, Thalas looked behind them, praying he was wrong, but the sight of a smirking Anieszirel telling him he was not.

"Run!" he bellowed.

"Help me!" Durlin cried.

But Thalas ignored him, grabbing Neremi by the arm and pulling her after him.

"Run, Neremi! Run!"

As the lovers ran, they ran to the sound of their friend screaming in pain. They were screams that grew louder and louder, until they abruptly ended.

"Keep running!" Thalas bellowed.

Neremi turned to glare at him. "Did you have to—"

But her words were cut short by the wind blade that sliced through her neck, severing her head from the rest of her and spraying Thalas with his beloved's blood. Startled, Thalas came to a dead stop as he watched Neremi's head roll away from him.

"A pretty sight, isn't it?"

Quivering, he turned to face Anieszirel.

"Though I wager you've seen such a sight many a time before."

"What do you want from me?" he quivered.

"Your life."

"Please," he begged, going down on his knees. "Please, I'll do anything you ask. I'll help you leave Merethia, I'll help you leave right now! I know many places you can go, places where you will never be found!"

Anieszirel smirked at him. "And you will take me there?"

"Yes! Yes!"

"And all from the kindness of your heart I wager."

"Please."

"Well, you see, the issue here is that Tip is angry. He is gloriously livid! And you are the object of his rage. So, I'm afraid I cannot let you live."

Thalas swallowed hard as he struggled with his self-control.

"But I *will* do you this one small favor."

"What?"

"Run."

"*No!*"

"What?"

"Go on, run. Run, little mouse, run. Let's see how far you get before I kill you. And do please make the chase worthwhile."

Scrambling to his feet, Thalas turned and ran with all he had, Anieszirel's mocking laughter ringing in his ears.

"No, Ani! He'll get away!"

"Oh don't worry, Tip, he won't get far." And smiling, Anieszirel floated on after him.

Quivering with rage, and no small dose of panic, Thuridan stormed through the square. He'd been right, of course, the Kin-Slayer had made good her escape. Worse still, the void sphere was gone. And to rub salt into the wound, they'd hadn't even bothered to close the secret passage behind them. It was almost as if she was taunting him. A part of him had hoped the Kin-Slayer wouldn't have realized the void sphere was within reach, a part of him had hoped she would've overlooked it, or even left it for fear of being trapped accidentally. But no, no she was too cunning for that, clearly.

As he walked past the Wyvern fountain, however, a disheveled elf burst into the square across from him. From where he stood, Thuridan could see the blood across the elf's face and clothes. But that was not all he saw.

"Thalas?" he said, slowing to a halt as the figure stumbled. His son was clearly under a haste spell, but was running with reckless abandon.

"Thalas!" Thuridan bellowed.

But Thalas did not look at his father. Instead, his gaze was behind him as he rose to his feet. Something was chasing him, and as Thuridan stared at his son, he soon realized, with sickening clarity, what was transpiring before his eyes. In a fit of rage, the Archmage flung a wind vine at the terrified elf, spinning it about his son's waist before pulling Thalas savagely to him, dispelling his son's haste spell as he landed clumsily before him. Startled, Thalas looked up from his father's feet to his father's furious face.

"Father!" he exclaimed, bounding to his feet.

"*You* stole the void sphere," he snarled, words that caused the other five mages with him to glare at Thalas.

"Father, I—"

"You tried to use it on the Kin-Slayer, and now she's hunting you, isn't she?"

"No, Father, we—"

"The others are dead, and now she's after you."

"No, Father, please—"

Disgusted, Thuridan waved his son to silence before turning to the youngest of his mages.

"Return to the storehouse, bring everyone here with all haste. We'll hold her here for as long as we can, but hurry."

"Nobody's at the storehouse, Archmage, they're all out searching."

"Then find them! Find them all and bring them here. Do you understand?"

Grimly, the battle-mage nodded.

"Yes, Archmage," he said before casting a haste spell upon himself.

Nodding, Thuridan turned back to his son. "Did she destroy it?"

"Father, please, you need to—"

Seething, Thuridan smashed the back of his fist against his son's cheek. "Did. She. Destroy. it?"

Dropping his gaze, Thalas shook his head. Thuridan looked at another of his battle-mages.

"Go with him, bring the void sphere with all speed. You are our only hope. Should you fail, we—"

"Archmage," a third battle-mage said as she pointed.

Turning, Thuridan's gaze fell upon Anieszirel floating eerily at the edge of the square, a chilling smirk upon her lips. The Archmage frowned at her.

"Be it fifty or five hundred," he continued, "we fail here without the void sphere. Bring it."

"Yes, Archmage," the second battle-mage replied solemnly before grabbing Thalas and pulling him behind the others. In response, Thuridan took two steps forward, motioning for the remaining three to follow him until Thalas and the last battle-mage were hidden behind them.

"Thalas," Thuridan said, his gaze upon Anieszirel.

"Yes, Father?"

"If you do not return with that void sphere, the Kin-Slayer will hunt you to the very ends of the earth."

"I will return, Father."

Thuridan nodded. "Good. And when this is over, you are to leave Merethia, never to return. Since you wish for freedom so much, it is yours."

"Father, I—"

"Should you ever return, I will fulfil my promise to you. Do you understand?"

"Please, Father—"

"Do you understand?"

"Yes…"

"Good. Now, go."

Taking a deep breath and letting it out slowly, Thuridan calmed his nerves as his gaze darkened.

"Prepare!" he barked, and as one, he and his remaining battle-mages strengthened their spells of protection and shielding.

"Summon," Thuridan ordered once all were done.

"But, Archmage," one of the three spoke up. "we're still in Merethia. We're bound by her laws and—"

"I said *summon*!" Thuridan bellowed, turning to glare at the outspoken battle-mage. Seeing the fear in his eyes, he relented and turned to face their foe.

"We need every advantage here."

"Yes, Archmage," the man said, and without another word, they did as he bid.

"Can't see him, Ani."

"Oh he's there, Tip."

"Don't let him get away."

"I won't. But I'm going to have to hurt the ones shielding him."

"Don't care. He can't get away."

"Oh, don't worry, Tip, he won't." Calmly, Anieszirel floated forward, but as she did so, four creatures burst into being about the mages, causing her to slow to a stop.

"Well, well," she said loudly. "I suppose I should be honored that you would fear me enough to violate one of Merethia's capital laws in such grand a manner." As she spoke, she cast her eyes upon the four creatures.

"*They have a dragon, Ani.*"

Smirking, Anieszirel stared at the winged wyrm floating above Thuridan.

"*They have a dragon.*"

"No, Tip, not a dragon, a wyvern. It's weaker, more pathetic. Nothing more than a status symbol."

Anieszirel then turned her gaze to the majestic griffin standing before all the others. As she stared at the creature, the rays of the night's sun glistening off the pure white feathers about its head, the smirk faded from her lips.

"That's the one we need to be wary of," she said, "not the wyvern."

"*Can you kill it?*"

"Oh, yes," Anieszirel replied, nodding as she smiled. "But first, let's put a little doubt in their hearts, shall we?"

Floating forward a few steps, she stopped before drifting slightly higher.

"You four, hear me and hear me well," she called out, her voice echoing about them like a tempest. "I care not for you; your lives do not interest me in the slightest. I only wish for Thalas Grovemender. Give him to me, and none of you need die here."

Each of the three cast sideways glances at Thuridan, but none moved.

"Thalas took the life of an innocent, and I am here for justice. Give him to me that justice may be done. Refuse me, and none shall leave here alive."

"Bold words, Kin-Slayer," Thuridan bellowed in response. "Let us see if you have the mettle to match."

"Your friends in the storehouse," Anieszirel continued, ignoring Thuridan, "they died because they tried to take the lives of my friends, Marshalla and Davian..."

Even Thuridan balked at this, the thought of his dearest coming close to death at the hands of his own people a thought that cut him to his core.

"...and know that I speak the truth. Return Thalas to me and you may live. Refuse and here you shall fall!"

"No, Kin-Slayer!" Thuridan roared, forcing the horrifying image in his mind's eye away from him. "No, it is *you* who shall fall! Attack!"

And with a thunderous cry, the battle was joined. As one, all four familiars lunged at Anieszirel, from the screeching griffin, its wings wide as it took to the air to dive down upon its prey, to the roaring wyvern, it's jaws dripping in anticipation as it flew straight at Anieszirel, from the large amarok bounding straight for its prey, its wolven teeth bared as a threatening growl rumbled deep within its throat, to the silent kitsune, the magic-wielding creature glimmering in the night's sun as it casts spells of enchantment and protection on the others, they all did as Thuridan bid.

But, for all their ferocity, for all their eagerness for battle, the first blood to be spilt wasn't Anieszirel's. As her enemies charged at her, their four masters readying a volley of death just for her, Anieszirel smiled, and, taking a deep breath, called forth blades of pure obsidian to grow from the back of each hand, and as her blades grew, Anieszirel let forth her breath along with a single word of arcane, and, like in the annex rooms, time slowed to a crawl. Then, like the annex rooms, she made to drink deep once more of the power within, only to stop herself.

"No," she whispered, smirking, "let's enjoy this one," then lunged at her attackers.

It was the amarok that was closest, and it was the amarok that fell first, Anieszirel plunging both her blades deep within the large creature's chest, her left blade slicing clean through its heart, while her right blade punctured its left lung. Smirking at the creature's impending demise, she pulled herself close to the amarok before leaping off it, launching herself over the wyvern. As she flew over it, she held her arms wide about her before spinning viciously, the arc of her leap and the speed of her spin allowing her to slice through the side and back of the wyvern again, and again, and again and again and again, before flying clear of the creature. Landing in a crouch, she threw herself forward, her final target being Thuridan himself, but as she flew through the air, her eyes grew wide as she realized one overlooked fact.

"Woah!" she cried as she brought her blades before her to stop herself from crashing face-first into the dome of protection Thuridan had erected about him and his battle-mages. But crash into it she did, her arms quivering greatly from the force of the impact. Gritting her teeth, the chronodragon pulled her feet under her and leapt off the dome, sailing through the air and landing safely away in a crouch as time returned to as it should be. It was the gargled gasp of the amarok that reached her ears first, then the pained cry of the wyvern. But it was the terror in the eyes of the battle-mages that brought a smile to her lips.

"Something wrong?" she asked, smirking, but a sudden darkening about her brought her back to herself, and calling forth her shield, Anieszirel sprang backwards, leaping clear of the griffin as it crashed into where she'd stood. The winged fury did not give her a moment's respite, however, swinging its tail at her as she sailed through the air, catching her in her chest before charging forward, barreling its head against her, the force of which sent her crashing through one of the statues lining the square.

"*Ani!*"

"We're okay! We're okay."

Rolling to her feet, Anieszirel stared at the griffin, but from the corner of her eye, she could see the four-tailed fox stood over the wyvern, a shimmering sheen about it as the wyvern thrashed in pain where it lay. Abruptly, the griffin took to the air, revealing the volley launched at Anieszirel from the mages, a volley that slammed against her shield but did little more, before a now familiar darkening surrounded her.

But this time, Anieszirel did not leap away. Instead she called forth a wind blade longer than the griffin was wide, and flung it straight up at the diving bird. With a startled cry, the bird flailed as it tried to avoid the blade, but it was diving too fast.

"Die!" Anieszirel screamed at it, only to watch as another wind blade slammed into hers, sending it careening into a nearby building.

Angrily, she looked in the direction of the caster. It was the kitsune, its four tails rigid as it glared at her. Worse, the wyvern was standing, its eyes fixed on her and its lips twisted in a snarl.

"Wonderful," she muttered, just as another volley slammed against her shield.

"Will you—" she began, but the darkening returned.

"Enough!" she bellowed and took to the skies herself, her blade aimed upwards as she flew towards the griffin. With a screech, the griffin spun away from Anieszirel, but not swiftly enough to prevent Anieszirel slicing two deep rivulets into its head. Sensing victory, Anieszirel slowed her ascent before turning and aiming for the retreating griffin. Before she could lunge at it, however, the wyvern smashed into her, its head barreling into her chest and forcing her against the building behind her. Though the sheer speed of the attack caught her off-guard, Anieszirel's shield held nonetheless, and as her rage mounted, she looked at the wyvern as it raised its head, ready to devour her. But she never gave it the chance, for the moment her arms were free, Anieszirel brought her blades to bear, slicing the wyvern's tongue in two with her left blade before burying her right deep into its throat. With a pained cry, it pulled itself free of Anieszirel before turning tail to retreat.

"Get back here!" Anieszirel cried as she pulled her feet under her to leap at the retreating wyrm and end its miserable existence once and for all. It was then she noticed the griffin hovering before her, and as she looked at it, the great bird brought its wings together rapidly, creating a vicious gust of such strength as to blast away much of the wall about Anieszirel, followed closely by yet another salvo from the mages below before the griffin slammed into her, both elf and griffin disappearing into the building as sounds of battle raged on.

"I can't see them!"

Thuridan stared incredulously at the battle-mage. "Of course you can't see them, you idiot, they're inside the damn building!"

He looked at his wyvern as it hovered above the glistening kitsune. "Help him!"

The wyvern hesitated a spell, but the four-tailed fox glared at the wyrm before barking angrily. With a pained cry, the wyvern picked up the kitsune and flew up to where the griffin and Anieszirel had disappeared before they too disappeared from sight.

As one, all four mages stared at the hole with bated breath, the sounds of battle becoming more and more frantic with each passing moment. Then, after what seemed like an eternity, an enormous explosion rocked the entire square as every part of the building above the hole erupted, spewing rock and stone far and wide.

"Get down!" Thuridan ordered as he poured every ounce of arcane strength he had into the dome, and before long, rock and stone great and small rained down upon them. There were three other things falling amongst the debris that elicited a howl from at least one of the mages. The first was the kitsune, the wounded fox landing on its head before bouncing limply across the square till it bumped into the dome. The second was the griffin, the majestic bird flung like an arrow against the fountain itself, the force of the impact obliterating the statue within and much of the fountain. The third was the wyvern, the defeated wyrm falling against the dome, and while the dome survived the impact, the wyvern did not, for the impact and the manner of its fall meant its back was now broken.

Hurriedly, all three summoners released their familiars before death could claim them, each praying fervently that it was not too late. Then, as their familiars faded from view, an azure glow emanated from the top of what was left of the building that had erupted.

"What is that?" one of the battle-mages asked Thuridan, his voice quivering as he spoke. Thuridan knew, of course, but, before he could answer, an object clad in azure flew straight at them, slamming against the ground just before the dome. The impact could only be described as earth-shattering, the energy released blasting all within the dome clean off their feet, the very ground beneath them cracking and falling away as fissures emanated from the point of impact and snaked far and wide, fissures so gaping as to cause two of the battle-mages to fall from sight almost at once, their cries brief as they fell. As Thuridan scrambled to his feet, his eyes befell the Kin-Slayer crouched before them, her fist against the ground as an azure glow covered her. It was a heart-stopping sight that brought with it one simple moment of brutal clarity. To face her on even terms was a fight they would not win. Unless...

Slowly, Anieszirel rose, her azure eyes taking in the remaining two mages. With a cry, the last battle-mage raised his hands at her, but she turned to him, calling forth her azure specter to breathe its flame upon him. As the flames died away, the chronodragon smirked as the mage fell on his knees, gibbering and screeching as he clawed at the ground. Then she turned to Thuridan.

"It seems the day is yours," Thuridan said calmly as he linked his hands behind him.

"Where is your son?"

Thuridan shrugged. "Racing back here, I expect, void sphere in tow. You know, you are quite lucky the shielding about it is too unstable to risk them teleporting back here with it, else this grandstand of yours would've been most ill-advised."

Snarling, Anieszirel took a menacing step forward.

"Did you tell Tip how we found him?" Thuridan asked.

At his words, Anieszirel halted.

"*Ani, what's he mean?*"

"Nothing, my darling," she thought in response. "He's just trying to tear us apart."

"Did you tell him of the pact between you and my son?" Thuridan continued.

Without warning, Anieszirel flung a gust of wind at Thuridan, one powerful enough to not only carry him off his feet, but smash him through the last remaining unbroken statue in the square.

"*Ani, what's he saying?*"

"I told you, he's just trying to tear us apart." Anieszirel took a step forward, but as she did so, she felt Tip fight her for control.

"Tip, what are you doing?"

"*What's he saying, Ani?*"

"Listen, Tip—"

"*No, what's he saying?*"

"Look, Tip—"

"*You lying, Ani. You lying!*"

A slight groan from across from them brought Anieszirel's gaze up to Thuridan as he rose to his feet.

"Did you tell him you offered my son wealth and knowledge if he killed his friend and left her for him to find?"

The silence that befell the square was deafening.

"Tip, listen to me," Anieszirel pleaded. "I—"

But it was too late, for even as she spoke, she felt her hold begin to wane.

"Tip, stop this! He'll kill us!"

But Tip ignored her, and if anything, his wrestles with her became ever more frantic. Anieszirel looked up at Thuridan, her eyes ablaze with pure hate. Then her shield flickered to nothing. Smirking, the Archmage raised his hands slowly.

"You should have told him," he said as magic crackled and swirled about his fingers.

Before he could complete his spell however, a lightning bolt as thick as an infant was tall tore across the yard, catching Thuridan on his side and flinging him across the square and beyond. Turning, Anieszirel looked for her savior, only to see Mardaley and another battle-mage racing toward them, the void sphere floating eerily between them.

"Tip, please." she thought.

No response.

"Tip, they will trap us in that thing! Please!"

Still, Tip kept his peace. Anieszirel watched as the pair neared her, her panic rising with each step they took.

"Tip, I beg of you, don't do this."

"*You killed Marsha, Ani. You killed her, now you need to pay.*"

"You'll suffer too."

"Don't care. Marsha's dead. Don't care anymore."

Anieszirel knew not whether it was the supreme sadness in Tip's voice, or the thoughts of her approaching end, but as she watched the pair close in on her, the chronodragon suddenly found herself awash with shame and guilt.

"Forgive me, Tip," she said softly as she sank to her knees. "As the stars bear me witness, I am sorry. All I ever wanted was freedom. I hope one day you will forgive me." And bowing low, she let go of what little control she had left.

"Bye-bye, Ani," Tip whispered as he regained control, tears filling his eyes as he looked up at Mardaley approaching. "Bye-bye."

At last, Mardaley and Baern reached them.

"Hello, Tip," the elderly storekeeper said.

Tip smiled in response, his tears finally rolling down his face.

"Ready," he said softly.

Taking a deep breath, Mardaley let it out slowly as he smiled at the little boy. "May I speak to Ani?"

Tip shook his head. "Don't want her in control anymore."

Mardaley went on one knee as Baern's gaze drifted from one to the other, his lips pursed in a tight frown.

"Then don't," Mardaley said. "I just wish to speak to her. Is that alright?"

Tip stared at Mardaley in silence a spell, then nodded.

"Good." Taking a deep breath, Mardaley rose, his face hardening as he did so.

"Anieszirel, Kin-Slayer, hear me and hear me well. Soon, Thuridan's people will be upon us, so I shall make you this one offer, and you will give me your answer swiftly, else I answer for you."

"No!" Tip shook his head, bounding to his feet, but Mardaley smiled, putting a calming hand on Tip.

"She can't do anything without your permission. It's quite alright."

Tip stared worriedly at Mardaley for a spell before finally relenting. Nodding, Mardaley's face hardened once more.

"You have the power to undo all that has happened here today, undo all that has happened right up to Marshalla's demise. You will do this, and you will do this now. Refuse, and we will trap you in the void sphere, then hand you back to the Tower. What say you?"

"Let me speak, Tip."

"No," Tip thought back.

"It's easier if I speak to him."

Tip shook his head vehemently.

"She wishes to speak?" Mardaley asked.

Tip nodded at him.

"Let her. If she tries anything, you can stop her."

Tip stared at Mardaley in silence a spell, gritting his teeth as he did so.

"Okay," he said at last, then stared into the ether. A moment later, Anieszirel stared at Mardaley with genuine sadness in her gaze.

"My answer is no."

"You would rather the void sphere."

"Better trapped than unmade."

"And if I were to tell you, you will not be unmade?"

"She has made her choice, Mardaley," Baern said, but Mardaley raised a pleading hand at his friend.

"I know, just…" Mardaley said, glancing at his friend before turning back to the chronodragon. "The vow your father made to you, he made on pain of you ever undoing the past for your own ends, am I correct?"

"His actual words mean—"

"Am I correct?"

"What are you implying, human?"

"You are the apple of his eye, the beloved of all his children. He will not unmake you without a reason too heinous to ignore, and undoing the past to return a fallen innocent to life is not a heinous act, is it?"

Anieszirel stared suspiciously at Mardaley.

"Is it?" Mardaley pressed.

"How do you know so much of my father and I?"

"Yes," Baern said as he stared at Mardaley with much the same gaze as Anieszirel. "How?"

"That matters little now. Do you agree that your father will not unmake you without a reason stronger than the one I present to you now?"

"Perhaps… But what you ask is beyond me. Too little of my power has returned."

Mardaley shook his head. "You're being stupid, Kin-Slayer. We know of the power within your grasp."

Anieszirel glared in silence at the human before her.

"Even if I do this," she said at last, "undoing the past won't stop it from reoccurring. They were outnumbered and tricked by Thalas and his friends. Friends who had a void sphere, I might add."

"Which is why you will undo the past to the moments before Marshalla's death, and you will convince Tip to allow you take control. Then, you will use that control to keep Thalas and his companions at bay until Baern and I reach you."

"To what end?" Baern asked.

"Yes," Anieszirel said, "to what end?"

Mardaley smiled smugly. "You and I are going to make them think you left Tip and possessed one of them. Then we are going to convince them that all our lives are in danger, and our only salvation is to trap you and your new puppet in their void sphere."

Anieszirel and Baern stared incredulously at each other before turning to Mardaley.

"That must be the *stupidest*—" Anieszirel began.

"You forget the audience that will be in attendance."

"He does have a point…" Baern mused.

"So, do we have an accord?"

Anieszirel stared at Mardaley in silence once more.

"Why help me?" she asked after a spell.

Mardaley shook his head. "I'm not, I'm helping Tip."

"But you're trusting that I won't turn on you afterwards."

Mardaley smiled. "Oh, I'm doing no such thing. I intend to dedicate my life to two things, Kin-Slayer. One is to train Tip to resist you. The more your power returns, the more his power will grow, and if I ever feel you are about to outstrip him, I will tell him of your accord with Thalas."

Anieszirel scowled at Mardaley.

"We caught up with him on the way here, took the void sphere from him and the one with him. He told us about the mouse, Kin-Slayer."

"I see." She sighed. "And the second?"

"I will look for a way to part you and Tip."

Anieszirel scoffed. "The only way to do that is if I were to find a new host."

"Which would be a completely stupid thing to do."

"Stupid?"

"Yes, stupid. You have a chance at happiness, at finally finding peace. You have been hounded for millennia, have you not? We are offering you a chance to no longer have to run, a chance to no longer have to fight and scheme—"

"By trapping me in Tip."

"By having you stay in Tip till we find a way to allow you have your own body. Is that not what you truly wish for? To be yourself once again? To soar and live in peace, away from plots and power-hungry madmen like Thuridan Grovemender. Is that not worth staying in Tip for a few decades?"

Anieszirel moved to speak, but words failed her. It was clear Mardaley's words had moved her greatly.

"Magister Meadowview!" a voice bellowed from behind them. "What are you doing? Trap her now!"

Turning, all three watched as battle-mages poured into the square, the mages taking up positions around them.

"I will have your answer now, Kin-Slayer," Mardaley said as he and Baern slowly set the void sphere down, his eyes scanning about them as he did so.

"I accept. And my name is Anieszirel. Or Ani."

Mardaley turned to smile at her. "Fine, Ani. Just be sure to shield Baern and I. We can't keep our end of the accord if we can't remember it, can we?"

"No," Anieszirel replied as she rose, smiling. "I suppose not."

"Can you really bring Marsha back?"

Anieszirel's smile grew.

"Yes," she thought.

Without being asked, Tip granted Anieszirel full control. *"Bring her back, Ani. Bring Marsha back."*

"Anytime now," Baern muttered as he threw furtive glances at the advancing mages.

With a nod, Anieszirel closed her eyes as she seized control once more. As her control grew, she drank deep of the arcane, of the power within the boy. As her control grew, she bowed her head and breathed deep, drinking ever deeper, and as the battle-mages raised their hands, she raised her head, opening her eyes, and whispered words of arcane, words she had not spoken in millennia. As she whispered, the world about her blurred. As she whispered, the events of the past few moments played themselves in reverse, from the lightning bolt striking Thuridan, to the defeat of the familiars, from the cowering of Thalas, to the death of Neremi. As she whispered, time itself unwound, the past undone, the slain awoken. Anieszirel whispered, till at last, she knelt once more beside Marshalla and Davian.

"Tip, this is important," she thought to Tip.

"What is it?"

"You're free, Marsha!" Davian exclaimed. "You're free!"

"I need you to let me stay in control a little longer." Anieszirel thought to Tip.

"But want to talk to Marsha."

"You will, my darling, but something's wrong."

"Come, let's get back. With luck, we can return before Mardaley awakes." Davian continued.

"What is it?"

Anieszirel's mind raced for an answer.

"I can sense the void sphere," was all she could manage.

"Oh no!"

"Yes. I'll get us out, but need you to trust me, alright?"

"Okay."

"Are you alright, Ani?"

Anieszirel smiled as she noticed both Davian and Marshalla staring at her with quite some worry.

"It's—" she began.

"Tip," a voice called out from around the corner.

Frowning, Anieszirel stared from Davian to Marshalla. "Whatever happens, whatever you hear, stay where you are."

Frowning, both nodded. Nodding herself, Anieszirel rose.

"What are you doing?" Marshalla demanded as she reached for her.

"Tip, I know you're there, I just want to talk," the voice continued.

"Stay," Anieszirel ordered before freeing herself of Marshalla's grasp. Rising fully, she stepped out into the open.

"Spare me, child. I have no time for your stupidity."

Her words caught Neremi by surprise, and it showed.

"I...I had words for Tip—"

"You had lies for him. I know your play. You mean to confuse him, fill him with doubt, fill him with hate for Marshalla. Then force him to run away, run into the open so you can trap him in the void sphere you have somewhere near here."

"I—"

"But you forgot about me, didn't you, child? You forgot what I can do to you. I shall make you *this* offer, though. Your friends will step into the open, with the void sphere, and I will not reduce you to ash."

"*Ani!*"

"It's only a bluff, Tip," she thought in response. "I need to see where the void sphere is."

"Well?" she barked at Neremi, who was backing away.

When no answer was forthcoming, Anieszirel raised her left hand as wreathes of flame erupted between her fingers.

"Thalas!" Neremi screamed.

"We're here!" Thalas cried as he, Thane and Durlin swam into view.

Turning, Anieszirel glared at the three. "Bring it closer."

"*Ani...*"

"I need it closer to destroy it. Don't worry, it won't be too close to hurt us."

Anieszirel watched as the three came steadily closer, and when she was sure she was within their striking distance, she raised her hand.

"That's far enough."

Nodding, they stopped.

"Now, step aside."

Nodding, Thalas looked at Thane, then Durlin, but Anieszirel understood that look all too well. It was a command, one she had hoped he would give, and without warning, Thane and Durlin flung spell after spell at her as Thalas turned to cast the spell of unbinding.

"You would dare?" Anieszirel bellowed as Neremi joined the onslaught.

Keeping her shield strong, she cowered from them until Thalas was close to undoing the shielding before sending a gust at him, knocking him away from the void sphere. Unfortunately, her spell also sent the void sphere rolling backwards away from them all.

"Bother," she whispered.

"The sphere!" Durlin exclaimed as he ran after it.

Just then, Mardaley and Baern arrived, charging into the opening with Drake in tow.

"Stay where you are!" Baern bellowed as he fought for breath.

Thalas and his friends did as he ordered, save Durlin, who'd finally caught up to the void sphere. Anieszirel turned to glare at Baern and Mardaley in turn, but her eyes carried a question, one answered in turn by their gazes. Smiling briefly, she turned to face the three men square.

"What are you doing here?" she demanded.

"To put an end to this," Mardaley replied.

Anieszirel laughed at him, her tone mocking. "Is that so?"

"What's he mean?"

"You remember that thing Mardaley said? About me pretending to enter one of Thalas' friends?"

"Yeah?"

"That's what he means."

"Oh! Yeah!"

"And how do you intend to do that, then, *storekeeper?*" Anieszirel asked Mardaley, sneering as she spoke.

"With this!" Mardaley bellowed before pulling out from within his pocket a gem, and, uttering words of arcane, held it aloft as an emerald beam struck Anieszirel from it.

"Ugh!" she cried and fell to her knees.

"Tip!" Marshalla cried, springing to her feet.

"Drake, stop her!" Baern ordered as she raced towards Tip, but Drake had already seen her, catching her before she'd taken her fourth step.

"Damn... you!" Anieszirel said as she crumpled.

"Get clear of the sphere!" Baern barked at Durlin.

"It's still shielded!" Durlin shouted back.

"What?"

Taking it as her cue, Anieszirel called forth her spectral form, roaring with all her might as she hovered above Tip, before flinging an azure flame at Durlin's chest, burning and paralyzing him in equal measure as she released her spectral form.

"Durlin!" Thane exclaimed as he turned to race to his friend.

"Stay where you are, Thane!" Baern ordered as poor Durlin convulsed from the pain, the flame burning deeper and deeper into him.

"Undo it!" Baern barked, turning to glare at Thalas as Mardaley turned the emerald beam upon Durlin, the beam taking on a darker shade once it struck the convulsing elf. "Now!"

"No!" Neremi cried.

"Undo it before she breaks free!"

Turning from Durlin to the void sphere, Thalas glanced briefly at Baren before, gritting his teeth, did as he was bid, and as the spell of shielding was finally undone, the void sphere burst into life, a swirling darkness emanating from it all at once. It was a darkness that seemed to latch onto Durlin, swirling higher and higher about him until at last it covered him completely, only to then pull him towards the void sphere. Then, in one brilliant flash of light, the swirling mass collapsed into the void sphere, and Durlin was no more.

EPILOGUE

As the sounds of revelry rang out from without, Neremi stood in silence as she stared at the center of the Tower Library. Everything was as it should be, with no signs of any life-altering events ever occurring there. Not even the podium remained. It was as if none of the madness of that fateful day had ever occurred. Sighing, she rested her head upon her beloved's shoulder.

"Did you ever think we would be standing here again, after all that's happened?"

Sighing himself, Thalas turned to her.

"We thought we might find you here."

Turning, both watched as Eldred and Thane wandered in. As Thalas watched, he noticed a certain reluctance about Thane, and it put him on his guard.

"They sent you to find us?" Neremi asked as they neared.

"Not quite," Eldred replied, forcing a smile. "Durlin's mother's asking everywhere for the both of you. She wishes to talk to you once more."

Sighing, Neremi looked at Thalas before turning to Eldred.

"I don't know what else to tell her," she said, shrugging as she spoke.

"You can't blame her, though," Thane said. "First Fallon, then Durlin. The poor woman's looking for closure."

"Is that what *you're* looking for, Thane?" Thalas asked suddenly, the tone of his words forcing all three to stare at the hulking elf.

"Ah… no," Thane replied. "No, I…" But his voice died in his throat. Looking to Eldred for strength, he took a deep breath and looked at Thalas once more.

"I said some things, hurtful things, and I came to apologize. You led us well, Thalas, you led us true. It's a shame we caught the Kin-Slayer with that busy-body around, else we would all be out of here. But at least, we're free of your father's grasp, and, hells, they're even throwing a party in our honor!"

"Yes!" Eldred exclaimed. "Things turned out rather well, all told."

"Precisely!" Thane said, grinning at Eldred. He looked at Thalas once more. As Thalas stared back at him, a thought wormed its way into his mind, one as simple as it was shocking.

"What I'm trying to say," Thane continued, looking briefly at his feet, "is, I am sorry I doubted you. Friends still?"

Thalas stared at Thane in silence for a spell, before at last smiling, nodding as he did so.

"Friends."

"Excellent!" Thane exclaimed, his grin returned. Turning to smile at Eldred, he looked back at Thalas and Neremi before nodding at them.

"I'd best get back, the spread they've laid out won't eat itself."

Chuckling, Neremi and Eldred shook their heads at him as Thalas grinned.

"Just save us some," Thalas said.

"You'd better hurry, then," Thane said as he hurried out.

"I'm so glad to see that settled," Eldred said once Thane was gone. "I hated seeing the two of you at war."

"Yes," Neremi said, looking up at her beloved. "I'm glad too."

"It was the only logical conclusion," Thalas said.

Eldred grinned. "You say that, but you're not known for your mercy."

Thalas shrugged. "Thane is competent, and useful. It would be a shame to lose him. And besides, his king-maker is gone."

"Who?" Eldred asked, frowning.

"Durlin, who else?" Thalas said, turning his gaze to the door.

"Dear gods," Neremi said as she turned to the door herself. "That conniving little bastard." But Eldred merely shook his head in wonder.

As the celebrations wore on within the Shimmering Tower, Magister Meadowview was in his office, busy at work as he entertained the festivity's honored guest.

"I still can't believe it all worked out so well," he said, checking once more that the dome of silence was firmly in place.

"Neither can I, in all truth," Mardaley said, smiling at his host. "And will you stop fretting? The dome will hold."

"Forgive me," Baern said, smiling as he fidgeted in his chair. "This is, after all, a rather risky place to be having this discussion."

"True," Mardaley replied as he nodded. "But refusing the Matriarch's invitation would've drawn too many questions, and it's a discussion we must have before the celebration is over."

"Quite right." Sighing, Baern looked at Mardaley.

"What was that gem anyway?"

"Which one? The one I held aloft?"

Baern nodded.

"Just some silly trinket I carry around for luck. It's quite harmless."

Baern frowned. "Then why did Naeve recoil from it when you showed it to her?"

Mardaley grinned. "That's because I showed her something else, an old phylactery I bought some years ago."

"You bought a phylactery?" Baern asked, surprised.

Mardaley grinned. "Oh, don't worry, the lich who owns it won't be returning for it for another century or two."

Sighing, Baern shook his head, smiling.

"I suppose it does make sense to show her a phylactery after telling her it was a necrotic beam you held Tip with," Baern mused after a brief silence.

"Precisely."

"But what was the beam though?"

"Just a beam of light. When I pointed it at Durlin, though, I channeled a binding spell through it."

"Yes, I noticed the binding spell," Baern said, nodding at his friend. "Quite clever, I might add."

"Thank you."

"Just wasn't sure about the other one."

Mardaley grinned. "Well, I had to put on a good show after all."

"Quite right, quite right," Baern replied. "So, what do we do about Marshalla and Tip?"

Mardaley's grin dimmed to nothing. "I truly wished you were wrong about the boy, Baern."

"You sound as if you no longer have any lingering doubts on the matter," Baern said, frowning

Mardaley nodded, frowning also. "Kin-Slayer didn't deny it when I confronted her about it. After that... well... there's little point in me denying it."

"I see," Baern replied, a sad smile upon his lips, for he knew how much such an admission would hurt his friend. "Any thoughts on what the source of that power could be?"

Mardaley shook his head. "Your guess is as good as mine. It's not unheard of for a skilled mage, or even a necromancer, to impart some of their power into a living vessel."

"But that much of it?"

Mardaley shook his head again, sighing once more. "In truth, Baern, I know not how a boy that young can have such power within him and not know, or even notice, but its existence is undeniable, as is its potency. Much of what the Kin-Slayer did should've been impossible given how long she'd been imprisoned."

"One more reason we cannot risk her taking full control of Tip."

Mardaley nodded. "Yes, one very good reason."

"So, what do you propose?"

Mardaley sighed. "Well, we need to have the boy in a place where we can watch him closely, learn more about this power while I try to part the Kin-Slayer from him."

"Yes, I fully agree."

Mardaley fidgeted as he nodded. "Yes, a place where, should the need arise, he can be quickly contained."

"Of course."

"A place where—"

"The answer is yes, Mardaley," Baern said, grinning.

"Oh, thank the gods for that," Mardaley said, sighing as he too grinned. "I was afraid I may have had to beg."

Baern chuckled. "I would've had it no other way, my friend. With him here, we can both keep an eye on him, and as for Tip's training, he will get no better training than here." Then he frowned. "Do you think that chronodragon will hold to her word and stay within Tip without issue?"

"You mean will the power within Tip prove to be too much of a temptation for her?"

Baern nodded.

Mardaley sighed, shaking his head. "In all honesty, my friend, I don't know. I'd like to think her desire for freedom outweighs her desire for power, but…I suppose only time will tell."

Baern sighed. "Not a very pleasant thought."

Mardaley shook his head. "No, it isn't, and I only have myself to blame."

Baern grinned. "We must all stay true to our convictions, for good or for ill, that is the only way to stay true to ourselves."

A wry smile parted Mardaley's lips. "Using my own words against me now?"

Baern laughed in response.

"Are you sure getting him past Naeve will be that easy though?" Mardaley mused. "If *you* can realize there is more to the boy, why won't she?"

Baern smiled. "You have Thuridan to thank for that."

"Oh?"

Baern nodded. "He managed to convince Naeve Kin-Slayer's escape must've been possible because of a flaw in the void-sphere design, something she hid from us all these years, until she found a vessel young enough that she could easily manipulate, one not attached to us."

Mardaley shook his head, smiling. "For once, Thuridan's arrogance actually proves useful."

Baern laughed as his friend's words.

"He does have no arcane training that you know of though," Mardaley added. "Will that not be a hindrance?"

Baern sighed. "He'll still have to undertake the Birthing, but I think I can persuade her to at least allow him try."

Mardaley nodded. "And with Anieszirel's knowledge, he should be able to pass it easily enough."

"But not *too* easily, we don't want to draw undue attention to the boy."

"True…"

Nodding, Baern sat back into his chair. "And then there's the girl."

"Yes," Mardaley replied.

"To allow her join the Tower is too great a risk," Baern continued. "Naeve cannot know who she is until we're ready… until she herself is ready."

"I know," Mardaley replied. "And besides, she hates magic."

"So, what do we do?"

"Well, she loves Tip more than life itself, so parting the two will be impossible."

"I agree."

"So, what if she joins the Tower Stables?"

"The Stables?" Baern asked, frowning.

"Or the Summoner Pens. Drake tells me she's good with animals, quite fond of them, and everyone knows the opposite holds true for Naeve, so it's safe to assume their paths will very rarely cross."

"That's a rather bold assumption."

Mardaley shrugged. "Do you have a better option?"

A brief silence fell on the men, till at last, Baern sighed at his friend. "No, I don't. But better the Pens than the Stables, I think. Naeve does have a horse of her own, but no familiar. You think you can convince Marshalla, though?"

Mardaley grinned. "It was actually her idea."

Baern grinned at his friend. "I should've guessed you would've said something to her already."

Mardaley shrugged in response.

"Well, we've dallied long enough," Baern added before rising. "Shall we?"

Growling, Mardaley rose too.

"Oh, do cheer up, old friend. Who knows, you might actually enjoy this one."

"You think so?" Mardaley asked sardonically, smoothing out his tunic as he spoke.

"No, but no harm in wishing."

Turning to glare at his friend, Mardaley held his peace as he headed for the door, Baern's chuckling following him as he went.

In the realm the gods call home, in that one plane of existence where flawless is normality, stands a tower, magnificent and ageless, the tallest in this domain of perfection. And, at this moment, resting upon the battlement at its zenith, was the great wyrm Cerunos, God of all dragons, and Lord of time. Resting his head upon his outstretched arms, he smiled contentedly as he stared at the swirling mist before him, a mist upon which he watched Baern shake his head and follow his friend out of his office.

"Father," a voice called out behind him.

Letting go of the swirling mist with but a thought, the great wyrm raised his head and turned his gaze to the eternally young human woman who stood behind him, her pure crimson eyes staring up at him.

"What is it?" he asked in much the same manner.

"Maena's returned."

At this, Cerunos huffed as he lowered his great head once more.

"I suspect she will keep calling till you grant her an audience."

Smiling, the wyrm king raised his head once more and stared at his daughter.

"Is that advice, Tessia, or admonishment?"

"Do you truly wish me to answer?"

Cerunos grinned as he rose to sitting. "Very well, send her in."

Bowing, the eldest of his remaining chronodragon children turned and did as she was told. Cerunos had not long to wait before Maena burst forth.

"What precisely do you think you're doing?" the god-queen demanded as she marched towards the dragon-god.

"So nice to see you too, Maena," Cerunos replied drily.

"Oh, don't start with me, wyrm, I am not in the mood!"

"Clearly…"

With a loud huff, Maena glared at him as she brought her ire to heel.

"What. Are. You. Doing?" she asked at last.

"I answer to your husband, Maena, not to you."

"Oh, for goodness' sake, Cerunos, it is I! We've been allies since the dawn of creation. Can you not confide in me?"

But Cerunos kept his peace.

"You are playing with fire here," Maena continued. "Sacrificing the soul of an innocent is never an easy thing to do, but you were there when Hazuel pleaded his case, and you agreed to this along with the rest of us!"

At her words, Cerunos looked away, wincing as he did so.

"And what you are doing now… you cannot tell me your daughter being in that creature came to be without your nudging, can you?"

Cerunos turned to Maena once more, and as their eyes met, the god-queen nodded.

"Precisely. So why, why have your daughter live within that creature? Do you not realize what could happen if it gained command of chronomancy? Can you not imagine the horrors it would visit on the mortal realm?"

"I am well aware of the risk, Maena."

"Then why do this?"

Once again, Cerunos fell silent.

Sighing, Maena took a step forward. "We have always been honest and fair with each other, so I came here to tell you something in honesty. I worry, Cerunos. I worry that your love for Anieszirel has blinded you completely. You seek to wash away her fall, have her return here to your side, but the risk you take is too great. I came here to beg you to reconsider. However, now that I am here, I see I will only waste my breath, so I make you this vow instead. Should that creature gain control of your daughter, should it bind and claim her, I will unmake her."

Cerunos glared at the god-queen, but she was unmoved.

"I will unmake her, Cerunos," she repeated. "Should the Beggar Prince get the better of her, I will unmake her. Better you lose her forever, than the mortal realm be plunged into darkness."

"She is my daughter," Cerunos growled.

"I am well aware of—"

"She is mine, Maena, *mine*! She is *my* responsibility, *my* burden. You will do no such thing!"

"She is your daughter, that I do not dispute, but the safety and harmony of the mortal realm is *my* burden, *my* responsibility. And letting that creature loose in that realm with full command of chronomancy is a danger I will *not* accept. You've clearly shown no risk is too great for you to see your daughter returned. Well, I am telling you now, no burden is too great for me to bear to protect those mortals from annihilation."

Cerunos glared in silence at an unmoved Maena, until at last, the god-queen turned and left. It was then that Cerunos finally lowered himself, an air of tired resignation hanging about him like a suffocating cloak.

"Father?" Tessia said as she returned.

Raising his head, he looked at her. "What is it?"

"Father, I have loved you, and I have served you all my life, and with every fiber of my being."

Cerunos smiled sadly at her. "You think I am wrong too."

"I think you are blinded," Tessia said. "I love Anieszirel, almost as much as you, and I have never held any ill will towards her, even after what she did. But Maena is right, the risk is too great. She is not worth it."

Cerunos chuckled. "If you think this, dare I ask what Etriazrine thinks?"

Tessia smiled as she lowered her gaze.

"I miss her, Tessia," Cerunos continued.

"As do I, Father," Tessia replied, looking up at her father once more, "but—"

"No, Tessia, no. You are wrong, you are all wrong. Anieszirel will prove she is ready to return. She will free the child, and the child will free her. You'll see."

"And if she fails? If the Beggar Prince claims her?"

"Then… Maena will unmake her." The words hurt the dragon-god, and it showed.

"I…I hope it does not come to that."

Cerunos sighed. "Me too."

And with no more words to utter, he lowered himself and stared into the mist. Not knowing what else to say, Tessia turned and left her father to his thoughts.

A Note From The Author

Firstly, thank you for taking the time to read my little tale, I do hope it was to your liking. There's a saying that the first time is the hardest, and that certainly held true for me on this. True, The Beggar Prince isn't the first book I've written, but it's the first I've taken through to publication, and that gave it a different feel to my other works. But I must say I rather like the result, and I do hope you did too.

If you'd like to know more about me, you're welcome to browse my nice little corner of the internet at https://jamesbdrake.com. Or, you can drop by and say hello on Facebook or Instagram (both as jbdrakeauthor). Alternatively, should the mood strike you, you can drop me a mail at jb.drake@outlook.com.

Now, if you'll excuse me, I'm off to work on the next instalment of our dynamic duo's caper!

J.B. Drake

WHAT'S NEXT

EXCLUSIVE OFFER – DELVING INTO THE PAST

One of the absolute best parts of being an author is building a relationship with my readers. For this reason, I send out a monthly newsletter where I share details of new releases, special offers and upcoming events. And every other month, I share a little short story following a set theme or other, all within this wonderful world of Tip and Marshalla's. Why not sign up?

If you do, you'll receive a free novel that takes a peek into the past of our daring duo, how they met, and what horrors drove them all the way to the jewel that is Merethia.

Just head on over to my website(https://jamesbdrake.com)to sign up.

J.B. Drake

Making A Difference

Reviews are the single most powerful tool in an indie author's arsenal when it comes to getting attention for their work, especially when they're growing authors like me. I don't really have deep enough pockets to be able to take out newspaper ads, or have posters put up in subways and billboards (not yet, at least!).

But honest reviews go a long way in bringing my books to the attention of other readers.

If you've enjoyed my little story, I'd be grateful if you could spend just 5 minutes leaving a review. It can be a single word, or a heartfelt essay, either would be greatly appreciated. If you're up for it, just click here to leave a review.

Thank you.

J.B. Drake

Other Titles Available

The Unbroken Bond Series

The Beggar's Wrath

With the hunt for Anieszirel over, and a home to call their own, Tip and Marshalla couldn't be happier. The nightmare is over, their prayers have finally been answered.

But for their dream to have come true, lives were lost. Because of this, there are those who would rather see the two friends dead than live happily ever after, and they will stop at nothing to make it so.

The Beggar's Past

No matter how far you run or how hard you try to hide, you can't outrun your past or hide from its reach, and Tip's past is as deadly as they come.

And now, it's caught up with him.

The Beggar Betrayed

Our daring heroes have fought tooth and claw to keep Anieszirel's presence a secret, but the bite of betrayal is a sting they know all too well, and it has come to claim their most closely guarded secret.

Worse, the Shimmering Tower knows about Anieszirel now, and all hells is about to be unleashed.

Made in the USA
Coppell, TX
07 January 2025

44075799R00163